THE WILD LIFE

DAVID GORDON

THE MYSTERIOUS PRESS
NEW YORK

THE WILD LIFE

The Mysterious Press
An Imprint of Penzler Publishers
58 Warren Street
New York, N.Y. 10007

Copyright © 2022 by David Gordon

MAY 3 1 2022

First Mysterious Press edition

Interior design by Maria Fernandez

Library of Congress Control Number: 2021925142

ISBN: 978-1-61316-277-4
eBook ISBN: 978-1-61316-275-0

10 9 8 7 6 5 4 3 2 1

Printed in the United States of America
Distributed by W. W. Norton & Company

For Matilde

PART I

1

Joe was afraid to move. He stood, holding his breath, listening intently for the creak of a floorboard, a telltale rustle or sigh. Every muscle tensed as he eyed the small bathroom window, doing the math—or, he supposed, physics—in his head: even if he managed to edge out sideways, onto the narrow ledge, could he make the reach to the fire escape without falling the eight floors to the sidewalk? Unlikely. But he would almost rather risk it than face what awaited him on the other side of the bathroom door. Why hadn't he thought to lock it? He stared at the flimsy handle now, waiting to see it turn from the outside, wondering if he could simply reach out and twist the locking mechanism, if he dared. Then he heard a voice. It was the law: Special Agent Donna Zamora of the FBI.

"What's the matter, honey? Why are you up? Do you have to make pee?"

Ears straining, Joe awaited the answer that could seal his fate. Why did the shower curtain have to be translucent? He heard the tiny voice of Donna's six-year-old daughter warbling in the living room.

"Don't worry, it was just a dream," Donna said. "Let's get you some water and tuck you in Mommy's bed."

As their steps faded, Joe breathed a sigh of relief, then smiled sardonically in the mirror. He'd hidden in sewers from cops and in bomb craters from jihadists without getting quite this tense. Then again, he'd sooner go up against a trained killer in mortal combat than have a small child discover him naked at two in the morning. Finally, there came a soft knock, at the height of an adult hand.

"It's me," Donna whispered.

He opened the door. Donna was in her robe, dark hair glistening in the shadows. She handed him his clothes, his Converse Chuck Taylors on top of his folded shirt and jeans. From her robe pocket, she pulled his crumpled boxers and one sock, with a hole in the heel.

"I couldn't find the other sock," she whispered, while he quickly dressed. "It must be under the bed."

He sat on the toilet lid to tie his laces. She ran her fingers through his hair. "Sorry if she startled you."

"She nearly gave me a heart attack."

He could see her smiling in the dim light that slipped in from the window. Joe Brody, veteran of ops so black his military record had been deleted, an ace criminal who commanded respect throughout the five boroughs, afraid of a little girl.

"Come on." She took his hand. "I'll grab your coat. You can get out through her window."

Joe followed her to Larissa's room, a magical, candy-colored cave where teddy bears and stuffed unicorns snuggled with lambs and frogs, Disney figures populated the walls, and shimmering stars hung from the ceiling. Glitter was everywhere. He drew on his jacket, pulling gloves from the pockets, winding a scarf around his neck, while Donna opened the window. That iron fire escape was going to be cold.

"It's your own fault, you know," she told him. "Ever since she spotted you that time she has dreams about a man creeping past her window."

"My fault?" He pulled his hat on. "In that case, I will just stroll out the door like a gentleman."

She shook her head. "You can't. You know Mrs. Ruiz will see you leave."

"Doesn't she ever sleep?"

"Not since 1975, according to her."

"That's what my grandmother says, too. Then you hear her snoring." He sat on the windowsill; already he could feel the chill from the river. She perched beside him.

"Point is, you're supposed to be a master at this stuff. Professional criminal."

He smiled. "I'm out of practice, thanks to you."

"Well, we are going to have to have a serious talk. Figure this out."

He sighed. It seemed like they spent half their time rolling deliriously in each other's arms, and the other half seriously discussing the problems with it. "I'm sorry if I traumatized your daughter. I will pay for her therapy out of my ill-gotten gains."

Donna smiled. "She's a city kid. She's seen worse. Luckily, she decided you were Spider-Man. God knows why. His outfit is way cooler."

"Because she's smart. She can tell we're both from Queens." Joe kissed her. "Speaking of which, come over tomorrow."

"Larissa has a playdate."

"Your mom can take her. We need a playdate ourselves. Gladys will be out all day."

"Sneaking a girl in when your grandma's out? Definitely not the solution to our problems."

Joe swung his legs out onto the fire escape and braced himself for the climb. "At least you get to come in the front door."

2

Swift and silent past the darkened windows, slow and careful past the few with lamp-yellow or screen-blue leaking through their curtains, Joe felt the cold leach up from the iron into his hands and feet, the wind from the river already stinging his cheeks and neck. The reason he was crawling up the fire escape now was not only because of Donna's impressionable young daughter, or her nosy neighbors, or even her mother who lived across the hall. It was not because of his grandmother, whom he had not told, or any family problems at all. It was not religion or politics or culture or any of those traditional issues. It was not even a romantic dilemma—they were both free and single. Donna and Joe were a twenty-first-century Romeo and Juliet, with the most modern of personal problems, a career conflict: Donna was a federal law enforcement agent, finally on the rise after thwarting a terrorist plot and saving much of New York. And Joe was a professional criminal, lifelong pals with a Mafia boss and deeply entangled with the city's top organized crime leaders, who had empowered him to hunt down a terror cell lurking in their midst. When that terrorist ended up with a bullet in the head, they declared him their "sheriff," giving him free reign throughout their territories, and making him the fixer they called on when they, too, needed 911 to protect them from the nightmares that kept even Mafia dons up at night: Al-Qaeda cells, white-supremacist plots, terror-financed heroin pipelines, home-made nuclear bombs. While the citizens slept, relying on Donna to keep them safe from dangerous criminals, the most dangerous criminals in the city relied on Joe.

For Donna, to have their relationship go public would mean the death of her career. For Joe, it would just mean death.

⊶

They were star-crossed from the start. They'd met when Donna arrested Joe during a raid on Club Rendezvous, the strip joint controlled by mob boss Gio Caprisi, where Joe, his childhood buddy, worked as a bouncer. They crossed paths again when Joe shot her with a beanbag round—something that a lot of women would consider a definite red flag—though he had done it to save her life, since he had infiltrated a group of weapons thieves who had ordered her death. Later, when she had to kill a terrorist to save Joe's life in return, he did the chivalrous thing and disposed of the body by taking it out on the Caprisi boat and feeding it to sharks. And that was how it went for them, always in danger, and often on different sides.

But the attraction, the strange magnetism, the electric charge, was there from the beginning, too, and the more Donna got to know him, the more fascinated she became, in spite of herself. She had dedicated her own life to serving and protecting the people around her. Joe had served his country and gotten nothing back but bad dreams and a PTSD-related drug problem. Seeing him continue to risk everything to save strangers who would never give him a medal or pay him a dollar or offer a word of thanks—who would, on the contrary, gladly lock him up forever—inspired a feeling in her beyond carnal attraction that was hard to dismiss. Not respect, exactly, since she could only deplore his methods; it was admiration, pure and simple. Her daughter had been right after all. Like Spidey, he was a working-class hero from Queens.

7

And for Joe? Donna was the answer to a dream he didn't know he had. A dirty dream at first, of course; she was sexy in a sly way, hot in a cool way, those dark eyes, exciting whether flashing with anger or lust, that raven-black hair, that body that made even a square Fed-suit somehow more X-rated than the nothings the girls wore at the club. But as he started to see how smart she was, and how brave, and how true to her own conscience, how much courage and honor she carried in her heart, he came to recognize a fellow warrior, one who somehow also lived in the light, in sanity, family, and peace. She seemed, just maybe, to offer him something he had never even imagined for himself: hope for a better future, a happy life.

3

Melody heard somebody coming. She had been locked up, chained to a pipe in this concrete hole, for what seemed like forever. There was little sense of time down here, but hunger, thirst, and discomfort told her it was at least a couple of days—days spent praying, crying, yelling, and, when exhaustion took her, dreaming in brief snatches about someone, anyone, coming to her rescue. Once she dreamed that she was home, really home, in Georgia, sleeping on a picnic blanket when she was a little kid, and she woke up crying. Once she dreamed that cops, whom she had feared and avoided her whole life, were coming to help her, and she woke up yelling. Once she dreamed that she was safe in bed in her apartment, under the covers, and her dog was licking her toes, and then she realized it was a rat, taking a tentative taste, and she woke up screaming.

But now she was awake, and like a dream come true, someone was coming. As the steps drew closer, she strained to see in the gloom, twisting her arm against the chain.

"Hello? Hello? Are you there? Help me, please." She tried to yell but could produce only a harsh rasp from her dry, sore throat. Her own voice shocked her. It was a ghost voice. She summoned the last of her strength, to wave her hand, to call.

Then he appeared, and she knew he was not here to save her. Too weak to cry, she shook her head as his hands curled around her throat.

4

"Just explore your options, that's all I'm saying."

They were lying in Joe's bed now. Gladys, his grandmother, was out gambling, playing cards. Not that it was really a gamble for her, nor was it play. It was work. She was an expert card hustler, an old-time grifter from a long line of thieves, who'd raised Joe herself when his parents died young. He grew up here, in this apartment in Jackson Heights. For Joe, this was not just home but the center of the world, most of which was represented in the neighborhood, more than at the UN across the river—from the clothes people wore in the street, to the hundred languages filling the air, to the markets and music and newspapers, and most especially the food. That was what Donna came for, besides Joe. Today it was Taiwanese seafood, then back to his place, the same apartment where she had once executed a search warrant, to make love. And then, of course, to talk.

"This is the perfect time for it," she continued now, curled up against him, his arm around her shoulders, while she absentmindedly traced the scar on his left side, over the heart. "You've got the money. It's not like you need that bouncer job. Why are you even going in tonight?"

Joe shrugged. His last caper had netted him more than two hundred thousand in cash. "My name's on the schedule." He looked at the clock on the nightstand. He had to get going soon. It was cold out there and so warm in here. "It's not like I can just retire. That money is in long-term savings."

"And by *savings* you mean your grandmother's mattress and Gio Caprisi's safe."

"That's right. It's a diversified portfolio."

She snorted derisively. Joe gave her a squeeze. "Snort derisively if you want. You know my grandmother's too smart to keep it all in her mattress. It's in her shoes. The walls. Even I don't know where. And Gio's safe? That is the most secure location in New York City."

"True," she admitted. Not even the most desperate criminal would try crossing Gio. "But it's not the safety of the money that worries me. It's yours. I mean, you can't do this forever. You'll run out of room for scars. And what about *our* long-term? You know you're going to have to quit sooner or later."

"Why me? Why do I have to sacrifice my career?"

She rolled her eyes at the word *career*. "Well, let's see. Because mine is legal. And it comes with a pension and health insurance. And I only rarely get shot at or almost blown up. And they gave me a medal for it. And a promotion. Not to mention a cool badge . . ." She paused there. Her finger stopped. Unconsciously, she'd been tracing the star that the city's top crime bosses had branded him with when they made Joe their sheriff. It wasn't a badge you could turn in, or throw away, or bury in a drawer to show your grandkids. It was a stark reminder that in Joe's world there was only one way to retire. She put her arms around him and squeezed tight. "Just take some time to explore your options," she said. "That's all I'm saying."

5

Gladys was working on an inside straight when she spotted it. She'd been coming to this casino for a few nights, always leaving with money in her pocket. She wasn't cheating—she didn't have to cheat to do well against this crowd—but she was on a job. She was looking for cheats.

The casino was in the basement of a storage facility in a commercial district with little activity after dark or on the weekends. No one noticed the vans that rounded up punters from nearby pickup spots and dropped them here to empty their pockets at poker, blackjack, craps, and a little roulette without the hassle of traveling to AC or the upstate casinos. The crowd was a mix—hardcore Chinese and Korean players who went all night, locals including everyone from retirees to public school teachers to lawyers and off-duty cops, and some visitors just passing through, dressed for a night on the town, stopping in between dinner and the club. The place had been set up by the building's owner—Max Morton, aka "Max the Mini King"—who ruled a small empire of mini-storage warehouses, where overstuffed New Yorkers paid to stash their extras, as well as a fleet of moving trucks. His face—cheeky, jowly, grinning, apple red under a cartoon crown—appeared on ads all over the subway, the billboards atop his places, and the sides of his trucks. Business was good, but not quite good enough.

The Mini-King had a major gambling habit. He liked high-stakes poker especially, playing at games held all over town, but he also enjoyed losing heavily at blackjack, sports betting, and even the lottery. Being the self-starting, bootstrap entrepreneur he was, his solution when he couldn't beat them was to join them and open his own casino. Why not? He had the space.

There was one big difference, however. When opening a mini-storage warehouse, there were local, city, and state authorities to deal with, tax people, inspectors, council members, homeowner's associations. When opening a casino in this part of town, there was only one authority whose blessing you had to obtain: Gio Caprisi. Max hadn't gotten to be the Mini-King by being stupid. He reached out to Gio, who considered the matter and agreed; he partnered on the casino with Max, and also had him grant a small slice of the pie to Uncle Chen, the boss of Chinese crime in Flushing, as well as to a Korean crime lord of Gio's acquaintance, to smooth any feathers ruffled by having pigeons fly over from the other casinos of Queens to be plucked. Gio also provided security, which in this case meant protection from both outlaws—a couple of Caprisi family associates worked the door, but it was widely known that robbing this place was suicide—and from the law itself—the local cops were paid to look away, and any other complaints would be routed to Gio's people.

After that, everything went smoothly, for a while. Fitting the name Mini-King, Max's joint was small but regal, with flocked rose wallpaper, gold trim on the pillars holding the basement ceiling up, brand-new card tables, professional dealers in white shirts and bow ties, a bar, even a roulette wheel in the corner. Then, after a few months, Gio noticed something weird in the weekly take—sudden spikes in poker winnings, always on busy nights and always at one or two tables. Now, Gio was in the gambling business, but he was not a gambler. He did not believe in luck. He wanted this oddity explained: maybe there were a few real pros in the mix. Or maybe there was a shark in his waters, cheating. And maybe they had inside help. So he called the sharpest card player and grifter he knew to come and check it out. She was perfect, someone no one would suspect, who looked totally innocent and harmless but was crooked enough to know every scam while also completely trustworthy in Gio's eyes: he hired Gladys, his best friend's grandma.

She spent a few hours a night playing poker at different tables, winning the occasional pot, losing enough to blend in, and mostly checking out the other players, the dealers, the security cameras, the door guys, the works. It took her two nights to spot it. Gio's new partner, Max the Mini-King, was ripping him off.

Max wasn't stupid, but he was greedy. His casino made a lot of money, but a lot was not enough to cover his own gambling losses, which only rose now that he was rubbing elbows with high rollers and meeting the guys who ran other joints, not to mention his usual nut—the big house, the big cars, and his wife and three daughters, all terribly spoiled: what was a Mini-King without a Mini-Queen and Mini-Princesses? So Max came up with the perfect scheme. Who was the one person who could go anywhere, look at anything? He was. He recruited a couple of sharp players from his old days as a regular customer, and had them sit in. Then he cruised around, meeting and greeting, shaking hands, checking up on the dealers, even visiting the camera room to check on the guys there. And the whole time, he was scoping out the cards, seeing what the people playing with his cronies were holding, who was bluffing, who had a winning hand. Then, when he saw a big pot, he'd signal his stooge: go all in, or fold.

It worked like a charm at first. But success made them even greedier. Soon the same two players were winning a statistically unlikely number of big pots, staking everything and winning but never going all in on any losers—creating an anomaly for Gio, and a pattern that Gladys could have seen even without her glasses. That night, when she cashed in her winnings and got up from the table, she smiled at everyone like the lovable granny she was—bright blue eyes behind huge round spectacles, a beauty-parlor-perfect halo of white hair, a wool sweater that matched her stretch pants, a cane. Like always, she gave a cheek kiss and a tip to the dealer, who was working her way through college. However, this time she also gave a cheek pinch to a cocky guy with a dark beard and black turtleneck who'd won the last two big pots. Then, as she made her way to the door, she gave a good night pat to a player at another table, a rotund fellow in a hoody, sweatpants, and bright sneakers.

"Don't stay up too late," she told him as she passed.

"'Night, Granny," he answered with a chuckle, as he went all in on another big hand. And won. When she reached the door, one of Gio's top guys, Pete, was waiting, along with Little Eddie—six feet two inches of muscle and wide as the door. Still, he was the son of Big Eddie, who had died protecting Gio, hence he would be known for life as Little Eddie. She caught their eyes as she passed. A beat later, they followed. In the parking lot, with his right hand, Nero, running the engine to keep the car warm, Gio Caprisi was waiting.

When he saw Gladys, Gio hopped out to escort her. She kissed him on both cheeks but declined his arm. "It ain't even icy, I'm fine," she said, handing him the cane, which was just a prop. "Now listen, you got two sharks in the tank there."

"Let's talk in the car," Gio told her. "It's freezing out here."

Nero opened the back door solicitously and Gladys patted his shoulder—"Hiya, hon"—as she got in. Gio sat beside her. Pete got in front with Nero, and Little Eddie stood outside, good-naturedly impervious to the cold, like his dad.

"I got the heat going and the seat warmers are on high," he told her.

"I can't stand those things," she said. "Make me feel like I peed myself. I'm not ready for diapers yet."

"Nero, turn off the seat warmers."

"Yes, boss."

"Now, I showed the sharks to Pete," Gladys said.

Pete gave Gio a single nod.

"They're small-timers," she explained. "And the boss, Mini-King Max, is strictly amateur. When he straightens his tie, it means bet heavy. When he shoots his cuffs, it means fold."

"Got it," Gio said. "Thanks, Gladys."

She shrugged. "It was nothing. Now what?"

Gio pulled an envelope, plump with cash, from his jacket and put it in Gladys's hands. "Now Nero drives you home. And Max, if he's smart, will be pissing his pants for real."

He and Pete got out, shutting the door. Nero popped the trunk, lowering his window to remind Little Eddie, "Don't forget the toolbox."

6

"I'm exploring my options," Joe said.

He was in the back booth at the club with Santa, who shrugged. Santa was a nickname, short for his last name, Santangelo, and he had the long white beard and big round belly to go with it. Santa's own options ranged from managing this joint for Gio, to training rescue dogs on the weekends with his wife, Kelly, aka Mrs. Santa, to doing what he was told and ignoring what he was told to ignore when Joe and the others needed to use his office. He was, on the whole, perfectly content with this destiny, if not quite jolly. "Sure, why not explore?" he told Joe.

"You can try what I'm doing, getting my GED," offered Autumn, a curvaceous redhead who danced at the club. It was early, and the crowd was thin, so she was wearing a pink silk robe over the G-string and bra she'd soon be taking off onstage. "Then I'm going to do either psychology or accounting."

"How'd you pick those?" Santa asked her.

She sipped her Diet Coke through a straw so as not to smudge her lipstick, which was an elaborate multiphase process, a lustrous red glazed with a gloss that would sparkle under the stage lights. "You learn a lot about psychology in this job, believe me, whether you want to or not."

Santa nodded in sage agreement. "Sure do. Male psychology up front. Female in the back."

"Half of these guys use me as their shrink," Autumn said. "My tits and my ass got me this job, but this"—she tapped her forehead—"is the body part that earns my tips."

"Sounds like your psych degree is in the bag," Joe said.

"I'm good with numbers, too. I already help the other girls with their taxes. Like, for instance, this"—she parted the robe, showing off her spangled pink bra—"is totally a write-off. Anything I wear onstage is. Though I guess I don't wear that much. Still, last winter? When I got that leather coat with the faux squirrel trim? I walked out in it, took it off, and voilà. Total write-off."

"What about implants?" Santa asked, stroking his beard thoughtfully.

"You don't look like you need them," Joe assured him.

Santa scowled, and Autumn laughed.

"Actually, that's a good point," she said. "I suggest amortizing the cost over a few years of projected earnings."

Joe could barely follow. He'd had two legit, on-the-books jobs in his life, the military and this. For the rest, he was an independent contractor who earned cash and paid "tax" only to people like Gio.

"So this program you're in," Joe asked. "After you get your GED, they help you with college? What about finding jobs?"

"You do like a whole career counseling, where they help you find your skills and talents and match them with career options and then make a step-by-step plan. But the first step is a diploma for me. What about you, Joe? Did you drop out?"

"Nope. Expelled." He neglected to mention that it was from Harvard. He was there on a scholarship, majoring in literature and philosophy and scoring straight As, but when he got caught fleecing the rich kids in card games, and broke a few frat-boy noses in the aftermath, he ended up bounced from the ivy halls and facing criminal charges. A judge, not a counselor, laid out his career options: jail or the military.

"Don't worry," Autumn said. "It's never too late to change."

"Speaking of which." Santa looked at his watch. "You're on in ten."

With a sigh, Autumn rose and went backstage. Santa's phone rang, and he retreated to his office to take the call. Joe sipped his black coffee and got out his book. It was his battered copy of *Ulysses*, which he'd bought used back at Harvard, and had decided to give another go. He was hoping for a quiet night.

1

"I got bad news and good news." Gio had entered the casino unannounced and caught Max just as he was coming out of the camera room, where he'd been spying on the players, hoping for one more big pot that night.

"Hey Gio, great to see you!" Max grinned big and shook his hand. "Uh . . . what news is that?"

"The bad news is, somebody's been cheating," Gio said. "But don't worry. The good news is, we caught them."

"What?" Max asked, his incredulity unfeigned. "Who?"

"Let's go see." Gio put a hand on Max's shoulder, calm but firm. Max's pants were not yet wet, but his armpits suddenly were.

They went upstairs to the closed storage facility, where one unrented space at the end of a windowless, concrete hall was now opened and lit. One of the men Gio had working casino security stood by the roll-down door, nodding as Gio and Max passed. Inside, the two players—the bearded turtleneck guy and the rotund sweatpants guy—were sitting in folding chairs at a folding table. They did not look comfortable. Pete stood to one side, casually holding a gun. Eddie stood on the other, holding a shiny red toolbox.

"What do you think, Max? Recognize these two scumbags?"

They both looked at him entreatingly.

"Me? Who? Them?" Max sputtered. "No. I never saw them before."

Beard gasped at this. Rotund squirmed, his eyes getting bigger. Gio shrugged. "OK then. Eddie, get the hammer. And, you two." He nodded at the two cheats. "Put your hands on the table."

Rotund began to whimper and shake his head. Beard tried to beg: "Look, I'm sorry. I didn't know—"

"Shhh. Stop whining, before I get annoyed," Gio told them, very calmly. "It's simple. You cheated at my table and got caught. You don't get to just walk away. You either lose the hand you cheated me with or you don't walk away at all." Gio stared at them, his eyes flat and opaque. There was nothing behind them. "Your call."

Reluctantly, they placed their hands on the table, still staring wildly at Max, who had retreated into a corner.

Gio nodded. "Smart choice." He stepped back. "Eddie?"

Eddie stepped forward, raising a small sledge, an iron head on a wood handle, but as he swung down, Beard instinctively jerked back his right hand. The sledge banged on the table. Both men jumped, and Max let out an involuntary gasp.

"Hey," Eddie said. "You moved."

"I'll hold them down, boss," Pete offered.

"New rule," Gio said. "Anybody who moves their hand gets both smashed. Fair enough?"

Eddie and Pete nodded. Rotund shrugged. Beard just sagged and put his right hand back on the table. Eddie brought down the sledge. Beard's howl echoed through the empty warehouse, echoing off the walls.

"Next," Gio said, looking at Rotund, who slowly laid his left hand on the table. Eddie raised the sledge. Gio put a hand up.

"Wait a second." He turned to Pete. "You were watching. He a lefty or righty?"

Pete grinned. "Righty."

Gio laughed. "Hustler to the end. Good for you," he told Rotund, who smiled shyly. "Now put out your right."

He did. And a second later his own scream was filling the hallway.

"OK," Gio said, clapping his hands together. "We're even. You two can go in peace." The two men rose, cradling their shattered hands.

Pete and Eddie nodded at them encouragingly.

"You did good," Pete told them.

"Thanks," Beard said, nodding and sniffling.

"No offense," Rotund added.

"None taken," Pete said as they shuffled off. "You get home safe." But as Max started to follow, Pete pointed the gun and shook his head.

"Max, have a seat," Gio said. "Let's review this security problem. Partners' meeting."

"I wish I could, Gio, but I really should get back. I swear it won't happen again. I'll double the guards. Get new cameras—"

"Sit down and shut up," Gio said. Max sat, shaking his head as Gio went on: "I know it was you. Stop shaking your head. You were spotted. Did you really think you could rob me with such a stupid play? What am I, running a church bingo game?"

"Gio, I'm sorry. I couldn't help it . . ." He began to blubber. "I have a serious problem."

"You sure do."

"I mean I need professional help. I have a mental condition."

"Really? That's two problems, then. I'm afraid none of us here are qualified—professionally, I mean—to help with the mental condition. But we can settle one problem right now."

Max sniffed. He took a deep breath. "OK," he said, nodding, "for my family. I'll do it." And he put out his hand.

Gio shook his head. "Sorry, but that won't do, Max. You see, those other two got caught cheating, so I broke the hands that stole food from my family's table." He looked at Pete and Eddie. "It's a cultural thing, I guess. Tradition."

They shrugged.

"But you were the brains. The head of the operation. I've got to set an example." Gio got very quiet and leaned in very close to Max. "It's not your hand that I want on the table." He stepped back. "Eddie, get out the saw."

"What? No! Please!" Max began to scream now, as Eddie pulled a hacksaw from the toolbox and Pete stepped in behind him.

"Don't worry, Max," Gio assured him. "We'll put all of you in one dumpster. That way your family can sew you back together for the funeral."

Max moaned as Pete began forcing his head down onto the table. Eddie laid the saw blade across the back of his neck. "No! Please! Just tell me what you want. I'll do anything."

8

Joe didn't get much reading done that night. By ten the place was packed and roaring, and there was no time to even think until past two, when they were wrapping up for the night. So when he stepped outside and zipped up his coat, the same page of his book was cornered as when he arrived. It was a brilliant night, though: one of those clear winter skies, sharp as polished glass, the pebble-faced moon leaning right over this neon-lit little roadhouse that, on a commercial strip not too far from the airport, suddenly felt lonesome and desolate as a prairie. The last few drunks howled as they stumbled away. The traffic moaned softly, rushing by like wind through wheat fields. Autumn exited, calling out a quick good night as she hurried into the cold, too exhausted by the long hours dancing onstage and on laps to want to chat any more about taxes.

"Night," Joe answered absently. He had the fat book tucked under one arm while he tried to get his zipper to bite. It was only when he looked up that he realized that Autumn, who had crossed the parking lot, was now backing away from someone, a guy in a plaid hunting jacket who was trying to present her with a gigantic flower arrangement. Joe walked over.

"No, thank you," Autumn was saying. "I'm sorry, but I told you, I'm not interested."

"But you said you liked red roses." Now that he was closer, Joe could see that it was a pudgy white guy with beady eyes, holding a bouquet of roses, complete with white baby's breath, a tiny plush bear, and one of those small heart-shaped balloons that said LUV U. He was brandishing it at her, and she was flinching away as if it were a weapon.

"No, Duane. That's not true. You asked my advice on what flowers to get someone and I said everyone likes roses."

"Excuse me," Joe said, stepping between them, legs planted firmly, upper body angled toward Duane so that he could strike fast if he had to. "Everything OK?" he asked Autumn.

"We're fine," Duane said, scowling at Joe. "This is a private conversation."

"I didn't ask you," Joe told him. He saw a black Town Car with a TLC plate roll in. "You all right?" he asked Autumn again.

She nodded. "My car's here."

"Why don't you go, then?" Joe suggested. "And I will have a little talk with Duane."

Autumn nodded quickly, mouthing *Thank you* to Joe, and then hurried off, waving at the car.

"Autumn, wait," Duane called, and started to follow.

Joe blocked his path. "Forget it, Duane."

"Get out of my way, man. Mind your own business."

"That's exactly what it is. My business. She and I both work here. You're a customer. That's all."

"But it's more than that. I can feel it . . ." He glanced forlornly at the car as it drove away.

"Your feeling is wrong, Duane. Walk away and forget it. Hug your bear."

"What if I don't want to?" he sneered, fist tight around the bouquet. The bear shook with his anger.

"Then walking away won't be an option anymore. Your choices will be crawling or being carried. Think about it."

Duane sniffed haughtily, clutching his bouquet to his chest. "Fine. I will," he said, and turned to march away, the LUV U balloon above his shoulder like a flag.

Luv u too, Joe thought to himself. Then, feeling how cold it was, he started to walk, eye out for a cab. He didn't have any credit cards, and he only used his phone for calls or texts, so ordering an Uber or a Lyft was out of the question. As he trudged along the road, cars whipping by, wind in his eyes, he sighed with deep exhaustion. Maybe Donna had a point.

9

Gio needed to unwind. He was not, generally, the kind of man who felt a need to hang out with the boys drinking beer or escape from his family to watch a ball game. On the contrary, he usually couldn't wait to get home. He adored his children, and not only did he love his wife, he admired and respected her. Carol was a child psychologist, brilliant in her field, and far more widely read and cultured than he was. But it was more than all that: Giovanni Caprisi, the son and grandson of mafiosi, from a loving but violent—or perhaps violently loving—background, had found real intimacy, real connection, and even a measure of peace and happiness in his marriage. His palatial home on Long Island, the routines of dinner and homework, family movie nights and soccer games were like a refuge, an oasis of sanity to which he was eager to return.

Except on nights like this. For one thing, his adrenaline was pumping. The rage at knowing that two-bit clown, Mini-King Max, had tried to cheat him, the excitement of catching him, the thrill of violence, the scent of blood in his nose: it was impossible to just shut that off and settle down to watch *The Daily Show* with Carol or hear the latest on his daughter's struggle with trigonometry or his son's possible allergy to mold spores. He knew it would be hours before he could sleep.

But the real reason he couldn't go straight home from the casino was that he didn't want to still be this person when he got there. He was not just another guy with a stressful job who needed to blow off steam. He was a gangster. What was more, he liked being a gangster. He had been licking his chops like a hungry wolf at the prospect of taking apart Max and his minions. He'd grinned as the hammer hit the hand. He'd fed on their fear and exulted in victory when he turned the whole situation to his profit. But now, as though hungover, he felt dirty, creepy, toxic. He didn't want to go home like this, with the reek of evil still on him. He imagined his wife could see it in his eyes. That his kids could sense it. That the dog would howl or bark as if scenting the wolf. That it would pollute his house, like some filth he tracked in on his shoes. That was the difference between the two halves of his life: Out here he walked, impervious, through blood and shit. Back there, Carol made him take his shoes off at the door so as not to dirty the nice, clean rugs.

That was why he went to Cookie's. Cookie ran one of the most successful, exclusive, and, most important, discreet dungeons in the city—located, as it happened, not in some dark depths but on the fifth floor of a large and nondescript office building in east Midtown. It was, essentially, a high-end brothel, but one that catered solely to more rarified tastes, employing specialists to satisfy every craving, from pain and humiliation to far more elaborate scenarios. Are you a cop who needs to be handcuffed and smacked around? A criminal yearning to be punished? A priest desperate to confess? A rabbi dreaming of being interrogated by a blonde in Nazi regalia? A black minister lusting to play plantation? A WASP banker who longs to have a tiny Asian woman trod on his balls in high heels? A macho movie star begging to be spanked by Daddy? A gay fashion icon hoping to be diapered by Mommy? Cookie could make it all happen for a price. And no one would ever know.

Or so Gio hoped. There was a certain risk involved, he knew. But after his last secret lover, a beautiful young accountant expert in overseas banking, had betrayed him to the government and then been shot to death by Carol, the idea of dating seemed unwise. His marriage had barely survived it. They'd tried everything, even counseling—hard when telling the truth meant confessing to felonies—and only really reconnected when an attempt on Gio's life reaffirmed their love and priorities. Since then, Gio had refrained; but the itch was still there, and he knew that Carol didn't share it. Their sex life was good, but this other, secret passion, this need, just wasn't part of their dynamic. It never would be, and they both knew it. So he came to Cookie.

She was the only person on the premises who knew who he was—and in fact, he was indirectly her boss. It was his influence with the authorities that kept this place safe from police and prying landlords, and his protection that kept out the predators who preyed on the sex trade. And if anyone did find out, Gio would know where it came from, making Cookie the one person more concerned with keeping Gio's secret than he was.

Security at Cookie's was always tight. You needed an appointment to get past the guard in the lobby. Then, when you were buzzed past the anonymous office door, you entered an antechamber where a camera scrutinized you further before the inner door unlocked. That let you into a tiny space with a desk, where a young woman in a tailored suit greeted you, took your money, and sent you to a private room. Appointments were staggered to avoid meetings among clients. But Gio was even more careful: that night he entered the building from a side door used only by staff during the day and rode the freight elevator to knock on a door that Cookie herself opened, avoiding even the receptionist.

"Giovanni," she said with a grin. "Come on in."

She stepped aside, a big woman, wide through her hips and shoulders, her deep brown skin set off by a pink silk dress that shimmered as she moved, her Louisiana accent firmly in place even after decades away.

"Hello Cookie, how are you doing?"

"As best as I can, baby. Same as always."

She turned slowly and led him in, her abundant flesh rippling as she stepped, lightly, on her remarkably tiny and dainty feet, which were encased in handmade designer shoes. The room was done in deep reds and dark greens, thick carpets and lacquer finishes, buttoned padding on the door, velvet couches, lamps with tasseled shades, standing art deco ashtrays and table lighters, a Chinese screen hiding the bed, and a black-and-white-tiled bathroom, complete with clawfoot tub. It was a sanctum within a sanctum, like a cross between old New Orleans and Weimar Berlin.

Cookie had come up in the world of sex work the hard way. A poor kid from an abusive background, she'd run away to the big city and fallen, like so many girls, into the clutches of a pimp. But by dint of her guts and brains, she found an angle: it paid much better to deliver the abuse than to receive it. Rich men, mostly white but later Asian as well, would pay very handsomely to be dominated, humiliated, and punished by her. A judge, old and skinny and rich, who loved to kiss her toes, took care of the pimp. She began to travel the world, to educate herself about culture, art, and food, and in each city she found at least one wealthy slave to support her. Those perfect feet were her fortune. Millionaires crawled to kiss them, begged to lick them, paid exorbitantly to help them into shoes. With the money she saved, she opened her own places, moving from labor to management, first in Tokyo, then London, then New York, where she met Gio. They hit it off immediately. And as their mutually profitable business relationship blossomed into friendship, Gio found himself stopping by to talk in this private salon, where during one very late, very Scotch-soaked conversation, they realized they shared something else: a fondness for handsome, young men, WASPy and preferably blond. No longer accepting clients for herself, Cookie now kept slaves of her own choice, and the young man she displayed to Gio looked remarkably like his own ex, Paul. Gio, at an impasse in his own life, confessed to Cookie that the only way he could find relief from his desires and the pressure that built inside him was to dress as a girl, Gia, and to have a young man like that whip him, a fantasy that had haunted him since early adolescence. Cookie understood. And with her exquisite taste and impeccable discretion, she made the arrangements, thereby solidifying her friendship with Gio, the only powerful man she still had any need to please.

But not tonight. "I'm so sorry," Cookie said, as she settled on the settee and poured them each a couple of fingers of her latest rare single malt. "I wish you'd called earlier. I'm afraid the only boy working tonight was Julian, and he went home with a cold."

"That's all right," Gio told her. "You know I really just come to see you."

Cookie laughed, her breasts trembling under their curtain of silk. "I appreciate your fine manners, but don't bullshit a bullshitter. If there's one thing Cookie knows, it's what people want. Still, I wonder . . ." She swirled her Scotch thoughtfully. "I normally wouldn't even suggest it, these new girls are so trifling, but . . ."

Gio smiled. "Now who's bullshitting? OK, I'm curious. Out with it."

"My newest protégé, Ioana. I know it's not your thing, but she really does have a flair. She's into it for her own pleasure, a natural domme. That's rare in this business."

Gio shrugged and finished his drink. "Give me another of these and I just might go for it."

Smiling discreetly, and saying no more, Cookie poured another drink, then tiptoed out.

A moment later, Ioana entered. A Romanian immigrant, she was tall, elegant for her age. Her head, with its broad, pale forehead, wide-set dark eyes, sharp nose, and red lips, seemed large for her small frame and long, stockinged legs, a pale flower on a thin stem. Her glossy black hair fell like a curtain over her backless gown. She was beautiful and beguiling. And Gio knew instantly that he was not interested. At least not sexually.

Ioana understood. She sat, legs crossed, and accepted a drink.

"We like what we like," she intoned in her Romanian accent, with its surprisingly deep tones and *W*s that sounded like *V*s. *Like Dracula*, Gio thought. "Actually, though, you are my type," she said with a shrug, and held her glass to the light, illuminating the deep golden liquor. "What can I say? I like my men like my Scotch: strong, mellow, a little bitter, and at least twice my age." Then she drank.

Gio laughed, deciding immediately that he liked this girl. Even if she was going to keep her clothes on, and he was going to keep his wig and gown concealed in a wardrobe. They spent an hour chatting, and then he left, tipping her heavily.

"Thank you for a lovely evening," she said, and kissed his cheek. "I hope we meet again."

"We will," Gio said.

He was wrong.

10

Donna had them wire up Fusco.

After years babysitting the tip line, she'd been assigned, finally, to field duties after she killed a domestic terrorist and deactivated his homemade nuke (with Joe's anonymous help), and had been given lead on a case involving a human trafficking ring. A group, suspected to be a mix of U.S. and Latin American criminals, were smuggling in illegal aliens, then forcing them into prostitution. So far, they'd remained one step ahead of law enforcement by moving up and down the Eastern Seaboard, setting up shop in a town, working the customer base via local connections and the internet, and then, at the first whiff of law, packing up and leaving in the dead of night.

The women were all young and from Latin America, the Caribbean, Eastern Europe, wherever life was hard enough that paying (sometimes a whole family's pooled savings) to sneak into a strange country seeking work seemed like a risk worth taking: if they got a good job—cleaning, taking care of kids, working in a factory—they could send home enough to support the family. That was what the traffickers promised and what the women were desperate enough to believe.

A couple of young Salvadorans had escaped, leaping out of a moving van and running barefoot across a highway in Virginia. One was hit by a truck and killed, but her friend was picked up by a passerby, who took her to a hospital. She ended up talking to the local FBI office, describing the leaders, a brutal enforcer named Chuko and the madam, a vicious and greedy woman they called just Senora but whom, she thought, Chuko had addressed as Flora. Then the INS deported the unfortunate young woman and that was that.

The case languished until Donna—who, as a Latina and first-generation American, felt a special kind of contempt for these particular scum who preyed on their own people—came across the file and had an idea. Using the fake names on the girls' false papers, as well as tiny facts the girl knew about some of her fellow victims, Donna had tracked their entry through Miami, and checked that against other factors, such as flights, ships, and staffing schedules in the airports. She came up with the name of a single passport control officer who'd been on duty when the women came through. A look at his finances confirmed her suspicions; he'd made large deposits and large cash purchases shortly after each woman had entered the United States.

They brought him in, or the Miami office did. As Donna watched through mirrored glass, he broke quickly. But all he had to cough up was his contact: the smuggler who organized the women, providing transport and fake IDs, then told the officer whom to let in without question. As for the American ring itself or the bosses ultimately behind it, he had no clue. Then Donna had an idea, and after pitching it to Tom Foster, her boss, he authorized it, making her officially lead agent.

And that was how, a month later, she found herself driving to Newark with her partner, Special Agent Andrew Newton; Deputy Marshal Blaze Logan, who was stationed in New Jersey; and Detective Lieutenant Francis Fusco of the NYPD's Major Case Unit. Andy had been Donna's best friend in the Bureau since training; as a gay black agent married to a Jewish man, he shared her struggle as she fought her way up from the literal bottom of the FBI, a basement room where she sat checking anonymous calls. As for Marshal Logan, a butch lesbian, she'd been assigned to escort Donna through the wilds of Jersey once before, and her demeanor had been chilly; but after a deadly gunfight, followed by a bar brawl and a successful investigation, they'd become pals.

And then there was Fusco. Francis "Fartso" Fusco was corpulent, truculent, flatulent, and as likely to belch out a borderline-inappropriate comment as to just belch. Plus, Donna strongly suspected he was a bit too comfortable with their counterparts on the other side of the law. But he was an able, dedicated investigator and a loyal comrade. Working together, they had built first a grudging respect and then something like a real emotional connection when his young partner, of whom Donna had been really fond, died in the same shoot-out that killed her estranged ex-husband. One thing no one could deny about Fusco—for better or worse, he was old-school; for him, an experience like that bonded you for life.

But that wasn't why she'd called him. It was when they got the tip on the prostitution ring's latest location, in Jersey, and were almost ready to move.

"I'm sorry," Donna was saying to Andy, "I just don't think you're believable."

They were in her tiny office, still in the basement. Blaze sat grinning as her friends faced off.

"I can pass for straight, thank you very much." He stood and turned, modeling his outfit. "This happens to be a classic Brooks Brothers suit, which I just had tailored a bit because my hips are slim compared to my shoulders. A very masculine pale blue shirt. And this tie and pocket square, while a bit assertive for some of these white boys from Utah, is very much in keeping for a cis straight African American gentleman. Am I right?"

"Don't ask me," Blaze said. She herself was wearing jeans, a flannel shirt, and a leather jacket, with her badge and holster clipped to her hip. "All you FBI wimps look like dress-up dolls to me."

"I'm not being homophobic," Donna told him in a reassuring tone, "I'm being lookist. You're just too damn young and handsome to have to pay for it."

"Well, that is a good point," Andy admitted. He sat back down. "Then who?"

Blaze shrugged. "Donna and I can be a couple looking to spice things up."

Donna rolled her eyes. "We're trying to blend in, not make a scene."

"Fine," Andy said. "None of us can play the part. So who do we know who's totally believable as a john and will fit right in among a bunch of sleazy lowlifes?"

<hr />

"Hold still and try not to sweat so much," Andy told Fusco.

"First of all, stop tickling me," Fusco barked. He was sitting in the back of the van, stripped to the waist, as Andy wired him up and Donna, earphones on, fiddled with the dials on the recording equipment. Blaze was behind the wheel, eating one of the donuts Fusco had brought along, a chocolate coconut. "And second of all, go fuck yourself. It's a glandular condition. I can't help it." He turned to Donna. "Agent Zamora, Andy's hurting my feelings."

"It's not my fault the tape won't stick." Andy glared at him. "I might have to shave you."

"Andy," Donna said, acting as ref. "Try some powder and be gentle with the tape. And Fusco . . ." She leaned over to him. "Stop pretending you have feelings."

<hr />

Fusco knocked on the door at 8:15 P.M. He was disguised, more or less, as himself: creased, baggy blue suit, sweat, mustard-and-coffee-stained white shirt, crooked red tie. He'd made contact through a call girl website and gotten a number. After answering a few questions, he'd been given this address, a generic extended-stay business motel near the airport, featuring suites with kitchens and conference rooms. A goon had answered the door—a very large, dark-complexioned guy with a buzzed, lumpy skull—checked his (fake) ID, and let him in. The conference room had several couches and a TV playing one of those *Star Wars* movies he'd never seen—how many were there now? The madam, a bony Latina with dyed-red hair who matched the description they had for Flora, came over and asked what he wanted. Playing shy and embarrassed, Fusco mumbled about a full-release massage. Cackling, she took his cash in her claw and pointed at the girls.

"Take your pick," she said in her heavy accent, so it sounded like *take you peek.* "All young beauties ready to be nasty for you." She smiled horribly. The half-dozen girls were a mix: three Latinas, two maybe Balkan or something, and one black girl he guessed, from her accent, was Haitian. The big blonde was his type, but he focused on the brown girls, fingering his tie like a nervous mook. Then he pointed at the one with the red ribbon around her neck.

"I . . . I'll take that one, please. Um . . . Sandra?" He repeated the ridiculous, Anglicized working name. If she was a Sandra then he, Francis Fusco, was bonnie Prince William.

"Good choice, sir. I'm sure she'll make you very happy," the madam told Fusco, then ordered Sandra: "Room three."

Sandra rose and took his hand. A compact, pleasantly rounded girl in her early twenties, she had long black hair parted in the middle and wide-set green eyes. She wore a pink negligee over her red bra and panties, and red heels that put her head only near Fusco's shoulder. With a sad smile she led him down the hall, passing the kitchen, where a big guy sat, long hair in a ponytail, with gold rings and a leather jacket, looking at his phone. Chuko. Fusco would have gladly ripped that ponytail right off his skull, but instead he nodded meekly, like a john, and followed the girl through another door.

It was a small bedroom, dimly lit with a pink bulb, furnished with a hotel double bed, a night table, and a chair. It had that industrial motel carpet and the heavy pleated drapes hiding the parking lot view. Fusco held out his hand. "Sandra, right? I'm Arthur. I'm a salesman. I travel a lot. I sell and lease copy machines."

Sandra shook his hand, looking him right in the eye. "Hi, Arthur. Why don't you undress and lie down?"

"Well . . ." Fusco smiled nervously. "I'd like to talk a little first. If that's OK?"

Sandra nodded and turned on the radio. Pop music blared out. Then Fusco sat next to her on the bed and whispered into her ear, "Agent Donna Zamora says hello . . ."

⚬⟊⚬

"Sandra" was in fact Daisy Gonzalez, a registered confidential informant working with the FBI. When Donna and her colleagues had busted the crooked passport control officer, he'd provided a list of women who were coming through, and agents had grabbed them up. Each was interrogated and offered a choice: return home, or work for them, reporting to the Feds about the ring in exchange for immunity, protection, and that grand prize, a green card. Two of the girls, already scared witless, were ready to head home. Daisy was not. She was smarter, or at least tougher. Born in a poor little town deep in Mexico, her stepfather had been ready to marry her off to the local drug lord's idiot son. So she'd fled. She'd hustled all the way to the tourist sectors of Cancun, where she picked up her English and eventually met the recruiter, who got her into the United States. She did not want to go back.

So she was let through, papers cleared by the passport officer, who was now working for the FBI. Claiming to be a virgin, she was spared the worst aspects of her new job—they were saving her for something special—and when the girls were allowed, once a week or so, to wire home their meager earnings, she'd used the FBI's fake Mexican bank address to signal Donna her locations as they made their way up the coast. Finally, they'd been permitted a phone call. She called collect and spoke to Donna in Spanish, giving her the Newark address. The red tie and red ribbons were signals, and she knew, too, to watch for a john named Arthur who sold copiers. Saying he wanted to talk was Fusco's coded way of asking if they were being bugged or spied on. They were not.

"I think we are moving soon," Daisy told him now, in a whisper. "Maybe into New York City, closer to the big shots, like Agent Donna wanted."

"Do you know where?"

"They don't tell us anything. We just move in the middle of the night. But a doctor's coming tomorrow, to give us STD tests." She frowned in disgust. "And they were joking about me being the big prize."

Fusco nodded. He tasted the bitterness that he heard in her voice. He took a small metal disk from his wallet. "Here. This is a transmitter. It will let us follow you more closely from now on. Hide it in your clothes or someplace safe. A shoe." She looked down at the tiny device in her palm.

He shook her hand. "And I promise, next time I see you, we will be locking up those fuckers, and setting you free."

She smiled ruefully. "I'd like that. Very much."

11

Joe walked to work from the train. It was dark and bitterly cold, but he still preferred to walk. It was like a little blank spot of open space and time between one engagement with the world and the next. He'd been told once by a doctor that walking served a particular function in healthy digestion, and he thought maybe the same was true for the mind: after so many thousands of years on the plains and hills, we had evolved into creatures who needed to move our feet, slowly and steadily, to clear out the crap.

The winter wind was good for that, too, and by the time he turned into the parking lot of Club Rendezvous, he was relaxed and warm from the walk, scarf loosened, book tucked under his arm, looking forward to a hot coffee and maybe some time in the back booth with *Ulysses* before work got too busy.

"Hey you, bouncer . . ."

Joe peered at the guy. He looked familiar under the parking lot lights, but it took him a minute to register him as Autumn's stalker. Partly because he wasn't holding a bouquet and a bear. Partly because he was flanked by two much larger versions of himself, bruisers in work clothes, breathing steam.

"Hey, stalker," Joe said. "I forgot your name."

"Oh yeah?" He jutted his head cockily now, from between his bodyguards. "Remember telling me to go home and think about it? Well, I did. And I told my brothers."

The goon on his left, who had MOM and DAD tattooed across his very big knuckles, asked: "This the guy? You the one trying to steal my brother's girlfriend?"

The one on the right grinned, showing what Joe thought at first was a missing front tooth but it was actually a dead tooth that had gone nearly black. "He ain't as big as you said. Let's break him in half."

Joe sighed. He guessed it was time to get to work after all. As the left brother, Knuckles, came at him, swinging those sledgehammer fists, Joe moved forward, not back, dropping low to let the mitt marked MOM clear his head, and coming up inside his swing. Clutching *Ulysses* hard, he delivered a sudden uppercut, bringing the book up fast and crushing Knuckles's nose with the fat spine. He heard the crunch.

"Oof," Knuckles grunted, grabbing his face as the blood gushed through the fingers marked DAD. Joe dodged left, circling behind him as the other brother, Tooth, came for him, arms out like Frankenstein. He clouted Knuckles again from behind, this time slamming the front of the book flat against his ear. Knuckles howled and bent double, holding the side of his head. Another Joycean blow across the back of the neck put him down. Now Tooth lunged for him from behind, grasping him by the back of his collar. Dropping the book, Joe shrugged off his sleeves, slipping free and leaving Tooth holding his empty coat in both hands like a butler. Joe pivoted right, twirling like a ballerina, and looped his scarf loosely around Tooth's neck, as if teasing a big cat with string. Tooth turned, tossing the coat in a rage, but he'd pulled the scarf taut with his twisting. Joe leaned back, yanking hard on the two ends of the scarf and choking Tooth's air off. The harder he fought, the tighter it got. He stumbled forward, Joe kicking him in the back as he pulled. Tooth dropped to his knees, fading out as he struggled for breath.

Duane, stunned at first, had stood by watching. But he quickly realized this date, too, was not going as he hoped, and decided to run. He took off across the parking lot toward the street. Unfortunately for him, Gio's car was just pulling in.

Gio was behind the wheel, with Nero beside him, holding the Chinese takeout they'd just picked up, and with Pete and Little Eddie in back. He was braking, and about to park, when he saw Joe knocking around the two lumbering goons and the third, smaller one taking off.

"What the hell is this?" he muttered. Nero shrugged.

Frowning, Gio hit the gas and accelerated across the parking lot, clipping Duane as he ran across their path. Duane hurtled over the hood and toppled onto the blacktop, where he lay, moaning softly. Gio put the car in park.

"What's all this about?" he asked as he got out, stepping over Duane. Joe was busy strangling Tooth, a foot between his shoulder blades. He eased up and left him gasping, then whipped off the scarf. Knuckles was on his knees, carefully probing his nose, which now looked like an overripe beefsteak tomato. Joe pulled his coat back on and wrapped the scarf over his shoulders. He brushed off his book. There was blood on the spine.

"That one was hassling a dancer," Joe said. "So I chased him off last night. He came back with his big brothers. I forget his name."

"Duane," Duane moaned suddenly. "And they're my little brothers. I'm the oldest."

Gio stepped on his hand. "I didn't ask you, did I?"

Duane shook his head. Gio turned to his guys, who had all gotten out. "Nero, park the car. You two . . ." He nodded at Pete and Eddie. "Clean this up. Joe, help me carry in this Chinese food. I'm starving." He smiled as he handed him one of the paper bags. "I couldn't decide, so I got us moo shu pork pancakes and scallion pancakes both."

12

Ioana knew she couldn't tell Cookie. Moonlighting was strictly forbidden. Her whole business was built on exclusivity. On the other hand, everyone did it, or was tempted to, at some point or another, if only by the alluring possibility of a way out of Cookie's. It was without a doubt the safest, cleanest, best-run, and best-paying dungeon in town, with the wealthiest and most exclusive clientele. But how much better would it be to not have any clientele at all, just a single client, a patron who would finally give her what she deserved? After all, that was what Cookie herself had done—according to the legend, at least. The money from those wealthy men had financed this very place. Cookie's example was the best reason to disobey Cookie's own rules. A girl had to think and act for herself if she wanted to help herself.

That was what she told herself, anyway, when Timmy gave her the gift. He was the senior security officer in the building, and his underlings all loved him for his willingness to work the late shifts despite having control of the schedule. They didn't know that Cookie doubled his salary; he really worked for her. But now a "wealthy admirer" had tipped him lavishly to break the rule and facilitate direct communication with Ioana. It was simple: a gift box with a thin gold chain containing a tiny gold lock—like a padlock—and a card with a phone number. Ioana grinned, her spine tingling with excitement. She affected a cynical, worldly air—"I am just a moody Romanian Lolita"—but of course even that was a kind of fantasy, a character she was playing in the movie of herself. And in that movie, this was exactly the kind of thing that would happen.

"All I can say is, whoever he is, he's rich," Timmy told her. "He had the messenger tip me two hundred just to pass this along."

She went and had a double espresso and thought about it. Then she called.

The man who answered told her that he was very happy she'd called, that he'd admired her when he saw her at Cookie's but wanted to meet secretly both for his own privacy and because he wanted to get to know her better, to spend more time. "I admit I don't like to share," he said with a chuckle.

"Good, neither do I," she said, deciding, on instinct, to take a chance.

He told her the address. "And wear the necklace" was the last thing he said.

Back in the van, Andy and Blaze had settled in, eating the donuts and gossiping. Fusco might have been a throwback, but he knew his donuts.

"So," Blaze said, dipping her old-fashioned into her coffee while Andy took a big bite of vanilla frosted with sprinkles. "Who do you think Donna is boning?"

Andy shrugged, chewing. "I didn't know she was boning anybody. She hasn't said anything about dating at all."

"Exactly. That's the first clue. Come on, use your investigative muscles. No whining about a lack of dates or bitter monologues about shitty dates for months now."

"True. And she brushes me off every time I try to set her up. Even when Ari's trainer, who she always lusted after, broke up with his fiancée. We saw it coming and had her positioned. Who turns down rebound sex?"

"See, that's what I mean. Factor in her glowing complexion. Girlish laughter. Even humming when we were driving over here. Who fucking hums on their way to a stakeout?" Blaze poked Andy in the chest. "A woman who is being righteously fucked, that's who."

Andy pursed his lips. "Well, you'd know, I suppose."

Blaze dunked the rest of her donut and popped it in her mouth. "You got that right."

"So then the question is, why isn't she telling us all about the lucky man?"

"I can only think of one reason," Blaze said. "It's someone at work."

⚬⟞⟝⚬

"So which one is Autumn again?"

Joe and Gio were in the back booth, the Chinese feast eaten and cleared. The other guys were sitting up front now, watching the dancers and happily handing over their money.

"The redhead on the right," Joe told him.

"And you're doing her? That why the creep was after you?"

"What?" Joe frowned. "No way. The only thing I'm doing is my job."

"All right. Never mind. Didn't mean to impugn your professional ethics. It's just that since Yelena . . ." He trailed off. Yelena Noylaskya was a world-class thief, a lethal combatant, and, until recently, Joe's on-and-off flame. But their last adventure together had ended with much of the Russian mob's ruling class bleeding out in a bathhouse, which in turn catapulted Yelena herself to a place of power. He hadn't seen her since. It was a different life she was leading now, traveling between Brighton Beach, London, Paris, and Moscow. That suited Gio: Anton, the old boss, had been his rival. Now he had a friend in charge. And he thought it was best for Joe, too. Their chemistry, as partners in crime and in bed, had been powerful but volatile, and not ideal for his friend's long-term stability and mental health.

And Joe knew he was probably right. He and Yelena were good and not so good together for the same reason: they were very much alike. If they stayed together, they might get killed, or self-destruct or just meet once every month or two, but neither of them would ever talk about the long term, or exploring options, or love. That was why he knew Donna was his chance, and why he kept his hands off Autumn and the other dancers. Though, of course, Gio couldn't know.

"I'm just taking some time for myself," Joe said. "You know, exploring options."

"You say that, but every time you mention it, you're here in this booth," Gio observed. "Which brings me to the matter I wanted to discuss. I have an option you might want to explore."

He paused while a passing barback filled their coffee cups, then continued. "I don't know if I told you what a great job Gladys did for me. I hope it didn't tire her out too much."

"You kidding? She loved it. I think it keeps her mind sharp, like doing crosswords is supposed to for other seniors."

"*Sharp* is putting it mildly. She's got lasers behind those big grandma glasses. Anyway, thanks to her you are now looking at the part owner of the Mini-King Storage and Moving Corporation."

Joe lifted his cup. "Mazel tov."

"And to show my appreciation to both of you, I was thinking: Why don't you come and run that casino for me? With Gladys."

"What? Really?"

"Sure. Why not? Like you said, it's good for her. And it would be for you, too. Your end would be extremely profitable, I'd know the place is in good hands, and Gladys would have something to sharpen her mind on."

"Wow, Gio, I don't know . . ." He pictured himself glad-handing punters while Gladys counted money in the back. Would he have to wear a suit? "I appreciate the thought. And the trust. But it kind of sounds like running this place, except with a lot more math."

"This place is what it is, but the casino business? That is a real growth opportunity. A long-term prospect, my friend."

"I'll think about it, Gio," Joe said, and he would, but he also knew he could never clear it with Donna. Moving from a semi-shady part-time job as a bouncer to a full-time illegal enterprise was not what she would call "growth." She would call it "racketeering."

"That's all I ask," Gio said, happily patting him on the shoulder.

13

"You know, I think I might have an option for him to explore," Carol was saying. Among all the people Gio knew, she had always taken a special interest in Joe. Partly because he was special to Gio, the one childhood pal he was still close to, the one "professional colleague" whom he fully let into his personal life. But Carol, as a therapist, also felt an empathic connection. It wasn't hard to see that the orphan and juvenile delinquent who became the battle-scarred Special Forces soldier with the substance abuse issues had some serious PTSD going on.

"I just offered him one," Gio said, checking the salmon. It was cold as hell outside, with their house right on the water, but he still preferred to use the grill when possible, so he was out on the deck, cooking in his parka over his sweatpants. Carol had the potatoes roasting inside and the salad and asparagus ready to go in the kitchen, and now she was out on the deck, sipping her wine. Their daughter and son were supposed to be setting the table, but there was no sign of it. "You know that storage company that I just acquired part ownership of? I offered him a spot running some aspects of that. He said he'd think about it."

"I'm thinking, this might be more up his alley than the storage business," Carol said. "Plus I think it could be very healing for him. A way to shift his energy flow from negative to positive."

"Sounds like you're going to give him shock treatment."

"Ha-ha. No, smart-ass. But I am going to give him a chance to use his experience to help others, to free himself from the past by freeing them from fear. To learn by teaching."

"Teaching what?" He took the wineglass from her and sipped. The salmon sizzled. It was almost ready. Where the hell were the kids?

"Self-defense. The community center's wellness initiative just approved funding for a free class in empowerment through self-defense, open to all. Maybe he could teach it. I'm sure I could arrange a trial class."

"Hmmm." Gio nodded, flipping the fish. "That's not a bad idea."

She took her wine back. "Don't sound so surprised."

Gio laughed. "Now the next problem is getting our children to set the table. Fish is done in five."

Carol slid the door open. "I'll go find them. I'm freezing anyway."

"Try texting them," Gio called as she went in. "They're a little more likely to answer."

"Good morning, everyone. My name is Joe."

Joe had them go around the room and give their names (he was unable to retain a single one), along with their reason for attending. The room, a harshly lit cinder-block box somewhere deep inside the community center of this suburban town, reminded him more of a military installation or a jail than anything else, though the coffee and snacks on the side table were much better, and neither of those institutions featured the kind of uplifting signs that lined the walls. *F.E.A.R.*, one read, *False Evidence Appearing Real*. Another declared, *You Have the Power to Empower . . . Yourself!*

The ten students included four seniors, two men and two women, who all stressed their fear of muggers and break-ins, three adult women in workout clothes, who mentioned a fear of sexual assault or carjacking, and three teens. The two female teens angrily specified "toxic masculinity" as their reason for attendance, and the boy, who stuttered, said he'd been a victim of bullying and hoped to become more assertive.

In fact he seemed terrified of everyone there, especially the two girls, who were a year ahead of him in high school.

"Great," Joe said. "I think we can do a lot to help defend ourselves from all of that." He cleared his throat and looked around, sort of like a platoon captain assigned a group of unpromising recruits, or a coach with the least likely baseball team imaginable. "Before we get into any actual fighting, let's just look at some very basic strategies."

One of the women, a fortysomething blond in latex running pants, a sports bra, and expensive sneakers, raised her hand.

"Yes, um . . ."

"Candice. Call me Candy."

"Yes, Candy?"

"Aren't we going to warm up?"

"Oh . . ." Joe hadn't thought of it. Nor had he considered his own outfit. He wore what he always wore: his black hooded sweatshirt over a black T-shirt, jeans, and his Converse high-tops, though in winter he often wore work boots.

"We can if you want, Candy, but the thing is, you mentioned being assaulted while walking to your car at night as one of your fears. Well, your attacker isn't likely to give you a chance to warm up, is he?"

"My trainer said I need to always warm up," she explained. "I'm in recovery from a stressed hammy."

"Then why don't you do some quick stretches while we talk? Anyone who wants to, go ahead and stretch."

Candy and the other women immediately commenced a series of bends and thrusts, while the others followed along half-heartedly.

"Where was I?" Joe asked the room.

The boy shrugged.

"Oh yeah. Like I was saying, a big part of self-defense is reacting quickly and aggressively to neutralize an assailant by whatever means are at hand. So even before we learn any new fighting moves, there is a lot you can do. For example . . ." He looked over his prospects, who seemed as doubtful as he sounded, then gestured to a heavy-set old man with a cane. "How about you, Mister . . . ?"

"What about me?" he asked defensively. "I'm just here because my wife said we needed to use the community center more, and the pottery class is full."

"Fine, but I was actually just going to mention your cane. You might think that having to use it is a disadvantage."

"It ain't for fun."

"But in a fight it makes a great weapon. Swing it hard and fast, and try to aim for the joints, behind the knees or the elbows. Those spots are sensitive to pain and they collapse easy." Joe flashed back to the Russian bathhouse, where he had used a similar tactic on a mercenary. Except he'd sliced his tendons with a knife. "Or you could even take that rubber stopper off and file the bottom to a point."

"Hey," the old man said, smiling as he swung his cane around, breaking the knee of an invisible enemy. "That's not a bad idea." The others stepped out of range.

Joe turned to the boy. "And I see you have a sharp pencil in your pocket."

The boy touched the pencils and pens that poked from his shirt pocket. He shrugged. "I like to draw?" he offered as one possible explanation.

"Can I borrow it a second?" Suspiciously, the boy handed it over. Joe wrapped his fist around it, thumb cocked behind the eraser. "Now, held like this it's a very effective weapon. I recommend getting in close, then aiming for a vulnerable spot, like the ears or eyes." In fact, Joe had done something quite similar to the massive terrorist and heroin smuggler who'd tried to crush him to death, though he'd driven the mechanical pencil straight through to his brain.

Now the boy smiled as Joe returned the pencil, gazing at it as if it were a magical sword. "Thanks!"

"No problem." Joe turned back to the group. "Anybody here smoke cigarettes?"

The women frowned, looking horrified at the idea. The elders shook their heads very seriously. Tentatively, the teen girls raised their hands, only shoulder height, as if uncommitted.

"That's great," Joe said. "I mean, no it's not, it's terrible, you should quit. But in the meantime, a lit cigarette also makes an excellent deterrent when pressed against any exposed skin. Again, aim for the vulnerable places. Believe me, shove a cigarette in your attacker's ear and he's going to let you go. No matter how toxic."

The girls laughed and nodded. "Hell yeah," one said, and they high-fived.

"What if I don't smoke or use a cane?" a dark-haired, heavily made-up woman asked. She was dressed like Candy but in white and seemed to be her friend.

"Well," Joe said, looking her over. "I'm sorry, I don't recall your name, but I notice you have long nails."

In fact they were claws, elaborately shaped and painted with a holiday motif of tiny Santas, elves, and snowflakes. "My name's Janice," she said, wriggling them.

"She's a cosmetologist," Candy explained on her behalf.

"I'm not surprised. They look great."

"Thank you."

"But they could also be serious weapons."

"You mean like scratch their eyes out?" She laughed and made a swiping motion, like a cat.

"Sure. But even more effective, if, as you mentioned, someone was assaulting you up close, would be to gouge their eyes out." He stepped up to the teen boy and held his hands over his face to demonstrate. "Grab on like this and force your thumbs in. The key is to keep pressing, hard as you can. Make sure you get those nails under the lid. And even when they struggle, don't stop until you feel the membrane on the surface of the eyeball give way. You can tell because there's a pop, kind of like if you bite through the skin of a grape—"

That was when Joe, who'd been focusing on correct stance and hand placement, glanced up to see the looks of mingled shock and horror on the faces of his class.

"Please sir," the boy whispered, afraid to move. "I don't want to die."

Ioana woke up in darkness and, for a split second, thought she was home in bed. Then, realizing she was tied down, her first thought was that she was in the dungeon, at work, and had somehow simply drifted off for a moment. It had happened before, after a long shift, when she was awaiting a client who'd requested a damsel-in-distress scenario.

But no. This was not the luxurious fantasy dungeon, this was more like a real cellar: a cold, damp concrete floor, handcuffs holding her to a wall, the sound of water dripping in the darkness. Then she remembered: the mysterious gift, the phone call and address that she thought told her who it was, the billionaire who would change her life, the ride in the elevator, the knock on the door—then nothing. She called out, but only her own voice echoed back, letting her know that the space was big and that she was alone in it.

Then her eyes began to adjust, and she realized, with horror, that she was not alone. Another woman was chained to the wall, though from the flies buzzing and the stench that drifted over, Ioana knew she was dead. And then slowly she made out the form of another chained prisoner, further away. This one she could only surmise was female from the long hair; she was nothing but bones. And beside that another . . .

And then, even though she knew only her own echo would answer, Ioana began to scream and scream.

14

"OK, so maybe let's say that class was a learning experience for you and the students both." Carol was passing the sautéed spinach. Gio was slicing bread. Joe was frowning. Her two kids, Nora and Jason, were grinning. She'd invited Joe to dinner after several of his students complained that the self-defense class was "triggering," "disturbing," and even "traumatic." To soften the blow, she made chicken marsala.

"Sounds cool to me," Jason said. "I want to learn how to gouge the eyes out of a foe."

"You don't have foes," Carol said.

"What about Dez?"

"Desmond?" Gio asked. "I thought he was your best friend?" He explained to Joe, "He lives across the street. His dad's a tax attorney."

"He was, but we are archrivals on Fortnite now."

"Well, you can't blind him. That's final," Gio said. "So you'll have to work it out."

"So I'm fired?" Joe said. "Already? That was quick."

"Screw it," Gio said. "You're too good for them."

Carol smiled and patted his hand. "The community center has decided to go with another approach that emphasizes flexibility and mindfulness."

"I hear that helps a lot with carjacking," Gio said, dipping his bread into the sauce and tasting it. "Especially flexibility. For running home after they take your car." He scooped potatoes onto Joe's plate. "Don't worry about it. Eat. There's lots of jobs out there for a guy with your talents. Like high-end corporate consulting. Believe me, they'd be thrilled to have you."

⚬━✦━⚬

"Don't worry about it. There's lots of jobs in the world. What you should be doing is corporate security consulting."

"That's what Gio said." Once again, he was in Donna's bed, happily exhausted, and not-so-happily discussing the future. Her daughter was sleeping—soundly this time, he hoped. This was a brief visit before she went on duty. She was the one working late for a change.

Donna shrugged. "Gio does have a head for business. You should listen to him."

"He also wants me to run a casino with Gladys."

"No."

"That's exactly what I said."

They kissed and she thought, *Why not, we have time,* and then, just as she was sliding on top of him, her phone. "Shit." She glanced at it. "It's work." Another kiss. "Hold that thought." And into the phone: "Yeah? What?" She stood abruptly. "OK, yeah . . . gimme five." She hung up. "Shit! Come on, get up. Quick."

"What? What is it? Somebody rob the Federal Reserve or something?"

"I wish. It's Fusco." They were due to relieve Andy and Blaze. "He was supposed to call and say he was on his way."

"Yeah. So? You told me."

"He was calling from downstairs. He, quote, needs to use the can."

"Shit," Joe agreed now, sitting up, feeling around under the covers for his boxers. "That's not good. He can't see me."

"And you definitely can't hide in the bathroom again."

Joe and Donna both slid into jeans. He found her bra and tossed it over as she took off his T-shirt and handed it to him. "I'll hide in here," he suggested, "slip out after you go."

"No way. My mom's coming over to watch Larissa. She'll curl up on the couch—and believe me, she sleeps like a cat. I spent my teenage years trying to sneak by her." Yolanda, Donna's mother, had somehow become great pals with Joe's grandmother, a high-risk situation for them both.

Joe yanked his socks on, while Donna, lying back, leg up, yanked down a boot.

"Fire escape again?"

"It's too early. People have their lights on. And their windows open. Including my mom and all her friends." Living in the same building in Washington Heights was terrific for safety, child care, and home cooking, but bad for privacy. It was essentially a small Puerto Rican village. And like many older New York buildings, in winter it was as overheated as a Puerto Rican village in the summer. Everyone kept their windows open till bedtime at least. Donna even had a shallow pan of water sitting on the radiator, as an old-school humidifier.

Joe laced his boots. "I definitely cannot meet Fusco, Donna."

"Agreed," she said, pulling on a sweater. They peered at each other, neither wanting to know exactly what the other was thinking.

"So?" Joe asked her. "What are we going to do?"

"Think of something, baby," she said, as she strapped on her gun and badge. "You're the criminal mastermind."

Teasing or not, she had a point: if you wanted to evade a cop, think like a thief. He stepped into the hall closet and pulled it nearly shut just as Fusco pounded on the front door.

"Yeah, yeah," Donna said, answering gruffly while she composed herself in the hall mirror. "Hold your water."

"It ain't my water I'm worried about," he called, knocking louder.

She unlocked the door and Fusco busted in.

"Keep it down, my kid's asleep," she told him as he hustled across the living room, already unbuckling his belt.

"It's an emergency."

"For Christ's sake, Fusco, have some decency. My kid bathes in there."

"Sorry. Here's a free tip. Don't eat the fried pork skins at Dino's," he said, hurrying into the bathroom and shutting the door.

Donna signaled to Joe, who was peeking from the closet as she answered Fusco through the door. "What are you, a rookie? Every cop in the Heights knows that."

Joe blew Donna a kiss as he slipped from the closet and out the door, shutting it carefully behind him. Collar up, hiding his face as he pulled on a hat, he hurried by Yolanda's door and down the stairwell, making good his escape. He was out clean. But like any sneak thief who'd just slipped through the fingers of a cop, he had to wonder how many more times he could do this before he was caught.

15

This time, when Gio stopped by, Cookie had made sure to have Brendan waiting for him. A strapping blond lacrosse player putting himself through NYU law school, he was enthusiastic about fulfilling Gio's fantasies—he helped him transform into Gianna, complete with long wig, makeup, dress and undergarments, and whipped him vigorously before they had sex—but without the emotional investment that had made Gio's relationship with Paul so complex and ultimately so dangerous. Afterward, rather than cuddle, Brendan liked to talk about school, his travel plans, and the kind of law he hoped to practice. Right now, he was in an idealist phase, wanting to battle discrimination and work for an LGBTQ-focused nonprofit.

"Sounds terrific," Gio told him. He'd showered and was getting dressed. "Except for the part about no profits. How will you pay off your loans?"

Brendan grinned. "Maybe I'll keep doing this on the side—it's all profit." He helped Gio on with his shirt. "Actually, we just had a seminar on sex workers' rights."

"Such as?"

Brendan shrugged. "Legalization, unionization, health care and safety, like that."

"Sounds good to me." Gio began to tie his tie while Brendan fetched his suit from the closet. Known as a sharp dresser, he'd been careful, when changing, not to wrinkle his clothes.

"You don't think decriminalization would be bad for business?" Brendan handed him his trousers and stood holding the jacket.

Gio shrugged. "Are the law firms worried about running out of clients? Why should Cookie?" He slid on his jacket and looked in the mirror, checking his cuffs while Brendan brushed off the shoulders. "As long as there is human nature, we will all be in business." Then he pulled out a folded clump of bills and put it in Brendan's hand: "But remember, if this job was legal, you'd be handing half of this over for taxes."

When Cookie popped in, carrying a tray with two glasses and a bottle of her latest Scottish love, Gio asked her how Ioana was doing. She shook her head. "She's up and gone, *cher*." Snapped her fingers. "Like that. Missed all her appointments. Didn't answer the phone. Not good. I think she ran into some trouble."

Gio, to his surprise, found himself a little disappointed. But he adopted a casual tone. "That's how it goes. You know that, Cookie. She took off with some guy. Or decided to quit the life. Happens all the time."

Cookie shook her head, waving a thick, heavily jeweled finger at him. "Sure, they come and go. But leave without her money? Never."

"She split without getting paid?" Gio asked, his eyes narrowing. "Maybe she's just on vacation or had to go home for an emergency and forgot to tell you."

"Without her passport?" Along with several thousand dollars in back pay, Ioana had asked Cookie to keep her passport in the office safe. It was still there. "No, my friend," Cookie said, pouring them more whiskey. "Listen to Cookie. She's been around a long time. Something bad happened to that girl."

Ioana ran. Or she tried to. She was weak from lack of food, water, and sleep, stiff from the cold, and her feet were bare, though mercifully numb, as she hobbled across the cracked concrete and broken glass.

She'd been chained up for hours, days, years. Who knew? It was eternal night down here, blackness relieved by shadow and the rustlings of rats. She was stripped to her undergarments, and that damned necklace, the lock, now a bitter joke, around her neck. And the bracelets, of course, the handcuffs attaching her to a pipe on the wall. It was her rage at the cuffs that first offered a glimmer of hope. As she freaked out, banging and yelling and twisting, working herself into exhaustion, she had felt the pipe shift, just slightly. It was decades old and caked in rust, and now she realized that it rattled a bit when she yanked her chain against it. It was crumbling away from the wall. So she began dragging her bracelet against the metal, again and again, ceaselessly, slowly wearing at the weak spot in the pipe, and digging her way to freedom. That went on for hours, days, years . . .

And then, suddenly, it gave. The pipe slid away from the wall, just a quarter inch or so, but as she ground her cuff against the opening, it gave a bit more, till she slipped the bracelet out, scraping her skin off, and she was free. Or perhaps that was the wrong word. She was loose. But she was still in this dungeon, this tomb.

Instinctively, she tried to jump up and flee, but she was too weak. She stumbled and fell, her legs simply folding beneath her. So she leaned on the wall, grabbing the pipes that lined the concrete for support, and pulled herself up, then began slowly stretching, moving, getting her blood flowing. And then, as best she could, she began to hobble across the chamber, not sure where she was going, but knowing her only hope was to get away from where she was.

Almost immediately she was lost. As she wandered in the dark, stumbling through tunnel after tunnel, turning randomly like in a maze, the brief rush of hope Ioana had felt gave way to panic and then despair. She stopped to catch her breath and, exhausted, sat on the floor, too disheartened to care when she realized she was in a puddle. Then she saw the light. It was a glimmer, coming from down the long hall, but it was light, external light. Reenergized, she stood and ran, and minutes later she was aboveground, passing through what looked like a crumbled, overgrown entrance into open space.

There was the night sky above her, starless and blank with fog, but glorious nevertheless. The wind stung her bare skin, but it was glorious, too, because the scent told her she was by the river. She almost laughed with glee, but her throat was too dry.

She looked around, trying to decide which direction to go. She had to find help, of course, police or a hospital. But part of her yearned just to find a taxi and go home and get in her own bed and pretend this had all been a dream.

Then she heard a shot.

It took a second to register what it was, that whistle and crack. But when the second shot rang out, hitting the ground just in front of her, she ducked low and bolted, running straight ahead, no longer caring about direction as long as it was away. And then the fog began to part and she saw the river around her and the sky above her and realized she'd made a mistake, she was running out onto a pier with nowhere to hide, and when the next shot rang out, she knew there was only one way off, one way to freedom.

So she jumped.

16

At first, when Joe called Integrated Secure Solutions, a boutique corporate security consultancy—he'd pictured a little shop with a cute display of billy clubs or a line of designer pepper sprays—they'd been enthusiastic. Ex-military were their top recruitment sector, even more than ex–law enforcement. Local law enforcement were useful, it was true, because of their connections and knowledge, but too much knowledge of what was legal could be a distraction. A soldier with black ops skills was exactly who ISS's clients wanted protecting their homes and businesses. The recruitment specialist Joe met with was a former Marine himself.

"Except there's no such thing as an ex-Marine, is there?" he said, laughing as he shook Joe's hand.

"Right," Joe said. "I've heard that."

"ISS is a great home for guys like us, who don't feel quite right out of uniform. Who need something to belong to."

"Sounds great," said Joe, who had never felt even remotely right in anything but his jeans and T-shirts. Nor was he big on belonging, as was made abundantly clear when they ran a background check and found no work record, no credit score, no college degrees, no club member-ships; nothing but a criminal record, an expulsion from Harvard, and a dishonorable discharge. It seems the only institutions to which he'd belonged had been very happy to let him go. And the feeling was mutual.

The recruiter shook his hand again, a lot less heartily, and said they'd keep him in mind, but Joe had the feeling he had not found a home after all. Still, he was in the city, not far from the river, so he decided to take a walk uptown and call Frank.

Frank Jones was a painter, well known in the art world, who had kept his studio in Harlem for decades. A Vietnam War vet whom Joe had met at the VA hospital, he'd become perhaps the only person he spoke to honestly about his PTSD and the difficulties of adjusting to civilian life. Maybe he'd know what kind of straight job Joe could get.

⚊⚊

"Don't become a fucking painter, that's all I know."

They were in Frank's studio, a large, open, raw space with a view of 125th Street sprawling below. Frank sat in his leather armchair, which was patched and scratched and disgorging stuffing. Joe sat in the straight-back chair, caked with old paint and worn smooth in the seat. The only other choice was an iron bed frame with a bare mattress. All these furnishings had appeared in many of Frank's paintings, but the one on the easel, from the glance Joe stole before Frank covered it with an old sheet, was of a steeply angled view down onto the street. There were worktables covered in half-squeezed tubes and brushes in jars and coffee cans, shelves heaped with books and magazines, and piles of splotched rags torn from old sheets. There was discarded mail, a pizza box, a rotary telephone, a broken umbrella, an empty caviar tin, and much more, but the main substance dominating the space was paint. Paint was everywhere, dripped on the floorboards, smeared on the walls and columns, splattered on the furniture. There was so much paint that the room appeared to be the inside of a magical cavern where time had built up an accretion of multicolored stalagmites and stalactites. Here and there, the markings showed signs of a human presence—a handprint, an image torn from a book and taped up, a row of phone numbers scrawled on the wall above the phone. Joe was happy to see his own among them as he sipped the espresso Frank had prepared in his living quarters, which were behind a curtain in the other part of the space.

"Why not?" Joe asked. "You seem to be doing all right."

"Now I am, sure." He gazed around his realm. He wore paint-splattered chinos with frayed cuffs, a thick cashmere sweater with a hole in the elbow, bedroom slippers, and a Rolex. His glasses hung on a piece of yarn. "It just took like thirty-five years."

"Is it easier? Now that your work sells, I mean."

"No. Paying the bills is easier, but not painting. It's harder. But then again, you don't want it to be easier. It's when I'm working on something that I don't know how to do that I'm excited to get up in the morning. Anxiety and despair keep me going. Not fame and success."

"So dramatic!" A lilting female voice with a slight South Asian accent came from behind the curtain. An Indian woman, small and fine-featured, entered carrying a tray. She wore scrubs and a belted sweater, all paint free. "My heart breaks for how hard your life must be, sleeping till noon, staring out the window, painting naked people, not going out or even putting on shoes unless you feel like it."

Frank laughed loudly. "Joe, meet Dr. Kiran Acharya. Brilliant ob-gyn, model, and snack maker." He reached for the tray and grabbed a grape, which he popped in his mouth, before slicing some cheese. "But she's got it severely twisted." He smiled at her. "I will have you know I was up at eleven this morning and working by twelve. And you see more naked people in a day than I do in a month. Though I hope you wear shoes."

Kiran shrugged. "I wouldn't know, I was delivering a baby at six. In clogs." She held a hand out to Joe. "It's a pleasure to meet you, Joe. Please have some cheese and crackers before he eats it all."

"Nice to meet you, too," Joe said. "And thanks." He took a few grapes.

"And please forget what he said about modeling. That's supposed to be a secret."

"Don't worry, Joe can keep a secret," Frank said. "Under torture if necessary, right, soldier?"

"Yes, sir."

"I don't think that will be necessary," Kiran said, spreading paté on a cracker and handing it to Joe. "But the real truth is, I am only doing it as a deal. For every hour I pose, Frank spends an hour birding with me."

"Sorry?" Joe ate the cracker. It was good, really good. "Birding?"

"Yes, I admit I am a fanatical bird-watcher. Maybe that is weirder than posing nude these days. And I am forcing it on Frank."

"Ever tried it, Joe? Not bad. Kind of like doing recon in the bush except with less killing."

"You joke. But of course there is a war going on, nature's war. Birds fighting each other to eat or to reproduce. Cats hunting birds. Hawks hunting everything. Not to mention our battle against the city and the developers. Which reminds me!" She pointed at Frank. "Don't forget you said you'd make a sign for our protest."

"Jesus, woman," Frank groaned. "I said I'd go to the protest and donate a painting to the fund-raiser. I'm not making signs. What is this, craft class?" He turned to Joe. "She's on a crusade to save the Wild Westlands for the birds."

"Not just for birds. For us. For all living things." She gave Joe a flyer from a stack on the table. "Here. This has all the information."

The Westlands were a patch of riverfront where a decrepit pier and loading docks, abandoned during the bad old days of the '70s and '80s, had reverted to a wild state, overgrown and teeming with birds, fish, and small animals, indigenous and feral. People had even claimed to see deer and the occasional misguided seal. Citizens groups had been fighting to have it declared a nature preserve and turned into a park.

But the city council was about to turn it over for development into a hotel / luxury housing / restaurant and shopping complex.

"Just what we need," Frank said. "More rich-people projects, tourist shopping malls, and overpriced shitty food." He sliced a hunk of cheese and tasted it. "Funny thing is, back in the day, that was a natural wilderness preserve of another kind. Notorious gay cruising spot. I mean full-on group orgies on the pier and all kinds of hooking up in the bushes. Hookers working the waterfront. Open drug use all over the place. That's why it was called the Wild Westlands. Early '80s, a bunch of us went down there and did paintings, too. A lot of graffiti but also murals, conceptual stuff. Like an underground museum. Probably worth something if you could get to it, and if it's still there." Then he stood, brushing crumbs onto the floor. "And speaking of art—it's time to get naked, my dear. Light goes early this time of year."

She laughed, happily. "Let Joe finish his coffee, at least."

"No, that's fine. I'm done."

"Guess we didn't solve your problem, did we?" Frank said, rooting through a thatch of brushes. "But what the hell do you expect? If a good-looking young white fellow like yourself can't hack it in this society, what's an old motherfucker like me going to tell you? Didn't you go to Harvard or something? What did you study?" He squeezed some paint from a tube onto a palette and began mixing it.

"Before they kicked me out I studied literature. And philosophy."

"OK then, forget that. Even more useless than art. Unless . . ." He paused, holding his brush in midair. A glop of paint fell on the floor. Kiran sighed. "You know?" He pointed the brush at Joe. "Old Alexis might be looking for a partner. And you two might just fall in love." He grabbed a sheet of newspaper and laid it on the floor, then leaned down to dab the spill. "Let me just give you the address."

17

The last thing Detective Mark Fry was in the mood for was a dead hooker. He had enough on his plate. And when the body popped up in the Hudson, literally bobbing to the surface as a horrified group of tourists cruised by on a sightseeing tour, it fell to the river patrol to scoop her up and drop her in the laps of detectives from Manhattan South. Manhattan South had followed the usual procedure. Accident was ruled out: she was in her very fancy underwear. Suicide was ruled out by the signs of abuse (though not sexual assault) and the evidence that she'd run barefoot over broken glass. Then there was the set of handcuffs hanging from her wrist, both bracelets locked. This was foul play, very foul.

However, no missing person reports matched up, or any open cases. Finally, after the pathologist got a few prints, someone thought to run them against the files in passport control. Bingo. She was Romanian, Ioana Petrescu. But she wasn't an unlucky tourist. She'd been stateside three years on a very sketchy student visa, and the precinct detectives suspected a working girl. That was when it became Fry's problem. He was Vice.

A lot of cops didn't like working Vice. They found it too upsetting, or depressing, or maybe too exciting, depending on their personal issues, but it suited Fry. A teetotaling, nonsmoking health nut who went to church with his wife and three kids every Sunday, he himself had only one vice: greed. It made him a perfect Vice cop: his abstemiousness protected him from temptation, his sanctimoniousness insulated him from the compassion that led to a savior complex and the ensuing burnout, and the rampant opportunities for corruption kept him happily filling his pockets. Shaking down brothels and sex clubs, leaning on hookers and pimps, blackmailing unlucky johns, or, better yet, earning the friendship of high-end johns by making their possible arrest or exposure go away—it was all extremely lucrative. It had even led to a plum side job, the kind of thing that set you up for a post-retirement career: a wealthy real estate guy had needed help making a call girl turned memoirist see reason. It worked out so well he'd been hired on as an all-purpose fixer and "security consultant." So the last thing he needed to be wasting time on was a dead hooker—who was, after all, worth nothing to nobody.

Still, he could always use a favor in his pocket along with the cash, so he took the picture around, visiting places in a widening radius from where she was found, and the security guard who shepherded johns into the Midtown office building where Cookie rented a discreet suite had given her the nod. He went back to the precinct dicks and told them she was definitely on the game. They thanked him and buried it under their pile of work. One less thing to worry about. The case would stay open, of course, murder always did, but a dead foreign hooker killed in the line of duty? No one was going to miss her, or claim her body, or complain to the bosses. Cops filed that, if only mentally, under NHI: No Humans Involved.

Then Fusco called. He'd flagged her name, and when it popped up in the system, he asked to see the file.

"File's pretty thin," Fry told him. "Anything I should know about?" He was happy to pass the buck but mildly curious about Fusco's interest: he was no choirboy himself, but Fusco was Major Case, the big time, plus the chief had just pinned a medal on him for helping foil that terror plot.

"Nah," Fusco grunted. "Just something the FBI asked me to keep an eye out for involving foreign girls. Nothing important."

"Damn Feebs should do their own work, right?"

"You said it," Fusco mumbled, thanked him, and hung up. Then, while he printed the file out, he switched to his burner phone and called Gio.

18

Perry Street Bookshop was two steps down from the sidewalk, under a crooked brick house, one of those deceptively deep shops that seems small from outside, set on a quiet corner in the far West Village, a spot that, even in the era of trampling tourists, movie star neighbors and *Sex and the City*–themed tours, still managed to get no walk-in traffic, unless you were lost. A bell tinkled as Joe entered, but no one seemed to care, especially not the white cat, long and languorous, who stared at him with pale blue eyes from its post in the window, behind the otherwise unguarded counter. The place seemed to be built of books. There were floor-to-ceiling shelves on both sides and more rows leading, at slightly off angles, into a maze of shelves, piled tables, and random stacks rising from the floor and tottering on the counter.

"I'm back here," a cultured but disinterested voice called, finally. "Should you need anything." It seemed to hope he didn't. Joe made his way back, watched suspiciously by the cat. He made a wrong turn into poetry, got waylaid by a large collection of atlases, emerged in the midst of French Modernism, passed under a special shelf for the Beats, and finally found what he suspected was a sign of life: smoke rising from behind a wall of books, haphazardly piled on a huge wooden desk.

"Hi, I'm looking for Alexis," Joe said.

"Are you?" the voice said from behind the books. A long-fingered hand, nails cut short, with clear polish, shifted some of the books, revealing a long, pale figure similar to the cat, dressed in a freshly pressed white shirt, blue bow tie, unbuttoned sweater cardigan vest, pleated woolen trousers. Another pair of blue eyes behind gold-framed glasses. A long draw on a cigarette and a plume of smoke. "And what do you want with her? I hope you're not here to sell me that."

"What?" Joe looked down. He realized he was holding his battered copy of *Ulysses*, which he'd been reading on the subway. Alexis fluttered a hand and Joe reluctantly handed it over. He ruffled the pages.

"No, this won't do at all, I'm afraid. I have three better copies of this Gabler edition right there." A finger pointed vaguely into the maze. Joe would learn that Alexis somehow knew where every volume in the avalanche was. "This one contains someone's scribbling, unfortunately . . ."

"Yes, that is mine . . ."

Alexis made a face. "And possibly their blood."

"Not mine," Joe said.

"If you're looking, I have two of the reinstated Penguins, one hard one soft, a fair 1961 Modern Library, reset from the Bodely, an acceptable 1960 Bodley. If you want to really upgrade, I have a very fine original Random House, 1934. My 1939 revised Odyssey Press is in the safe, and I'd need to know you were serious about buying before I got up and bent over." The thin lips pursed over another stream of smoke. The cat popped out of nowhere and walked across the desk, ignoring Joe and sitting on his book to be pet by Alexis.

"Actually, it wasn't the books I was told to come and look at," Joe said. "It was the shop."

⟜

Alexis was a fixture from another Village era—certainly not kinder or gentler but somehow easier—when rent was cheap, attitudes were lax, and smoking, apparently, was harmless. He (or she; Alexis seemed to vary pronouns based on mood as much as anything) had owned the shop and the building for decades, living in the apartment above and renting out the others. Still, business, never all that swift, had been slowing for decades, and he was behind on mortgage and taxes.

He waved a hand, drew a smoke circle in the air. "I admit, I could use an infusion of fresh blood." He pushed Joe's book back across the table. "But not literally."

Joe took a look around. He could, in theory, buy in with a chunk of his savings, work here part-time, learn the trade. Not exactly a booming industry right now, but as Frank said, "They told me painting was dead before I even started. We're both still alive. People are even buying records again. Maybe paper will be the new vinyl."

It would, in any case, be a nice life, down here in this labyrinth of books, talking to the Minotaur, ignoring customers, and someday, if he was patient, petting the cat. Joe breathed it in and felt something new: it was peace. A calm, pleasant, slightly boring life. But could it be his? Then his phone rang.

"Hey, Gio, what's up?"

"Where are you? What are you doing?"

Not wanting to answer the second question, he answered the first, vaguely. "At a bookstore downtown. Why?"

"We need to talk. It's urgent."

Suddenly worried that Gio knew about Donna, he answered, voice level: "Sure, what's up?"

"I'll tell you when I see you. But career development is over for now. You've got a job."

PART II

19

The Golden Dragon was crowded. The palatial Chinese restaurant did a booming business, and the main room, a vast hall with large circular tables on several levels, was buzzing with activity. Waiters in black pants and white shirts hurried everywhere with heavily laden trays, setting the tureens of hot soup, covered serving dishes, and bamboo steamers stacked with buns and dumplings onto the lazy Susans that rotated among the hungry diners, while busboys cleared dishes and unfurled fresh white tablecloths, and hostesses in brightly colored cheongsams escorted the next extended family or laughing gaggle of coworkers. Several weddings were happening in the ballrooms upstairs, and here and there young people in tuxedoes or elaborate bridesmaids' gowns rushed by. As Joe hesitated in the entranceway, a bride appeared, climbing from a white stretch limo, helped by a retinue of family holding her train, veil, and bouquet. He stepped back and held the door, then entered in their wake, feeling a little dazed. The only other non-Asians he saw were wedding guests: a black couple holding hands and carrying a wrapped gift; a college-age white groomsman in a tuxedo and cummerbund.

"Good evening, sir." A woman in a cheongsam approached him, holding menus.

"Hi, sorry, I'm not here for dinner actually . . ." Joe began, but she gestured toward the interior.

"Your party has arrived. Please, right this way."

She turned and began to quickly make her way through the crowd, like an expert tracker. Joe followed. She led him into a back hallway where waiters bustled, silverware clattered, and busboys snuck cigarettes. They got in an elevator, the woman smiling pleasantly, still holding her menus, while they rose a few floors. The doors opened onto another hallway, also lined in wood paneling with potted jade plants, but empty this time. The quiet was noticeable, the roaring restaurant now a dim murmur. Pointing gracefully again, she guided him to the end of the hall and slid open a door, then held it, nodding, and slid it shut behind him.

He was in a private dining room, ornately decorated with elaborate woodwork and beautiful scrolls, tasseled lanterns, a long lacquer table surrounded by upholstered chairs, a view of the busy Chinatown street behind thick glass. There were five diners gathered around the table. And no food.

"Joe," Gio said, standing, "thanks for coming so quick. You know everybody here."

Joe approached the table, smiling. Sitting before him, impassively, was a Who's Who of the underworld's ruling class. At the head of the table was Uncle Chen, the Chinese crime boss, a short, wide man who had to be in his seventies, though unwrinkled and smoothly bald, and dressed, uncharacteristically, in a tuxedo. To his left was Menachem "Rebbe" Stone, who controlled the illegal side of ultra-Orthodox life in Brooklyn and beyond. He too was oddly formal, in a silk robe and fur hat. Next was Jack Madigan, eldest of three brothers who ran a small but still powerful Irish gang on Manhattan's West Side, and whom Joe and Gio had been instrumental in helping take power. Jack's youngest brother, Liam, had become one of Joe's crew. Next was Little Maria. Just under five feet tall (without her very high heels), Maria was the unchallenged queen of the dope trade in much of Washington Heights and the Bronx. She'd lost her boyfriend, her aunt, her dog, and her foot in a raid on her home but had made a strong recovery. She was dressed in red leather, pants and jacket, her prosthetic slotted into a red stiletto shoe, and she held a gold-tipped cane. Across from her was Alonzo, boss over the black gangs of Brooklyn; a sharp dresser who often shared tailors with Gio, he was in a pinstripe suit and purple silk tie with a camel hair overcoat. And beside him was Gio, impeccable as always in a gray suit, white shirt, and crimson tie that matched his oxblood shoes. He clapped Joe on the back as he took the next seat, and then sat back down, too, crossing his legs and unconsciously hitching his trousers to preserve the crease. A file folder lay before him on the table.

"Before we get down to business," Gio said, "I want to thank you, Uncle Chen, for accommodating us on such short notice, especially on the night of your grandniece's wedding. I'm sorry to darken a happy occasion with such matters."

Uncle Chen smiled mildly. "Business has to come first, we all know that. But never let it spoil your life, either. You are all invited to the party. I promise you a ten-course feast. You can sit at my old friend Rebbe's table."

Rebbe smiled and held up a gnarled finger. "Don't worry, you won't have to eat my kosher dinner."

"You can cheat a little," Uncle Chen said, patting his hand. "It's a party."

Everyone laughed. Rebbe went on: "I also want to say that our friend Yelena from Brighton Beach sends her regards. She is out of town but also concerned about this problem. And very glad to know you are handling it, Joe."

Joe nodded. He had not seen Yelena since their last job ended, when she had been at a different table, representing the bosses of the Russian mob.

"We're all glad to see you, Joe," Alonzo said. "Thing like this, who are we going to go to? Not the cops. That's for damn sure."

Maria shrugged disdainfully. "What do they care if someone is killing us?"

Joe was confused. "Sorry. What exactly is going on?"

"Women are disappearing," Gio said. "We want you to find out what happened to them."

He slid the file over, and Joe opened it. A dead body, female and young, he thought, though it was hard to tell much more than that.

"Her name was Ioana Petrescu. She worked at a dungeon, Cookie's, which is—well, should have been—under my protection." Gio frowned as if he'd bitten into something bitter. He swallowed it. "She was also a friend. The cops say she was imprisoned and tortured, and they think she died trying to escape. Anyway, they fished her out of the Hudson yesterday."

"But she ain't the only one," Alonzo said. "Once Gio started asking around, we realized we'd all lost people. At least seven girls we can think of. Could be more."

Joe shut the folder. "Girls come and go. If they're lucky they grow out of it, or meet Prince Charming, or go home to Kansas. Or worse if they're not so lucky."

"We all know the life," Maria agreed. "But this is different. These are all top earners from our best places. They didn't get killed on the street."

Jack leaned across the table, a big hand tapping the folder. "Whoever is doing this has money, access, power."

"And they didn't just retire, my friend." Rebbe leaned forward, wagging a finger. "I knew one of these young ladies personally. Melody. A lovely person who worked at Alonzo's fine establishment."

Alonzo nodded. "Her real name was Maxine."

"She had a dog, a little fuzzy thing," Rebbe went on, "and she loved it like a baby. A week after Melody vanished the neighbors finally got sick of the dog crying. They found the poor thing half starved. No way on earth she would do that. Someone took her."

"It's the same with all these girls," Gio told him. "They left behind clothes, money, passports, phones."

"They had friends and lovers," Jack said. "One had a kid, for Christ's sake. No way they just took off."

"Some sick fuck kidnapped them," Alonzo said. "And then tortured them to death."

"A monster," Maria said.

Rebbe nodded. "A serial killer."

Joe sighed. "All due respect, I think you should bring this to the law. You've all got people you can reach out to."

"We did," Alonzo said. "But it's not like we can file a missing ho report. These girls have no one looking for them but us. And you know nobody they know is going to talk to the law."

"The cops don't even believe it's a pattern," Rebbe said.

"Not without bodies," Gio said. "And even with Ioana, they basically stopped investigating when they found out she was a pro. They're just hoping she drifted over from Jersey."

"Just because they sell sex, they think their lives are worthless," Maria spat out venomously. "I know. I worked the street for a few months before I met my husband. The police don't care about a *puta*. Only us."

"She's right," Rebbe said. "These are our people. No one will protect them but us."

"And who else are we gonna ask," Alonzo said, "but you?"

"I'm a thief, remember?" Joe said. "Not a goddamn private eye."

"You're our sheriff," Uncle Chen said with a shrug.

Maria leaned over and tapped Joe's chest, on the left, under the heart. "That's why we gave you the star."

20

Joe went to Flushing first, since he had Cash there to drive him. Cash took care of all sorts of things for his uncle, but his specialty was anything to do with cars—driving them, stealing them, taking them apart and putting them back together before selling them here and abroad. He'd also done several jobs with Joe, but since the large payout on their last caper, things had been quiet, and he'd been focusing on having fun and spending that hard-earned money.

"Sorry to pull you away from the party," Joe said.

"I'm happy to get a break. Little fresh air," Cash said. "You know what these big family events are like. Hours of eating and explaining why I'm not married yet." He glanced over at Joe. "Or maybe you don't. Anyway . . . I get to show you my new pride and joy." He jingled a set of car keys as they turned into the entrance of the garage.

"Wow," Joe said. "That's not something you see every day."

It was a 1965 Pontiac GTO with a 389-cubic-inch V8 engine, Tri-Power induction, and a four-speed manual transmission. Gleaming black, it seemed to rest there, with its angled grill, double headlights, and a hood scoop like the nostrils of a glossy beast. Cash unlocked it himself; he'd refused to even let the attendants park it.

"Want to give her a try?"

"I wouldn't dare," Joe said, walking around to the passenger side. "At least not until you put the first scratch on it." He got in and slid on his seat belt. "I almost feel sorry for whoever you boosted this from."

"What? Dude, I bought this at an auction. Legit. And restored it myself. Redid the engine. Rims. Paint." He seemed a little insulted that Joe would even suggest such a thing. Now Joe understood his reluctance to let the parking lot attendants touch it. For Cash, stealing a car was simpler than hailing a taxi. He drove them hard, parked them anywhere, and forgot them, or else took them back to headquarters to be stripped for parts. Now, suddenly, he was afraid that someone else would treat his baby like that. He grinned as they moved smoothly into traffic. "Though I do have a little job in mind. You should come in on it with me. Imports."

As they drove, Cash told him about a luxury auto dealer he'd been eyeing on the West Side. "It's like when I was a kid cruising past a candy counter, my mouth waters."

"Except most kids don't smash the window and take the candy."

Cash was indignant. "Neither did I. I used a trick lunchbox to boost it and took off on my bike."

As they approached their destination, Cash began to fidget in his seat. "I should mention, there's another reason I wanted to drive you here. It's kind of an excuse to see this girl I like." He'd developed a crush on a girl named Lulu, the reigning princess of Uncle Chen's most exclusive brothel.

"Talk about candy in the window," Joe said. They pulled into the underground parking lot beneath a tall commercial building that contained several floors of shops and a food court. The brothel was in a suite of rooms far above them. "Don't let that sweet tooth get you in trouble."

"Yeah, but that's just it. I don't just want to buy her time, you know? I want to take her on a proper date. So I'm going to wait till I pull off this next caper and then take her out to celebrate."

Joe was about to tell him that getting personal with a professional was always tricky for people like them, but then he thought about himself and Donna and decided to mind his own business. "Good luck," he said as they got on the elevator and rode up.

The clientele were rich civilians: advertising execs, hedge funders, tech starter-uppers, as well as some entertainment types and a few athletes. Most were white or black men, with a few Chinese mainlanders in town on business, being hosted by their U.S. colleagues. No locals. They were all in Brighton Beach, chasing blond girls. That's how it was: whether it was cars or wine or sex, the customers craved what was rare and different, and they were ready to pay. Not Cash. He liked American muscle cars and drank forty-ouncers. And he liked Lulu, whose real name was Mingmei. She came from a small village and sent most of her earnings back home. A sweet, ordinary girl, but pretty as a movie star. At least Cash thought so.

Joe thought she looked like a cute kid dressed up for the prom, and from the way she smiled and waved shyly at Cash when Madam Wong herded all the employees who were not with clients into a room, he didn't think he needed to wait for a special occasion to ask her out.

Madam Wong was an old lady who smoked incessantly, with lipstick on her cigarettes and her teeth, and played epic all-night mahjongg games when she wasn't haranguing the women in her employ, and sometimes the customers, too. She was tough and ran this place like a platoon, but she was polite to Cash, because he represented the boss. However, she launched into a long opera about how hard it was to keep these girls under control, especially considering how little she earned, and so on. When Joe asked about girls who were missing, about whether anyone knew if they had been dating clients outside or working elsewhere, about whether they'd talked about stalkers or other worries, she not only translated his questions, but amplified them into a harsh rebuke. Working outside the brothel was strictly forbidden. Unsurprisingly, no one said a word. They barely blinked. The row of young women stared impassively, as if they spoke neither English nor Mandarin, except for Lulu, who blushed at Cash a couple of times.

"Now what?" Cash asked him.

Joe shrugged. "I guess I'll try a couple places in Brooklyn."

"Want me to drive you?" Cash asked, unenthusiastically, one eye still on Lulu. Just then, the madam barked her name. She had a client, and after checking her hair in the mirror, she hurried out.

Joe clapped Cash on the shoulder. "Why don't you get back to your party?" he said. "I'm sure you're missed."

⚬⭤⚬

Lulu did end up going on a date the next night, though unfortunately not with Cash. Although it was forbidden, she had given her phone number to one or two extremely generous clients, rich, old, married white men who tipped heavily and made her feel safe. After all, the best hope for her to make big money and eventually bring more of her family over was to become the mistress of such a man, kept in an apartment with an allowance, and perhaps access to his resources, his connections. So when the millionaire businessman called her, just as she was leaving work and heading around the corner to the noodle shop, she picked up. And when he offered her an exorbitant sum to come to him right then, she agreed. She even called a car, rather than take the 7 train, which would take an hour and a half to reach Midtown Manhattan. It was worth it. Who knew? Maybe her dream was about to come true.

21

Joe went to Brooklyn. He took a cab and had it drop him a block from the place Nell ran for Alonzo. It was upstairs from a row of storefronts—a tailor, a barber, a fruit stand, a hair salon—all but the corner bodega now closed for the night. There were buzzers for four apartments, but the names were years out of date and only the top button got a reply, since they'd opened up the flats to form one large warren of interconnected rooms. You walked up a narrow flight of stairs to what looked like a cheap dentist's waiting room, where a bored-looking Caribbean guy with braids checked you over indifferently and then, based on his private criteria, decided to buzz you through. Now you entered a kind of lounge—dim lights, comfortable modernish furniture, women in negligees trodding the soft carpets to serve drinks or sit on laps. Most of the laps belonged to Hasidic or ultra-Orthodox men, though there were some Asian businessmen and black guys in track suits. All the girls were black or brown. Alonzo had called ahead and personally instructed Nell, who came out to greet Joe. She was a petite woman in her early thirties, braids in an updo, glasses, gray wool suit, clearly an executive of some sort, management, not talent. In fact she had taken this place in hand, after running a nightclub for Alonzo, and turned it around, eliminating the rowdiness, fighting, and drug use, and making it a safe harbor for married men and those with carnal tastes forbidden in their own communities. Most of the clients were regulars, and some even lingered, drinking with friends and watching sports on the flatscreens.

"Good evening, I'm Nell," she said, shaking his hand. "Please come this way." She led him down a hall to a small but very neat office, and sat behind a desk with a computer. "I've gone ahead and pulled the relevant files."

Joe sat across from her. "You keep files?"

"Certainly. We need to organize bookings, for one thing. The names are fake, of course, and everything on my hard drive is encrypted, with an auto-destruct fail-safe. Plus all services are listed as massage or herbal therapy, so there's nothing anyone could prove on paper. But this way, employees who want to be on the books can be, and we can offer inducements to top earners. Along with discounts for repeat customers. Some even pay by credit card."

"Impressive."

"Thank you." She smiled quickly, looking down as she opened a folder. "I've identified three women who match the criteria."

"Someone mentioned a Melody to me?"

"Yes. Her real name was Maxine Waters. She is the most recent. A top earner with a lot of VIP regulars, even . . ." She hesitated.

"I know. A distinguished gentleman in black with a long gray beard."

"Yes. Exactly. But other than him, I don't know that she saw anyone outside."

"It happens, though."

She shrugged. "Of course. I mean, we discourage it. It's poaching customers like with any business, a fireable offense. But for some it's too tempting to resist."

"And the other disappearances?"

Nell tapped a nail on the paper. "This woman, she went by Karamel, with a K, seems to have surfaced in Atlanta. It appears she ran off with a client, an osteopath who left his wife and kids. But number three, Jeri Calvert, she looks suspicious. It was about a year ago, but from what I can see she called in to say she was taking a sick day and then disappeared. Left a paycheck and a locker full of personal stuff behind."

"You have sick days?" Joe asked.

She smiled, for the first time. "Don't you?"

⌐━━━○

As in Flushing, the workers were called in and told to answer his questions frankly, but the results were the same, with the slight difference that no translator was needed. They all told him nothing in English, their accents ranging from Caribbean to African to Alabaman to hometown Brooklyn. Then Nell walked him out; the lounge was full of harmless and hapless husbands who now seemed, to Joe, like a lineup of suspects. A lifetime had taught him to spot a shoplifter, a dealer, a mugger, or a cop from a block away. But what did a psycho killer look like? He had no idea. But he suspected they looked like a regular, square guy. A citizen.

At the exit, Nell shook his hand, a little tighter than before, and asked, "Do you really think there's a murderer out there? I mean, one man behind all these disappearances? A serial killer?"

"I don't know. It's starting to look that way. Anyway, something happened to these women."

"You know, I try to run this like a regular business, like a legit enterprise, which in my opinion is what it should be." She looked up at him, distress on her features. "But it's not, is it? I mean, women don't get preyed on at regular everyday jobs."

"Don't they?" Joe asked.

The door buzzed and a client came in, a shy-looking man in a North Face jacket with glasses and a yarmulke. Nell smiled, holding the door, but as Joe left, she said, quietly: "Catch him. Please."

Joe nodded and went down the stairs.

⌐━━━○

By the time he got to Brighton Beach he knew how it was going to go: another brothel, another accommodating manager, another passively mute bunch of women, this time from Russia, Eastern Europe, and the Balkans. Still, the manager, a svelte, copper-haired Russian woman in her fifties, was eager to accommodate Joe.

"Yelena is on vacation, in Miami, but she gave strict instruction," she said, with an ingratiating smile. "Joe must have whatever he wants." This waiting room was like the others, but with more of a British gentleman's club vibe—buttoned leather couches, standing ashtrays, floor lamps lit low. There was also a tremendous amount of smoke, from cigarettes, pipes, and cigars. She gave a slight wave over the room, indicating a wide range of possibilities.

But no one was talking, in any language. They'd learned that honesty got them nowhere: with cops, bosses, customers, and neighbors. Why would that change now?

Thoroughly discouraged, he found a cab and headed home. Then, on impulse, he texted Donna.

Are you up? I need to talk.

The answer came back:

L is asleep but come over, Romeo.

Smiling, he tapped on the Plexiglas partition and asked the driver: "Sorry, can you take me into the city? Uptown."

"Yes sir," he nodded, a bearded Sikh in a turban. He didn't mind, the meter was running, and he resumed his heated conversation over his headset. Joe stared out the window, wondering idly what sort of vacation Yelena was on. It was hard to picture her lying poolside and sipping a margarita.

22

Yelena was poolside sipping a margarita. She couldn't have been happier. True, she hated the sun and would have vastly preferred a shot of cold vodka to this insipid fruity concoction. And she would have liked to drown a few of the men who paraded by her in their swimsuits and insisted on talking to her despite her earphones. Some were still dripping from the pool, an unpleasant drizzle pooling between their legs and running under her lounge chair. But none of that could dim her mood. Finally, after months of work and stress, she was going to reward herself. A fabulous and rare antique necklace, studded with rubies and diamonds, was on display in the hotel prior to going on auction tomorrow. And Yelena was going to steal it.

As the tattoos that covered much of her skin revealed to the knowing reader, Yelena Noylaskya had begun her life in one of the worst places on earth—the Russian prison system, her mother a drug-addicted prostitute who died soon after. Born into the underworld (symbolized by her Madonna and Child back piece), she had thrived, becoming an expert thief, a virtuoso safecracker (a dollar sign), and a lethal assassin (the skulls). But the authorities kept tabs on her and eventually sprung a trap: she would go back to prison, or to New York, where she was expected to report to Moscow on the Russian mob. That was when she met Joe. As a result of their collaboration, both profitable and bloody, she not only got revenge on the Russian agent who had controlled her (devil's face) and eliminated her rivals (more drops of blood from the dagger on her thigh) but rocketed to the top of the food chain, a boss herself (the stars on her shoulders and knees, the crown on her finger, and more). But despite the many perks of power, the job was a bit tiresome—mainly administrative, solving problems, resolving disputes, and juggling egos like any female executive at any big business—and Yelena found herself growing restless. She was finally safe, but safety was not her natural state. Her comfort zone was danger.

That was why she was in Florida for a brief vacation. It was why she was wearing a loose cover-up with makeup expertly applied to her tattoos. At this point, a lot of American hipsters would just find them fashionable, but she didn't want to be too memorable—just another languid blonde in a long white shift reading under an umbrella. Besides, in a wealthy vacation enclave, it was always possible to run across someone who knew what her tattoos really said.

It was also for the sake of appearance that she had booked two rooms under two different names but made sure they were next door to each other. Now she walked past the necklace in its display case, glancing over the uniformed guards, the discreetly plainclothes but still armed backup guards, and the cameras, then riding the elevator upstairs to her room. She knocked on the wall, then went out to her balcony, where Juno hopped over the dividing wall.

Bed-Stuy born and bred, Juno had been a delinquent minor and a major hacker on the same job where Yelena first met Joe. They had saved Juno's ass that time, and then a couple more times, and they'd all grown close. Juno became Joe's go-to genius for anything tech-related. The task at hand was child's play for Juno, but it was always a pleasure to watch Yelena at work, in more ways than one.

"How's it looking down there?" Juno asked. "Any gators in the pool?"

"Only sharks in Speedos," she told him. "Security is the same as yesterday." She checked her watch. "So an hour till they move the necklace into the vault. And I go down an hour after that."

"How about we eat in the meantime?" Juno asked. He wasn't much of a sunbather himself, since he spent most of his time in his mom's basement, but he was a foodie, and he'd found a Cuban place he wanted to try. "I can order us in a feast. My treat for hooking me up with this gig."

"OK," she said, then poked his shoulder with a stern finger. "But really pay for it. No stolen cards or other tricks. Remember what Joe always says."

"Yeah, yeah, wear your seat belt and don't commit any misdemeanors when you're on the way to commit a felony."

So they ordered, paid cash, and ate on the balcony. Then Juno got on his laptop while Yelena changed into a slinky black dress and heels. Then she went down to the office and asked the manager to let her into the safe.

Two days earlier, Yelena had checked in, pretending to be a wealthy Russian tourist, and asked to store her valuables in the hotel safe. The manager obligingly provided a metal box for her to fill, but she'd insisted on seeing the facilities and placing her goods into the safe with her own hands. The manager was not surprised. This was a very fancy hotel, with many clients who were both wealthy and fussy. Besides, he knew the security was serious. The safe room had a reinforced steel door with its own time lock; once closed for the night it could not be reopened. And the safe was a beast, a new model, top of the line. Even Yelena was impressed. Happily, she put her jewelry case into the metal box and then slid it into the spot the manager indicated. He even bragged about how the dazzling necklace, once worn by princesses, would sleep in there awaiting the auction.

As it happened, Yelena was already quite familiar with the necklace. She'd commissioned the most talented crooked craftsman in New

York's diamond district to make her a duplicate, perfect in every way except made of glass and worth a couple of hundred dollars on the open market. That was in her jewelry kit, along with some real diamond earrings and a tennis bracelet—both quite nice but nothing anyone would fly to Florida to bid on. Now she appeared again, looking like a lady headed out for the night, and asked the manager to let her into the safe room.

"Of course, madam," he said, grinning obsequiously. "You're just in time. In fifteen minutes the door locks till tomorrow."

"Oh, I'm so grateful you're here to help me, then," she purred. "I feel naked without my jewelry."

He led her into the room, opened the safe while she discreetly looked away, and was unlocking her metal box on the table when the lights went out. The power had gone down in the whole building, but while emergency exit lights were dotting the halls and lobbies, this window-less inside room was pitch-black.

"Oh my God!" Yelena squealed like a cartoon girl seeing a mouse. "Help!" She purposely knocked over a chair.

"Please, madam, remain still," the heroic manager declared. "For your own safety, I beg you, just wait here calmly while I go see what's wrong. I promise to fetch a flashlight." And he hurried out.

Yelena didn't need a flashlight. She opened her box and removed the fake necklace. She then moved quickly to the safe, and with her fingertips counted down the row of boxes to find the one containing the real necklace. With a pick she had tucked into her dress strap, she easily popped open the flimsy lock on the box and removed the necklace from its velvet-lined case, replacing it with her fake. She put the box back, tucked the real necklace into her purse and sat back down.

About fifteen seconds later, she saw the beam of a flashlight bouncing over. "In here," she called. "Help, please."

"Don't worry," the manager said, entering bravely and shining the light on her. "Everything's OK. We called the electric company and they said . . ." But then he stopped because the lights came back on. "Oh. There we go. See?" He patted her arm. "I told you there was nothing to fear."

"Oh, thank you, you're so kind," she cooed, as he beamed. "And I know you'll think I'm a silly coward, but I'm so exhausted now, I think I'll just stay in."

The manager understood. He made a big show of replacing her box and locking the safe, then sealing the door for the night behind them. The next morning, the necklace was transported via armed guard to the auction house, where bidding was intense. The buyer took possession and of course quickly realized the necklace was fake. But who had made the change? And when? Everyone, from the seller to the hotel staff, transport security, and auction house were suspects. Yelena waited patiently while the police checked each guest's box, and consented to let them open her case, confirming that the few lovely but unremarkable pieces were hers. Nothing was missing. Thank you so much, officers. And she checked out, cool as a margarita. Unlike Juno, who was already back in New York with the real necklace in his pocket, nervous he might somehow get randomly mugged, until Yelena got back and took it off his hands.

"By the way, have you heard from Joe lately?" she asked as she paid him for his excellent work hacking into the hotel's master power controls.

"No. Why? You want me to call him?" He knew Yelena and Joe had taken some space since the last job, but like a kid whose parents have separated, he was keen to see the crew reunited.

"No." She shrugged. "Just making conversation."

23

"What the hell are you up to now?"

Donna was waiting by the open window when Joe came creeping down the fire escape. He'd taken the elevator to an upper floor, then the stairs to the roof, then back down to the window. He'd warned her he was thinking about doing something that might keep him busy for a while and that he couldn't tell her about it but that she shouldn't worry.

"Do you really want to know?" he asked her, now that she was confronting him in her bathrobe, fists on her hips.

"I don't know." She frowned and sat on the bed. "Can you give me a hint?"

"Like what?" He sat beside her.

"Something that won't make me an accessory?"

So he told her in a roundabout way—the dead girl in the river, the other missing women, the lack of evidence.

"Sounds like a police matter," she told him.

"A dead Romanian prostitute and possible illegal alien? I'm sure the police will make it a top priority. As for the others . . ." He shrugged.

"There's missing persons. They'll look into it."

"Only if someone is missing them. The straight world doesn't care. The cops can't be bothered. And no one is going to talk to them anyway. They won't even talk to me."

"You're not qualified. You're not an investigator."

"I raised that point." Joe leaned back, suddenly exhausted. "Honestly, I have no idea where to even begin."

"But why is it your problem?"

Joe shrugged. "There's no one else."

She lay back beside him. They both stared up at the ceiling.

"Do you really want me to just walk away?" he asked the ceiling fixture. "Forget these girls existed, like everyone else? Do nothing?"

Donna sighed. "No."

Then her phone rang. Neither one of them moved. Donna reached her hand out and found the phone on her night table. It was her mother, calling from across the hall. Someone had reported a suspicious character on the roof. Should they call the cops?

"No, that's all right, Ma, I'll check it out."

"Be careful, *mija*. Take your gun."

"Don't worry."

"Do you want me to stay on the line?"

"No, Mom, it's fine. I'll call you back." She clicked off with a sigh. "Oy."

"I'm guessing that's my cue to leave?" Joe asked from his supine pose beside her. "Or maybe you can tell her you have a suspect in custody and you're busy making him talk."

She turned to him, their faces an inch apart. "Actually, I'd very much like it if you stopped talking," she said, and kissed him. Then her phone rang again. "Jesus . . ."

"Maybe there's really another intruder on the roof," Joe suggested.

Donna reached her hand out. This time it was work. She sat up as she put the phone to her ear. "Blaze, what is it? Right. Got it." She turned back to Joe. "Sorry. But that *is* your cue to leave."

⁘

The brothel moved to New York City.

While Blaze and Fusco sat in their dirty van, arguing sports, a long black passenger van, of the sort that delivers people to airports or out to the Hamptons, had pulled up. Chuko emerged from the rear exit, dressed for travel in a puffy coat, his hair in a ponytail under a beanie, and oversaw his thugs as they hauled out luggage. Then the Senora came along, in a leather and fur-trim coat, herding the girls, who huddled in a group as if for warmth.

"This is it," Blaze said. "We're rolling."

"Finally," Fusco said, sliding behind the wheel. "Get me the hell out of Jersey."

With a last eye roll, Blaze slipped out the rear of the van and jogged to her own unmarked car nearby while Fusco started the engine. Although disguised as a plumbing truck, the van was too conspicuous to simply tail them the whole way. He'd follow from a distance for a few blocks, while radioing with Blaze, and let her pick them up.

Meanwhile, Blaze called Donna, who hurried down to her own car. She'd be in position to switch off with Blaze when the van came over the bridge. Donna sat behind the wheel, jiggling her legs nervously as if pacing in place. The tracker they'd given Daisy was working fine, but it didn't have much range, and Donna would be on edge until she knew for sure where they were going. Of course, the bridge traffic made it worse, as the suspect van waited in line to pay cash for the toll. Finally, she heard Blaze's voice crackle over the radio:

"We are heading south on Broadway, should be coming into view."

Donna sat up straight and started the engine. Then she saw the van in the rearview. "I got it," she reported, pulling out and falling a few cars behind. "You can drop back."

"Roger that." Blaze slowed down and changed lanes, letting Donna stay behind the van. In busy traffic there was nothing suspicious about riding fairly close. When the van turned, Blaze would be ready to slide back into first position.

Finally, they stopped in front of a building in the far West Forties. The ground floor was a restaurant-supply place, above that offices, then a few overpriced apartments. It was the kind of block that would empty out at night and where few people knew their neighbors. Ideal for a brothel. Chuko and the Senora hustled their charges inside. As Donna cruised by, she saw that the lights on the fourth floor were on. She turned the corner onto the avenue and pulled over at a fire hydrant. Cops and criminals: the two groups who parked wherever they wanted.

And how did she feel about Joe being back to work? She didn't like it, of course. How could she? He was not only placing himself, inevitably, in danger, he was threatening their still brand-new relationship. And yet, she had not been able to ask him to drop it, even if he would. How could she? If there was any chance of flushing out a killer, then he had to try. But that was the part that ate at her, now that she had time to think. Despite all the talk about exploring options and retirement, when push came to shove, there had never really been any question, and they both knew it.

◦━━◦

It was Fusco who spotted her first. He'd driven the van back into the city, then parked it a few blocks from Donna and Blaze. Then, on foot, he'd taken up a spot in a doorway down the block from the brothel's new address, realistically fading into the background by sitting on a stoop and slowly munching through several slices of dollar pizza and drinking a bottle of Diet Coke. Actually, he was annoyed to have to stop before finishing when Daisy emerged. She was with a group of women escorted by two of their thug minders. As Fusco watched, they were walked two blocks across town and into the gigantic drugstore one corner up.

Donna, too, had been walking over, following Fusco's directions, and now she wandered into the drugstore a few steps behind the group.

They dispersed, some heading for the makeup counters, others for toothpaste or tampons. Daisy, after saying something to a thug who grunted his assent, went downstairs. Grabbing a basket and adding items randomly as she went, Donna cruised for a few minutes until the thug went back to staring at his phone, and then drifted downstairs as well. She spotted Daisy in the medicine aisle, reading a bottle of Pepto-Bismol, and made sure she was seen before turning down the next aisle over. Just her luck, chips and candy. She grabbed a few items as she sidled alongside Daisy.

"Hey there," came a low voice.

"How are you?" Donna asked.

"OK. Nothing like saying you have diarrhea to get a little privacy. Not even creeps want to be too close to that."

"Smart thinking." The two women met at the end of the aisle, loitering casually, one eye on the stairs. "When are they going to start seeing customers here in the new spot?" Donna asked.

Daisy shrugged, dropping the Pepto-Bismol into her basket. "They gave us money to buy makeup, and they're bringing racks of new clothes tomorrow. Supposedly there's a big party with high rollers over the weekend."

"Do you know who?"

"No way. They'd never tell us. But I think that's when . . ." She looked over and made eye contact. "You know, they're going to auction me off or whatever. I think they have someone lined up."

Donna sighed. She didn't like the idea of leaving Daisy out on a limb longer than absolutely necessary, but she also knew this could be the bust they'd been waiting for, the chance to roll up the whole operation bottom to top.

"OK, listen," she said. "You're doing a great job. Just hang in there a little longer. Soon you'll be done with this forever, starting a new life with a green card."

"Can't be soon enough." She frowned. "Honestly, I really need this Pepto. My stomach's in knots from stress."

"I know. I'm sorry." Donna reached out, instinctively, squeezing Daisy's wrist, then dropped it and stepped away, checking. The coast was still clear. She leaned in to whisper, "Remember, we have people watching twenty-four seven now. And maybe, if we really bag some big players, we can arrange some kind of financial assistance, too, to help get you on your feet, find a job."

"Really?" Daisy perked up. "That would be awesome. Like a bounty for catching a big fish?"

"Exactly. So just be strong a little longer. All right?"

She nodded.

"And keep that tracker on you."

"I will, thanks. Better go now," she said, and left. Donna dawdled, adding a large bag of Reese's Pieces and a bag of salt-and-vinegar potato chips to her basket. Between Daisy and Joe, it was going to be a stressful week.

24

Joe went to visit Cookie's dungeon. It was not your typical brothel. In many ways it was like an X-rated amusement park, or better yet a play camp for perverts. The main room, expressive of Cookie herself, had an old New Orleans atmosphere, with deep couches, wingback chairs, tasseled lampshades, and lots of pillows, shawls, sheets, and curtains draped and drooped and billowing everywhere. The walls were wood-paneled halfway up, then the pink-washed plaster—or was it just the red lampshade's glow?—held Postimpressionist daubs and vintage French posters for absinthe and perfume. But this old-fashioned drawing room inserted in a bland New York office building was also a kind of sci-fi spaceship—the rooms that opened from the hall were portals leading into wildly divergent worlds: a police holding cell, complete with barred door and steel toilet; a classroom with a teacher's desk, an uncomfortable student chair, and a blackboard, not to mention a paddle and a ruler; a doctor's office—examination table, scale, cabinet of stainless steel tools—with an experimental lab attached, featuring electrodes, probes, and blazing lights. Nursery-themed rooms were so popular that Cookie had two: one with a crib, stuffed animals, and a changing table; and a second playroom with toys, little stools and tables, and a selection of baby clothes, school uniforms, and pretty little dresses, all in adult sizes. Then there was the more traditional castle-keep vibe: fake stone walls, chains, whips, and spinning torture wheel, as well as the throne room, where slaves groveled, kissing feet, or lay prostrate beneath the open-bottomed seat, acting as a human toilet.

No desire was beyond the pale here. Nor did the talent conform to the mainstream body stereotypes that made the cash rain down at Club Rendezvous. Here, two of the biggest earners were hugely overweight women—one black, one white—while a tiny, boyish Asian woman earned a fortune trodding men under her perfect feet. There was a woman in a hijab and a rabbi's wife in a wig. There were strong, glamorously buff young men who were paid handsomely to "force" straight customers to play gay. There were trans men and women with mixed characteristics. There was an eighty-year-old with a cane addressed as Grandma. A double amputee, in the office Wednesdays only, had a loyal following of clients with standing appointments.

By definition, this unusual business model created a no-judgment, all-are-welcome tone for both workers and clients, and Cookie acted the part of den mother, gathering her oddly matched household of misfits. Those with secret selves and hidden cravings found acceptance. Those fleeing repressive or unsympathetic or, worse, abusive and traumatic pasts found refuge. Those with bodies or identities or desires excluded by the mainstream found a warm harbor where they too were desired and adored. Cookie's "kids" tended to hang out together, room together, form an ad hoc substitute family. She hosted big dinners for Thanksgiving and Christmas, and the Halloween and New Year's parties were legendary. And, of course, it all paid extremely well.

But it was still a business. And that also meant that, as in any business, you didn't really get to pick who your customers were. Working for Cookie offered you the chance to be paid and desired: but the desire you were fulfilling was the paying customer's, not yours. Few of the pros at Cookie's shared their clients' fetishes. Many of the women didn't even like men. They were playing the roles that they were paid to.

Joe understood that. They were hustlers, outsiders finding a way to survive or maybe even thrive, like Cookie herself, beyond the bounds of square society. Everyone he knew, from his grandmother to his friends to the people he worked with, got by by getting over, one way or another. You used whatever you had.

And so the most common fantasy among Cookie's employees was to somehow escape from having to work there. For many, that meant a different, better career—there were aspiring artists, designers, stylists, models. Others were going to school or using their time in the dungeon as "experience" to be channeled into their writing or films. And for some, escape meant love with a client—the client's love, that is. The rich, generous, exclusive slave who became so enamored he wanted all your time. The one who would give you an apartment, an allowance, a car. That was the wild fantasy that tempted many of the tempters, and that, Joe suspected, led at least one of them to her death. Because the fantasy of the perfect client was as unreal as the perfect fantasy projected onto the sex worker. You didn't ever really know what lay in another's heart.

<hr />

As in the other brothels, Cookie called the employees together, told them to speak to Joe openly, assured them their honesty would have no repercussions, and left, shutting the door behind her. And just as in the other places, no one said a thing. Or rather, no one provided any useful information, a clue. Most of them had known Ioana. They were clearly distraught, some grief-stricken, some afraid for themselves. Darla, a young black woman in thigh-high boots and a corset, announced her intention to go back to waiting tables until she finished her degree. "I mean, let's face it, it's flirting with guys that earns my tips. That's who pays me. Not women. Not gay men. Straight dudes. At least here I get what I'm worth. But getting paid what I'm worth is not worth dying for. I'd rather be poor and just worrying about a creep grabbing my ass."

Meanwhile, a plump blond woman dressed as a nurse wailed while a younger white girl, with jet-black hair and black-lined eyes and lips, rubbed her back. She was dressed in Goth bondage gear—high-wedge boots, torn fishnets, a tightly buckled dress—and heavily tattooed, with lots of cursive black writing. After a moment Joe realized she was trans.

Joe nodded. "Sounds smart," he said, because he didn't know what else to say. "It's a good time to be careful." Nevertheless, this was getting him nowhere. He scribbled his number on a pad and told them to call if they thought of anything. Then he left.

He rode the elevator down, passed the security guy, who didn't look up from his *Post*, and turned to walk toward the subway, pulling his phone from his pocket. Why wait? He felt ready to call Gio and report total failure. Joe sighed. If someone identified the target, he would not hesitate to take him out, then go home and watch *Jeopardy* with his grandma. Assassination. That was what he was trained to do. That was his very dubious talent. But this . . . unlike murder, this was out of his comfort zone. This was law, not crime.

Then, before he could make his mind up to dial one of the very few numbers saved on the flip phone, it beeped. A text from an unfamiliar number:

Please turn around

Joe stopped and turned, quickly, hands rising in front of him, instinctively ready for defense. No one was there. Then he saw the trans girl from upstairs, the Goth one, standing across the street. She nodded at him and then walked down the block. He crossed the street and followed around the next corner, where she waited in a doorway.

"I want to talk to you but not here," she said, before he could say anything. "And definitely not up there."

They went to a diner. One of the remaining old-school places, where you got a cheeseburger deluxe or a club sandwich or breakfast twenty-four hours, though according to the menu you could also get fettucine alfredo or surf and turf. Had anyone ever ordered that? He imagined the big moment, the excitement in the kitchen as they scrambled, digging deep in the freezer. Someone had finally ordered the trout almondine. Perhaps it was the same person who drank the dubious "wine" that sat in the fridge beside the beers and sports drinks.

But that night wasn't tonight. It was late, after two, and the crowd was sparse. An old man at the counter crumbled crackers into pea soup. A tired woman in scrubs—a real nurse, not a roleplay nurse—read a book while she ate an omelet. At a big table, a bunch of kids laughed and took pictures of each other, dressed up for a club or party. Two men in heavy leather gear kissed in a booth. From behind the counter, the Greek manager chatted with the Mexican waiter, who nodded and grabbed two menus when they came in.

They took a back booth and both ordered coffee. Joe took his black, while she slowly added a little plastic creamer and a long pour of sugar. She stirred.

"My name is Jem. Sorry about before. Cookie's OK, as far as it goes, but she is severe about moonlighting."

"Is that what Ioana was doing?"

Jem hesitated, regarding Joe thoughtfully and licking the spoon clean before placing it on the table. She nodded.

"Yeah. Not a lot. Just a few rich guys now and then who asked for her number. She was looking for like a sugar daddy to set her up and maybe pay to get her a green card. That was her dream guy, a submissive immigration lawyer with a foot fetish." She chuckled sadly and for a split second looked like she might tear up, then it was gone.

"You know this because you were friends?" Joe asked.

She nodded. "Roommates. Well, I was staying with her till I found a place. I still am." She shrugged. "It feels weird, but the rent is paid up and someone has to feed the cat."

"You're new in town?"

She smiled. "How can you tell?" She spoke in a flat Midwestern accent that could have been from anywhere. "I'm from Oklahoma. A small town. I went to Tulsa, then Chicago, then here. The big time."

Joe nodded. He'd never been to Oklahoma or Chicago. In his own way he was just as provincial. Connecticut seemed far. Unless, of course, he was working, then he might be sent anywhere around the world. To him, Bangkok or Dubai were less exotic than downtown Tulsa.

"Was Ioana seeing someone the night she disappeared?"

Jem nodded again. "Yeah, some big shot, supposedly. At least he acted that way, came in all loud and boisterous. But he was well-connected, and he spent a lot. Anyway, Cookie set him up with Ioana."

"What was he into?"

She shrugged. "Roleplay, naughty-boy stuff. He wanted to be humiliated and punished."

"Like how?"

"She said she walked on him with these six-inch heels I lent her." She smiled faintly at the memory, then it faded. "He gave her a huge tip, so when he asked for her number, she said OK."

"What did he look like?"

"I just saw him briefly. Big guy. White. Red face, suit and tie, you know, a stockbroker type, maybe? Thinning hair. Overweight."

"Age?"

"Sixties?"

"And you never heard a name?"

"No one asks for names there."

"How do you know she was with him that night?"

"I don't. But I got a text, asking me to feed the cat."

She scrolled through her phone:

Big shot called!!! I am getting car now.
Can you please take care of Midnight? You can use my Uber.
Thank you!!!

There was a row of emojis: heart, dollar sign, diamond, smiley.

Joe asked the waiter for a pen, then dug in his pocket for something to write on and found the creased and folded flyer about the Westlands. He noted the date and time, handing back the phone. "She says you can use her Uber. So then, you have access to her account?"

"Yeah, she was sweet that way," Jem said, smiling sadly as she wrote it down for Joe. "You know, kind of harsh and European on the outside, but so generous if she liked you. Midnight is a stray we found at midnight. A black cat. She was crying under a car in the rain. Do you know . . ." She hesitated, searching for words. "About her body. Do you know what's going to happen?"

"Eventually it will be released, if there is anyone to claim her. Otherwise . . ."

"I'm going to go down there. I mean, I'm not family or anything, but she deserves something at least." She seemed about to tear up again, but then sat up and put her phone away, turning to watch a waiter pass by, his tray loaded with plates.

"Are you hungry?" Joe asked. "My treat, for taking the time out to talk."

Jem shrugged. "Are you eating?"

"Yeah." He waved at the waiter. He was suddenly ravenous, now that he felt he had a direction, a next step. "I'm starving. I think I'll have fettucine alfredo and then surf and turf with a half bottle of muscatel."

"Really?" she asked, opening the menu. "Is that good here?"

"No."

He had a club sandwich. Jem had a tuna melt and a chocolate shake. It sounded good, so after a moment's hesitation he added a shake, too, black and white. They shared a plate of fries. When they were done, Joe went up to the counter and paid the check in cash.

"Here's my number," he said as he sat back down, flipping and unfolding the flyer to find an unused bit. "Call me if you think of anything else."

"I already have it," Jem said with a smile. "I texted you, remember?"

"Oh yeah," Joe said, laughing as he stood and counted out a tip. Then Jem pointed at the flyer.

"That's him. That's the guy."

"Who?"

"Ioana's big shot."

Joe looked closely at the flyer for the first time. Photos of the politicians and developers behind the project had red Xs through them. The name beneath the smooth, smiling face that Jem tapped with her nail read James Hackney.

<hr />

At first Lulu thought she was dreaming. Her eyes opened on total darkness. She couldn't move. Her arms were held somehow—chained, it felt like, to metal—and she lay on bare concrete. She was very cold. She'd had nightmares like this, as a kid and again when she first came to New York, anxiety dreams of being lost or helpless. Then she began to remember: she'd been on her way to see the rich man, but then it all went fuzzy. Her head ached. She blinked in the blackness. Then she heard footsteps and saw a flashlight approaching, and she knew. This was no nightmare. This was real.

25

Next day, Joe slept in, then went to see Juno. He'd had a long, late night, and Juno never got up before noon anyway. He spent the nights in his hacker's den, also known as his mom's basement. But, with the money he'd made working with Joe, he'd helped her pay off the mortgage, then turned half the basement into a recording studio. Now he was pursuing his dream of producing, though at this point it was mostly just creating beats and cutting demos with local kids, who preferred to pay with weed, food, or swag they'd pilfered. Joe brought grape Snapple.

"Ah, thanks, dude," Juno said, still sleepy, when he let Joe in the side door and took him downstairs. He wore a black hoody, sweats, and slippers. In his lair it was still midnight. Waves crawled on screens. Power lights flickered. The internet jazz station played. He flopped into his executive desk chair and cracked the day's first Snapple, while Joe sat on the couch. "So how might I be of assistance this time?"

"For starters, I need you to check this Uber account. Tell me where this girl was dropped off." He tossed Juno the flyer on which he had written out the details. Juno was shocked.

"Wait. You've got her account number and password right here? Don't get me wrong, man, I'm always happy to see you, but you do know anybody with a phone could just log in and do this?"

"Not my phone," Joe reminded him.

Juno smiled. "I mean anybody besides you." He spun around in his chair and tapped some keys. "Let's see . . . it's a Manhattan address, West Side." He mapped it. "OK, she was dropped off at Hackney Tower Hotel."

"Great," Joe said, handing him a second sheet with a list of names and dates. "Now tell me if these other women have accounts and where they went those nights."

Juno grinned. "Now that is a bit more of a challenge. Why don't we order some pizza for breakfast? I'll be done by the time it gets here."

Sure enough, by the time Juno had folded his first slice and popped open a fresh Snapple, the pattern was clear: on the evenings they disappeared, the missing women had taken cars to Hackney Tower Hotel, the large Midtown hotel owned and operated by James Hackney.

"Do me a favor, Juno," Joe asked. "Find out everything you can about this guy."

"Aye-aye, captain," Juno said, rubbing his hands together like a musician warming up before hitting the keys. "He our new target? We taking this sucker down?"

Joe shrugged. "Maybe. For now just put it on my tab."

"Aw, come on, man, you know with you it's more than money. Don't make me get all sentimental or we'll both be crying soon."

Joe laughed. "OK. Thanks, Juno."

"Besides, you bought the pizza. And I made out pretty good on this last caper with Yelena, down in Florida."

"You two were in Florida?" Joe asked. "Her people told me she was on vacation."

Juno laughed awkwardly, a little sorry now that he'd mentioned it. "You know she ain't the vacation type. That's like you playing golf. We heisted a necklace."

Joe smiled. "For Yelena that is a vacation. Stealing relaxes her."

Joe spent the rest of the day asking around about Hackney, adding to the little he already knew. Jim Hackney was a local fixture—a player on the social and political scene, whose ups and downs had been followed by the media since the '70s, when he emerged as the socialite son of Dick Hackney, who'd made a fortune building low-income housing developments in Queens and Brooklyn that quickly devolved into slums. The younger Hackney was a lot more grandiose and a lot less successful: he launched a series of high-profile buildings, casinos, and resorts, all of which featured a lot of glitz and gold, and most of which went bankrupt or were sold off, leaving disgruntled partners. He currently lived and worked from the penthouse atop the hotel that bore his name, but of which, apparently, he owned only a small share. Now he was launching his biggest and most controversial project: the Westlands development.

His wife, Anne, was confined to a wheelchair. He had a son, also a James, known as Junior, who worked for Dad. He'd had a respectable career in amateur martial arts circles and was known as a big-game hunter who had courted controversy by posting his trophies online, proud pictures of himself with dead lions and tigers.

Privately, Jim Sr. was known to be a serious philanderer as well as a heavy gambler, and he was a familiar figure at brothels, casinos, and high-end poker games, where he often had a hired girl on his arm. Nevertheless, his strong political and press connections, as well as the code of silence that pervaded his circles, had kept his profile more or less clean—if being a blowhard real-estate tycoon with smarmy politicos and shady foreign bankers as friends was your idea of respectable.

But could he be a killer, responsible for the serial murders of at least four women, possibly many more? For Joe the question was irrelevant. His basic view of humanity was such that, outside of the small number of people he knew well and had formed close personal opinions about, anyone was capable of anything. The fact that Hackney belonged to the straight world, the world of supposedly legitimate fronts and conventional moralities, only muddied the waters. Thieves stole, grifters grifted, hustlers hustled. Killers killed. No one who knew Joe had to wonder what he was capable of. But who knew what lay in the heart of a supposedly regular guy?

If anyone did, Joe suspected it was Cookie. So he made another appointment, this time for a private chat.

⚬━╼⚬

"You know who did this?" Cookie asked him straight out, as soon as the door to her room was shut.

"No, not yet. I just have someone I'm curious about. One of her clients."

"A person of interest." She smiled. "As they say."

"I'm hoping you can provide some . . . let's call it psychological insight."

"Like one of those profilers."

"Exactly."

She held a hand out toward an upholstered wingback armchair. Joe sat while she settled herself on the love seat and fixed him with a steady gaze. "I am at your service."

"What can you tell me about Jim Hackney?"

She breathed deeply and sat back, considering the idea. "Not who I'd pick for most likely to kill someone, but I suppose anything is possible."

"Who would you pick?"

Cookie gave him a reproachful look. "I've been in this business a long, long time. Anyone I thought was dangerous wouldn't get past the door."

Joe nodded. "OK then, why not Hackney?"

"He's all show. You know the type, *cher*. Lion in the boardroom, mouse in the bedroom. A sub, but a difficult one. Always topping from the bottom."

"How so?"

Cookie leaned forward, heavily ringed fingers weaving in the air as she warmed to her topic. "He craved domination, but still kept trying to control things, ordering the domme around, trying to tell her how to dominate him." She laughed. "But Ioana could handle that. She had the knack. Guys like that were her bread and butter."

It was a truism in Cookie's world that many of her clients were powerful and wealthy men: bosses, politicians, cops, even ministers and rabbis. Big shots. Men who were dominant out in the world. "But why do you think that is?" Joe asked. "Besides their being the only ones who can afford it."

Cookie chuckled. "It varies, of course. Some crave release from the pressure. They want to give up control, let someone else be the boss. Some really are submissive inside, weak, scared, insecure, and the big-shot routine is all an act. In here"—she looked around at her domain—"it's safe for them to finally be themselves."

"So they're compensating," Joe said. "Puffing up their egos, like bullies."

"Oh yes." Cookie smiled and nodded. "We get lots of bullies in here, *cher.*"

"What else?"

Cookie thought about it. "Then there are some who feel guilty."

"For what?" Joe asked.

She shrugged. "I once had a client, in the '90s, Mergers and Acquisitions I called him. You know, a corporate raider. He'd buy a company, fire everyone, sell its assets, make another fortune. Then he paid me to whip him for it. I've had judges, police chiefs, even generals come asking me to punish them for sending others to jail or maybe to death. It's a big burden. I ease it for them."

Joe sat forward, hands on his knees. "So you think maybe this man Hackney has something to atone for? Something weighing on his conscience?"

Cookie nodded. "Oh yes. He puts on a show, but deep down he knows what he deserves. A punishment."

"To fit his crime," Joe added, finishing the thought.

Cookie said no more. She just sighed.

***

Joe still didn't know much. He had no proof of anything. All he knew was that the evidence led him to Hackney. And that was what he told Gio when they met that night in the back booth at the club.

"Jim Hackney?" Gio asked, not looking as impressed as Joe expected. "The Westlands guy?" He winced. "Are you sure? It would be better if it wasn't him."

"What's wrong with Hackney? I thought you'd be happy I got a lead so fast. If you had someone else in mind you should have told me."

"It's not that. You did a great job, but maybe it was too fast? I mean, are you sure it's him?"

"Sure? Of course not. You want fingerprints, maybe? DNA?"

"It wouldn't hurt."

Joe waved at the dancers, the wiseguys drinking at the bar. "So send your forensics team in."

"I'm just saying. We don't want a rush to judgment here. He's innocent until proven guilty."

Joe scowled. "Fair enough, counselor. But neither of us know shit about being innocent, do we? That's what happens when you send a criminal to do a cop's job. Why don't you drop a dime and let the law take it from here?"

"You know, I might just do that if it was anyone else. I'd call that FBI chick, Zamora, kick this over to her."

"Why not?" Joe said. "Let her figure it out."

"If only we could control her. Had leverage, something to make sure she'd play ball. But she's a true believer, isn't she? Straight as they come?" He regarded Joe hopefully.

Joe returned his gaze, then shrugged. "How would I know? Seems like a Girl Scout. But what's wrong with that? Give her the tip, let her win another merit badge."

"That's the problem," Gio said. "We can't risk it. We handle Hackney ourselves. Strictly in-house."

"Why? You pay taxes, sort of."

Gio hesitated, shrugging sheepishly.

"Oh . . ." Joe said then. "I get it." He sat back with a long sigh. "He works for you."

"Not for me, personally," Gio objected, but then he sat back, too. "But yeah. For us." He took a deep breath and leaned forward, as if he and Joe were hunched over a chessboard. "It's this Westlands development. A lot of our friends stand to make a lot of money on this deal. Including all the people at the table the other night. He's got a connection to Rebbe going back to his father's time. The city councilwoman who reps that district, Schlitz? The Madigan brothers own her. And Little Maria's man from uptown is helping swing the votes, too, get this thing approved. They all have contracts lined up. Uncle Chen is going to arrange the steel from overseas, and a lot of the workers, once it's up and running."

"And you?"

"Concrete. Trucking."

"And?"

"Fine . . . and the unions. And garbage pickup after it's built."

"So I guess a few dead girls aren't so important after all."

Gio flared, poking a finger at Joe. "I didn't say that, did I? If this is the piece of shit who did this to Ioana and those other girls, then I will personally take him apart piece by piece, and fuck however many millions it costs, understand?"

Joe held his gaze without reacting. "Understood."

Gio ran a hand over his face. "Sorry. I just . . . I knew that girl. Just as a friend, I mean, it was nothing. I only met her once. We just talked. But I liked her, and nobody deserves to have this happen to them just because sexually they're . . . outside the norm. People have needs, they have desires, and society makes it impossible to fulfill those desires in normal life, so they come to us and OK we profit from it, so I'm not saying we are better than the law and the churches and the square fucking world, but at least we're not hypocrites, pretending we're above these perverts, pointing the finger and saying they had it coming. These were our people and we should have protected them, and we didn't. So now we get them justice."

Joe nodded. "We will."

Gio pressed his hands together as if praying. "But that's why we need proof. If he did it, we show that to the others and then we make him disappear. You're telling me you're not a detective? No kidding. Do I look like the DA? We ain't making a *Law and Order* episode here. But this happened on our turf, so yeah, we are the law."

Now Joe was the one to run his hands over his face, as if trying to clear his mind. "You know I'm used to tricky jobs, but this time . . . I don't know."

Gio smiled and patted his friend on the shoulder. "Lucky for me that badge we gave you doesn't come off."

<hr />

Joe took the train back and then walked through the neighborhood, lost in thought, barely aware of the daily life swirling around him. People yelled and horns blared, the elevated train roared overhead, yet Joe heard nothing, saw nothing. Like a fish in a stream, he flowed with the currents, following his thoughts. He passed his grade school, PS 69. He passed the pizza place where he often used to buy a slice and Coke with stolen coins. He passed the store where he once bought comics, which was now a shoe store. When his feet got cold, he went home and watched an *NCIS* episode with Gladys, vaguely hoping it might give him some investigative tips. No luck. Then she went to bed and he sat up reading *Ulysses*. That didn't help either.

In the morning he had an idea. It was as fragile as a smoke ring, so he didn't speak or make any sudden moves as he brushed his teeth and pulled a robe on, and Gladys, who knew his moods, ignored him as he drank coffee and stared out the window. Then for no reason she heard him laugh out loud to himself, seemingly at nothing, and she knew he had it cracked, whatever it was. A caper.

Joe grinned at her as he passed by, and then he got on the phone.

Madam Wong called Detective Fry. She didn't consider herself to be any sort of traitor. Maintaining good relations with the police was part of her job, after all, though her boss, Uncle Chen, did not know about this particular relationship. Still, when they met years ago, Fry had made it clear that there would be rewards for helping him and penalties for refusing. She helped him. And her place, Uncle Chen's place, was never disturbed. Not to mention the cash Fry slipped her for special favors. After all, she earned so little, considering how hard she worked. She had her own future to consider. She hoped to move back to Shanghai, buy an apartment, and retire or own a small shop. So when she was asked about Mr. Hackney, whether he was a regular, if he might have been there on such and such a night, she answered honestly, as she had been instructed to—she was a loyal employee and wanted no trouble with the boss—but she also called Fry, who had first brought this very regular, very welcome, and very big-spending customer to her establishment. Fry thanked her and promised to bring a gift soon. The truth was, if she had twenty more customers like Mr. Hackney and ten more cops like Fry, she'd be on her way to retirement.

26

When Joe's call came, Josh and Liam were already at work. They'd been up before dawn, brewing coffee in the apartment they'd bought by pooling the proceeds from their last job with Joe. The top floor of an old Chelsea brownstone that looked out on a garden, it was close to everything, but felt far away, especially from the Hell's Kitchen haunts where Liam's oldest brother, Jack, ran the rackets, and the ultra-Orthodox Brooklyn kingdom ruled by Josh's boss, Rebbe Stone. Rebbe had brought Joshua over from Israel, fresh out of the army. Liam and his brothers had been brought over as muscle for Pat White, a distant relative and the last of the Westies, the old Irish mob. When Pat turned rat and got exterminated by Gio Caprisi, the Madigan boys took over and formed a new alliance.

It was also during their first heist with Joe that Liam and Josh fell in love. In the beginning, they kept their romance secret, but soon, like so many others before them, they discovered the wonderful truth about New York: Nobody cares. They'd had to come a long way to be themselves and find each other, but in this megalopolis, just being a couple miles from family and work meant they were anonymous, free to live as they pleased, and their fellow New Yorkers responded with an indifferent shrug. They were all too busy minding their own business.

They had coffee and Irish-style oatmeal at their kitchen table and then they went to work. Josh headed out to Brooklyn while Liam drove to a truckyard in Queens. By six Liam was cutting a hole in the truckyard's wire fence and slipping in to affix a small device to a tire.

By seven he was following that tire, and the empty truck it carried, toward its scheduled pickup, a liquor warehouse in Westchester. But it didn't make it. On a quiet patch of road, Liam hit the radio transmitter resting on his dashboard, and the tire blew.

The driver swerved, the large empty trailer rattling, and pulled to the side. They were on a highway with woods on both sides, and a landscaped median dividing the flow of traffic. Liam drove past the disabled truck and then circled back, cutting through the next access and then pulling over across from and slightly behind the truck, hiding his car in the trees. The driver was out, shaking his head over his tire, and then pulling out his phone. Reaching into the back seat, Liam drew a bazooka-like device, specially smuggled in from Israel, and aimed it carefully. Then he pulled the trigger.

The driver felt nothing, heard nothing. Nothing seemed to happen at all. He merely shrugged, putting his phone away, and then went back to the cab of his truck, presumably to call for help on the radio there. Liam knew it wouldn't work. The gun he'd fired was not designed to kill people or blow up trucks. It knocked out cell, Wi-Fi, and radio transmission with impressive accuracy.

Many people would love to see such devices in the U.S., temporarily killing all cell phones in a movie theater, for example, or in the quiet car on a train. But they are illegal here: FCC regulations protect the freedom of our airwaves.

Meanwhile, Josh had picked up another truck. It was from a fleet Rebbe owned but painted for this job to match the one that Liam had just put out of commission. While Liam watched the disabled truck's driver begin the long walk down the highway to find help, Josh drove his imposter truck to the Westchester warehouse and waited while it was loaded with single-malt Scotches, artisanal bourbons, and other fancy whiskeys. Now they would be sipped and admired in establishments owned or controlled by Rebbe, the Madigan brothers, and a few of their closest associates. They were just meeting back up in Brooklyn, where Josh was dropping off Rebbe's unloaded truck, and looking forward to going home for a nap, when Liam's phone rang. It was Joe.

◦──▸──◦

Cash was casing Championship Motors, again. It had become a private obsession: that row of gorgeous exotic collectibles, each one glistening and perfect—the vintage Mercedes coupe, the James Bond–style Aston Martin, the Ferrari—lit up in the dealership's window like jewels in a case, begging to be smashed and grabbed, the other gorgeous Lamborghinis and Porsches and Jaguars scattered about the pristine white showroom like toys in a gift box, waiting to be taken out and played with. Cash was, first and last, a car thief, and this prize drew him like a bee to honey. But that was where it ended, with him buzzing around, pressing his nose to the glass.

When it came to driving, stealing, chopping, selling, fixing, and reconstructing cars, there was no one who could keep up with Cash. If any one of these cars had been parked on a street or in a lot, in a garage or on a moving flatbed, it would already be his. But that wasn't the job. The job was breaking into a highly secured location with a very sophisticated alarm system and live guards, in a prime, well-lit, glass-box location with a busy avenue full of witnesses, including plenty of cops. Not to mention, once you got in, you had to get all those cars out.

That was why he wanted Joe in on it and had floated the idea when they'd been together the other night. But Joe was busy playing Sherlock for the bosses, and Cash's proposal had barely seemed to register. Now, as he idled up the block from the dealer, the powerful engine under the hood of his GTO growling, waiting to be unleashed, he too idled restlessly, wondering: What would Joe do?

Then his phone rang. It was Joe. He needed Cash's help on this new job, and he wanted Cash to tell him more about that car thing, too.

⚊⚊⚊

Juno was cutting a track. Since his big payday, Juno had sunk about fifty grand into his home studio, buying mics and musical equipment, installing soundproofing, and upgrading his internet and computing power in the bargain. It was a dream come true. Among real-life gangsters and career criminals, Juno was not only accepted as an equal, a pro, he was respected as a master of his craft. But as a DJ and producer he had nothing more than amateur status, spinning records at family parties, jamming with friends. He was still seen as the same nerdy kid he was in high school.

Cash had sent over a couple of rising rappers, Fazed and Dazed, Richmond Hills corner boys who, when they heard what Juno charged for an hour of studio time, promptly robbed the organic muffin shop that had just opened on the rapidly gentrifying avenue, which led the neighbors to complain to his mom. Everyone loved those muffins. Plus, all the weed fumes gave him an asthma attack, so he had finally hung a *No Smoking* sign prominently on the wall.

As a result of these issues, his clients so far tended to be a bit less hard-edged: His neighbor, who worked for the MTA as a dispatcher, wanted to record a proposal rap to go with the engagement ring he'd just bought. A Syrian Jewish kid from Midwood, whose parents were powers in the designer jeans world, wanted beats for the rap he would give at his upcoming bar mitzvah. And now, a sixtysomething friend of his mom's who helped lead the gospel choir at her church wanted to record a hip-hop song to help lure the youngsters back into the fold.

"Are you ready, Mrs. Clarkson?"

She did not look ready: Juno had her in the Plexiglas booth, at the mic. She was holding the earphones up to her head, under the chin, since she had refused to let them mess up her hair.

"What did you say?" she asked now, sticking her head out of the booth.

"I asked if you were ready. Remember, you have to speak into the mic and listen over the headphones, OK?"

"Right. Sorry, baby. Everything here is so technical. No wonder your mama was bragging."

"Thank you. But please get back in the booth and let's record one . . ."

She eased back inside, smoothing her dress and checking her hair, not quite getting that there would be no visual record. Juno spoke into his own mic at the control panel. "'My Lord Is Lit,' take one . . ."

Who's the savior who's got the flavor?
Who's so dope that he fills me with hope?
He parts red seas and dropkicks Pharaoh to his knees.
He's a number one hit! My Lord is lit!

They were on take twenty-one when Joe called. It was, Juno had to admit, a relief.

⚬━━⚬

Yelena had to admit, she was relieved when Joe called. She was in her new apartment, a pristine loft with a wall of glass overlooking the ocean, a view that befitted the new Queen of Brighton Beach, a sweeping panorama of waves, sky, beach, and boardwalk that changed constantly with time and tide, sun and moon, while also remaining essentially, eternally, the same. It was a luxury dwelling, but aside from the view, the main luxury she indulged in was empty space. She'd always been a minimalist. At first that was because she was poor and could afford little or nothing. Then it was because she was more or less in a permanent state of transit, always ready to fight or run, and thinking of whatever room she used to sleep, eat, and store her clothes and weapons in more as a camp or hideout than a home. She needed to pack light. Now she could afford as much of everything as she wanted, but, if anything, her aesthetic had grown even more severe: she'd bought this place because it was a good investment and she loved the light and air, but the rooms were emptier than ever.

Her giant living and dining room, which seemed to take up a block of beach frontage, contained a white couch, two modernist black leather chairs, and a glass-and-steel coffee table, like islands in a polished hardwood sea. A flatscreen TV and expensive audio equipment lined one wall. The dominant objects were the giant white lambskin throw rug before the cold and empty fireplace and the dazzling glass chandelier over the dining table where no one had ever eaten. Her closet contained rows of expensive black, white, and gray clothes, her bathroom, with its sunken tub, held rows of expensive skin and hair products of the sort that look like medicine, in white or gray or black tubes and boxes. The small exercise room where, if she thought about it, she felt most at home, contained free weights and a bench, a stationary bike, a mat for Pilates, and a mirror and barre. It also held the padlocked locker, stenciled in Russian, which contained her stash of weapons. The lock was just to discourage nosy visitors or cleaners. As one of the world's most talented cat burglars, she had a low opinion of security devices and didn't bother much with elaborate locks or alarms, though she slept, always, with a loaded Glock in a holder under her bed and kept knives in several places other than the kitchen. That was her idea of a deterrent.

The bedroom contained a king-size bed on a steel frame, a night table with a lamp and a cut glass vase with an orchid, and another large lambskin rug, this one black. That was it, usually, though this morning there was also a very attractive nude body snoozing in the bed. That was Deena, a young black woman with a shaved head whom Yelena had met running on the beach. Another luxury. She liked running, talking and having sex with Deena, but admitted she was a little uneasy with this other person still here in her lair. Deena, however, liked to sleep over and cuddle. And when Yelena had mentioned the guest room—which had never seen a guest—Deena had assumed she was kidding.

So, when the morning sun woke her, Yelena had tiptoed out into the living room herself and taken a catnap on the couch, wrapped in her lambskin. Then she did her Pilates and made coffee, pausing while it brewed to play with the necklace she had stolen in Florida and had buried in coffee in her freezer. She didn't really want to wear it, and unique items like this were hard to fence, so in the end she would most likely sell it back to the insurance company for a percentage. A nice score, but hardly worth the trouble now that she was a boss. But that was the problem: being a boss was boring, managing other people while they stole and fought and ran. She'd needed the release, and smiled now at the memory, dangling the necklace in the air and watching the light that bounced off the ocean pass through the jewels to dance across her white walls.

That was when Joe called. It was a very short and simple conversation. Could she come to a meeting later? He had a new job and was getting the crew together. Yes she could. She wanted to say, *Thanks, I'd love to*, but this was a job, not a date.

Though she and Joe had had good sexual chemistry from the beginning, that had been the easiest part of their partnership to let go. She was a sexual athlete and could find another playmate, fulfill those needs, which came and went regularly, with Deena or someone else. What she missed about Joe was exactly what her job and apartment and money were supposed to insulate her from: Danger. Difficulty. Trouble. Circumstance and necessity had made her, born and bred her, to be a very specialized being, like one of those champion horses who had to run, or a jungle cat who went nuts if she couldn't hunt and prowl. That was why she had gone down to Florida, and that was why, when she saw Joe's name light up her phone, she smiled, and the same tingle, the same charge that she got holding the necklace, came tickling down her spine. They were going back to work. She stashed the necklace, then poured the coffee and went to wake up Deena.

27

"Thanks for coming. This is a weird one. The only thing we are really out to steal is evidence, and there may not even be any. There's a reward, but we may never be able to claim it. We are doing the job that the cops should be, but if we get caught, we still go to jail."

He looked around the room. Once again he was in the manager's back office at Club Rendezvous, sitting at Santa's desk. Liam and Josh were together on the couch beside Juno. Cash perched on the coffee table. Yelena was in the other roller chair, legs tucked up under her.

"Actually, this whole thing is fucked," Joe admitted. "So if anyone here wants to walk away, now is the time. I will totally understand. No hard feelings."

They all listened to him and then looked at each other and grinned. Juno and Cash giggled. And then finally Liam and Josh burst into laughter, too.

Joe scowled. "What's so funny?"

"Don't you realize?" Liam asked. "'This whole thing is fucked' could describe every job we've done with you."

"That should be your business card," Josh said.

"Why do you think we're here?" Cash asked. "Not because we expect an easy payday, that's for sure."

Juno laughed. "We're buying a ticket for the roller coaster."

Yelena, who'd been watching all of this with a faint smile, finally spoke: "You see, Joe, we all know you very well. So stop teasing already and just tell us. Why are we here?"

Joe told them about Hackney, what he knew and what he'd come to suspect. When he finished, there was a moment of silence.

"Fucking hell," Liam said. "This one is simple. I know what we do with a vile bastard like that back home."

"Same as here, brother," Juno said.

"Free of charge," Josh added. "I'd pay."

"A flash fucker, too," Liam said. "I loathe his type."

"Thinks he owns the world and everything in it, because Daddy got rich exploiting poor people," Juno chimed in. "Only thing lower than a slumlord is the big-mouth son of a slumlord."

Yelena smiled. "It will be my pleasure to cut this monster's throat."

Cash, who'd been quiet, spoke up: "If he really killed Lulu, then I'm going to chop his head off and throw it in the trash."

"Killing him is the easy part," Joe said. "What I need help with is getting the proof."

"For what?" Cash asked. "Let him sue me."

"You're missing the whole point of being a criminal, Joe," Liam said.

Joe stood. "Because the people who stand to make millions off of this Westlands development are the same people who protect all of us. We need to get the OK on this or we will be next in line to lose our heads." He shrugged and leaned back against the desk. "Plus it might be nice to be sure we killed the right guy."

"Fair point," Juno said. He patted Cash on the arm. "Could be embarrassing if we chopped him up and it was all a big misunderstanding."

Cash nodded half-heartedly. "I guess."

"Now that you mention it," Liam said. "Me brother Jack is into this for a fair slice of the pie."

"I know he is," Joe said. "So is your uncle," he told Cash. "And Rebbe and Alonzo." He turned to Yelena. "And your new best pals out in Brighton Beach wouldn't be too happy, either, if you killed the golden goose."

Yelena shrugged and pursed her lips.

"Fine," Cash said. "If we're not here to kill him, why are we here? What are you thinking?"

Joe sat down again, leaning back in Santa's executive chair. "I'm thinking, what if, through no fault of ours, this project ran into trouble? What if Hackney became a liability instead of an asset to protect?"

"You're saying we sabotage the Westlands?" Juno asked. "How?"

"We'd have to be sure it didn't connect back to us," Liam said.

"Damn sure," Josh said. "I'm not telling Rebbe I cost him and his hundred grandkids a fortune."

"Exactly," Joe said. "But if it was Hackney who cost them the money . . . and we had evidence linking him to the killings . . ."

Cash grinned for the first time. "Then they'd not only OK the hit, they'd thank us."

Juno sat forward, rubbing his hands together. "Excellent. What's the plan?"

Joe shrugged. "I don't know . . ." Everyone groaned. "Yet," he added. "But I know we've got to get in close, learn a lot more about him and his operation. And that means getting inside."

"All right, then," Liam said. "That's step one."

"Actually, that's step two," Joe told him. "Getting close to a flash fucker, as you called him, takes flash. And that takes money." He grinned at Cash. "And a really nice car."

Fry got a call from the morgue. Some friend of Ioana Petrescu's had turned up, a roommate who confirmed the identity of the deceased and inquired about claiming the remains. As he was the investigating officer on file, they were giving him a heads-up. Normally, he would pass this along to Fusco, who seemed happy to take this case, and wash his hands of it. But since the last call he'd received from that Flushing madam, he'd taken more of an interest.

"I know Fusco in Major Crimes flagged this," the morgue tech went on, "so I will tell him, too, but I figured, dot the I's, you know . . ."

"Actually," Fry said, "could you send that friend's name and address straight to me? I'll circulate it to the interested parties. Thanks."

28

Much like Cookie's, Championship Motors was a toy shop for very rich (mostly) men, a chance to live out fantasies, to project dreams and desires onto idealized fetishes, polished to perfection. The big difference was secrecy. Cookie's was all about a safe place to hide. Champs, as its customers called it, was all about display. Big glass windows, big white showrooms, big shiny cars, or small cars with big engines, incredibly loud or, just as impressive to the right ear, incredibly quiet. Even closed, as it was now, at six on a frigid morning, it called attention to itself: the windows onto Tenth Avenue were lit, the Ferrari on the rotating stand rotated, and the neon sign was aglow. Only a few rats, a passing garbage truck, and a bum camped out on a warm vent across the street were there to appreciate it, but the owners thought it was safer. Most times they'd be right. Not today.

"I'm shutting the security system down," Juno said. "Now it's just the door alarm." He was in a white van that sat idling around the corner from Championship Motors. It was equipped with a high-powered satellite dish that let him hack into the shop's Wi-Fi system and disable the motion detectors as well as the connection to the alarm company, leaving only the loud bell that would sound if the doors were opened. That was hardwired into the electric. The van also featured special hazard lights and a spinning flasher on top. Joe, who was driving, hit the lights: pulsing yellow arrows that ran down the back of the van and a spinning red light on top. Yelena, who was sitting in back, couldn't help laughing. Normally a thief tries to enter like a ghost, unseen and unheard. Now they were rolling in, trying to attract as much attention as possible.

"Showtime," Joe said over his walkie-talkie, and put the van in drive. They were rolling.

Because Juno had cut the connection to the alarm company and replaced it with a normal, idling signal, neither the security firm nor the guard on duty noticed anything. The guard was also distracted when a van with flashing lights came down the block, leading three full-size trucks, painted white and bearing the Championship Motors name and checkered-flag logo. He stood and pressed his face to the window as this impressive convoy stopped in front of the shop windows.

Joe hopped out, dressed in white coveralls and a red cap, carrying a clipboard and shoulder bag. He waved at the guard, who gaped until Joe rapped on the glass and pointed at the door. The guard jumped and fumbled with his keys. He slid one into the alarm panel and turned. Now the bells were silenced. Then he unlocked the door.

"Good morning," Joe told him. "We're here for the pickup."

"Pickup? What pickup?" He peered suspiciously at the clipboard.

Joe held it up. "This one right here. See?" He pointed to a printout. Sure enough, it listed nine of the shop's most expensive cars. "It's for the movie shoot in Connecticut. You know, the one where George Clooney plays a billionaire car collector who is also an amateur spy." Joe shrugged. "Your company is handling security. They got people on-site already. Waiting."

"A movie shoot?" The guard shook his head. "Nobody told me about this."

"Typical, right?" Joe said.

"You said it. Nobody around here tells me anything. Well, you better come inside while I call this in."

"Righto," Joe said, whistling cheerfully as he followed him around the corner to his desk. As soon as they were out of sight, he slipped the blackjack from his pocket and knocked the guard unconscious, catching him to be sure he'd suffer nothing more than a headache and some embarrassment when he woke, and easing him into his desk chair. Joe spoke into his walkie: "Come on in." Then he pulled out rope and a soft breathable hood and began to tie up the guard.

Juno and Yelena came in from the van, also dressed in white coveralls and red caps. While Juno went to raise the large rolling metal door that sealed the loading entrance, Yelena took Joe's clipboard and went to the boss's office. In minutes she had picked the lock on his door handle, proceeded to the keyboard, and begun selecting the keys for the cars on the list. Joe rolled the guard, now bound to his chair and snoring peacefully through his hood, into the boss's office and parked him in a corner. Then he and Yelena went to the loading dock, where Juno was directing Cash as he backed in one of the trucks. Cash hopped out. He was wearing the same uniform, as were Liam and Josh, who idled outside in the other trucks.

"Let's do some shopping." Joe tossed a set of Lamborghini keys to Cash, who laughed gleefully.

"Joe, you've made my childhood dream come true. Even if I'm only driving it fifty feet."

Cash, Yelena, and Joe hustled to the showroom floor. Juno, a typical New Yorker, didn't know how to drive, but he lowered the platforms so the display cars could be moved. In minutes, two Lamborghinis and a Ferrari were on the truck. Cash pulled it out, rejoining the convoy on the street, and Liam backed in. They loaded a Rolls-Royce, a Maybach, and a vintage Mercedes coupe. Next were a Bentley, the Aston-Martin, and a Porsche. At the last minute, Joe unlocked a red Ducati motorcycle and rolled that on board. Finally, Juno lowered the gate, and while he and Yelena got in the van, Joe locked the front door behind him with the guard's keys. That was when the cops pulled up.

"Morning officers," Joe said, strolling over to their window. Two cops, big men with buzzed heads, one white, one black, gazed at him from within.

"Morning. How's it going?"

Joe glanced at his watch. Six thirty. "Not bad. Running a little behind, but what else is new?"

"You plan on blocking this lane much longer? Rush hour starts early here."

"We're moving right now, sir," Joe said. He pointed at Juno, who climbed from the van wearing a reflective vest over his uniform and holding a signal flag. He carried one of each for Joe, too. Yelena started the van up and hit the lights.

"Great," the cop said. "We'll help." They hit their flashers, too, backing up to the rear of the trucks. Then, while Joe and Juno stood in the middle of Tenth Avenue, diverting the sparse traffic—mostly cabs and black cars along with a few trucks and buses—Cash, Josh, and Liam put their trucks in gear and hit their headlights. Slowly the convoy got rolling, with Yelena in the van leading the parade. At the corner, Juno hopped in next to Yelena. And as the last truck pulled up, Joe climbed in next to Liam and waved his flag to the cops in thanks. They flicked their lights in acknowledgment and drove off.

⌐╍╍○

First they went to the docks. Within the hour, eight of the cars were in sealed containers bound for mainland China and Russia via the Balkans, and Joe had his stake. The Rolls and the Ducati they kept, transporting them in a truck to Reliable Scrap in Queens. The large decals with the Championship Motors logos were removed from the trucks, revealing the Mini-King Storage and Moving logos beneath, and the plates were switched back: they'd been replaced with sets from

131

wrecks in Cash's lot. Joe took everybody to breakfast at a diner, and then suggested they all head home for a nap. They had a busy night ahead.

They split up shortly before nine, right as the manager of Championship Motors was arriving and noticing something strange: the bright white jewel box was empty, the alarms were back on, and the security guard was snoring peacefully in his office. He notified the police, of course, but if anyone on patrol saw anything that morning, they were too embarrassed to report it. The only witness was a homeless man camped on the hot air vent across the street, but he took no interest and went on with his day.

By the time Joe got home, Gladys was up and about. She offered him coffee or toast, but he explained that he'd already had breakfast and was now going to sleep, which made perfect sense to her. She turned down the radio. He went to his room, drew the curtains, peeled his clothes off, lay down on the bed, and was just drifting into oblivion when the phone rang. He'd forgotten to turn the ringer off. He reached for it in the dark. He didn't recognize the number.

"Hello?"

"Hi . . ." There was a long pause. "Sorry to bother you, but you said to call if anything came up. Well, something has definitely come up."

"Sorry," Joe said, clearing the sleep from his throat. "Who is this?"

"Jem."

In a flash he was fully awake, sitting up and reaching for the lamp. "What happened?"

29

Jem was feeding Midnight. She knew she couldn't stay at Ioana's forever. Even someone with her gift for optimism (or self-delusion, depending on whom you asked—who else would head off to New York with nothing but a suitcase?) had to accept that. But her native optimism was matched by a keen survival instinct that had let her escape first a brutal home life, then foster care, and then more than one death trap on the streets, to arrive here, in relative safety, at least till the end of the month. By then she would know what to do next—as if by magic, she thought.

She remembered one of the few fond memories of her barren child-hood, a trip to the circus on free tickets organized by a social worker. It was a crappy, run-down, threadbare circus, with what even then a streetwise kid recognized as a junkie sword swallower, a very angry, very butch bearded lady, meth-head dwarves, and some seriously alcoholic clowns. The animals were behind bars, something no kid in the system could pretend was fun. But the magician, in his top hat and pointed mustache, and his wonderful assistant, a long-legged, long-haired brunette in a sparkling leotard and fishnets, appearing and disappearing, spinning on a wheel while every blade missed her, even getting sawed in half (one of the kids in her group home's dad had actually sawed up his mom, though he had already strangled her first) and then coming back, whole, happy, beautiful, and smiling like a starlet. And she did it all in red heels. That was how Jem wanted to be. And here she was. After all, she had transformed from Jeremy to Jem, had transported herself from Oklahoma to Chicago to New York, all without money or connections. She would, she knew, slip free again. Abraca-fucking-dabra!

She smiled, whispering it to herself, or to Midnight as she scooped out her food—holding her breath because it smelled horrible, though it was the fancy cat food—and spooned it into the bowl, while the cat swam, purring, rubbing figure eights between her ankles. "Here you go, baby," she said, petting her as she set the bowl on the floor. She was the perfect magician's cat. A coal-black familiar with yellow eyes.

Then she heard someone trying to open the door. She froze, wanting to shush the cat but realizing that it was far more risky to be heard herself. Whoever it was clearly didn't expect anyone to be home—but they also had no key. She could hear them breathing and whispering to each other as they worked on the lock. Trying to stay calm as her pulse and breath accelerated, she reached into the drawer for a short, sharp knife, then bent to pick up the cat, who mewled in protest, her meal not yet done, and tiptoed from the kitchen, shutting off the light. She hurried to her bedroom, where, just as she heard the door give, she dropped to the carpet and slid under the bed, hugging the cat to her chest and clutching the knife.

"Shhh . . ." she whispered, stroking the cat, feeling her own heart pound. Her own ears pricked, she heard voices and steps from the other rooms. There were three voices, she thought, all male.

"What are we looking for?" one asked.

"Anything that connects us. Anything with my dad's name, the business, whatever." She heard drawers opening, cabinets banging. "Look," the commanding voice resumed. "I've got to go. You're in charge, Riley. Just do a thorough search and let me know."

"Yes, sir," the first voice responded, and then, as the front door shut: "I'll finish in here."

"Right," said a second, younger voice.

A moment later, Jem heard her bedroom door creak open, and light fell across the floor. He flicked the switch and she saw shoes appear. Cop shoes, she thought at first, black and chunky, with some kind of polyester blue cuffs above them. But they were too blue for cops and had a gold stripe. Security guards? Sighing to himself, the guy moved around, opening her closet, riffling through her things. He did not seem to be doing a very thorough search, she thought, but he did a good job of making a mess, as she saw her belongings gather into piles on the floor. Then he paused, and with a groan, he got to his knees. He was going to check under the bed! Jem held her breath as two large hands, also clad in blue cuffs, came creeping toward her. One hand, searching blindly, touched Midnight and she flinched, yowling loudly and squirming free. Instinctively, Jem lashed out to protect her charge, stinging him between the fingers with the tip of the blade.

"Shit!" he yelled, pulling his hand back and jumping up as Midnight ran past him out into the hall. "Fuck!"

"What's going on?" the other voice called, louder now, as the man ran into the room.

"There was a cat under the bed. Goddam thing scratched me. I hope it doesn't get infected."

"Are you kidding? It's nothing."

"It's bleeding. Plus you know there is that cat scratch fever."

"That's a real thing? I thought it was a song."

"It can be fatal, I think. Or maybe that's raccoons."

"Well, if you're done crying, let's get out of here. I go on duty in an hour."

"I'm not crying, dickhead. I'm bleeding. And I got a shift coming up, too."

"Oh yeah, hotel? We can order dinner. I'm thinking cheese steaks."

"No, I'm at the site tonight. My luck. That place gives me the creeps."

"Yeah, better watch out. Might see raccoons. Or a mouse."

The voices and footsteps faded, and then the door opened and shut. Jem breathed. When it seemed like five minutes had passed—it was probably thirty seconds—she slid out and stood, stretching her back and feeling the dread-sweat dry on her skin. Then she tiptoed to the door and peeked through the peephole. Empty hall. She relocked the door, packed quickly, and found Midnight hiding under the couch. She coaxed her out and then, feeling guilty for tricking her, immediately zipped her into her carrier. And then she left. She ran aimlessly, just wanting to be clear of the building, the block, and then, as she tired, she walked, and finally, as she got colder, she went into a café, ordered a tea, and thought about what to do next. Then she remembered that guy, Joe.

She was pretty sure she woke him, and there was a terrible moment when she realized he had no idea who was calling, but as soon as she explained, he was on it, calm and alert.

"Get in a cab and come to this address," he said, reciting it slowly and then waiting while she repeated it.

"It's in Queens," he said. Then, as if reading her mind, he asked, "Do you have enough money for the cab?"

"No, but I bet Ioana's account still works. I can call a car."

"No. Just hail a regular cab and call me back when you're close. I will come down and pay. Go now."

"OK," she said, suddenly realizing she knew nothing about this man but deciding, intuitively, to trust him. *You told yourself you'd know what to do when the time came, Miss Magic*, she thought to herself. *Well, here it is.* "But . . ."

"But what?"

"There's just one more thing."

"OK," Joe said patiently. "What is it?"

"I have a cat."

30

When Josh and Liam got home, they crashed. But while Liam took the opportunity to sleep in, knowing he'd be busy later, Josh took a quick nap followed by a shower and a special quadruple espresso latte that he made with the contraption in their kitchen. Then he put on a suit and tie and went to the Hackney Tower Hotel.

The executive offices were far above, along with the premier suites and Hackney's own penthouse, reachable by private elevator. But the regular staff offices were in a warren of hallways on the ground floor, behind the lobby, shops, and restaurants, with locker rooms, CCTV station, and so forth in the basement, along with the laundry, kitchens, and other services. Below that was the parking garage.

Josh wandered the lobby, window-shopped, and generally loitered, noting the comings and goings of the security personnel, who wore blue slacks and jackets with gold piping and an emblem that he assumed was the Hackney family crest stamped in gold over the jacket's breast. He quickly picked out the supervisor: a typical meathead, thick neck and buzzed skull rising from his too-tight collar, arms too big to rest comfortably against his body in the jacket. He barked and bullied as he came and went, checking up on the guards at the front desk, crossing and recrossing the lobby. Then, like a faithful dog, his ears perked. The light over the private elevator dinged, and his masters emerged. The Hackneys, father and son. The dad was overweight, lumbering, but in a custom-made blue pinstripe suit. The son was in fighting trim, wearing a slightly more hip version of the same clothes; his jacket had vents and four buttons, his tie was a lighter blue, and he moved lightly, on the balls of his feet. Josh walked right up to them, deliberately cutting in front of the eager supervisor.

"Excuse me, sirs," he said, letting his Israeli accent thicken a bit. "A moment of your time."

The two paused, curious.

"My name is Joshua—" Josh began, pressing closer, hand out for a shake, but before he could even speak his (fake) last name, the supervising meathead was grabbing him by the shoulder. Josh spun right, elbow out, stomping on his foot and holding him in place while his elbow drove deep into his solar plexus. The supervisor grunted, caught off guard and out of breath, while Josh grabbed the hand on his shoulder and, in a second, was bending it up behind its owner's back while he plopped him facedown on the floor. The big man howled as Josh applied pressure. The Hackneys stared.

"What the hell are you doing?" Senior asked.

"Do you know this man, sir?" Josh asked.

"He's our security supervisor," Junior said. "Let him go."

"Oh . . ." Josh looked down at the squirming body. The thick neck was beet red. "Sorry, sir." He hopped up, brushing off his suit. "I apologize. I am just out of the army last week."

Senior grinned. "Not the U.S. Army with that accent."

"No, sir. Israel. I was in a commando unit, so I am trained to react quickly. I apologize for hurting your employee. Don't worry. His arm is not broken."

By now the supervisor was sitting up, tenderly rubbing his arm. "How do you know it's not broken? It's numb."

"I depressed the nerve but did not break any bone," Josh explained. "The feelings will return soon. Painful feelings. Ice will help." He leaned over to help him up, but the supervisor shook him off angrily and got carefully to his feet.

"Well, now that you got our attention," Hackney Sr. said, "what do you want?"

Josh grinned sheepishly. "I wanted to apply for a job, sir."

"As what?" Junior asked.

"Security."

"What?" the supervisor bawled. "That's a hell of a way to apply. You've got to be kidding if you—"

"You're hired," Hackney Sr. said. "When can you start?"

"Right away, sir."

"Good," Hackney said. He frowned at his supervisor. "Dickerson, take the rest of the day off and ice that arm. Junior, walk him through the process and get him a uniform." He held out a hand to Josh. "You start tonight."

"Yes, sir!" Josh clicked his heels and gave a smart salute, then shook hands. "Thank you, sir."

Junior held his hand out, too. "I'm Jim Hackney Jr., executive vice president in charge of operations." They shook hands. "Now come on, commando, let's get you on board."

31

After the call from Jem, Joe went to talk to Gladys, who was still in the kitchen, tidying up after breakfast.

"Listen," he said. "I want to talk to you about something."

She dried her hands on her housedress and sat at the table, where the paper was open to the crossword. "Did you change your mind about the casino? You realize Gio is offering us a percentage? I could finally retire in style."

"Retire from what, doing crosswords?" he asked, pouring coffee. "The stash you've got stuffed in that mattress, how do you even sleep on it?"

"Like a baby. So then, what?"

"There's someone coming over. Kind of a witness. She might be in danger." He shrugged. "She's kind of a lost sheep, too. I don't think she had anyone else to call."

"She on the game?"

"Yeah, but not for long. She's just a kid. Someone killed her roommate and now some heavies tossed the crib."

"Poor kid." Gladys shook her head. "Sure, let her come."

"Also, I should tell you, just so you know, she's a trans woman."

She tapped her pencil thoughtfully. "You mean like an illegal immigrant?"

"No. She's from Oklahoma." He sighed. "You know, when she was born, she was considered male but now identifies as female."

"Oh!" Gladys nodded, happily. "Tranny! Of course, there were always lots of tranny hookers on the game. Tough girls, too. They had to be. Always the most glamorous, too, let me tell you. Gave me a lot of tips on makeup. But don't let the hair and nails and sweet voice fool you. You don't want to fuck with a tranny. Those bitches will cut you."

Joe squirmed, foreseeing disaster. "Just, when she gets here, be, you know, respectful."

"I always respected them. Everyone did. One time, this friend of mine, Fantasia, a pimp tried to bitch-slap her, and like that"—she snapped her fingers—"she had her razor out and—"

"No, what I mean is, that language, some of those terms aren't really considered polite anymore. Like *tranny*. Or *hooker*."

"*Hooker*? What do you say?"

"*Sex worker*."

Gladys shrugged. "Fair enough. It's still sucking dicks. But it's honest work, and you should never be ashamed of a job well done." She stood and pushed the paper toward Joe. "Anyway, don't worry about me. You know I get along with all types. You just help your old granny with the crossword while I put on a fresh pot of coffee and get ready for our guest. Five across is kicking my ass."

Feeling less than reassured, Joe picked up the pencil as Gladys kissed his head, walking by. "Oh, one more thing," he called after her. "She has a cat."

Gladys put some milk in a saucer. Midnight, wary but thirsty, crept slowly from the carrier, taking these new humans and their space in with big yellow eyes before daintily dipping her whiskers in the milk and taking a tiny spoonful on her tongue.

"There you go, hon," Gladys murmured, slowly stroking the cat.

Jem added milk to the coffee Gladys had poured her and told them about what had happened at the apartment. Joe took it in thoughtfully, tapping a finger against his lips.

"Good for you," Gladys said, when she got to the part about slicing the guy. "Don't take any shit off nobody. I'll show you how to hide a razor in your hair."

"I'm just lucky," Jem said, then shivered, though the apartment was, if anything, much too warm. "I keep thinking about Ioana. Would it have mattered if she had a razor?"

"Well, hon, there's always that risk when you're on the—" She caught herself. "You know, sex working. The money's good, especially when you're young. But there's some sickos out there."

Jem nodded. "I know it. Ioana always thought she was going to meet the right guy, you know? The one who would save her. Instead she met her killer."

The tears began to trickle down her cheeks, and Gladys began slowly rubbing her back. Joe got up, silently, and went to get his coat and shoes. He had to meet Yelena at her tailor.

Later, after Jem had washed her face and Gladys had spent some time playing with Midnight, making her a toy out of a pencil and some string, Gladys got to thinking. "I've been thinking," she said. "A nice, smart girl like you. We need to find you a new career. Something with a future."

Jem smiled, watching Midnight swat the spinning pencil that Gladys held above her. "I dropped out of high school. And I never learned to type or cook or anything. The only other job I ever had was cleaning houses."

Gladys curled her lip. "I was thinking of a nice, safe grift. Like fortune-telling. Or poker. Marks would never see you coming with that innocent, corn-fed Indiana thing you got going."

"Oklahoma."

"Right, right. You play cards?"

Jem laughed. "The only thing I ever did with cards was make them disappear."

"How so?"

"Oh, nothing. I just always liked magic shows, you know? So I learned some dumb tricks."

"Show me," Gladys said, getting out a deck of cards and sliding her glasses on.

So Jem ran through her small repertoire of tricks, floating cards to the top of the deck, vanishing them up her wrist, and making them reappear. Gladys sat back, watching with a smile.

"You've got fast hands, kid. With enough practice, you could be a cannon."

"A what?"

"A top pickpocket. You've got the grace, the long fingers. Those hands were made to dip."

Jem laughed. "No way."

"Don't laugh. It's a nice, steady line of work. I know what you're thinking—people don't carry cash anymore. Well, first of all, that's not true. You just have to know how to spot them. But the real dough nowadays is in credit card numbers and IDs. And it's safe. People don't get killed over a pulled wallet."

"I guess . . ."

"And the best part is, if you do get pinched, so what? It's a minor beef. You're back out in a few hours."

Jem was grinning now. "But it seems pretty difficult. How would I ever learn?"

Gladys stood, gathering the cards. "Of course it's difficult. It's an art. That's why everybody respects a good dip. Come on, let's make some lunch." She led Jem into the kitchen, brushing against her as she opened cabinets and the cat circled their feet. "Tuna OK? For you, me, and kitty?"

"Sure."

Gladys got out a bowl and took two tins of tuna from a shelf. "What you need is a good teacher and a lot of practice."

Jem shrugged. "If you say so. When do I start?"

Gladys grinned, holding up the wallet she had slid from Jem's back jeans pocket. "You already did."

32

"Which side do you . . . tend toward, sir?"

"Huh?" Joe was spacing out while the tailor fitted him for the suit, trying not to squirm like he did the last time this happened, which might have been with his grandmother, buying the suit he wore to his mother's funeral. Now he looked down at the head of the tailor, a corona of white fuzz around a bald center as he knelt between the pinstriped pants, his tape measure out, chalk in his hand, needles bristling from his lips.

Yelena was watching from a stool. This was her tailor, and under her direction he'd pulled a rack of clothes for Joe, including several exquisite suits intended for other customers. Now he was altering them to fit Joe.

"What he means," she explained with a smile, "is which side does your shlong hang down when you put your pants on?"

The tailor shrugged in agreement.

"Oh . . ." Joe said. "I'm not sure."

"Right side," Yelena told him, and repeated it in Russian. "*Pravaya storona.*"

He nodded and got back to work. Finally, Joe was allowed to get back into his own sweatshirt and jeans, the last time he expected to wear them for a while. They'd chosen four suits and a camel hair topcoat. Then, while the tailor finished up, they went shopping for more, hitting the high-end shops, paying cash. They bought dress shirts, expensive khakis, a couple of cashmere sweaters and silk scarves, even

T-shirts and boxers and black dress socks. Yelena picked out ties and Joe bought three pairs of shoes, including a brand-new pair of high-tech running shoes to replace his beloved Converse. They even got cuff links, cologne, a razor and fancy shaving cream, and some kind of British toothpaste. Most of this stuff Joe never expected to use, but it didn't matter. It was set dressing. Props. The illusion had to be complete.

They bought luggage to put it all in—Louis Vuitton, but from a vintage resale place; it was more realistic a bit worn—and unwrapped everything before packing it. Then they went to a barber, and Joe got a tight haircut and a close shave. By then the tailor was done, but they stopped in first to eat lunch at a place Yelena knew—hot borscht, kielbasa, kasha with mushroom gravy—because Joe didn't trust himself not to get mustard or gravy or, worst of all, beet juice on his new clothes. The tailor smiled, proud of his work, as Joe buttoned up the gray pinstripe, which now fit perfectly, and Yelena came over to help with his tie.

"You look so good even I would be seen with you," she said, and kissed his cheek. He laughed and paid the tailor, double the regular price. Outside, the early winter dusk was already falling, blackening the sky, turning the shop window into a mirror. He looked, to himself, almost ready. Then he heard a honk.

"They're here," Yelena said, opening the door, letting in the noise and light of the street. Joe pulled on his overcoat, shook hands with the tailor, and carried his luggage outside. The Rolls and Ducati were waiting. Liam hopped out of the car while Cash climbed off the bike. Both men wore suits, though not quite as refined as Joe's. Liam was in a loose-shouldered Italian number, Cash in a plain black suit that buttoned up tight.

"Somebody call for a ride?" Liam asked.

"What do you think?" Cash asked, presenting the bike like a game show host. "Cheesy enough for you?" Along with providing both vehicles with clean plates and papers, he'd repainted the motorcycle, replacing the bright red with an even more garish yellow and adding a truly eye-scorching bolt of orange down the side.

Yelena laughed. "Even in Moscow this would get attention."

"It's perfect, Cash, good work," Joe said, holding out his hand. "Now hand over the keys."

"I was afraid you'd say that." He dropped them in Joe's palm and then put a cap on, completing his chauffeur's look. He got behind the wheel of the Rolls while Liam helped Joe load his stuff into the trunk. Yelena got in back; she'd be dropped off at home to prepare for her own part.

Joe slid onto the Ducati. It was like strapping into the cockpit of a jet, one of the new stealth fighters that streaked across the sky, a blurred scream unseen on radar. He started the engine, a low, liquid rumble, like a dragon clearing its throat. He pulled out, getting used to the instrument, going slow. He had one more stop to make. He had to see Princess.

Princess was a fence. She had been one as long as anyone could remember, and her line reached back even further. Her father had run the business before her. Whether by DNA or osmosis, Princess had a gift. She could assess the value and authenticity of any object at a glance, but she often relied on her other senses as well. She was said to weigh jewels by hand, listen to watches, sniff antique silver, even taste gold. They even said that fake or inferior pieces, if she tried them on, would raise a rash on her skin. People said that's how she got her name, supposedly, from "The Princess and the Pea." Though really it was what her dad had called her when, as a kid, she had played in the underground store he ran, a cabinet of wonders.

Now she sat in the same throne-like chair, salvaged from an eighteenth-century church, behind the huge French Empire desk, with, that evening, a Persian rug, a Japanese scroll, and what, to Joe, looked like a Basquiat painting on the wall behind her. More treasures were heaped everywhere, but Joe wasn't there to buy or to sell. He was renting.

Princess gave him a hug, waved him into a Danish modern chair, and disappeared into her labyrinth, returning with a gold-and-diamond Patek Philippe watch worth about a hundred grand.

"The only reason I'm not asking for a deposit is I know your people," she said, strapping it on his wrist. "Your grandma used to sell me engagement rings she boosted from Fortunoff's." She breathed on the watch and gave it a quick wipe with a cloth. "That and Gio said that if you get killed, he'd pay."

Joe kissed her cheek. "Thanks, Princess, I love you, too." Then he looked at his reflection in a standing gilt mirror. He shot his cuffs. Now he was ready.

PART III

33

Donna was reading the paper. She was in a Con Ed van, which were ubiquitous all over New York, keeping an eye on the brothel. Business had been slow, a trickle of men whom she dutifully photographed. The rest of the time she read the news or gossiped with Blaze, who was flirting with women on Tinder.

"Hmm . . ." Donna mused, turning a page. The photo was of a car dealership just a mile or so away, its windows empty.

"What?" Blaze asked without looking up.

"You hear about this heist at the fancy car dealership? They showed up with trucks, pretending to be legit movers taking the cars to a movie set. Then they disabled the alarm, and the guard, and cleared the place out. And somehow nobody saw a thing."

"Injuries?" Blaze asked as she swiped.

"Just a minor bump on the guard's head. He woke up in the boss's office."

"Nice work," Blaze mused. "Think what a pleasure this job would be if we just had real professionals working on both sides. Instead of dirtbags and dumbasses."

"Also on both sides?"

"Exactly."

Donna reluctantly agreed. Clever, audacious without being foolish, intricately planned and executed with minimal force and zero evidence. It sounded like someone she knew. But it couldn't be Joe, she thought with relief. He was chasing that killer. *What has my life come to?* she thought ruefully. *I'm happy my secret part-time boyfriend is busy with another illegal enterprise and not stealing cars.*

"Damn it. Lying bastard." Blaze muttered curses under her breath.

"What?" Donna asked, turning the page as if clearing her mind.

"I think this woman I've been talking dirty with is a dude."

"That's what you get for trawling the internet. At least he wasn't a maniac white-supremacist terrorist." She was referring to the chief suspect in her last major case, who had targeted her on a dating site.

"At least you got to shoot him."

"True. That was very satisfying. Also I stopped a nuclear attack."

Blaze waved her phone in the air, clearly incensed. "Here's the thing I don't understand about this needle-dick. I mean, I know I'm hot. I know straight guys are into me. I can't blame them for trying. Look how many straight girls I've converted."

"That's why they call you the Lesbianator."

"You're one of the few who were able to resist."

"I didn't want to jeopardize our friendship. It's too precious."

"But what does this guy get out of just pretending to be female online? He can't meet me. He can't get anything out of it. There's a million porn sites and stuff way more X-rated than my very vanilla pictures of me walking my sister-in-law's dog. What's the point? Is he just whacking off with one hand while he texts me, pretending to be a girl?" Her lip curled, as if she wanted to spit on the floor of the van, but she did not. "I'd feel sorry for the loser, if I didn't want to kick his ass so bad."

Donna shrugged. "Who knows? The human heart is a mystery."

Blaze gave her a look. "Well, you would know."

"What's that supposed to mean?"

"Nothing. Just that you're a top investigator. You solve mysteries."

"Yeah, yeah. I know you. You meant something."

Blaze waved her off. "Seriously. I was kidding." She looked down at her phone. "Anyway, I'm busy."

"Come on. Spit it out."

"Spit what out?" Andy opened the back door. He was dressed in a Con Ed uniform, coveralls and helmet, though freshly laundered and better fitting than most, and carrying a cardboard tray of coffees and a bag of snacks.

"Ask her. She's got something on her mind." Donna crossed her arms, regarding Blaze. "And it must be major. Considering how shy and quiet you are."

Blaze looked at Andy, who shrugged, then nodded as he handed out the drinks.

"Well . . ." Blaze turned her phone off and put it in her pocket, as if preparing to have a private talk. "Here's the thing." She took a big sip of coffee for strength. "Speaking only as friends, Andy and I have noticed that, as of late, you seem . . . different."

"You know, just a little weird," Andy said, handing Blaze a chocolate croissant and taking a cinnamon bun for himself. "Not your usual self."

"What do you mean?" Donna asked. "I've been in a great mood lately."

"That's it," Andy said, pointing at her. "Exactly."

"Yeah," Blaze concurred. "You seem—"

"—happy!" Andy concluded.

"And that's weird?" Donna asked.

He shrugged. "For you it is."

"Most of our conversations are bitching, right?" Blaze said. "About the job, about dating . . ."

"Well, the job's going good," Donna said.

"Sure, sure," Blaze said, waving that off. "But nobody's happy when they have to get up at five A.M. to follow some miscreant or stays cheery all night, squatting in a cold van just because they love their job. You're not an elf."

"Plus your skin is clear. Your eyes are bright. Even your hair is more lustrous." Andy sniffed. "The only job that gives you that is trophy wife."

"You're not the only investigator here, kid." Blaze held a palm out, as if presenting her case. "We are capable of making a logical deduction."

"Which is?" Donna asked, both flattered and annoyed.

"You're getting laid," Blaze said.

"Good and regular," Andy added.

Donna said nothing.

"But then," Blaze went on, holding a finger up, "we asked ourselves, like good investigators, why, if you finally got lucky, wouldn't you tell your two best friends, who you tell about every bad date and lame guy you run across?"

"So we looked at the common denominator," Andy said. "And came to the only possible conclusion."

"Which is?" Donna asked flatly, but she swallowed hard and her hands curled into fists, nails digging into her palms. Ever since her first night with Joe, she had dreaded this moment. Now it was here. They knew.

Blaze pointed an accusing finger at Donna. "You're boning a coworker."

"I just hope it's not Tom," Andy blurted out. "Because he's married with kids, and the scandal will ruin both of your careers."

"Tom?" Donna recoiled. "I am not even remotely attracted to him."

Andy shrugged. "But I am. You know I have a thing for silver daddies. Plus the whole boss's-office scenario gets to me."

Blaze shook her head. "I told him that was crazy. You'd never do the boss man. You're a woman of the people. I'm rooting for Tadeusz."

"Who?" Donna asked, incredulous.

"Tadeusz. The hot janitor. You know, the big one with the hairy forearms. That smoldering look in his eyes. That accent from I don't know where. Don't tell me you haven't noticed him mopping up. I figure you came across him cleaning the women's bathroom and it just happened. Nobody's fault."

Donna burst out laughing in relief. "You're both out of your minds. Maybe I look good because I tried a new shampoo and some moisturizer. And unlike some"—she wiggled two splayed fingers at them—"I have cut way back on my sugar." She saluted with her coffee, skim latte and no sweetener. "You both need to eat some veggies, get a good night's sleep, and focus on solving this case, not the mystery of my cold, cold heart."

That shut them up, Donna was happy to see. But still, it got her thinking. Blaze finished her croissant and left, her shift over, for a Tinder date made with an attractive and (she was reasonably sure) female French teacher. Andy was now reading Donna's discarded newspaper, poring over the same article on the car heist. Fusco was due any moment, to relieve Donna. His bear claw was waiting in the bakery bag. Acting casual, Donna slid her phone from her bag and checked it. No messages.

"You know," Andy mused, "I bet those cars are halfway to China or Russia already. Which could make it federal. I might ask to see the file, just for kicks."

"Uh-huh," Donna answered, typing with one thumb and sending a secret message to her own mystery lover.

I get off work soon. Want to get me off? Soon?

34

"Good evening, sir, and welcome to Hackney Tower Hotel. Will you be checking in?"

"That's right. The name's Bloom. I'm checking into the penthouse."

Joe leaned casually on the counter, as though it were a bar and he was ordering a martini from the young clerk. Freckled, with her auburn hair cut in bangs, she seemed nervous, like she was out of vermouth. Liam stood to one side, briefcase under his arm, slowly scanning the room like a not-very-worried bodyguard. Cash came in next, cap on, followed by two bellhops wheeling a cart heaped with luggage, the LV trunk on top. He stepped up on the other side of Joe, removed his cap, and clicked his heels. Everyone looked.

They'd made a similar splash in the parking garage beneath them. Joe had gunned the Ducati's monstrously powerful engine, announcing to everyone in earshot that he'd arrived. Behind him came the Rolls, stately and calm, purring along with Cash at the wheel. He pulled right into the best spot, beside the elevators, and Cash slipped into the second-best spot beside him. From there, they waltzed right into the elevator, ignoring the valets who came scrambling over, only to find both vehicles locked. As it happens, both spots were clearly marked *No Parking* and named *J. Hackney, Sr.* and *J. Hackney, Jr.*

Now the desk clerk squirmed, caught in the cross-fire stares of Joe, Liam, and Cash. "I'm terribly sorry, Mr. Bloom, but the penthouse isn't available. I mean it never is. That's where the Hackneys live."

"Who?" Joe checked his watch, as if late for another, more important meeting. The clerk caught its glow. She lowered her voice deferentially.

"Um . . . Mr. and Mrs. Hackney and their son?" She tapped the coat of arms on her jacket. "The owners?"

"Oh right. Well, then the best suite you have. And the biggest."

"Yes, sir, well, I'll have to see what's available." She tapped the keys. As it happened, Juno had hacked into the booking site and, pretending to be the assistant to the son of an important oil-rich sheik, had canceled a reservation. The nervous clerk continued: "I'm afraid our premier suites are usually . . . oh." She smiled in relief. "It looks like the Imperial Suite is available. That comes with—"

"Imperial sounds about right. We'll take it. Open-ended stay." He started to turn away, as if bored with this interaction and ready to move on.

"But, sir, your card . . ." the clerk pleaded.

"My associate here will handle the details."

Liam opened the briefcase, giving everyone a brief glimpse of the cash stacked within it (actually, a top layer of genuine bills covered sheets of blank green paper), and slipped out a stack of hundreds. "Now then," Liam said, eyes twinkling, rolling his brogue, "shall we say a week in advance?"

<hr />

While Joe's entourage moved toward the elevators, with a concierge leading the way, one bellhop pressing the button while two more rolled the luggage, all smelling juicy tips, and the desk clerk waved and smiled, a limo was pulling up to the front doors. A sheik swept in, robe fluttering, flanked by assistants and bodyguards, and another couple of bellhops wheeling luggage, and descended on the front desk, ready to claim his suite. The clerk turned to greet him, her warm smile slowly freezing. But before he could even state his name, the private elevator opened, revealing Hackney and son, both dressed in golf clothes, pink slacks, and blue sweater for Junior, and gold pants, a checkered polo, and windbreaker for Senior. Both wore Kangol caps.

"Going up?" Joe asked.

Hackney frowned. "This is a private elevator." He pushed by Joe and charged into the lobby, cutting off the sheik to demand of the terrified clerk: "Who parked in my goddamn spot?"

<hr>

The Imperial Suite lived up to its name. There was a large living room, as well as a full dining area, sumptuously furnished, carpeted, decorated, and lit, like the set of a play about glamorous millionaires, all perched over a glass wall that vertigoed out over Broadway. An office, three bedrooms, three bathrooms, and a kitchenette opened off the main space.

"Not bad," Joe said upon entering. He told the concierge, "Book us a table for dinner."

"Yes, sir!"

Liam tipped everyone lavishly and Cash shooed them out the door. It shut. Joe immediately began to remove his tie, then thought better of untying it, since he didn't have Yelena here to help, and pulled it over his head.

Cash and Liam explored the other rooms. "I call this room," Cash shouted from the master.

Joe followed, hauling his giant LV case. The bedroom was huge, featuring an acre of bed with a carved wood headboard reminiscent of a cathedral altarpiece, heavy bureaus, and end tables and vanities, another sweeping view.

"Sorry, but we'd better stay in character," Joe explained to Cash and Liam, who were both sprawled on the covers. "The maids gossip and so forth. Though I guess if you two slept at one end of the bed, I'd probably never notice." Joe kicked off the unfamiliar shoes and stretched out his arches, flexing his toes in the soft carpet.

"Not I," Liam said, staring up at the ceiling. "I need privacy. Might have a sexy security guard stopping by."

"I'll pass," Cash said. "I know what a racket you make when you're sleeping." He turned to Liam on the next pillow. "All that cursing and thrashing around. I don't know how Yelena stands it."

Liam shot him a look, and Cash fell silent, worried he'd gone too far.

Joe looked at his watch. "Speaking of Yelena," he said. "Shouldn't you be heading to Brooklyn?"

"Right." Cash jumped to his feet, heading toward the door.

Liam stood, too. "I'm going to call Josh. See if he can give us an update."

"Good idea," Joe said. Emptying his suit pockets, he found his phone and saw the message from Donna. It was true what Cash said: he had a history of nightmares and panic attacks, flashbacks triggered by old wounds and bad memories he managed to hide from himself when awake. For a while booze and drugs helped. Then they became the problem. And now? It seemed to be getting better lately. Since Donna. Anyway, he didn't remember them as often when he woke up, and Donna didn't complain. On the other hand, he realized, they hadn't ever really slept a whole night together. He wished he could invite her over, to share this big bed and the sunken tub, order room service and try on the white robes—inscribed, of course, with the Hackney coat of arms. He sighed and began to laboriously peck out an answer.

Sorry. I'd love to. But I'm on a case. You know what that's like.

35

Yelena made her entrance at eight.

Cash pulled up in the limo and leapt out to open the rear door and help her emerge, like a butterfly from a gray steel chrysalis, then proceeded to the garage with her luggage. The doormen, two of them, backed in, pulling the doors wide, with a mixture of delight and fear. There was no possibility of a tip, as her tiny metallic purse could never hold a wallet. She wore a vintage ermine cape, which flapped like a vampire's cloak behind her as her red-tipped heels clicked across the marble floor to the restaurant. The maître d' rushed over to unwrap her, revealing a black sheath, tight enough to be certain there was nothing under it and slit high enough to show her stocking tops. Once again, theatrical makeup covered her tattoos. Her nails and lips looked bloody. Her shining gold hair hung straight down her bare back. And around her neck, her only other adornment: the Miami necklace, a couple million in diamonds, rubies, and sapphires, glittering like a cold fire.

Her eyes darted toward Joe, sitting at a central table with Liam. The maître d' scraped and bowed as they stood and she strode over. All eyes followed. Most particularly, two belonging to Jim Hackney, who sat in his reserved booth with his son and his wife, whose eyes followed his but with much less pleasure.

Anne Hackney was a birdlike woman in a wheelchair. Still striking, with light hair and eyes, she seemed brittle, both fragile and tense. She was in an expensive gray suit and covered in jewelry—fingers, wrists, neck, ears. But nothing quite matched the power of Yelena's necklace. She flinched and turned back to her food, her son squirmed and blushed, and her husband licked his chops, openly gawking as Joe kissed Yelena, then called for the wine list.

Joe sniffed the wine. It was the most expensive bottle in the cellar, a prize Burgundy, and the sommelier, after opening it with a flourish, had poured him a small taste, watching with pride while a waiter and busboy looked on. But his smile faded as Joe frowned, wrinkling his nose. Joe took a small sip, swished it thoughtfully, then abruptly spit it back into the glass. The sommelier stared in horror as Joe stifled a gag with a napkin.

"Corked," he rasped, coughing as if he'd just slugged vinegar.

"I assure you, sir, it's one of Mr. Hackney's own personal bottles."

"Water, I need water," Joe croaked to the waiter, who rushed over. Joe passed the wineglass to Liam, who took a sniff and then pulled away.

"It's foul, man." He handed it back to the sommelier. "Like the bog at a Guinness festival on a summer's day."

Yelena shuddered. "I can't bear rude odors," she declared, and took a small, ornate bottle from her purse and sprayed perfume in the air.

As if at the dentist, Joe rinsed his mouth thoroughly, spit into the water glass, and gave it back to the waiter. "Thank you," he said, clearing his throat.

Once again, from their corner banquette, the Hackney family looked on, annoyed by the disturbance. The dining room was generally hushed, full of wealthy people, men in sober suits, women in shimmering gowns, their arms and throats and earlobes lit with gems. The waiters moved swiftly and silently, whispered and cooed. It was all a backdrop to the Hackneys, who presided as if from a stage. But tonight, everyone was watching Joe's table.

"You don't mind if I sample it, sir?" The sommelier snapped his fingers and a minion ran up with a clean glass.

In fact, Joe had made a big show of examining the bottle, searching for his reading glasses, which Liam found, and demanding the waiter bring a candle closer to read the label. All of this distracted everyone's attention while he popped a small plastic bubble concealed in his palm and smeared the cork with a gel containing an intense concentration of trichloranisole, the generally airborne fungi that causes wine to become spoiled. Then, when the sommelier opened it tableside, his corkscrew had pushed the substance into the wine.

The truth was that Joe, whose own taste had run more to cheap vodka, couldn't even tell the difference, but every minute the bottle sat there, the chemical reaction that would transform it from exquisite to worthless was rapidly occurring. The sommelier poured himself a drop, took a concerned sniff, then a pinched sip, and then frowned.

"I'm terribly sorry, sir, but you're absolutely right. I will remove it immediately."

He would try it himself in the kitchen, decide it was fine, and split it with a friend.

Meanwhile, Hackney was fuming, waving his arms, while his wife and son tried to calm him. Finally, Junior rose and reluctantly approached.

"Excuse me," he said, smiling stiffly. "Sorry to interrupt, but I'd like to offer you another bottle, anything you choose, on the house, with our compliments."

Yelena looked at him like he was panhandling for change.

"Just bring us some mineral water, please," Joe said. "And waiter, I need a new napkin as well." He handed over the crumpled, damp linen.

Junior twitched a little around the eyes but kept his voice steady through gritted teeth as he reluctantly accepted the napkin. "Sir, I think you're confused. I'm not a waiter. I'm vice president in charge of operations. My family owns this hotel." He marched off in a huff, handing the napkin to a waiter and muttering, "Mineral water over there."

Joe leaned over the table to Yelena and Liam. "God only knows what peasant pissed in that bottle back in France, but I'll bet he died of a kidney infection." They laughed. Hackney stared, and stewed.

The rest of the meal did not go much better. Joe sent his steak back as overdone, Yelena sent her fish back as underdone and her water as too cold. At last they asked for the bill. Meanwhile, having made finishing their entrees a point of honor, Hackney and his wife declined dessert. While a waiter pushed her chair, Hackney muttered to the maître d', who nodded effusively and scrambled over to Joe, offering the bill in its ceremonial leather folder.

"Just make sure that wine's not on there," Joe said, barely glancing at it. "And charge it to the room." He slid a folded hundred into his hand. "This is for you."

"Thank you, sir," he oozed, "but about the suite. I'm afraid there's a small problem."

"I know it," Joe said, helping Yelena on with her fur. "The towels are too thin and the sheets are too rough, but what are you going to do?"

He took Yelena's arm and they cruised out, Liam tossing a healthy tip onto the table. The maître d' scrambled after them.

"No, sir, sorry, that's not—"

Hackney, who'd been watching gravely, left his wife by the private elevator and crossed the lobby, Junior a step behind.

"Excuse me," he spoke up gruffly. "Maybe I can help clear up this confusion."

Joe turned to him, smiling patiently. "Why? Are you in charge of laundry?"

Hackney bristled. "I own the place."

"Ah, right, you're Hackley." Joe nodded at him. "Listen, if you need a new wine guy . . ."

"It's Hackney," he corrected, waving his arm over his domain. "My name's on the wall. And on your damned towels."

Joe noted the logo on the wall. "Right. My mistake. My assistant handles these things. To be honest, the Carlyle and the Pierre were both full. And let's face it, the Plaza's not really the Plaza anymore, am I right?" He shrugged. "But don't worry. It's fine. A very nice hotel. We can always send out for towels."

Hackney closed in, confronting Joe with his bulk, while Junior hovered. "Actually, that's the problem," he said. "You see, that suite was already booked, to a family friend. So the dinner's on me, but . . ."

"Wait a second." Joe perked up, affronted. "What are you trying to pull here? Think you can rent it for more?" He pointed at Hackney. "I paid a week in advance. Cash. I'm not going anywhere."

Hackney seemed to swell, his face growing red. Joe's eyes remained locked on his. Junior stepped in.

"Let's keep this calm," he said, speaking low. "Or do I have to call security to escort you out?"

Joe grinned. "You're welcome to try."

Hackney grinned back. "They're ex-military. Trained in Israel."

Joe nodded at Liam. "He's an ex-bartender. Trained in Ireland."

Junior put a restraining hand on his dad's arm. Hackney shrugged it off. "He's right," he told Joe, with a hollow chuckle. "No reason to get angry here. Maybe there's another way for us to settle this like gentlemen."

Joe laughed. "You challenging me to a duel?"

Yelena laughed at this, delighted. Hackney forced a smile. "I was thinking of something more like cards. Or billiards."

"You've got a pool table here?" Joe said, glancing at Liam, who stepped away discreetly. "Why not? I don't mind shooting some pool, if the stakes are worth my while."

"Fine," Hackney said. "One game of pool. Upstairs in the library in one hour. You win and you stay the week for free, with a full refund. I win and you leave tomorrow, without a dime. Deal?" He held out a hand.

Joe stared at it, then shrugged and shook. "Why not?"

36

It was Josh's first night on duty. In his uniform—navy pants with gold piping, the jacket with the crest, crimson tie—he'd been given a tour of the whole building, bottom to almost top (the penthouse was off-limits, along with its private elevator), and then sent to observe various new colleagues as they patrolled the lobby, checked the exits, and responded to mostly very minor complaints. The biggest event so far was chasing away some paparazzi who had gathered by the rear door, hoping for a glimpse of a K-pop star supposedly staying in the hotel under a fake name. Josh had kicked one in the butt hard enough to bruise, which earned him backslaps from his comrades and a big grin from the new head of security, a beef-faced bully named Riley.

Now he was on a break, but he had headed up to the library instead, as soon as he got Liam's call. The room, all dark wood, wingback chairs, and buttoned leather couches by a fire, was dominated by the stuffed and mounted heads of animals Junior had slain, which gazed down, plotting revenge. Tonight was quiet, just a couple of older businessmen drinking cognac in a corner. Josh went to the pool table in the rear of the room. It was a beauty, with gleaming wood and hand-carved legs. He dropped to his knees and began examining the underside, using the flashlight on his phone. He found what he was looking for, traced a cord to where it led under the carpet and carefully scraped away with his pocketknife.

"Hey, Josh, there you are!"

He clicked the knife shut and slipped it into his pocket, then stood, brushing off his pants. It was Riley. "What the hell you doing here? Break's over."

"Sorry," Josh said. "A guest stopped me in the hall and told me she lost an earring when she was playing. So I came to look." He shrugged. "I can't find it."

"Did you tell her to check lost and found?"

"Yeah."

"OK, well, there's some homeless begging out front and they're scaring the guests. Get down there."

"Right," Josh said, and hurried to the elevator. As soon as he was alone, he texted Liam.

Found it. All set.

⚊

Joe was late. He wandered in with his entourage in tow, Liam smiling the patient, stiff smile of the long-suffering retainer, Yelena climbing atop a high stool, letting her coat slide off her bare shoulders while she yawned, the distracted distraction.

"You're late." Hackney stood beside his son, jacket off, sleeves rolled up, cue in hand.

"Gave you a chance to practice," Joe said as he selected a cue and started chalking it.

Junior smiled a vicious smile. Hackney reddened.

"The game is nine ball," he said. "The terms are set. The guest breaks."

"Thanks, Hackley, that's very gentlemanly of you."

"Hackney."

Joe shrugged as he leaned over the table, set his cue, and broke. The balls scattered. The ten ball rolled into a corner pocket.

"Stripes," Joe said, rechalking his cue. Then he cleared the table. It had been a while, but he'd spent many hours of his youth, especially school hours, in pool halls, and the basic skills were in place. He'd never been a real hustler, but he'd lost to a few, and the lessons had stuck. Now he moved systematically, taking his time, knowing that the slower he moved, the more it would aggravate his opponent. Finally, he called the eight ball and sunk it in the corner pocket.

"That was fun," Joe said. "I will send Liam around for my refund." He started slipping his jacket back on as he added: "You're no good at choosing wine or shooting pool, but I have to admit you are a gracious loser."

Hackney flinched visibly at the *L* word. "Double or nothing," he barked.

Joe paused, jacket half on, half off. "I think that suite's two grand a night. So that's twenty-eight you will owe me."

"If you win," Hackney said. "My break. Rack them," he told his son.

"Do you mind, babe?" Joe asked Yelena. "I know how boring this must be." He turned to Hackney. "I promised Olga I'd beat you quickly. She tires easily."

She shrugged. Her necklace flickered. "Boys need to play their little games."

"All set, Dad." Junior stepped back from the table and took up a casual stance by the bar. Hackney broke, and the one ball rolled in. "Solids," he said, glancing over at his son, and while he lined up his next shot, Junior surreptitiously slid a hand under the bar and flipped a switch.

Many commercial pool tables, for instance those in bars or arcades, contain magnets. They cause the cue ball, which is specially made with an iron core, to travel down a different track than the colored balls when sunk. That's why, during a round at a pay table, the cue ball returns to play while the other balls vanish into the pockets to await the next game. Trick players take advantage of this feature to perform fancy shots, using magnets to guide the cue in loops and whirls.

The Hackneys took it a step further. They ordered a whole set of trick balls. Once Junior hit that switch, turning on the electromagnet hidden in the table, any shot that came even close to a pocket would be pulled right in. Smiling now, he made eye contact with his dad, who made a big show of draping his form over the table and gracefully stroking the cue. He missed. His ball hit the bumper and rolled away, knocking against several others.

"What?" he snapped, and looked at his son, who shrugged. Then he recovered himself.

"Aw, nice try," Joe said. "Let's see. I'm stripes?"

Frowning, Junior made sure he flipped the switch off. Joe sank two and then missed. Hackney gave his son a knowing look, and he flipped the device back on. His dad sank one, an easy shot straight into a side pocket. Then, feeling more confident, he tried a tricky bank shot. Miss.

"Damn it!" he yelled, and smacked his cue against the table.

"Take it easy," Joe said with a laugh. "It's just a game. And never bet more than you can afford to lose." Then he cleared the table, pausing before the last shot. "You know, Huxley, you're a great host. I've had so much fun, I'm going to give you another chance to win your money back tomorrow. Be my guest at a private high-stakes poker game. Normally the casino is members only, but I think I can get you in."

"Fine," Hackney muttered, glaring at his son.

"Eight ball, corner pocket," Joe said, and sunk the ball.

<hr />

They made sure they were back in the suite, with the door shut, before they burst into laughter.

"You don't know how hard it was, keeping a straight face," Liam said, "when Junior kept hitting that switch and nothing happened."

"Not as hard as it was for Hackney," Joe said. "I thought he'd have a stroke right there and save us the trouble."

"And the look on his face," Cash said, flopping onto the couch. "I've never seen a white face turn quite that shade of purple."

Yelena kicked off her heels and slid into a chair to rub her feet. "All I know is I am not wearing those shoes tomorrow."

Joe pulled his tie off and tossed it on the coffee table, then sat and removed his shoes, too. "Tell Josh I said thanks for a nice job."

Liam checked his watch. "You'll get your chance. He just came off duty, I think. Should be here soon."

As it happens, Josh had been about to clock out, changing from his uniform into his street clothes, when Riley stopped by the locker room.

"Good, you're still here. Boss wants to see us."

"Is there a problem?"

"Hell yes. But not with you."

"Should I change back?" he asked, pointing at his uniform hung in the locker.

"Nah, this is after hours, off the books, like."

Josh shrugged and shut the locker.

Riley clapped his shoulder. "Come on, let's go, they're going to be in the gym. I don't want to miss the fun."

"What the fuck happened?"

Hackney led his son onto the private elevator, punched the Basement button, then got impatient and hit the Close Door button.

"I don't know. The wire was frayed."

"Frayed? What does that mean? Could they have cheated somehow?"

Junior shook his head. "I think maybe the cleaning crew ran it over with a vacuum, or maybe it got disconnected when the guy was installing the new fridge behind the bar."

"I don't want to hear excuses. Remember what your grandfather said. Only losers need excuses."

"Right," Junior said, straightening up as though he'd been goosed. "Sorry, sir."

Hackney shook it off, glanced at his watch. "Anyway, we'll deal with that another time. They ready for us downstairs?"

"Yes, sir."

"Good, good."

The doors slid back and they moved through the basement into the now-silent gym, where the empty machines sat waiting, and on into a room used for classes or private training. The room was a mirrored box with a polished wood floor, with mats, balls, and other gear stacked in a corner. Dawkins, the hotel manager, waited nervously, his tie knotted tightly, while Riley and the new Israeli kid, Josh, stood off to the side.

"Good evening, Dawkins, thanks for staying late."

"Yes, sir. It was my kid's birthday, but Riley said—"

"Well, I won't keep you, then. You're fired. Enjoy the party."

"Sir? I don't understand . . ."

"Don't you? Well, it's been a full day. First, we had to fire the head of security when our young Israeli friend here made a puddle out of him in two seconds. So I hired Josh and promoted Riley. Congrats, by the way."

"Thank you, sir," Riley said, punching Josh playfully in the arm.

"Then under your watch, my dear friend and, did I mention, key investor Sheik Ibrahim's son got his reservation canceled. And then you let someone park in my spot."

"Both of our spots," Junior added.

"So that's three strikes. You're out."

The man looked stricken. "But . . . that's only two."

"Two parking spots," Junior reminded him, holding up two fingers.

Hackney frowned at his son. "Actually, I was counting the security fuckup as yours, since technically you were manager when that staff

171

was hired. Whatever, three strikes and a foul. But don't worry, I'm still giving you a choice."

While he said this, Junior took his jacket and tie off, rolled up his sleeves.

Dawkins stared. "Choice?"

"You can just walk out, with nothing," Hackney explained. "Or you can have a month's severance." He pulled an envelope from his inside pocket. "But you've got to get by Junior."

"Sir?" Dawkins looked from the father to son. "How do you mean?"

"Come at me," Junior said, hands up, legs set.

"Junior does MMA," Riley bragged to Josh from the corner of his mouth. "Made it to the state championships last year. We spar sometimes."

Josh nodded, trying to look impressed. Dawkins just looked amazed. Grinning, Hackney stood behind his son, waving the check.

"Come on, Dawkins, it's easy. Just get past Junior and it's all yours."

Finally, in a burst of desperate energy, Dawkins ran, trying, like a running back on a football field, to duck and weave past Junior. Junior jumped in his path, swinging, and clipped him across the jaw, knocking him back, then put him down with a roundhouse kick.

Hackney chuckled. "Nice try, Dawkins. Get up."

Junior grinned, bouncing on the balls of his feet, while Dawkins climbed to his feet, rubbing his jaw.

"Come on, Dawkins," Hackney taunted. "You can do better than that."

Junior and Riley both laughed. Josh watched as Dawkins made a fist.

"Fuck you!" Dawkins yelled, finally erupting, no doubt after years of repressed rage, and charged forward, swinging hard and catching Junior off guard with a shot in the mouth.

"Nice shot!" Hackney yelled, as Junior licked his split lip. "You gonna take that, Junior?"

Junior spit blood, smiling through red-stained teeth. Then he took Dawkins apart. It was ugly to watch. Junior was, Josh had to admit, expert: fast and graceful, with a clear understanding of how to inflict pain and damage, but Dawkins was hardly a worthy opponent. At last Dawkins lay in a heap, moaning, eyes blackened, nose bloody, limbs oddly bent. Hackney clapped his son on the back, well pleased.

"Nice work," he said, then turned to Dawkins's inert form. "And here you go." He tucked the envelope into his limp hand. "You earned it." Then he waved to Josh. "A word."

Josh trotted over, resisting the urge to help Dawkins. "Yes, sir?"

"Your first day on the job, it went all right?"

"Definitely, sir."

"And what you saw here tonight, you got any problems with that?"

Josh shrugged. "What did I see, sir?"

Hackney grinned and shook Josh's hand. "Good. I knew you were a good kid. Report at nine tomorrow. I've got something special for you. Now help Riley take this trash out."

<hr />

Hackney felt better. Losing at pool had flooded him with shame. He wanted to wipe the snide grin off Joe's face, to make him pay. And the woman, Olga. The memory of that beautiful, mysterious woman, icy and imperious, sneering at his food, his wine, even the hotel with his name on it, then laughing at his defeat. He burned at the thought of it and, finding that intolerable, flipped instantly into rage, directed at anyone else who might be at fault. Like his son.

But now his anger had been exorcised and his ego reasserted. He was proud of the kid. Not that poor Dawkins, a born loser, was any kind of real match. But that was the point: Junior had the killer instinct, the will to win at any cost, and by any means. His own father, Dick Hackney, had done the same thing, taking him out in his Cadillac, one of the old-fashioned Fleetwoods, to watch from a discreet distance, as his own security forces beat up unionizers or evicted deadbeat tenants, piling their stuff on the street. He was schooling him in the one great truth of real life: winning was all that mattered. The loser was forgotten, along with their complaints about fairness. That was why, to Hackney, a trick pool table was perfectly reasonable; it was actually part of the game, just another way to outfox your opponent. The strong won, that was business. And life.

At home, his father had applied the same principles more directly. Hackney remembered how his father had cured him of wetting the bed: he was whipped with a belt in front of the family and staff, then sent to sleep in the garage in his wet pajamas. He cried all night but he didn't resent his father now. He understood. He'd been preparing young Jim for the real world, which ate the weak alive. (Though actually it had not stopped the bed-wetting. Instead he had learned to rise early, change his pajamas, and wake the maid.)

With his own son things were different. Times had changed, and Anne absolutely forbade even spanking, much less whipping. And when Junior showed little aptitude for sports and was even bullied himself at school, Hackney blamed her. When, like his own dad, he started taking him to brothels in his early teens, Junior was shy and disinterested, and Hackney even started to worry he had some kind of a queer on his hands. But Junior found his own way, first with the martial arts, and then with the hunting, and now Hackney knew he'd be just fine. In the ring, on the African plains, or in the jungle of New York real estate, the same rule applied: winners killed.

Josh knocked softly on the door. Liam let him in, and they joined the others in the living room. He'd performed first aid on Dawkins, sent him home in a cab, then waited for Riley to leave. Now he briefed the others on what happened and what he'd learned about the security setup and the layout of the hotel. Plus his assignment for tomorrow: There was a demonstration planned at the site of the new Westlands development. They were adding extra security and Josh had been recruited.

"I know somebody who is going to that," Joe said.

Josh stretched out on the couch, his limbs entangled with Liam's. "Tell them to be careful. Looks like they expect trouble. And I've seen their idea of security."

Joe looked at his prize watch. "Looks like another long day, then. We all better get some rest."

Everyone slowly stood, and Cash exchanged a curious glance with Liam, who shrugged.

"OK, good night then, everybody," Cash called, and retreated to his room.

"We're turning in, too," Liam answered, tugging Josh.

"Yeah, I have to slip out early," Josh joined in. "Sleep well." They shut their bedroom door, leaving Joe and Yelena alone. She stretched, yawning luxuriously. She then headed into the big bedroom, a shoe swinging dangerously in each hand. Joe followed, awkward.

"So listen," he said, as she hung up her fur.

"Unzip," Yelena instructed, turning her back on him.

"Right." He unzipped her, then stepped clear as she let her dress fall. "Listen, this whole job happened so fast, we haven't really had a chance to talk about, you know, us."

She turned to him, dressed only in her stockings and G-string, and gave him a dubious glance. "Talk? About us? Since when?"

Joe nodded in acknowledgment. "Fair enough. But I still think it's best if maybe, just to keep it professional, we don't share a bed."

Yelena shrugged. "Fine. But if I am playing a mistress, then I am sleeping in the master bedroom." She grabbed a robe and slipped it on, then bent and slid off her underthings, leaving the stockings like discarded snakeskins as she crossed the room. "After I take my bath."

"Right." Joe smiled, grabbing a pillow and the extra blanket. "I'll be outside if you need me."

"Don't worry," Yelena assured him. "I won't." She shut the bathroom door.

—◦—

In the penthouse, seeing that her light was still on, Junior stopped in to say good night to his mother. He knocked softly, and she called, "Come in." She was in bed, reading her Bible. Her room was palatial—a huge bed, wheelchair set to the side, thick carpets, fine antiques, religious paintings in heavy gilt frames and colorful landscapes—and commanded a stunning view of the night skyline, but the heavy curtains were drawn. Seeing that it was him, she set the book down and smiled, waving him over. His mother had been a beautiful woman, and in this golden lamplight, in her ruffled pink nightgown with her blond hair brushed out, she still was. Junior sat on the edge of the bed.

"What happened?" she asked, pointing to the cuts on his hands.

"What? Oh, that's nothing."

"You didn't get into a fight with that man in the restaurant, did you? The rude one?"

Junior shook his head. "No. Nothing like that. Just a session in the gym."

"Good. You're my good boy." She patted the hand. "You know, I'm very grateful to you for defending my honor, but it's much more important to me that you learn self-control. That's what your father never had." She shook her head, bitterly. "Every impulse, no matter how selfish or stupid, every appetite, rage, pride, greed. All seven sins."

"I know, Mother. I'm not like that."

"Lust," she added, spitting that one out. "That worst of all. His sins are on all of us. That's why you have to make sure that you don't turn out like him."

"Don't worry," he said, "I'm not."

"I love him, I do, he's my husband. And I pray for him every day. But he is a sinner, and I know, in the end, where he will go. But not you."

"No," he said, firmer. "I'm not. I told you. He's my father and I respect him. And I need to learn the business, so I can take care of you, of us, when he's gone. But I will never be like him."

She smiled. "Yes. You're right. You're my sweet boy."

He smiled and put her Bible on the side table. "Now it's late. Time to sleep."

"Yes," she said. "Will you pray with me first?"

"Of course." He knelt beside her bed.

She clutched his hands in hers and began to pray, asking God to forgive their sins and those of their family, asking Him to protect them from evil, within and without. It took almost an hour before she finally fell asleep. When Junior stood to shut the light, his knees ached.

⚬━━⚬

Later, when he was lying on the couch, *Ulysses* open unread in his lap, Joe wondered whether he should call Donna. It was late. Still, he could possibly slip out, catch a cab uptown, and sneak into her place. Finally, after tossing and turning awhile, he sent a text:

You up? I miss you.

But she was asleep. Or in any case, she didn't respond.

37

The demonstration started at eleven. It was cold, and the constant wind off the river made it feel even colder, but it was bright and clear, one of those surprisingly sunny New York winter days—a fine day to get out and yell, at least until your ears and fingers went numb.

The space they were fighting over was also typical of New York—a weird patch of urban landscape combining the ruins of a past civilization, the pressure of future development, and the stubborn persistence, or resistance, of nature. It was a narrow strip of riverfront, comprising a concrete dock and walkway, a derelict, half-collapsed pier, and some ruined buildings, along with scraps of greenspace: the whole thing had been more or less abandoned in the '70s, when the city hit bottom and went broke. Nature reclaimed it, and as the man-made structures failed, a wilderness erupted, trees and bushes filling in the blanks, sending their roots through the concrete, while new weeds and flowers and mutant city plants appeared, even on the tops of buildings. Through the '80s, it became outlaw territory, notorious for drug sales as well as cruising and all manner of sex trade. You could basically get anything you were seeking in that jungle, if you were brave enough. Graffiti writers covered walls in bright paint, and then more organized groups of artists joined in, decorating the old buildings and tunnels, holding parties. On a wall by the entrance, someone spray-painted *Welcome to the Wild West*, and the spot became known as the Westlands.

Time moved on, the city calmed down, grew richer, safer, and less exciting, and the area became less a pirate's cove and more of a safe harbor for other, nonhuman wild things: especially birds, who populated the overgrown trees and bushes and didn't mind the old structures, either, but also all manner of critters, from feral cats to raccoons and possums. And along the river, in the rushes and among the old pylons, waterfowl, fish, and mollusks multiplied. These days, the only ones having orgies there were mice, but urban hikers, bird watchers, sport fishers, and plant collectors had made the place their own, until now. For now it was due for reclamation by society once again, rebranded as the Westlands Development. The city council was about to vote on a plan to let Hackney's company and its investors build apartments, shops, and a hotel, granting them a ninety-nine-year lease for a billion dollars in rent. Neighborhood groups and environmentalists wanted it to become the Westlands Nature Preserve. And while the battle raged and dragged on, for months now, the whole thing had been fenced off.

That was why Josh was here. For the most part this was a low-key, even boring post compared to working the hotel, but Hackney expected an aggressive protest today and he wanted a show of force, so he'd put his new security chief, Riley, in charge, and told him to include his newest recruit, the Israeli ex-commando, on the team. So far, standing outside the main gate with the other guards, Josh was bored and cold, a sentiment he seemed to share with the protestors, who stamped and clapped, listening to the speakers, whose amplified voices were distorted as they were torn in the wind. It was a mixed crowd, including lots of locals, retirees, families, and moms with kids wielding homemade signs, as well as dedicated environmentalists in camping and outdoor adventure clothes, with professionally printed signs, petitions, and hats emblazoned with group logos; and an angrier segment, young and clad in black or in surplus gear, chanting, focused, and ready for trouble. At the far edge were a ring of media wielding cameras, and then some bored cops, mostly leaning against their cars, waiting for something that concerned them to happen.

Meanwhile, Councilwoman Amy Schlitz tried to placate the crowd. She was bundled in a white wool overcoat over her red pantsuit, her hair strangely motionless in the wind. Her makeup, which would look natural on camera, now looked like she was on her way to perform at a carnival. She was assuring them that no one loved nature more than Jim Hackney.

"You spoke and we heard you! That's why the Hackney Corporation has generously agreed to reserve a large portion of this property for parkland, free and open to the public."

The crowd was not impressed. They booed and yelled: "Only seven percent!" "You traitor!" "Bird killer!"

But apparently the councilwoman couldn't hear well, either, because she smiled and waved as if they were cheering, then hurried back to her heated car.

Next up was Dr. Kiran Acharya, who was greeted far more warmly by the even colder crowd. She wore a parka, gloves, jeans, and Wellington boots, and her hood kept blowing off, at which point her long black hair would begin to whip around wildly. Not only did she demand that the city council reject the deal (which was not going to happen, it would be a mere rubber-stamping), she insisted they abandon the project altogether and create a public park and wildlife refuge. Lastly, she deplored the fact that the grounds had already been sealed off. "I demand that these gates be opened! This is public land and it belongs to all living creatures!"

With that, she turned to face the fence, and the crowd started moving in behind her. Their plan was to crash the gate, or else get arrested for trying, an act of civil disobedience that was sure to make the news and draw more attention and sympathy to their cause.

"Parks belong to the people! Parks belong to the people!" The crowd began to press against the gate, rocking it back and forth, hoping to collapse a section of the wire fencing. The security guards pushed back. And the cameras zoomed in on it all. Several of the hardcore kids began to climb the fence, and guards scrambled to intercept them.

"Head them off! Don't let them get into the tunnels!" Riley yelled, rallying his troops and grabbing the first invader over the fence, a teenage girl in a hoody, whom he dragged off by the hair, hoping to kick her around a little off-camera. By this point, things had escalated enough to interest the police, and uniformed officers waded in, shoving protestors aside, bludgeoning those who didn't move, and making for the presumed leader, that little Indian woman who'd been doing all the yelling.

The first cop to reach Kiran grabbed her by the hood and pulled her back from the fence, totally ignoring the man beside her, an old guy in paint-spattered pants and an ancient parka, walking with a cane.

"All right, lady, that's enough," the cop said, pushing her to the ground and reaching for his cuffs.

"Keep your dirty hands off her," Frank said as he tripped the cop with his cane. As the cop fell, Frank thwacked him hard across the back of the neck. Seeing this, more cops began pushing through the crowd to help their fallen comrade, while the protest descended into chaos.

That was when Josh got to work. He'd been keeping an eye on Kiran all along, slowly edging closer as the protest picked up speed, and now he moved in, taking her arm and helping her to her feet.

"Dr. Acharya?" he began, but before he could say any more, Frank came at him, cane swinging.

"Joe sent me," he yelled as he warded off the blow, deflecting the cane with a forearm. Frank and Kiran both started, taking in this stranger who was dressed like an enemy but invoking the name of a friend.

"This way, quick," he whispered, grabbing them both by the arms, and began to guide them through the crowd, while yelling, loudly:

"Get the hell off! This is private property!" Another civilian, in a dark parka and hat with a scarf over his face pressed in to shield them from view. This was Liam.

"Come on, folks," he said, "let's get you out of here. The filth won't much like you knocking their mate about."

Together, Liam and Josh hustled them along the fence line until they were clear of the crowd. Stepping into the street, Kiran and Frank stared as a Rolls-Royce pulled up.

"Get in," Josh said, opening the rear door as Liam got in the front. Stunned, they obeyed, and the car was rolling smoothly away by the time the door was shut.

"Hi," Joe said. He was sitting on the jump seat. "You two look like you're freezing." He leaned over the front seat. "Cash, can you crank the heat up in this thing?"

Around the next corner, Cash pulled over and Josh and Liam jumped out—Josh to fade into the crowd, Liam to handle other matters—and then proceeded uptown to Harlem. Along the way, Kiran and Frank filled Joe in on more details about the Westlands.

"I know a billion dollars sounds like a lot of money," Kiran was saying. "But this is one of the last chunks of open land in Manhattan. Think about what that's worth. And it's publicly owned. Factor in the tax breaks and other incentives, and they're practically giving it away. Divided by ninety-nine years, that works out to a little more than ten million a year in rent. Ten million! One single condo in the new development will be worth more than that."

"So, all Hackney has to pay when he closes this deal is ten million?" Joe asked.

"Up front? Yes. And the rumor is that even that is being supplied by his silent partners." She bent her nose in the familiar gesture. "You know who."

Joe did indeed. Frank winked at him.

Kiran went on: "He has to raise two billion in construction funds, but the foreign banks are ready. As soon as he has the land it all starts flowing."

"Lots of construction jobs," Frank put in. "Union jobs."

"Sure. For the next couple of years. But then what? Regular New Yorkers won't be able to afford to live there, big corporations will take up the stores and offices. Hackney and his pals get a priceless piece of public property for ten mil a year. And the only jobs long-term will be janitors and security. Or maids cleaning the bankers' apartments."

"Strip clubs, too." Frank laughed, slapping Joe on the thigh. "They always do well when more money guys come around."

Joe nodded. "And brothels." Cash met his eye in the rearview. Then he turned to Frank. "And art collectors."

"Touché," Frank said. "Speaking of which, I kind of wish we had torn off those gates. There's a big painting I did down in those tunnels that I'd like to see again. Work by friends of mine, too. Some long gone. AIDS, mostly."

"Tunnels?" Joe asked.

"Yeah, there's a bunch of them, building basements and loading, I guess, from the docks. A whole maze. People lived down there—the troglodytes, we called them—or partied, or did drugs. But there were art crews, too, that went down, and everybody took a wall or a room and did something. It was really cool."

"Those tunnels caved in years ago," Kiran explained. "It's not safe, especially for old men with canes and fake knees." She eyed Frank. "If you could even find it after thirtysomething years."

"Oh, I could find it," he said. "I'm an old tunnel rat, remember."

Joe did. In Vietnam, Frank had been sent into the underground networks built by the enemy, with a gun and a flashlight.

"Doesn't matter if it's Cu Chi or the West Side," Frank said now, "last week or last century, a good tunnel rat never forgets. Might have to get back out."

Kiran watched the cityscape roll by, concrete, metal, and steel. "We worry about jobs and housing and park space, sure," she said. "What about the wildlife? We think of these creatures as free, living and hunting in their own world. But really they are desperate, fighting for life in the margins and cracks of our world. We have to save that tiny little breathing space for them, too."

They stopped the Rolls in front of Frank's building, and several neighbors stared as they got out. Joe walked them to the door.

"Thank you again," Kiran said. "You and your friends saved my life."

"Not quite," Joe said, though he was familiar with central booking and he didn't think she'd like it. She kissed his cheek, then went to open the door.

"Come up for a coffee?" Frank asked.

"I can't. Work."

"The club?"

"No . . ." Joe smiled evasively. "I've got a freelance gig at a casino tonight."

"I won't ask for details," Frank said, giving him a hug. "And I probably shouldn't ask how come all of a sudden you got a fresh shave and haircut and are cruising around town in a chauffeur-driven Rolls, either."

"Probably not."

38

The casino was humming. Still known as Max's, and with Mini-King Max still working as the front, in reality it was now run by Gio, who had installed dealers, security, and managers to watch the money come and go, making sure Gio got his share and no one else got more than theirs. And so, when a limo pulled up in front of the storage warehouse, where the Rolls was noticeably parked in front, and disgorged Hackney and Junior, Little Eddie, who was at the door, signaled the arrival of the marks, then used his considerable bulk to block them.

"Can I help you?" he asked, looking down at the two men.

"You can make some room," Hackney said.

"The name's Hackney," Junior explained. "We're expected."

"Sorry, this is a private club, gentlemen. Members only."

"Like your jacket?" Hackney said, flexing his own expensive suit, carefully tailored to hide his gut.

Eddie was wearing a leather jacket buttoned over a black shirt and red tie. "Huh?"

"It's a joke," Hackney explained. "You know, the brand . . ."

"Naw, this is Italian leather," Eddie said.

Hackney drew a folded hundred from his pocket and pushed it into Eddie's palm.

"Hey, thanks!" Eddie said, and pocketed it.

"Now why don't you check your members list?"

Eddie shrugged and reached for a clipboard. He flipped a page. "Nope. Sorry."

"I just gave you a hundred," Hackney complained. He turned to his son. "Is he too dumb to know he's been bribed?"

While Junior tried to calm his dad, Liam came wandering out for a smoke. "Hey, it's the Hackneys."

"Good evening, sir." Eddie turned, giving Liam a light. "You know these two?"

"Yeah, they're with us."

"Oh, well, that's different, then." He looked them over again, then opened the door. "Go right on in."

Liam took a deep drag and flicked away the cigarette. "I better come along. Make sure they don't card you for drinks."

As they entered the casino, Hackney's nerves began to buzz. He felt that tingle in the spine that real gamblers get when they know they are close to the action. All around them luck was changing, wheels spun, cards turned, dice rolled. Winners cashed in piles of chips while losers drank at the bar, fortifying themselves to lose more. Max, who knew nothing but to mind his own business, saw Liam coming and showed them to the special table that Gio had ordered set aside.

"The buy-in is ten thousand." Liam explained as they crossed the room. "It's a gentleman's game, so your credit's good, but we settle up for cash at the end. Understood?"

Hackney pulled a fat wallet from his inside jacket pocket and showed Liam it was stuffed with bills. "I'm ready," he said, and replaced it.

"Good luck, then," Liam told them.

At the table, Joe, in a black suit and tie, was settled in behind a wall of chips. Yelena, in another slinky gown, this one red with a white mink stole, perched on the arm of his chair. There was a house dealer and three more empty seats. Two were for the Hackneys. The remaining player was Gladys, dressed in a white pantsuit and pink shirt that set off her rosy cheeks and halo of white hair as she made her way slowly over.

"There you are," Joe barked at Liam. "Where the hell you been?"

"I went for a smoke, sir," Liam replied calmly. "And to greet your guests."

"Smoke on your own time. I'm sitting here with an empty glass." Joe rattled the melting rocks in his glass, which had actually contained water.

"They have waiters here, sir," Liam countered. "That's not my job."

"Here. A bonus," Joe scoffed. He tossed Liam a hundred-dollar chip. "Now fetch my damn drink."

Liam caught the chip and tucked it quickly into his inside jacket pocket. "Sorry," he muttered to the men. "Would either of you like a drink?"

"Glenfiddich Eighteen," Hackney said.

"Just a Heineken," Junior said, and added, "but you don't have to get it."

"It's fine," Liam told him, "I'm used to it." Then he headed for the bar, and the rest of the team went to work.

The first move was Yelena's. She set her high heel on the edge of Joe's seat and bent to straighten her stocking, immediately drawing the eyes of many in the room, but most importantly, magnetizing the attention of Hackney, who was drooling. That was also the signal for Jem to move.

Jem had spent the last two days with Gladys, who, along with enlisting her assistance with the crossword, hunting under the couch for a lost remote control, and watching *Jeopardy*, had been schooling her in the fine art of picking pockets. She was far from ready to take the starring role, but the sleight-of-hand skills she'd developed as a magic nerd, and her eager willingness to learn, convinced Gladys she would do just fine as a stall and helping with the handoff, two essential roles. Dressed in a tight skirt, hair and makeup perfect, she started walking, contriving to bump into Junior just at the moment when Senior's attention was on Yelena's leg, and to spill her tray of chips.

"Eek!" she squealed. "My chips!"

"Sorry, miss," Junior said, turning to her as she knelt, setting her purse down, and grabbing at her scattered chips, which rattled around the legs of the men. He knelt beside her. "Please let me help."

"Thank you, you're so kind," she chirped, playing up her Oklahoma accent. "I'm just so nervous being in a place like this."

That was the stall: Yelena and Jem had both successfully distracted the marks and stopped them long enough for the cannon to make her move. That was Gladys. When Jem stumbled into Junior, Hackney had to step back, and that was when Gladys made sure to be passing, so that he backed into her.

"Help," she called, faking a fall. "My hip!" Hackney turned, and she grabbed on to his jacket for support. That was when she made the dip. Liam had signaled to her which pocket when Joe tossed him a chip and he put it away in the corresponding place in his jacket. Now she expertly slid her fingers into Hackney's jacket, drew out his billfold, and slid it up her sleeve.

Meanwhile, Jem had gotten back to her feet, thanking Junior profusely, and while he handed her the tray of recovered chips, she let her open purse dangle from the crook of her elbow, behind the backs of the two men. Gladys slid the wallet in.

"Are you all right?" Hackney asked her. "Sorry about my son. He can be a clumsy fool sometimes. Apologize!" he ordered.

"I'm sorry, ma'am," Junior told Gladys, as Jem hurried off, closing her purse.

"That's all right, sonny," Gladys said with a smile. "I'm getting too old for these fancy shoes is all."

At the bar, Jem handed the wallet to Liam. "Thank you kindly," he said. He took the money out and folded it into his pocket, then found a security ID and slid it across to Juno, who was pouring drinks for him. Juno was dressed like a waiter in a white shirt, black bow tie, and vest.

"Jem, this is my good friend Juno," Liam said.

"Nice work, Jem," Juno told her. "That was super slick." He drew a small portable card reader from his pocket and slid in the ID.

"Really?" She beamed. "It was my first time."

"I'd never know it. You're a natural."

"Well, Gladys has been teaching me. I spent the whole day practicing with her and Yelena."

"There you go. Learning from the best."

Liam snapped his fingers. "Card, please, Juno?"

"Couple more seconds." The little light on his gizmo turned green, and Hackney's card popped out. "Here you go." He handed the card to Liam and turned back to Jem. Liam put the card back in the wallet.

"You want a drink or something? I don't really know how to mix anything fancy. I'm not a bartender in real life. I'm a hacker. And I produce. Music, I mean . . ."

"Really? That's so cool. I'm kind of a geek that way myself. I'd love to hear more about—"

"Sorry to interrupt," Liam said, lifting the tray of drinks, "but Cash is waiting, Juno. Jem, I will see you again." He smiled at her and left.

"Right," Juno said. "Got to work. Let's do it later. I mean," he stumbled, "I mean we can talk more later."

Jem giggled. "I understand. Nice to meet you, Juno."

"Yeah," he said, dashing toward the rear of the bar. "You too, Jem."

By now, Hackney had helped Gladys to her seat, and he and his son were sitting. Liam arrived and circled the table, handing out the drinks. He also slid the cash from Hackney's wallet into Joe's side jacket pocket and slipped the wallet to Yelena. She stood.

"Honey, you know how boring I get watching you play," she said, her accent extra thick. "I want to shoot the shit."

"You mean shoot craps. At least I hope." Joe shook his head. "Foreigners," he said to the Hackneys. Then he pulled out Hackney's cash and peeled off a few thousand. "Here you go, babe. This should get you started." He winked at the men. "Always keep them coming back for more."

"Thank you, honey," she said, and kissed him, a long, lingering kiss that ended with a little bite. "Good luck." Then she turned to Hackney. "And fair's fair," she told him. "Good luck to you, too." She bent over, giving him an eyeful, and kissed him on the forehead. He was dazed, too dazed to notice that as her hands brushed over his body, she slid his wallet back into place.

"Have fun, boys," she said, and sauntered off.

"Well then." Gladys spoke, stacking up her chips. "If you kids are done fooling around, let's play some damn cards. Dealer?"

⚬━✦━⚬

The first few hands were normal enough. Modest pots and realistic plays. Gladys won a hand with three of a kind. Joe won with two pair. Hackney won two hands, one with three of a kind and one with a pair of kings. At least he was quieter when he was playing, thinking hard and staring at his cards through the reading glasses he slid on, half-moons that made him look a bit more studious. All the pots were in the $500 to $1,000 range. Then it started to get heated. Hackney got bolder, making big bets and raising, and Junior, while more modest, always

190

called him. Joe and Gladys both folded on one hand and Hackney won with two aces. The next hand he drove up to five grand. Joe and Gladys both called, and he drew an inside straight. He cackled with glee as he raked the chips over.

"You can shoot pool, I admit. But it looks like poker's not your game."

Gladys started to stand, leaning on the cane. "Sorry, boys, but I need a quick break."

"Already? Come on," Hackney wheedled. "The game is just getting interesting."

"I'm an old lady, and I didn't wear a diaper tonight. Need I say more?"

Joe stood. "The ladies' is right over there. I'll help you." He looked at the Hackneys. "For all our sakes."

"Fine." Hackney sighed. He turned to Junior. "How about another round of drinks?"

<hr />

Cash sped. The Ducati had been parked around back, and as soon as Juno was ready, they were off, as fast as possible. Cash glided them through traffic while Juno, in back, watched the police scanner on his phone. They didn't worry about cameras—the plates were fake, so it didn't matter if they were flashed—as long as they didn't waste time getting pulled over. Cash blew stop signs and rolled through reds, making many illegal right turns, and even humped onto a sidewalk once to cut a corner. But as any city dweller knows, making good time isn't just about speed; it doesn't matter how fast you are when there is nowhere to go. It's about grace, rhythm, instinct, knowing when to turn and when to pass, floating in and out, seizing those moments to leap forward when you can, and, most of all, maintaining forward momentum at whatever pace. If "Don't get busted" is goal number one, number two is "Don't get stuck."

As it was, the clock showed just twenty-two minutes had elapsed when Cash pulled to a smooth stop in front of the Hackney Tower Hotel's garage, discharging Juno before circling right back to the casino. Juno hurried in, waving a paper bag and talking on his phone about a delivery, and was ignored by the valets. He rode the elevator up but got out a couple floors below the executive offices, then made a left down the hall.

"Psst." It was Josh, in his security outfit, waiting in the stairway door. "We'll walk the rest," he explained as they trooped up. "No cameras in here. You got the card?"

Juno drew the magnetized card from his pocket. It was blank, just a white plastic card with a black strip, but it was coded with the information stripped from Hackney's card.

"Good work," Josh said. "The offices are closed now, so we should be clear."

Josh peeked out from the stairway. The hall was empty. He led Juno quickly to the executive suite. Juno swiped them in, and they crossed the ornate waiting room to the large wooden door of Hackney's private office. Juno swiped that, too.

"Presto," Juno said, opening the door.

Josh slapped his back. "Genius."

—✦—

"He's daubing," Gladys told Joe as they chatted in the handicapped stall in the women's room. She'd leaned heavily on the cane walking, but now it was propped in a corner, unneeded. "Using juice dust, probably. Doing a nice job, too."

"The glasses?" Joe asked.

"That was the giveaway. And I spotted the kid marking cards. He's feeding one to Daddy now and then, too."

"Can you beat him?"

Gladys raised her eyebrows and sighed. "How long have you known me?" She opened her large purse and handed it to Joe. "Hold this." She dug in and came up with two little squirt bottles, one containing a mild solvent, the other a sticky mixture. She tucked them in her sleeves. "And the finishing touch . . ." Searching again, she pulled out a lipstick, a pack of tissues, a pack of cigarettes, a lighter, a switchblade.

"You got a date after this?" Joe asked.

"Ha-ha, wise guy. You're lucky I come prepared. Where the hell? Oh, here it is." She found some glasses, identical to her own, and switched them.

"Voilà," she said.

"Ready?" Joe asked.

"Almost." She opened the lipstick, puckering up in the mirror. It was a dark red. She wiped a smudge off her teeth with a tissue. "OK, kid," she said with a grin, and took Joe's arm. "Let's go pick those suckers clean."

Joe had assumed that the Hackneys would cheat, but he didn't know how. That was one of the things he needed Gladys for. She'd spotted it immediately. They were good, for amateurs, but only good enough to fool other amateurs. They were daubing: using an invisible sticky substance, they were marking their cards, or some of them, with a simple system. Treating the back of the card like a clock, the ace was twelve, the king three, the queen six, the jack nine, 10 in the center, and lower cards unmarked. Suits might also be marked with tiny daubs on the corners. In some cases, the cheater went by feel, using a substance that was slightly rough or gritty. But Gladys had guessed that Hackney's glasses, like 3-D or black light glasses, let him see the tiny marks. In this way, within a few rounds, enough cards had been marked for

Hackney to make some good guesses about what his opponents held. It only revealed a portion of each hand, of course, but that was plenty to judge who might be bluffing or holding high cards. Even a small advantage like this made a gigantic difference, letting him know when to bet heavy or fold. It was, Joe had to admit, a pretty good system and tough to beat if you didn't want to call him out for cheating.

That was the second reason Gladys was there. Now that her own glasses let her see the marks as well, she could begin messing with them, using the solvent to erase their marks and making her own deliberately inaccurate daubs, marking low cards high and so on. She could also, of course, read the Hackneys' hands, since they were marking their cards.

<hr />

"There you are," Hackney barked as Gladys took her seat. "I thought maybe you fell in."

The dealer, a young black woman working her way through school, frowned distastefully at his comment, and Junior muttered, "Dad, come on."

But Gladys took it in stride. "Almost did. But my big ass saved me," she said. "Now let's play. I smell blood in the water."

Joe took his seat as well, and the dealer shuffled and dealt. The difference was subtle at first: Gladys could see that Hackney had two kings and folded, signaling Joe to do likewise by scratching her ear. Then she saw he was bluffing and ran up the pot, with Joe following along, and won with three of a kind. The third pot Junior won, but it was modest, under five hundred dollars. By then she had tampered with enough cards, erasing and re-marking the ones that passed through her hands, and a more pronounced and remarkable change began to occur.

First Hackney, spying through his glasses, thought that Joe had a bouquet of mixed garbage, though in fact he was working on a straight, helped along by the nine that Gladys palmed and then gracefully slipped onto his lap. Hackney figured he was bluffing, and holding three kings himself, he went in for the kill.

"I don't know about you," he said, "but I'm getting a little bored. Let's liven things up." He grabbed a handful of chips and let them tinkle into the pot. "Five thousand dollars."

"I call," Junior said.

Gladys smiled. "I admire someone who's not afraid to make mistakes. I'll see that five and raise it another five." She brushed two stacks of chips into the center of the table.

"That's ten to you," Hackney told Joe.

"Is it?" Joe asked, and chuckled. "I guess I miscounted. I thought it was twenty." He pushed four stacks across. "Let's just round up, why don't we?"

"I fold," Junior said. He had nothing.

"Well I think you're bluffing big-time, buddy." Hackney smiled behind his magic glasses. "I see right through you."

Joe shrugged. "Time to put up or shut up. Fifteen grand. Unless you're getting nervous. You already owe me what? Twenty-eight?"

Hackney grinned like a wolf. "Good point. Let's just settle that debt now, shall we?" He pushed fifteen in, and then another pile. "Here's fifteen, and then another fifteen. Now you'll owe me."

"You boys are getting personal," Gladys said, folding her hand, and knowing she would lose to Joe anyway. "I'll leave it to you."

Joe smiled and pushed another fifteen thousand into the growing heap. "She's right," he said, "this *is* getting personal. So we might as well see how big those balls really are." And he shoved the remainder of his chips into the pot. "I'm all in."

Hackney calculated. It was another twelve thousand. He pushed in his own dwindling pile and scooped up most of his son's. "I call," he said, tossing the last chips onto the heap.

"Showtime," said the dealer. "Let's see your cards."

"Three kings!" Hackney yelled, and gleefully flipped his hand. "Now who's the loser?" He stood and leaned forward to rake in the chips.

"You are," Joe said, and showed his hand: a straight 6, 7, 8, 9, and 10.

Hackney goggled. "But, but, but . . ." he stammered. He turned on his son, who gaped back, wide-eyed.

"I don't know what happened," Junior said.

"You're useless, that's what happened!" Hackney cracked.

Junior flinched as if he'd been hit, eyes burning with shame, as everyone in the casino turned to look.

Hackney pointed a finger at Joe. "You cheated! I know you did!"

Joe smiled wide. "How do you know exactly?"

By now Little Eddie had come by, casting his looming shadow over the table, with two other suited heavies—casino security—looking on. "There a problem here, sir?" Eddie asked.

Yelena floated over, placing a hand on Joe's shoulder. Everyone waited. "I don't know," Joe said, staring at Hackney. "Is there?"

Hackney boiled, locking his jaw. His fists clenched. His whole body seemed to wriggle with the strain of containing himself. "Fine . . ." he croaked. He cleared his throat. "Fine," he said, again, louder. "What do I owe?"

"You're down forty-seven thousand, sir," the dealer said.

"Plus the original twenty-eight," Joe reminded him. "As long as we're settling up."

"Is that all?" Hackney chuckled drily. "Hardly worth all the fuss. I earned more than that while I sat here." He reached into his pocket and drew out his wallet, waving it as the whole place looked on. "Here's your damn money," he declared, and opened the wallet. It was empty.

39

Josh and Juno set up the cameras. Together they figured the best spots and Juno checked the angles, watching the image on his phone, while Josh stood on a chair. They concealed one in the ceiling molding and another on the underside of a shelf. Finally, they planted a mic under the desk. The cameras were motion triggered and the mic keyed to start recording when the cameras turned on.

"One last thing," Juno said. "Joe asked me to sweep for safes." He pulled out a handheld metal detector and ran it over the walls and along the floorboards. "Nothing here." Juno was checking the sound levels, listening on headphones while he moved around the desk reciting the alphabet, when Josh's walkie squawked.

"Nighthawk One, you there, over? This is Command."

"Shit," Josh said. He told Juno: "Don't say anything."

Juno saluted mockingly.

Josh gave him the finger as he clicked on the walkie. "This is Nighthawk One, I read you Command, over."

"What is your twenty?"

"I'm on break—"

"Please report to the kitchen. I have an assignment for you."

"Roger. On my way."

He turned the walkie off and pointed at Juno. "Don't laugh."

"Laugh? Bro, I'm impressed. You're Nighthawk One already."

Josh rolled his eyes. "Yeah, yeah. Come on, I've got to get out of here. See what this ass wants."

They left, shutting the lights and locking the door behind them.

Joe was concerned.

Cash had texted Liam as soon as he parked the bike around the side of the storage facility, and then circled to the back entrance used for the casino, where the Rolls was waiting. By the time Liam came out with the Hackneys, Juno had also checked in to report that he and Josh were done.

But while part of Joe's plan involved infiltrating Hackney's world and planting the electronics, much of it also depended on Joe's reading of Hackney's character and on their ability to manipulate him, to trigger his behavior by playing on what Joe saw as his main weakness: pride. He was, Joe thought, a narcissistic personality, an egomaniac so extreme that he would do anything to win, to feed his monstrous and ever-growing ego—lie, cheat, steal, even kill. Perhaps the dead women rejected him. Perhaps they made him feel inadequate sexually. Perhaps his all-consuming self-obsession made it impossible to see them as real people with lives of their own, rather than toys to be played with and smashed. Perhaps it was torturing and killing them that was in itself the pleasure: a sadistic thrill based on the ultimate power trip, something that would swell his ego to satanic proportions.

Joe hoped that by setting himself up as a rival and constantly challenging his ego, wounding his pride, Hackney would have no choice but to respond, even if it went against his own interests and ultimately exposed him. But now he worried that he had gone too far, that Hackney would cut himself off from Joe and, feeling too threatened, simply retreat into his bubble where he felt safe.

That was why Liam followed them out, apologizing for Joe's rudeness, assuring them that their credit was good. Liam was the roper, his job was to hook the marks and keep them on the line. Now they were climbing into their limo, crestfallen and silent. Cash, posing by the Rolls, tipped his hat as they passed, but they barely noticed, and Cash sidled up to Liam as the limo's taillights disappeared.

"How'd it go?" Cash asked him.

Liam shrugged. "We'll see."

And this was also why, when the two went back inside and through the casino to the private back room where the rest of the crew were laughing and toasting each other with champagne, Joe was brooding in a corner with a Coke. He was concerned.

Jem, on the other hand, was delighted. "Golly, what a rush!" She was flushed with excitement, eyes glittering while the bubbles raced up her flute of champagne. "Is it always like this?"

Now Joe had to laugh. "Yeah, it's pretty damned good."

"Thank you for letting me be a part of it," she said. "For Ioana."

Joe nodded. "Sure," he said, not feeling very sure, and tapped his glass to hers. "Welcome to the team."

Jem ran over to pour champagne for Juno, who found it a bit tart compared to grape Snapple.

Joe sidled over to Yelena. "I want to get back soon," he told her. "Just in case."

Yelena nodded, eyes on Jem. "She did good," she said. "I like her. She's been staying with you?"

Joe shrugged. "For a couple days, while I'm at the hotel. Then I don't know." He watched her watching Jem.

"You know," she said finally. "I have a guest room now."

"Oh yeah?"

"Maybe she can come stay with me. Just for a little bit."

"I think that's a good idea," Joe said.

Yelena smiled, then downed her champagne. "OK, I am ready."

"Good," Joe said. "Let's get Cash and Liam." He signaled Liam, who nodded and poked Cash, then grabbed his coat. He held Yelena's fur while she slid back into it, like a wolf slipping into sheep's clothing. Liam would bring the bike back while the others took the Rolls.

"Oh, one more thing about Jem," he remembered, as he felt the smooth pelt shimmer. "She has a cat."

"It's Missus Hackney," Riley told Josh when he reported to him in the hotel's basement kitchen. "She wants you to bring up her dinner."

"Me? Why?" Josh was thrown off guard. He'd never even met her. He'd been ready to accept a task like drunk wrestling or chasing dumpster divers with equanimity, but this weirded him out. "How does she even know me?"

"She don't," Riley said. He shrugged. "You know how old people are."

"How?" Josh was worried.

"She's all alone up there. And the two room service waiters on duty tonight are Jose and Felecia."

"So?"

"Well, you know, they're Spanish."

Josh was perplexed. "They're from Spain?"

"No, they speak Spanish. Look, it's not like she's racist. It's just that being a cripple and all, she has to be extra careful. And you're the only white guard here right now. You understand?"

He nodded, but he wasn't sure he did. In the corner of the world he came from, Sephardic Jews of Mediterranean descent were often discriminated against by the more fair-skinned Ashkenazi Europeans. He was actually darker than Jose, with thick black curls, dark brown eyes, and coffee skin. Plus, a big nose.

"I'm a Jew," he pointed out.

"I told her," Riley assured him. "I said, 'He's Israeli, so a type of Jew.' She was OK with it."

(Really, she had shrugged when he told her this and said, "If he was appraising my pearls then I'd expect him to Jew me, but I don't think he'll riffle through my underwear drawer.")

"I'm supposed to be on break," Josh said finally.

Riley nodded in sympathy. "I know. Do me this solid and you can take a longer break later. Thanks, man."

He lumbered away, back to his headquarters, and Josh stood by the swinging kitchen doors, waiting awkwardly. Jose gave him a dirty look when he wheeled out the cart. Josh wanted to say something—*Sorry, man, you can go ahead and spit in her food*—but he had his own role to play. This was the first peek they'd gotten inside the penthouse. It might be good luck after all.

<hr />

"Mrs. Hackney?"

The doors opened directly into the living room, which was enormous. It felt more like the lobby downstairs than a home, but it was even more ornate, more columned and gold-leafed and chandeliered. Josh wanted to say it looked Roman, or even Vatican, but that wasn't quite right; it was the Vegas version of that, or, even further down the evolutionary scale, the Atlantic City version, way more Mafia don than Roman emperor.

"Hello?" he called out. "It's your dinner!" He wheeled across thick carpets and gleaming floors, passing a piano and a harp. Silent behind thick glass, the world tinkled and blinked below. He could see how, staring out over it every day, you might begin to think it belonged to you.

"In here," a voice came. "Follow the light. I'm in the boudoir."

Josh grimaced, fearing some sort of Mrs. Robinson scenario, but he followed, rattling the cart along a dark hallway to where light spilled from an open door. The room was warm, cozy, if such a word could be ascribed to a space larger than most family apartments. It was stuffed, padded with cushions, blankets, drapes, and rugs, packed with toy-like French antiques, lit with the candied light of Tiffany lamps. Most striking were two large crosses—one elegant gold, one a full treatment, complete with writhing Jesus—plus religious paintings, mostly Marys, on the walls. He felt more Jewish than ever.

In the center, gold-lit and shadowed by lamplight, Anne Hackney sat in her wheelchair. Her hair was carefully coifed and she wore a Chanel suit, although she was clearly going nowhere. She also had black heels on, Josh noted, for some reason.

"Your dinner, ma'am."

"Leave it there," she said, pointing vaguely beside her. "What's your name?"

"Josh."

She considered him curiously. "Is that Hebrew?"

"It's short for Yoshua."

"Right." She nodded. "Jericho." She patted a book on the table beside her that Josh realized had to be a Bible. "Joshua, do you pray ever?"

He shrugged. He'd had a lot of worries about what might happen on this visit, but this was not one of them. "I guess."

"I've been praying all night," she said, then leaned, waving him closer. "There is evil in this house."

Josh tingled. Was this it? A revelation about the murders? A clue? He couldn't wait to tell Joe. He leaned closer. "Where?" he asked. "Who?"

"Everywhere!" She waved an arm. "Sluts and whoremongering! Evil harlots!"

"Oh . . ." Josh nodded, trying to hide his disappointment. "That."

"In the Bible they call them succubi. In my Bible, at least."

It's the same Bible, Josh thought. *You guys stole it and added a lame sequel.* But he just nodded again. He was ready to leave.

"You should eat your soup before it gets cold," he suggested. But she reached out and grabbed his hand.

"They are female demons," she went on. "They invade the hearts of men, weak men like my husband, and poison their souls with lust. It's not his fault. I can't be a wife to him anymore. I pray for him every day and night."

Her eyes blazed. He wanted to run, but she had a good grip on his arm—in fact, her nails were digging in a little. "Would you pray with me? Please? Say a Hebrew prayer?"

"Um, sure . . ." Josh said, totally confused, but hoping to placate her somehow.

"Kneel here," she said, patting the air beside her.

"Right," he said, and awkwardly knelt on the carpet. He cleared his throat. "OK, ready?"

She nodded vehemently, eyes shut tight, and Josh haltingly began to chant the only prayer he could call to mind: *"Baruch Atah Adonai, Eloheinu Melech ha-olam, asher kid'shanu b'mitzvotav v'tzivanu al achilat matzoh."* It was the prayer you said at Passover when you handed out the matzoh.

40

"Thanks a lot," Liam said, handsomly tipping the room service waiters who rolled in two heavily laden carts and whose name tags read *Jose* and *Felecia*. As soon as they left, he knocked on the bedroom doors. "Food's here."

Yelena, Cash, and Joe all emerged from hiding and began to remove covers from trays, digging into their late dinner. Yelena sprinkled cheese over her pasta.

"Man, I'm starving," Cash said, dipping a shrimp into cocktail sauce and stuffing it in his mouth while simultaneously pouring ketchup on a cheeseburger and fries.

"Fuck," Liam muttered, his mouth full of club sandwich, as his phone beeped. He checked the text. "It's them."

"The Hackneys?" Joe asked.

"Yeah. They invited us up to the library for a drink."

"Good." Joe was hungry but also relieved. The hook was in; they had not wriggled free. He stared longingly at the covered plate that he knew contained his veal piccata. "No one touch my food."

"Don't lie to yourself, dude," Cash said. "Veal piccata will suck if you wait. Gets all gelatinous."

"He's right, Joe," Yelena told him solemnly, as she twirled linguine on her fork.

"OK fine, eat it," he said, as Liam scarfed down the last of his sandwich and stood, brushing off crumbs. "But nobody touch the Toblerone in the minifridge. I fucking mean it."

Agent Donna Zamora was ready to move. After days and nights of squatting in a squalid van, becoming far too intimate with her colleagues, and eating way too much junk food, it seemed like the promised big fish were finally swimming into the net. The operation was essentially over, or ready to be, but her CI, Daisy, had passed word that a special party was being organized for VIP clients tonight. And so they had waited, despite the additional expenditure, the fatiguing stakeout, and the eagerness of her bosses to roll this up and move on. Mostly though, they were bored. And restless. Till now.

"Hey! It's What's-His-Name, Doctor Hair," Fusco chuckled, munching from a bag of Doritos as he stared through his lens.

"Who?" Donna asked.

"Clearly you're not an insomniac," Fusco said. "Or you have better things to do at 3 A.M. than watch TV."

"He owns a chain of hair-loss clinics," Detective Fry explained. He was NYPD Vice, brought in as a courtesy, since this was his patch and so he could help connect this operation with any other open cases.

"That explains it," Donna said. "I don't care because I'm not a middle-aged balding man."

Andy, who was young, with a dense, closely cropped head of healthy curls, laughed at this, but Fusco tutted.

"That's stereotyping, Zamora. A lot of their clients are women, too. You should see the testimonials."

"Now here's a celeb in my world," Fry said, as a diminutive fellow in an overcoat and bow tie climbed from a town car. "That's Johnny Eggs, the bookmaker."

"How'd he get that moniker?" Andy asked.

Fry shrugged. "He carries hard-boiled eggs in his pockets to eat when he goes to the track. Brings his own little salt shaker, too."

"Colorful," Donna said.

"Hey!" Andy said, brightening. "I know this guy. It's Max the Mini-King. His ads are all over the subway. And his face is on the trucks."

"Oh yeah," Fusco chimed in. "I stored my stuff in one of his places after my last divorce." He grinned, as if brushed by fame. "Not that he was there personally."

Donna sighed. "I don't think this is what the boss expected when we promised him big fish. It's more like a sad commentary on contemporary male life."

Fusco nodded sagely and waved a hand dusted with orange. "That's what a brothel is, Zamora. What'd you expect, a musical number from *Moulin Rouge*?" He popped a few more Doritos and crunched thoughtfully.

A pensive silence descended. Cold wind whistled along the block. The radio crackled like a fire in a hearth. Fusco burped softly and chewed a Tums. Then a cab pulled up.

"Bingo," Andy said, as two men got out, both well dressed and in their sixties, one in a fedora, one with a skullcap. They paid and went into the hotel. "Madam," he said, grinning at Donna, "I believe it was you who ordered the big fish tonight?"

"Oh my God . . ." Donna said softly. "Is that who I think it is?"

"Yup," Fusco said. "His Honor, Federal Court judge Romeo Garcia."

"Jesus, I just testified before him last month," Donna said.

"Next month, maybe you'll testify against him," Andy said.

"And who's his pal with the beanie?" Fusco asked.

"That," Fry said, "is Assemblyman Aaron Berg."

⁘

"I hope it's not small bills," Joe said, grinning, as he and Liam walked in. Hackney and Junior were by the small bar, a bottle between them. The rest of the room was empty. "Like if you stole the valet's tip jar."

Hackney laughed. "I'm starting to like you," he said. "You can always be counted on to be a total prick."

"We told you," Junior put in. "You'll get paid tomorrow."

"You said it was in the safe," Joe corrected.

"The hotel safe. It's on a time lock. Eight A.M. tomorrow."

Joe waved a hand. "Fine, fine. Liam will be there with an empty pillowcase. I'll be sleeping." He looked at his watch. "So why am I here?"

"We have a surprise for you," Junior said. "Drink first?" He held up the bottle of single malt Scotch.

"Sure, why not?" Liam said. "It's not Irish but I'm an open-minded man."

"None for me," Joe said, and burped loudly. "I just had your kitchen's veal piccata, and it's repeating on me."

Hackney laughed. "No wonder—we just put that on the menu for the pansies. Should have had a steak."

Junior handed Liam and his father drinks and then raised his glass. "My father and I are going to a very special private party. We thought we'd invite you along. Show there's no hard feelings."

Hackney raised his glass, a big grin on his face. "At least not till we get there. Then it's every man for himself."

⚬━┿━⚬

Donna was waiting to move. She'd called for backup, Bureau troops to take down the traffickers, support staff to process and care for the women, and local PD to handle the johns and manage any civilian bystanders. As the players made their way through the dark streets to muster a block north, out of sight of the happily clueless targets, Donna also waited for an answer from her other call, to her boss, who was busy conferring with his own bosses in his pajamas, deciding what to do about this suddenly very high-profile event. Fusco and Fry had made similar calls to their respective captains, who were no doubt having similar late-night conferences.

"This is bullshit," Donna announced after a long silence. "I say bust them all and let the chips fall where they may."

"That's why we love you," Andy said.

"And why you're not a boss," Fusco said. "See, they're figuring out how to cover their asses now, before time. Not after the shit starts to fly."

"Let's face it," Andy said. "None of those big-timers are going to take a fall."

"She's right, though," Fry said. "Do them good to take the walk of shame. Even if they make the charges go away."

"Exactly," Donna said. "Fry knows what I mean. At least let them know we know. Let them look us in the eye after that."

A limo pulled up and four more men got out, all dressed in expensive suits and well-fitted overcoats. "Here we go," Andy said. "More contestants on Name That John. The old guy is what's his name, the real estate dude. You know, he's a real show-off. Owns that hotel."

No one else spoke. He snapped his fingers. "Come on, help me out here, Donna. It's going to drive me nuts. Starts with an *H*."

The door opened and the four men went in as their limo pulled away. Donna shrugged.

"Hackney," Fusco said at last.

"Right, thank you!" Andy slapped his leg. "Jim Hackney. And that's his son with him. Anyone make the other two?"

There was a long quiet moment.

"I better check in and see what's what," Fry said finally.

"Yeah, me too," Fusco quickly added.

Donna said nothing. She just glared.

41

The Senora greeted Hackney and his son like old friends, kissing them on both cheeks, though she quickly showed Joe and Liam the same warmth as soon as they were introduced.

"Gentlemen," she said in her thick accent, "please come meet the ladies. Don't be shy. We are all one big, happy family here."

They'd rented a floor of nondescript corporate housing near the convention center, and the furnishings and décor in the main room were more regional sales office than den of decadence: modular couches, glass coffee tables, thin woven carpets in grays and tans, wall sconces. It felt like you were walking into a dull marketing conference, except for the fact that half the women were dressed in lingerie while the others were dolled up as if for a glamorous nightclub, while the men who weren't in suits were in bathrobes, their legs bare except for socks and shoes.

Chuko and his men had made an effort—this was a VIP gathering, after all—but they still stuck out as what they were—thugs. The two hoods' suits were cheap and tight across the chests, the ties too wide, the pants too short or too long. One wore white socks. Chuko himself had dressed up by slicking his hair back and donning a tie and blue silk shirt under his leather trench coat, and succeeded only in looking even sleazier.

Hackney immediately strode across the room to where two men sat on a couch and slapped one jovially on the back, an older black man in a white bathrobe with a gold cross on a chain nestled in his gray chest hair. "Reverend," he boomed, "I should have known you'd beat me to the good stuff."

The Reverend laughed, shaking his head. "Hackney, you old goat. Don't worry. I left you some scraps."

Hackney shook hands with the other man, portly and white, and in a matching robe but with a yarmulke on his head and a chain with the Hebrew word *chai* in gold. "Assemblyman! Shouldn't you be up in Albany doing your job?"

The man guffawed, holding his gut. "You know it's too cold for me up there." He patted his friend's arm. "Anyway, I had important meetings with constituents like the Rev here. And our friend on the city council. I told her I'd be seeing you tonight, by the way. She sends her regards. Said you'd understand if she took a pass on this party."

Hackney shook a finger at them: "Don't believe it. Her balls are bigger than anybody's."

The men roared. "I'm going to take your word for that," the Reverend said. "And not check for myself."

The assemblyman gasped with laughter, wiping his eyes. "How could you? She's always in a pantsuit."

"You remember my son?" Hackney said now, as if remembering the others were there.

The two men shook his hand heartily. "Junior. How's it going?" the Reverend asked.

"And I brought a couple of new friends along." Hackney waved at Joe and Liam. "Show them how the big-timers live."

"Evening, gents," Liam said, bowing slightly.

"I've got to admit," Joe said, taking it all in, "you do look like two sultans in a harem."

"Dive in, the water's warm," the Reverend told him.

"And the booty's hot!" chimed in the assemblyman. The two men laughed again.

"Think I'll browse a little before I pick," Joe said. "And Hackney," he added, holding out a hand, "I got to hand it to you, this is first-rate. You finally impressed me."

Hackney beamed as they shook. "Help yourself. Best in town. And it's all on me. Of course," he added, full of pride, "I've already saved the sweetest plum for myself. Or should I say cherry?"

The robed men laughed as Hackney waltzed off, his son in tow. "Oh, Flora, where's my private stock?"

Smiling wide, the Senora took Hackney's arm and led him away. "Sandra," she called. "Come and meet your date."

"What the hell's that all about?" Joe asked the giggling men.

The assemblyman shook his head. "Jim's like one of those gourmets with the jaded palate. He's had it all, so now it's got to be caviar stuffed up a quail's ass and poached in fresh cream. I'm a meat-and-potatoes guy myself, right, Rev?"

The Reverend laughed. "Though I won't say no to extra gravy."

"Anyway," the assemblyman went on, "this time Flora has promised Hackney a treat, a totally new girl. A first-timer. That turns the old devil on."

"Think it's true?" Joe asked dubiously. "A lot of girls make a good living out of every night being the first."

The assemblyman shrugged. "Who knows?"

"Let's face it," the Reverend added, "half of what they sell is the fantasy. Otherwise you could be screwing your own wife."

"Still schmoozing?" Hackney swung by, his arm around a young woman. She was small-boned but curvy, with a lot of very long, shimmering black hair. She wore a red satin dress, tight and shiny. Even with heels she barely reached Hackney's shoulder. "Well, you snooze you lose. I've already won this prize." He leered at her, hugging her tighter. She giggled and then squealed as he squeezed.

Joe smiled at the girl. "Good evening."

She nodded back shyly.

"Better get in there, or you'll be stuck with leftovers." Hackney laughed wide, clearly feeling better. "Let's go, baby."

As he smacked the girl on the bottom and led her toward the hall that opened on the bedrooms, Joe saw Junior watching intently from across the room, his gaze like a beam finding its way among the shifting bodies, the laughing men, the dancing women, the shadows, the smoke. His jaw was set, his eyes narrow, and as his father disappeared with the girl in red, he turned abruptly and left. Joe caught Liam's eye. He shrugged, raising his eyebrows.

"Think I'll go out for a smoke, boss," he said.

Liam stepped out onto the street. It was like a plunge into cold water, the wind smacking his face like saltwater spray. He ducked back into the doorway and lit a cigarette, aware of Junior watching him from a few yards away. The street was empty, except for traffic slowly passing and the occasional solitary walker. The storefronts were dark, the buildings were quiet, or as quiet as this part of town ever got; there was just the low roar from the avenues and the groaning wind. He pretended to notice Junior now, nodded, and strolled over, holding out the pack.

"Smoke?" he asked, and stood beside him, leaning on a wall, a narrow setback that hid them from the wind.

"No," Junior said, then, "Thanks."

Liam nodded, leaned, smoked, waited.

"Not getting your dick wet tonight?" Junior asked finally.

Liam shook his head. "I keep it dry on duty. Like my gunpowder."

Junior laughed, the first crack in his dour demeanor. "Are you really strapped?"

Liam glanced up and down the empty block. Then he leaned over and lifted a trouser leg, revealing the .38 revolver in an ankle holster. He straightened up. "My boss tends to piss people off."

Smiling now, Junior opened his coat, revealing an automatic in a shoulder holster. "Mine too." They both laughed. "Got to admit," he added, "your boss is pretty good at poker."

Liam shrugged that off. "He cheats."

"You admit it?" Junior was affronted, looking Liam up and down. His breath steamed.

Liam smoked coolly. "If you're daft enough to quote me I'll deny it. And what would you say—he cheats better than you?"

Junior was taken aback by this, literally. He rocked on his heels, as if avoiding a punch on the jaw. Liam braced himself. Junior was big, with chunks of back and shoulder muscles swelling his overcoat, bulked up in that way where even expensive clothes fit wrong. Liam was fly, thin. His plan was to stick Junior with his cigarette butt, then kick him in the balls, then shoot him or run, depending. Then Junior's grin broke again, and he started laughing. Liam joined in, making him laugh harder.

"You're right!" Junior gasped, howling with laughter now, the kind that came from the release of deep tensions. "The look on his face when he saw Joe's hand. I almost lost it."

Liam laughed for real at that. It was true. Hackney had shit a brick. Liam had to dig his nails into his palms to keep a straight face when that happened.

Junior caught his breath. "You're all right," he told Liam now. "I'm part Irish too. On my mom's side. O'Shaughnessy."

"That's a fine name."

Junior straightened his tie, smoothed his hair. "I've got to tell you, though. My dad won't ever give up. This, tonight . . ." He waved up at the brothel. "This is just another part of the game.

Show off. Scope out the rival. Whatever girl your boss goes with, he'll pay her off to find out more, anything he can use against him. Any weakness."

Liam nodded. "We figured. I don't know if he will even dip his wick. He just came out of ego. Because he couldn't back down, either. Like with poker. He has to call or raise."

"Let me ask you," Junior said, serious now. "Honestly. Why are you even working for that guy? Eating his shit?"

Liam sighed, eyebrows raised. "I was an orphan in Ireland. I've eaten worse. I may be a flunky but I'm very well paid, thank you. Someday I'll make enough to go home and buy a pub."

Junior shook his head. "I don't know how you stand it."

"How do you?" Liam asked.

Junior froze for a moment. Gave him a hard stare.

It was a bad couple of seconds, but Liam played it off, dropped his butt, and ground it on the sidewalk. "All due respect," he continued, "but they're two of kind. That's why they butt heads, isn't it?" He shrugged. "Maybe that's what it takes to be boss."

Junior took this in. "My dad can be difficult. But it's different. It's family."

"Of course. But then I wouldn't know, would I?"

"Oh yeah, right. Sorry about that . . ."

"Still, it can't be easy, having him as your old man. A lot to live up to, I suppose."

"It is, man, it really is." Junior shook his head. "A lot."

⚬━╾╼━⚬

Joe approached the women, who were draped over the couches and chairs, as if arranged for display. Some looked him directly in the eye. Some glanced away shyly. Some seemed absent, their eyes vacant, as if they had already given up and left the room. Joe smiled nervously, as awkward as if he were at a junior high school dance. He'd been around the sex trade his whole life. His grandmother used to work as a manager in a brothel, answering phones, booking clients, taking money, and keeping an eye on the girls. A call girl neighbor who entertained visitors at night would be home and free daytimes to let Joe in after school if Gladys was out. It was normal, another hustle, one of the many ways a person got by in the world. Hanging out with strippers in the club, after a while you almost forgot they were half naked. Almost. But he'd never been a customer, a square john with his money in his hand, and the feeling depressed him. He felt bad for the women, of course, but in a strange way he felt sorry for the men, too. For the women he had compassion, for the men something more like embarrassment. The whole thing made him sad, and what he really wanted was to go home and sleep. Or get high and shut his eyes. Or maybe, he thought, a new thought, talk about it with Donna, or not talk about it, just be silent but not alone with her.

But he couldn't do any of that. Like them, he was working.

<hr />

"You know," Junior was saying, "if you were to help us win a rematch, take him down at poker, you could be buying that pub next week." He was relaxed now, smoking a cigar, one of his Cubans.

Liam, who was trying one as well, shook his head. "Never happen. He's too crafty for that. Why do you think he plays at that casino? He runs it. Nah. He'd never play if he can't win."

"That's too bad, Liam. Thing is, I like you. I think we could work well together. And we do have a new opening for a manager at the hotel. Just saying. If you could help us get to him. Find his weak spot. My father would be extremely appreciative."

Liam considered. He shifted from foot to foot, automatically checked the block, although no one was in sight except an old man dragging a wheelie bag very slowly along the sidewalk. One wheel squeaked, maddeningly. A cab slid by. Otherwise it was only parked cars, dirty vans, and a silent ConEd truck. Finally, Liam spoke.

"Olga," he said.

"What?"

"The woman, Olga. That's his weakness."

"How do you mean?"

Liam hesitated. He took a breath, like at the edge of the diving board. Then he jumped. "She's his mistress."

"So?" Junior was confused. "I didn't think she was his wife. He's married? Big deal. Unless his wife controls the money or something . . ."

"No, you don't understand. I mean *mistress* like 'Yes, Mistress. No, Mistress.'" He leaned in, confidential. "Look, he plays up being the big shot tough guy, but behind closed doors, he's a sub. You know, like he fancies being flogged and such."

"A masochist?"

Liam shrugged. "Yeah, I guess. He's always been a bit kinky, but it was more like dommes he hired or clubs he went to."

"Dungeons, they call them."

"Right. Then he met her. She's Russian but they met in Berlin. Anyway, since then she is with him full-time. He plays the boss, but she controls him completely. Pays her a fortune. You saw that coat. The jewels. All from him."

"Wow. He's her slave, like."

"That's the real reason he wouldn't do aught with that lot upstairs. She won't allow it."

"How would she even know?"

Again, Liam hesitated. "This is just between us, right?"

"Of course, I swear it."

"And that manager job, it pays well, does it?"

"Double whatever you get now. For starters."

"Right." He lowered his voice. "She keeps him in chastity."

"What the fuck does that mean?"

"It's this apparatus, like. Goes around the cock and locks like a collar, it does. You can have a pee but you can't, you know, stick it to anyone."

"Get the fuck out of here."

"I'm fecking serious. She holds the key."

"You mean he has it on now?"

"Of course. She won't let him out otherwise."

"Damn. I don't think I can look at him the same way."

"You're telling me. Anyway . . . he's terrified she'll leave him. That's his Achilles' heel. I mean, we're all led around by our dicks, right? But not with an actual collar and leash on it." Then Liam straightened abruptly and cleared his throat. Junior looked over as Joe came striding out.

"There you are. What the hell? On a break? Or did you take early retirement?"

"Sorry, boss. We were just talking."

"Talking? About what? Unionizing the flunky business?" Joe considered Junior as he buttoned his overcoat. "Shouldn't you be upstairs wiping off your dad's dick or something?"

Junior bristled, then relaxed. "You know what, I'm not even going to rise to that occasion." He stared at Joe's groin for a beat, then shook it off. His phone rang and he glanced at it. "I've got to take this. Have a nice evening, both of you." He turned to go back inside, answering, "Yeah?" Then walking faster. "What? When?"

42

Daisy had hooked her big fish. But where was Agent Zamora with the net?

As promised, the VIPs had filled the place that night, a bunch of big shots showing off for each other. And the Senora's number one customer, the one she had bragged about, had indeed paid big for her supposed deflowering. And if that was what it took to buy her own freedom and security, so be it.

But the whole idea was that the Federals would swoop in and catch him in the act. She had done her job as the bait. Why didn't they spring the trap? Instead, as this fat cat—"Jim," he called himself—grabbed her, his hand squeezing her ass like an orange he was thinking of skinning and juicing, she felt her skin crawl. It was impossible not to recoil in revulsion, but she played it off as shyness, smiling coyly and giggling as she wriggled out of his grip. When he kissed her, his breath reeking of booze and food, she felt like she was going to throw up in her mouth, and maybe even in his. *Maybe that's how this will end*, she thought, joking darkly to herself, as Jim took her into the room and shut the door behind him.

But as soon as they were alone things changed. He seemed awkward suddenly, even a bit shy, and almost as uncomfortable as she was.

"So, uh . . ." His voice still had its gruff, commanding tone, like a minor tyrant, a bus driver or factory manager, pushing people around, but his body language shifted. He shuffled his weight from left to right and looked at his toes. "I know this is your first time and you're nervous," he said, avoiding her gaze.

She nodded, wondering if he really believed that. But men were often eager to believe their fantasies were true. "Yes, sir," she said softly.

"Well, let's play a game then," he said. "I'll go change and you take off that dress, but when I come out, you act like I'm not even worthy to be your first. Understand?"

Confused, she shook her head. "Not really."

"Make me beg," he ordered. "Slap me if I try to touch you."

"Slap you? You mean it?"

"Hard as you can," he instructed. "Got it?"

"Yes, sir. I mean—"

"Look, just get ready." He was growing impatient. "I'll be right out, OK?"

So she did. He went into the bathroom, and she took off her dress and got between the sheets, ears straining the whole time for the sound of Federal boots kicking down the hall door. Unfortunately, it was the bathroom door that opened, though from Daisy's vantage point, it seemed there was no one there. She sat up, craning her head. And there he was, in a white T-shirt, white briefs, and black socks, on his hands and knees. Her first urge was to laugh, more out of shock and embarrassment than humor, but she stifled it. She was also afraid. The situation was so bizarre, and she was so unsure of where it was headed, that she feared what the wrong reaction might trigger. Breathing heavily, he began to crawl across the room. She pulled the blanket higher. He reached the bed and began to reach for her foot, which was exposed, poking out from the blanket. She froze.

And then came a pounding on the door.

"Go away!" Jim yelled. "I'm busy."

Thank God, thought Daisy, *they're here.*

The door opened, but it wasn't cops or Feds. It was another, younger blond man. "Dad," he blurted as he rushed in. "We have to—" He stopped abruptly at the sight on the floor. "Are you OK?"

Jim looked stricken, then furious. "What? Yeah, of course, I'm OK. I dropped something."

He hoisted himself up while his son hovered.

"Dropped what?" he asked, examining the floor.

Jim faltered, and Daisy, watching awkwardly from beneath the sheets, piped up. "I lost an earring."

"Never mind that." Jim waved it off. "What are you doing in here?"

The two men conferred in whispers. Then Jim looked at her for a long moment, and said to his son, "Get her number," before rushing back into the bathroom.

⚬━╾━⚬

"So?" Joe asked, as he and Liam walked back across town.

Liam grinned. "The hook's in deep. Now you just wait for them to jump in the net."

"Nicely done." Joe patted his shoulder. "I'm impressed."

"One small thing, though. Just a detail."

"What?"

They turned uptown now, taking Broadway. There were more people and more cars, and the rows of traffic lights blinked green and yellow and red, like holiday decorations. "Well, I might have given him the impression, that, you know . . ."

"No. What?"

"That Yelena keeps your lad in a cage."

"My what?"

"You know. Your flute. I told him Mistress Olga keeps it under lock and key like, in this chastity device."

"Jesus . . . how'd you even come up with that?"

"I saw it online by accident, didn't I?"

"'Accident'?"

"I was looking for gay porn, I swear. But *bottom* has that other meaning over here. Next thing I knew I was seeing all that, women locking up a fella's mickey. Anyway, it stuck in me head."

Joe frowned. "And now it's stuck in mine, thanks to you."

"Stand down."

"What?" Donna barked into the phone, then caught herself, "I mean, what do you mean, sir?"

In the van, Fusco, Fry, and Andy were staring at her, while she sat on the phone with Tom. Outside the van, a block away, others, too, waited unseen.

"You know what I mean," Tom said. "Do not move in until further notice. Fall back and observe."

"But, sir, my CI is in there, possibly in danger and—"

"—and you postponed this action, because she told you about a bunch of big shots. But that was never the focus, was it? So keep your eye on the ball. You'll make your bust, and maybe, if you listen to me, you'll still have a career. Understood?"

"Yes, sir."

"All right then," Tom said, suddenly sounding exhausted. "Good night, Donna."

"Good night," she answered softly, and ended the call. No one spoke. While it was silent in the van, she stared out the one-way glass as Joe walked by, talking and laughing with another man.

"What did he say?" Andy finally asked. He was holding the radio, with the troops on the end of the line. "What are we going to do?"

"Let them walk," Donna said, her eyes on Joe.

***

No, Daisy was thinking. *No fucking way.*

At first, when the son—Junior, the old man called him—had interrupted her "deflowering," Daisy had been confused and then relieved. Then she realized something was up. Something was wrong. She dressed quickly as the son gallantly looked aside, and she was just shifting from relief to disappointment, realizing this big fish was swimming away, when Junior approached, phone in hand.

"Listen, my father would love to see you again. Privately. It would be worth a lot to you. Much more than here . . ."

Of course the girls weren't allowed to have phones. But Daisy thought, *What the hell, maybe I can get another shot at this.* She gave him the number to her own cell, which Zamora was holding, along with some personal effects, for safekeeping.

Then Daddy came out, buckling his belt. "Um . . ." He hesitated, suddenly unsure. He put out a hand. "I apologize for leaving like this," he said. "I hope you find your earring."

Too stunned by it all to know what to say or think or feel, Daisy shook his hand.

***

Back in the main room, something was definitely going on. The customers were mostly all gone, with the few stragglers leaving in a hurry. All of the overhead lights were on, revealing the place for what it was: a shabby hotel suite, cheaply furnished and not very clean. Towels and robes and sheets were dropped here and there, as if the ghosts they once clad had vanished. Chuko and the Senora were yelling, while their two stooges rushed around following orders.

Daisy turned to Amarylis, a sweet, plump young woman she'd befriended. "*¿Qué pasa?*" she asked.

"*Nos estamos mudando a Boston, ahora mismo,*" she answered, frantic, wringing her hands. They were moving, Chuko had said. Right now. To Boston. Amarylis was from Ecuador, and each move north took her further from home and deeper into a cold and empty future.

That, Daisy decided, was not happening. She had no way of knowing what happened to the raid, why the trap hadn't sprung, but she knew that Donna and the team had to be close, watching or listening. She noticed the remains of the fruit and cheese platter that had been laid out for the clients. While everyone was distracted by the chaos of packing, she grabbed the cheese knife and concealed it in the bodice of her dress. In the confusion, as the stooges began rushing luggage out the door, getting ready to load the van, Daisy slipped out into the hallway. She ran to the corner and found the fire alarm. She pulled it.

As the clanging sounded, Chuko stuck his head out the door, a clutch of women spilling after him. "*¡Maldita perra!*" he hissed, and came for her.

"Go! Run!" she yelled to the women. "*Vamos. ¡Trae ayuda!*"

They ran, in a sudden rush for freedom, screaming as they made for the stairwell, with the stooges right behind them. Daisy faced Chuko, one hand curled in a fist, the other reaching for the blade.

Junior hustled his father into the waiting car. Fry's warning had sent them both into a panic. Hackney had been sweating bullets in the elevator, and they raced out of the building like they'd just robbed a bank, necks craning for the cops. They even ducked in the back of the limo, hiding from view, too freaked to speak, until the car turned the corner and joined the flow of traffic.

"Sorry you didn't get to close the deal with that girl, but I got her number," Junior said.

Hackney nodded, regaining his composure, smoothing his tie and hair in the reflection of the window. "Probably safer to stick to in-call for a while anyway. That was too close."

"Still, it wasn't all a waste," Junior said. "I had a very interesting conversation with our Irish friend."

"Oh yeah?" Hackney turned to him. "Any dirt on his boss?"

Junior smiled. "Wait till you hear. I know all about Olga, too."

Donna was being stubborn. They were stood down, the troops were dispersed, and Fry was no longer needed. Although it was Andy's turn to keep watch with Fusco, she'd refused to give up and go home. She sat behind the wheel of the van, brooding.

"Go home," Andy told her. "We'll bust these assholes tomorrow. And the rest, we'll get them another time."

"He's right," Fusco said. "You got to learn to pace yourself. There's a lot more of them than us."

"I know. I just can't walk away. Not yet. Maybe I'll sleep here." She looked at the floor of the van and considered curling up on the filthy carpet. Maybe not. She sighed, resigning herself to one more day of this. Then she heard a ringing sound.

"What's that?" she asked.

Fusco shrugged. "Car alarm? Fire? Either way, not our problem."

"Hey, look," Andy called, pointing out the windshield. A handful of young women, some in street clothes, some in lingerie, none with boots or jackets, were running from the door of the building, screaming and waving. Right behind them were two big angry-looking dudes with guns.

As the women ran by, passing the side of the van, Fusco and Andy rushed to climb out the back door. Donna paused, hand on the door handle, and as the big thug came charging past, she kicked the door open so that he ran flat into it, full speed and face-first. With a grunt, his upper body flipped back, while his legs ran on, and he flopped backward onto the pavement, his gun skittering away. The door bounced closed and Donna caught it, pushing it back open as she dropped from the van, one boot pinning his throat, and drew her gun. She held it with both hands, and stared down the barrel at his face.

"Don't move," she said. He didn't.

Meanwhile Fusco and Andy had wrestled the other thug to the ground and had him cuffed.

"Cuff this guy and call for backup," Donna called, as Andy hustled over. She hurried across the street. Body low, weapon up, trying to be careful, she moved as fast as she could, pushing through the doors and up the stairs, heart pounding as she burst from the stairwell and into the hall, where she saw three more women proudly pinning the Senora to the floor and taking turns slapping her across the face while they laughed with glee. Daisy, clad in a slinky dress, was sitting on Chuko's chest. While two women held his arms and legs down, she was pressing the forked tip of a cheese knife into his throat.

43

By the time Joe and Liam got back to the suite, Josh had finished his shift and was watching soccer on cable while Cash played chess with Yelena.

"How'd it go?" Josh asked Liam as he sat on the arm of his chair.

"All I will say," Liam replied, "is thank God we are not heterosexual," and kissed Josh's upturned face.

"I agree," Yelena said, grinning, as she moved a piece.

"It's not so bad," Cash countered, then added, "Shit . . ." as Yelena took his queen.

"Anyway," Liam continued, "I expect you'll be getting a call soon, Yelena."

"And you?" she asked Joe as he bent over the fridge and grabbed the chocolate bar and a bottle of mineral water. "How was it being a heterosexual man tonight?"

"Exhausting and depressing," he said, and flopped into a chair. "Especially with a tie on. And these shoes." He began to loosen and remove the offending items.

The soccer match ended, and Cash conceded to Yelena. Soon Joe was alone. Suddenly thirsty, he guzzled from the seltzer bottle and unwrapped the chocolate. Leaning back, he took a big bite, snapping off a triangle. Immediately, a splinter of nougat wedged in the crevice of a tooth. He sucked on it for a while and tried to wash it out with seltzer. Then he went to the bathroom and brushed his teeth, but the bristles couldn't budge it. The light was out under Josh and Liam's door.

Cash was snoring. So he knocked on Yelena's door, which showed a stripe of light.

"Who is it?"

"Me."

"Come in."

He opened the door. Yelena was naked on top of the bed, facedown, reading a magazine. "Yes?"

"Do you have dental floss?"

"Floss?"

"I got something stuck in my tooth. It's driving me nuts."

She frowned. "Is this your way of saying you want to have sex?"

"Nope."

"Good, because it would be pathetic." She rolled over and stood, then walked to the bathroom and emerged, still nude, with the floss. She unwound a couple of feet and snapped it off. "I'm not giving you all," she noted, and handed it to him.

He smiled. "Thanks, that's plenty." He turned to go. "Good night."

He went back to the bathroom mirror and flossed. The nougat, which felt like a boulder but was in reality a tiny speck, popped out. Relief. He rinsed his mouth. He checked the time on his phone. After midnight. He hesitated for a moment, bringing Donna's number up, staring at it, thumb hovering. He went to the window, parted the drapes, and looked at the endless city, its million lights each burning for a soul, asleep or awake, together or alone. He called Donna. She did not pick up. So he lay on the couch and read *Ulysses* until he fell asleep.

⊶

Daisy was finally free.

After Agent Zamora talked her out of slicing Chuko's throat and letting him bleed out like the pig he was, she rode down to the federal building, where the suspects were officially processed, as well as the victims. For tonight they received medical care, shelter, and clothing. Tomorrow their journey would continue, ending in deportation for most, and while some just wanted to go home to their families, some were already afraid of what would come next, a fight to remain in the country they had been so desperate to reach in the first place.

"The Bureau has arranged a hotel for the night," Donna had told Daisy, as she sat across from her desk. "And here is some money for clothes and a toothbrush and things." She counted out two hundred in petty cash and had Daisy sign. Knowing how exhausted she was, how trying and traumatic the last days had been, Donna told her she could come back for debriefing and paperwork tomorrow. She opened her bottom drawer and handed Daisy a ziplock bag containing her own cell phone, ID, and wallet. Donna shook her hand.

"I know you're going to be hearing about it from a lot of people, and officially, too, but let me be the first. Thank you, Daisy. You did a hell of a job."

Daisy fingered the money. "And what about the bounty?"

"Bounty?"

"The extra we talked about for the VIPs?"

Donna sighed. "Sorry, that was a no-go. Not your fault, Daisy. Or mine. But we'll get those bastards one day. We know who they are."

Daisy did not seem reassured. Donna sent her off in a car, then waited for the last victim to be tucked in and the last dirtbag locked up before she called a ride for herself.

That was when her phone rang. It was Joe.

When she saw him there, dressed up and polished like she'd never seen him, laughing and smiling with those other pigs, she had tasted bile and blood, pure fury, while also knowing her rage was foolish, pointless. She knew he was tracking a killer, that the killer preyed on sex workers, and no doubt that was, somehow, the reason he was there.

Or not. It was impossible to say. That was part of what infuriated her. Joe's presence at a brothel when she thought he was busy working might mean just that—he was working. Like his job at the strip club, which was actually the humdrum, workaday cover for a far darker, deadlier career, so secret that even if they spent their lives together, she would never really know what went on.

She understood, in a way. She, too, belonged to an insular organization that forbade her from revealing its deepest secrets to any outsider, even her family or closest friends. It was, paradoxically, part of what made their time together so sweet: no stupid questions they couldn't answer, no need for excuses or guilt.

And yet, if the bosses hadn't put the kibosh on it, she would have busted him that night, swept him up with the other trash, and cuffed him herself, just like the night they first met. That wasn't a good sign. Or maybe it was the sign of a good agent, but it also signaled some deep, unresolved conflicts in her feelings for Joe. She knew they had to talk. But not yet. She wasn't ready. So she didn't answer his call. And he didn't leave a message.

⚬━━⚬

Daisy found the message when she got out of the shower.

> *Hey it's Jim from before. Sorry we were so rudely interrupted. I know it's late, but if you would consider meeting now I promise it will be very much worth your while. I will send a driver. I have a private suite at the Hackney Tower. The champagne is chilling, or the brandy warming as you prefer. Please come.*

She sat, wrapped in one thin towel with another wrapped around her hair. Yes, it was safe, and private, but the FBI's hotel was no better than the hotels the prostitution ring had provided. It had rankled her, letting this big fish go unspeared, and here he was, basically begging for it, though not in the way he thought. Maybe there was another chance to bag him and win her reward. Or maybe she could earn her own reward, work one more night and have a nest egg for her new life in America. Resolved, she tapped out a reply:

How much?

The driver was waiting when Daisy went downstairs. She'd put her dress and coat back on, done her makeup and hair. He hopped out to open the door and then, once she was settled in the back of the limo, he handed her a small box. It contained a little gold lock on a chain, with a *D* inscribed on the back.

"The gentleman would appreciate if you wore that, miss," he said into the rearview mirror. Then he drove through Manhattan, all cold glitter and moonlight. When he pulled up in front of the hotel, and the doorman rushed over to open her door, the driver gave her a card key.

"Suite 3003," he told her. "Please go right up."

She checked herself in the polished mirror of the elevator. The lock looked good, gold against her skin, and she touched it as she walked down the silent hallway to 3003. She gave a quick knock before swiping and going in.

It was a gorgeous suite, definitely a big step up, lit with small lights, done in black and white, lilies in a vase, the view. She stepped in, heels sinking into the thick carpets, a bit dazzled, actually, to suddenly be thirty floors up. She barely had time to register it when the door shut behind her, and she heard only a soft pop before everything went black.

PART IV

44

Juno got the passwords around 10 A.M. He was in his bathrobe, on the couch in his studio, eating some leftover pizza and watching the live feed from the first camera they had mounted in the upper corner of the office. He had been there since eight, but at first nothing happened, just an image of an empty office, the only movement shadows shifting with the sun. Then around eight thirty an off-screen door opened and a maid came in. She gave the place a quick dust, vacuumed, and emptied the wastepaper basket. Then quiet again till nine thirty. At that point the man himself, Jim Hackney, strode in, suit and tie, trailed by his son, Jim Jr., similarly garbed, gesticulating earnestly. Waving him off, Jim Sr. made a call. Juno turned the sound up, triggering the mic under the desk, but he was just ranting about somebody "trying to fuck me on monogrammed towels," and Juno hit mute, deciding it was time for breakfast. Of course, just as Jim sat down at his desk, Juno's mom interrupted.

"Juno," she called, sticking her head down the opening for the stairs. "Can you fix the toaster oven? It's doing it again."

"In a minute, Ma," he yelled, trying to zoom in with one hand.

"But don't electrocute yourself," she cautioned.

"Did you unplug it?"

"Yes, of course, as soon as I smelled the burning."

"Then I can't electrocute myself, can I?" By then, of course, he'd missed it. "Damn . . ."

"What?"

"Nothing. I'm working."

Luckily the video was automatically recorded so he just ran it back, zoomed in tight, slowed it down a bit, and there it was: Hackney's fingers on his computer keyboard, entering his passcode: BIGJIM001!!! Which, honestly, Juno felt like he should have been able to guess. In minutes, he had hacked in remotely, using the information he had already gleaned from examining the Wi-Fi server in the office. Soon, along with the live video feed of Hackney drinking coffee and reading the *Post*, Juno had an exact copy of whatever was on Hackney's screen up on another of his screens, and a complete copy of his entire hard drive on his own system. He called Joe.

"Good morning."

"Hey, what's up?" Joe said.

"Just letting you know, we're in."

"Already? That's great, Juno. Thanks. Keep me posted."

At ten thirty, Liam showed up at the office. The receptionist buzzed and Junior let him in, then shook his hand. His dad was behind the desk, leaning back, staring out at the city, his city, while he drank coffee and ate a blueberry bran muffin. He waved him in, wiping his lips on a linen napkin. The coffee and muffin were served in china marked with the Hackney family crest—which he had hired a Chinese design firm to create. (This explained why the motto, *Magnidicum Aeditus*, which he thought meant "To Build Greatness," actually meant "Bragging Temple Janitor.")

"Good morning, Liam. Have a seat. Coffee? Muffin? It's the kind that's good for heart attacks but pretty tasty. They bake them fresh downstairs."

"Thanks, but I had breakfast. I just came by to fetch the money you owe."

"Yeah, about that . . ." Hackney grinned at his son. "We're not paying."

"You're not?"

"He cheated. That voids the debt."

Liam looked at Junior, who shrugged. "Sorry."

"But you cheated, too," Liam said. "Your son admitted as much."

"Yeah, but technically that doesn't count since he won, so-called," Hackney reasoned. "And *he* was cheating, so he didn't really beat me."

"He still beat you at cheating," Liam pointed out.

"Look," Junior interceded, "the point is that, in light of these facts, we are released from any obligation to pay. I mean, who's he going to tell? He'd be admitting his own culpability."

"And if the whole town finds out his casino is rigged, then what?" Hackney finished his coffee and smacked his lips. "He screwed himself. Nobody beats me."

Liam shrugged. "He won't like it."

"Let him try something. My security will throw him out on his ass, no problem." Hackney leaned back, brushing crumbs from his belly. "And if he thinks about getting smart, he doesn't know who my friends are. Believe me, I'm connected. Big business. We're talking billions. A lot more than any two-bit casino in a warehouse."

Liam stood. "I'll deliver the message."

"Easy, not so fast," Hackney said. "There's more. Sit down."

Junior smiled now. "I'm sorry I told my dad about the cheating, but I had to. You see, I told him the rest of what we talked about, too. About how you could help us. And how we can help you."

Liam sat back down. "I'm listening."

Hackney smiled. "I know Junior told you we're looking for a new night manager," he began, "but potentially it could be much more." In fact, his gut told him that this Irish kid was going to work out great. Once they broke ground on the Westlands, he and Junior would be focused there. This Liam could run the hotel, maybe with Josh, the Israeli, as head of security after he moved Riley to the new site. Or maybe he could use Josh there. He liked the way Josh had dealt with those protestors. Those Israelis knew how to handle nonsense. "The main thing is, we need to know we can trust you. That you're on the winning side."

"I always am," Liam said. "Despite my tragic Irish nature."

Hackney stared.

"A joke."

Hackney laughed, sort of, and Junior patted his shoulder.

"I told him you were our kind of guy," Junior said.

Now Hackney stood and opened a desk drawer, removing a small box wrapped in plain brown paper. "That's good, that's what I like to hear. And just to show us you're serious, and to kind of, you know, make up for the cheating, I hope you'll do me this little favor."

"What kind of favor?" Liam asked, staring dubiously at the box.

"It's nothing, really. Just deliver this to the Russian girl, Olga." He held it out.

Junior leaned in. "And make sure your boss doesn't know."

Back in the Imperial Suite, Joe, Yelena, Josh, and Cash were watching this scene unfold on Cash's tablet, beamed in from Juno's headquarters. The screen was propped up against a vase on the table. Cash was eating a bagel and lox. Josh was eating granola. Yelena drank tea and picked at croissants. Joe drank coffee and picked over his plan.

"Looks like someone's got a secret admirer," he said.

"Yeah, Josh," Cash said.

Josh laughed at this. "He's just got a thing for Israelis. Happens all the time." He was wearing his shirt and tie, with his uniform jacket over the back of the chair. Cash was in his chauffeur's outfit. Yelena wore her robe. Joe was in suit pants and an untucked dress shirt, the tie loose around his neck, as he postponed tying it to the last second.

There was a knock on the door—two short raps, a pause, one more, then two again—Liam. He swiped and came in.

"Special delivery for Yelena," he sang out. "Did you catch all that?"

"Brilliant performance," Josh said, squeezing his hand.

Cash had turned down the volume on the office feed. Junior had left and Hackney was on the phone again, yelling at someone else. "You were disturbingly compelling as a double-crosser."

Liam took a seat. "I saw my character more as a frustrated soul lashing out at a toxic father figure." He clapped Joe on the back and placed the package on his empty plate. "There you go."

Joe pushed it toward Yelena. "It's addressed to you, Olga."

She wiped the crumbs from her hands, then grabbed a knife and slit the paper. It was a small gift box. She looked at the others, who were all watching expectantly, and shrugged. Then she pulled off the lid. Wrapped in red tissue, there was a small gold lock on a golden chain. She drew it out.

"It has an *O*," she said, showing the engraving. "And there's a note." She pulled the paper out and handed it to Joe, while she inspected the lock.

Joe read aloud, "My Dear Mistress Olga, Please accept this small token of my esteem. I invite you to join me for a private meeting to discuss a matter of great mutual interest and profit. One P.M. Suite 3003. Yours sincerely, Jim."

Yelena got up and went to her room, returning with a small leather fold full of lock picks. Joe turned to Josh.

"Thirty-oh-three. Does that mean anything?"

Josh shook his head. "No. But I'll try to check it when I go on duty at twelve."

Joe rubbed his head, irritably. "I wish we had time to get cameras in there."

Yelena grinned. "Why? You want to watch us, Joe?" She held the lock up under the light. "See? There is a little keyhole but no key." She slid a pick in and probed delicately for a moment. It popped open, a locket as well as a lock. She held it up, a tiny hollow. "Empty."

⚬━╾⚬

Daisy woke up in darkness. She was someplace cold and damp, on a hard surface, concrete or stone. Her wrists were manacled, chained to the wall, so movement was constrained. She could tell she was stripped to her undergarments from the air on her skin. But there was something around her neck. She strained to touch it and then suddenly she recalled: it was the gold lock on the chain.

Panic surged, and she thought she would scream or puke or faint, but she forced herself to breathe deeply, steadily, calming her nerves, slowing her heartbeat. She reconstructed the course of events, the last things she remembered: the message from the old guy—Jim, he was called—the big shot. The driver, with the gold lock in a box. Then walking into the suite and being momentarily distracted by how nice it was, candles, flowers, a view. Then something moving behind her. Then blank. He knocked her out, maybe? Her head hurt. No, she'd have a sore spot, not this throb coming from the inside. Drugs. He injected her or something. That was all she recalled. Except for the suite number: 3003.

Then, as her eyes adjusted, she saw more. She was in some large barren space, a basement or warehouse or something, with exposed pipes rusting away on the walls. She heard rats scratching. Water dripped. Flies buzzed. And something smelled very bad. And then, slowly, in the shadows, she made out the forms. They were bodies.

Several skeletons close enough to see, and others that were just silhouettes. And one, still recognizable, sort of, was a woman, flesh rotting, teeth and eyes bared, but she could see the swollen rotten wrists still chained to the wall, like she was. And then, without being able to stifle it, she started to scream.

45

Cash wired up Yelena. While Juno directed him, monitoring the sound from home, he attached the tiny mic to her dress, a tight black number that clung to bust, ribs, hips, and thighs, leaving her shoulders bare. He attached it at the back, by the zipper, and hid the tiny wire that acted as a transmitter behind the label. Her hair, brushed out, covered it all. Her receiver, a tiny earpiece, fitted into her left ear, invisible unless you got in there and really peeked. She taped a combat knife inside her high-heeled boot, which slid over her calves to just beneath the knee.

"We'll be listening from here," Joe reminded her, pacing nervously, reminding himself really, while she sat calmly and regarded herself in the mirror. "And Josh is going to find a reason to be on that floor."

Josh had checked the registry when he began his shift. Suite 3003 was held in reserve, in theory for in-house needs such as a comped guest or extra office space, but there was no record of it ever being used. It was technically occupied but empty. A ghost room.

"So if anything goes wrong," Joe continued, "if he tries anything at all, just say the word and we're there."

Yelena lifted the gold lock to her throat and held the ends behind her.

"If he tries anything," she said, while Joe bent over and shut the clasp, "I will stab him through the heart. Don't forget"—she patted him reassuringly on the hand, then touched the bright lock—"I have killed bigger men than him, with smaller knives."

"Come in!"

Yelena opened the door marked 3003 and entered. It was a suite—bedroom and sitting room—all done in elegant black and white: polished black or glass tables, white or black leather modern chairs and couches, thick white throw rugs on gleaming dark floors. There were white flowers. The view was, needless to say, spectacular.

Hackney was there, posed in an armchair, in a blue suit, gold cuff links, gold tie, and pocket square sprouting like a napkin from a goblet at a wedding. Yelena could smell the cologne. She had an acute sense of smell and knew that his cologne was quite expensive, but it was not one of which she approved. She was severe in such matters. She remembered noticing, during their first job together, that Joe had a pleasant natural scent. Without that nothing else would have been possible. It was difficult for her to even be friends, for example, with someone who used a skin cream she found repellent. Once, she had stopped going to a hairstylist who used the cologne this Hackney person had on now.

"Thank you for coming, and welcome to my little private retreat," he intoned as she entered, sweeping a hand over his domain. But he got no further with his planned speech. As soon as the door shut behind her, Yelena marched across the room until she was standing right over him. She ripped the gold lock from her neck, breaking the chain, and threw it at him, catching him in the eye.

"Ow! Shit!" he cried, clutching his eye and ducking as she glared down.

"How dare you send me this piece of worthless shit!"

"But it's gold—"

"Bah," she spat. "Eighteen-carat crap at best. Do you think you can buy me with such a cheap bauble?"

"No I . . ." He tried to rally while still shielding his face. Also she was too close now for him to stand up, looming down. "It was merely a token—"

"And a lock?" she hissed. "Do you dare to think that I, Mistress Olga, would submit to you, you little piglet? You're not worthy to lick my boots, one of which costs more than this tasteless gift. I have come only to spit in your face personally." She did so, spraying him full in the face. "And now I leave."

He sat stunned for a moment, staring, but as she turned to go, he jumped to his feet. "You bitch," he roared. "Who the hell do you think you are? I own this goddamn place. Don't you know who I am?"

As she reached for the door handle, pulling it open, he hurled himself against it, slamming it shut, and grabbed her by the arm. "Nobody spits in my face. Especially not a worthless whore!"

Without hesitating, Yelena smacked him, hard, right across the face. Hackney froze, his red face white where she'd hit him. His eyes bulged. A tremor ran through him. Some spittle bubbled at the corner of his mouth.

Yelena held her breath and waited to be murdered. She'd come here as bait, and now here she was, face-to-face with the beast in his lair. She'd maneuvered herself close to the door, with her back to the wall, to make it as hard as possible for him to knock her out or surprise her, though she still had his bulk, and now his fury, between herself and freedom. But she didn't want to escape, not yet. She needed to see what he'd do. So she waited, judging the seconds it would take the others to kick the door in, figuring the distance from her fingertips to the knife in her boot, and weighing it all against how quickly he could get his hands, which shook in fists before her, around her throat.

Outside, in the hallway, Josh held his breath. When the sound of Hackney's shouting and a scuffle in the room came over the wire, Joe, Liam, and Cash had all flinched. Cash had gasped audibly, standing up as if ready to fight himself. Liam had blurted: "Josh, get over there!" Only Joe had stayed still, and silent.

Josh hurried from the elevators, where he was loitering as if waiting for a car, down to the door of 3003. He had his all-access key card out and was ready to go in.

"I'm here," he'd whispered into his own mic.

"Wait," Joe said in his ear. Back in their suite, Joe was straining, listening hard, as if to make sure Yelena was still breathing. There was no one whose ability to survive and escape he ranked higher. She had more moves, and more lives, than a cat. But every now and then even a cat takes a leap and misses, and falls. "Hold steady, Josh," he whispered, as if right into Josh's ear, and Josh waited, holding his breath, while Yelena faced Hackney a few inches away, behind the door.

Then Yelena spoke, her voice clear and defiant in all their ears: "Don't you ever touch me without permission again." And they all exhaled.

<hr />

"Don't you ever touch me without permission again," Yelena told Hackney, her voice cold and hard, her eyes on his, close enough to smell not only his cologne but his coffee-flavored breath. "You call me a whore? Well then, this whore is too expensive for you. Men pay all they have just to kiss my feet or sniff my panties. And what they buy isn't sex. It's something too rare for you to understand." She looked him up and down. "Now get out of my way."

He took a breath. His blood pressure seemed to decrease as he stepped back and smoothed his hair and jacket. "Now hold on just a second," he said. He held up his hands, as if offering a truce, and then drew a plump envelope from his pocket. "Let's both just calm down. The necklace was just a token. This is what I wanted to give you." He handed it over.

Curling her lip, Yelena slit it open with a nail. She sniffed slightly as she riffled the bills. Ten thousand in nice crisp hundreds.

"I'm sorry if we got off on the wrong foot here," Hackney continued. "Let's just sit down and talk."

"For this," she declared, folding the envelope, "I will hear your request. That is all." She sat in the armchair he had occupied and crossed her legs as she removed a cigarette from her purse. "I'm waiting," she said, holding it between two fingers.

"Right, sorry . . ." He looked around, grabbed a table lighter from the coffee table and gave her a light, then drew his cigar case. "Mind if I join you?"

"Yes I do," Yelena answered, blowing smoke. "I find cigars disgusting." She tapped ash onto the carpet. "Now what do you want? Time is running away."

"Right." He sat on the couch. "First let me be clear, that envelope is of course just a down payment. All the money that he thinks I owe him, I will give you all of it, and more, if you'd . . ." He paused, not sure how to phrase this. "If you'll provide the same . . ."

"You want me to be your mistress?" Yelena asked drily.

He nodded vigorously. "Yes. And whatever he is giving you, I can double . . ."

Now he trailed off, as Yelena, chuckling softly as at a private joke, drew one of the hundreds from the envelope and, with the tip of her cigarette, slowly lit the corner.

"Why?" she asked. "Because you are jealous of him? Because he bested you in the, how do you say, pissing contest? You silly men. Like children in the playpen." Here the bill caught, and flamed out, and she dropped it in the ashtray, then tapped more ash on the white rug. She lit another bill. "I am not a school prize. Not a horse or some kind of car to be shown off or sold for new model." The bill flamed and she dropped it. "That is what wives are for." She lit another, thoughtfully, watching it curl, then added it to the tray like a pile of autumn leaves. "No. Sorry. I am not interested." She stood, tossing the cigarette onto the pile of money, where it smoldered. "Time is up."

As he rushed to put out her cigarette butt, she started to leave again. From behind her she heard him again, but it was almost as if another person, a brother or twin, perhaps, had stepped into the room. This version of his voice was sincere, plaintive, lacking the bark and bluster. "I need to be punished," he said. "Please."

She stopped. She turned. She stared and waited, impassively. He got on his knees, kneeling slowly on stiff joints. The crumpled suit, which had seemed a bit tight, now seemed big, drooping off his shoulders, bunching up. Yelena considered him gravely. The look in his eyes was desperate.

"For what?" she asked.

⚬━╾⚬

"Twenty years ago, my wife and I, and our son, he was five, we were in an accident. A car crash. I was driving. It was a snowy night, the road was icy. This was in Vermont. It was an accident, we hit a patch of black ice and skidded. But I'd been drinking. And going too fast. And my wife had begged me not to drive, to spend the night at her family's place. But I didn't listen. I'd been arguing with my father-in-law. Anyway, I wanted to go home, back to our condo, and we crashed. We skidded off the road and down a hill. It was my fault. My son was OK. He was in his car seat in back. But Anne, she . . ." Here he stopped. He was looking at the carpet. Yelena stood very still. "The car came down on her side, the passenger side and her legs were crushed. Also, she"—he gulped air, as if gathering the strength to lift something—"she was pregnant. We lost the child. And after that she couldn't. We couldn't." He broke off. "I haven't even talked about this in years. Centuries, it feels like."

She sat back down, this time with her back straight, watching him. She spoke softly. "Go on. I'm listening."

"Well, after that my wife got very religious—she thought it was some kind of punishment from God. Anyway, that was her way of dealing with it. And coddling her son. I didn't like it. Boys need to be tough to face the world, like my dad showed me, but she was so afraid that God would take him, too. And yet at the same time I think she felt ashamed, guilty, that she couldn't be, you know, a wife to me in that way. In bed. And me . . ." He shrugged. "Well, I've been through a thousand women since then. But all of them, you know . . ."

"Professionals?"

"Yeah, right, call girls, women at brothels. I became known as a ladies' man, a philanderer, I guess. But I didn't want a girlfriend. I love my wife, and I thought it was better to keep things business-like. No strings. And it does make me feel better. You're right. Like a good cigar or a great meal. Like a luxury I can afford. But the thing is, usually, when it comes down to it, with most of these girls, I can't really . . . you know . . . perform. Unless there's some kind of element of domination. Them punishing me, humiliating me. That seems to help."

He cleared his throat now. He seemed relieved, over the embarrassment. He looked up at her and she held his gaze. "That's why I wanted to see you. I mean, at first, I admit, it was just competition, like you said. I wanted to steal his girl, his prize. But when I heard how you control him, how you have him in that thing . . ."

"In chastity."

"Yes. Collared. Owned." Now he inched forward on his knees, and she could see it wasn't easy, at his weight and age. He knelt low, his hands together, more in supplication than desire. Like a prayer. "Please, Mistress," he whispered now. "Please give me what I deserve."

Yelena took a moment. Partly for effect, she was playing her part, but partly to think. This was not the sort of confession she had hoped for. Finally she spoke: "I accept you as my slave."

He exhaled heavily. His body slumped in relief.

"Now strip."

"What? You mean right now?"

"Yes. Right now. And the correct reply is 'Yes, Mistress.'"

He nodded. "Sorry, sorry. Yes, Mistress." He stood, leveraging himself on one knee first, then grabbing the couch and rising. Then he sat and began to disrobe, folding his clothes.

"Faster," Yelena ordered. "I want to see my property."

"Yes, yes, Mistress," he stammered, and quickly stripped down to his briefs. He was pale and blotchy, flabby but not that hairy. He was clearly embarrassed, arms crossed. Despite his many trysts, this arrangement, being stripped while a woman was dressed, was obviously new to him, and he looked vulnerable. He seemed about to ask something, and then, thinking better of it, he held his tongue and slowly lowered his briefs.

Yelena chuckled. "That little thing is the cause of all this trouble? Too bad we can't just snip it off." She waved an arm. "Very well. Go shower now. And make sure you are clean. Shampoo and everything. The smell of your cologne nauseates me."

"Yes, Mistress . . ." He hesitated, wanting to gather his clothes.

"Go!" She pointed and he went, shuffling in his socks. She heard the bathroom door shut and then the shower. Immediately, she spoke into her mic. "You hear all that?"

Joe spoke. "We sure did."

"Jesus Christ," she whispered. "That was not what I signed up for."

"I know, just finish up quick."

She reached into her purse and pulled out the device Juno had provided, a small metal detector made to look like a phone. Switching it on, she moved around the room, waving it in front of walls and over shelves. Finally, it lit up over an abstract black-and-white painting and she checked: a small safe.

"Found it," she said.

"Good. Any trouble?"

"Not for Mistress Olga," she answered, replacing the painting, while steam began to drift in from the bathroom. Then she gathered Hackney's clothes—suit, shirt, underwear, everything but his tie, handkerchief, and shoes—and she left, shutting the door behind her.

46

"Want something to drink?" Juno knelt over the minifridge he kept stocked downstairs.

"Thanks. I'll take an orange pop." Jem walked a slow circle, checking out the gear. Juno was glad he'd cleaned up, or at least hidden the dirty laundry under the covers when he made the bed, though it now looked kind of like somebody was sleeping under there.

"I don't have pop," he said. "Just Coke, orange soda, water, seltzer, grape Snapple . . ."

"Sorry, *pop* is what we call soda. I keep forgetting you don't say that here."

"Really?" Juno had barely ever been anywhere. Down south to see relatives in Georgia and North Carolina, this last trip to Florida with Yelena, not that he even got to swim. He tried out the word: "Pop!" He liked it but couldn't see it catching on. "You know my cousins down in Georgia call all sodas Cokes, like even if it's grape or whatever."

"Really?" Jem frowned. "That sounds confusing."

"What do y'all call Snapple?" he asked now.

"Snapple," Jem said, and that seemed to exhaust the topic. He gave her a can of Fanta and took a grape Snapple for himself.

"Thanks. I love your setup," she said. "It's really cool."

"Thanks, it's coming along," he said, smacking the lump under the cover a few times as he passed the bed to smooth things out and make it clear there was no one sleeping or dead in there. "Got the recording booth set up now for . . . recording." He cleared his throat and sat in his Aeron swivel chair, where he felt more himself. "Pull up a seat and I'll show you what I've got going."

She took the second-best chair, which was just a regular desk chair, but it had wheels.

"That is the live feed from the cameras in Hackney's office." Juno pointed his Snapple at the screen, which just showed the empty room. "Nothing much happening there now. This is what is currently on his screen," which was also nothing much, a screensaver with his family crest. "But this," he said proudly, pointing to another screen that showed a host of open tabs and documents, "is the fun part—a full copy of everything on his hard drive."

"Sweet," she said. "May I?" As she leaned in over the keyboard, Juno smelled expensive shampoo. It was actually Yelena's.

After the casino, Joe had sent Cash, in the Rolls, to pick her and Midnight up at Gladys's place and bring her to Yelena's, where she settled into the guest room. In some ways it was all over the rainbow: suddenly she went from near-homeless couch surfer to a luxury condo overlooking the ocean, but she felt useless, restless. She couldn't work, of course, or see clients, and she wasn't sure she'd want to when she could. Gladys thought she'd make a great pickpocket, but that was a long way off. But most of all, she wanted to help, to be part of the team that was avenging Ioana's death and taking a killer off the streets. That had been the real thrill at the casino, the feeling of empowerment, of being activated. So when she mentioned how she had some basic skills in web design, and Juno said she could help with his next task, she happily agreed. Plus she thought he was cute. And sweet. And clearly a brilliant hacker.

"Help yourself," he said now, and rolled his chair right so that she could get in there. She clicked the keys and started opening things, as he went on: "Now, I already pulled the info Joe wanted, the records and stuff, so what we got to do next is figure out which sites to clone."

"Let's see what sites he visits most often," she suggested, then: "Oh . . ." There was an embarrassed silence as porn sites and call girl agencies popped open on the large screen. Juno had never realized quite how large it was.

"We definitely don't have to clone those," he said finally.

"Right. I'll just shut them then," Jem said, and began hastily X-ing them out, when Juno's phone mercifully rang.

"Yo, Cash, what up?"

Cash was on his way over to get the swipe card Juno had made. And Yelena needed her safecracking gear.

Where the hell was Daisy?

Donna looked at her watch. The day was flying by. She dialed the phone between bites of her sandwich. "Daisy, it's Donna, Agent Zamora. I'm sure you're wiped out, but we need you down here to finish your debriefing. Please call me back as soon as you get this. Thanks."

Donna had an uneasy feeling. If anyone deserved to sleep in, it was Daisy, but this was not the day to play hooky. And while CIs, by their very nature, were flaky, Daisy's eagerness to get her green card processing in motion made it unlikely she'd simply blow Donna off. Then she checked her own cell just to be sure she hadn't called that or texted. No. And nothing from Joe, either. Not that she was ready to talk to him, but still some part of her, illogically, wanted him to want to talk to her. Instead, like a lovesick teenager, she listened again to his last message, thought about deleting it, then saved it and put her phone away. For later. For now, she finished lunch and got back to work. The previous night's bust had triggered an avalanche of paperwork. It would be hours before she could dig herself out, and she couldn't drop it all to chase a CI or an MIA boyfriend.

What the hell was Joe up to anyway? And where the hell was Daisy?

47

Joe swiped them into Suite 3003.

He and Yelena were dressed as a waiter and a maid, respectively, in uniforms that Josh had borrowed from the basement. Joe had a fake mustache and glasses, Yelena a maid's cap and glasses of her own as well as different makeup. They were not hoping to completely alter their appearances, only to disappear into the atmosphere, to become invisible to ordinary guests and upper management. Their stolen name tags read *Svetlana* and *Franco*. Hackney and Junior were in the office, where Juno was monitoring them. Josh was watching the security cameras, doing his job, sort of, but keeping a special eye on that floor.

"Housekeeping!" Yelena trilled as they entered, just to be sure, and Joe checked the bedroom and bathroom. There was no one around. Yelena slid on surgical gloves then removed the painting and got to work, unpacking her stethoscope, her little notebook, her mechanical pencil. (This stuff was new. Her last stethoscope had melted in a fire set to destroy evidence, and Joe had buried her favorite mechanical pencil in a terrorist's eye.) Joe stood watch by the door. Through his earpiece and the mic under his collar, he kept in communication with both Josh and Juno.

"Try to be quick," he told Yelena. "We don't know when they'll come back here."

"If you want quick, I can cut it. If you want clean, it will take as long as it takes."

"Right," Joe said. "That's what I meant."

And then she had the stethoscope in her ears as she slowly clicked the dial, listening patiently for the first of the numbers she would record in the elaborate and painstaking process of elimination, and he was silent, peeking through the peephole at an empty patch of hall, until Juno spoke in his ear.

"Yo, I think it's showtime. That City Council lady just got to the office."

"Good," Joe said softly into his mic. "Tape it."

"Already am, but it ain't been tape for decades."

"Whatever," he replied. "Thanks, Juno."

Councilwoman Schlitz was in a hurry.

" Jim, Junior, good to see you," she greeted them as she hustled in, wearing a white belted cashmere coat over a dark blue pantsuit, chunks of gold at her neck and wrists and fingers.

"Amy!" Hackney stood but remained behind his desk, while his son came over and shook hands. "Thanks for coming. Have a seat. Junior, help the lady off with her coat."

She sat but kept her coat on. "Sorry but I can't stay long. I've got that zoning thing today."

Junior perched on the corner of the desk. Jim leaned back into his chair. "We won't keep you from the people's business. Speaking of which, you were very impressive at the demonstration."

She laughed, a short bark, and tossed her hair. "You know how the folks love a show. Let them get their frustrations out. It won't make any difference when we vote." She wagged a finger at him. "But you need to reign your goons in. A grandma got knocked over. I took care of it, sent flowers and posed for a picture. But if she'd broken a hip or something, Jesus, the headlines."

"My son handles site security," Jim said.

Junior leaned toward her. "We've had to tighten up, bring in new people, but I will make sure they are careful with civilians."

"*Constituents* is what I call them, kid."

"Yes, ma'am."

"But the council vote," Hackney added, leaning forward now, elbows on desk. "That's a done deal?"

"Bought and paid for, as you well know. The question is, do you have the funds on hand?" She sat back, looking like a stern vice principal. "I know you had some issues there."

Hackney took out a cigar and lit it. He grinned. "Ten million, courtesy of our friends who shall remain nameless. I can show you the bank balance if you want." He held a hand out toward his computer. Junior tapped some keys and swung the screen toward Schlitz. She lifted her reading glasses over her eyes and gave it a glance.

"Fine." She sat back, crossing her legs. "But it's the balance in *my* bank that I care about." She lifted her purse and opened it, removing a slip of paper. "Which brings me to the reason for my visit." She handed the paper to Junior, who glanced at it then put it on the blotter before his father. "That's my Caymans account."

"Wise choice, the Caymans are lovely. And convenient. You can fly down anytime and visit your money."

"And when will that be?" Schlitz asked.

Hackney shrugged. "Government bureaucracy is your department, you tell me. But paperwork aside, after the vote, the lease becomes official, and we make the payment. Then we can start awarding the contracts and taking in investment."

"There's no problem there," Junior said. "Two hundred million from Russian banks, ready to flow."

"And the first round of bids on excavation, hauling, concrete, steel, already set with our friends," Hackney said, blowing blue smoke at the ceiling. "Don't worry, Councilwoman, you're going to have a very well-feathered nest down there in the Caribbean."

"That's what I came to hear," she said. She stood, hand out. "Gentlemen."

"Ma'am," Junior said, shaking her hand.

Hackney leaned over the desk to shake hands as well. "Councilwoman, it's always an honor."

⚬━━╾⚬

"Got 'em," Juno said, grinning big.

"So that's it then?" Jem asked. They were watching the live feed from Hackney's office. The lady politician, Schlitz, was shaking hands with father and son. "That's what we've been waiting to see?"

"It'll do nicely." He replayed the recording on another screen, checking the sound on his headphones. "Now we need to prep our little news bulletin," Juno said.

"Coming right up." Jem clicked the keys. Sifting through Hackney's browser histories and tabs, they'd found some news websites that he checked daily, especially *Celebrity Report*, *Real News*, and *Top Secret International*, trashy sites specializing in scandals and rumormongering. They had copied the front pages of each site and now began to use these as scaffolds on which to construct their own versions. While Juno handled the heavy coding and the video edit, Jem wrote the copy. They worked in companionable silence. At one point Juno retrieved another orange pop and purple Snapple from the fridge, opening the can before he set it before her.

"What a gentleman," she commented. He grinned but said nothing and they kept at it, fingers flying over the keys, until Jem sat back and took a deep breath. "I think I've got something."

"Hit me with it," Juno said, swiveling her way.

"It's just a first draft, but—"

"Come on, quit the hemming and hawing, let's hear it."

She took a deep breath. "OK, here's the headline. 'Caught in the Wild Westlands: Dirty Developers Collude with Corrupt Councilwoman. Jim Hackney, would-be developer of the controversial Westlands project, along with his son, party boy and big-game hunter Jim Jr., have been caught red-handed conspiring with Councilwoman Amy Schlitz, as the treacherous trio discuss payoffs, fixed city council votes, and rigged contract bidding on the multi-billion-dollar deal . . .'"

<hr />

"Open," Yelena said, as the dial clicked, and she pulled back the door of the safe.

Joe hurried over. "Nice work," he told her, reaching for a pair of gloves. "What have we got?"

"I'm not sure," she said, pulling out some family memorabilia: a framed photo of Mr. and Mrs. Hackney at their wedding, a bronzed baby shoe, a silver spoon. Some antique jewelry and an old pocket watch in a felt bag. She handed each item to Joe, who examined it impatiently. Then she removed a wooden box lined in velvet. She opened it and sighed heavily.

"Anything good?"

"I don't think *good* is the word," she said, and showed him. The box contained at least a half-dozen gold locks on chains, just like the one Yelena had been given, each inscribed with an initial. There was also a small gold key. She held it up and he nodded. She opened a lock. Inside was a tiny bundle of black hair.

"Yuck," Yelena said. "It's hair. What the hell does that mean?"

Joe shrugged. "In the olden days, women gave men a lock of hair as a token. Try another."

She did. This one was blond. Then next was reddish auburn. Then black again, but finer, Asian hair. The same key fit them all.

Neither of them spoke until they opened all six. Then Yelena asked, in a whisper: "You think they are, what is the word? Not *keepsakes*. Souvenirs?"

Joe nodded. "Trophies."

Joe thought about what to do. Then he searched Yelena's tool bag and found a roll of tape that she would use on glass before breaking it or to help rig a safe she wanted to blow. He tore off small strips and wrote the initial from a lock on each. Then, while Yelena took photos of the locks and their contents, he got the tiny tweezers from his utility knife and removed a hair or two from each lock, fixing it to the appropriate strip of tape. Then he stuck them all to a sheet of paper. He was especially interested in the one marked *I*.

Together they repacked the locks in their box, then replaced it and the other items in the safe. Yelena relocked it and Joe rehung the painting. Yelena straightened it.

"We're coming out," Joe said to Josh over his mic.

"You're clear," he said. "Just take the service elevator right down."

They left the suite, locking the door behind them. A guest, bundled in a puffy coat, came out of her door as they passed, but she just nodded vaguely and walked by. She didn't even see them.

Back in his suite, Joe removed his disguise and dropped it all in a plastic bag to be thrown in an outside trash can. Then he called Gio, staring at the row of labeled tape on the sheet of paper that lay on the table before him.

"What's up?" Gio asked. "I can't really talk. I'm shopping with the kids."

"Your friend on the force," Joe said, keeping it general. "I have a little errand for him."

"What kind of errand?" Gio asked suspiciously.

"Detective work."

48

Fusco didn't want to know.

He didn't want to know who this kid on the motorcycle was and was glad he didn't take off the helmet. He just pulled up at the Midtown corner where Fusco was told to meet, and where he sat in his car with the heat cranked and the engine running, smoking and brooding on his latest football losses, as a second line of smoke rose like a tail from his exhaust pipe, a gray thread unraveling in the frigid air. He heard the bike before he saw it, a fancy yellow number. Without dismounting, the driver leaned over and thumped the window with a heavy glove. He lowered it.

"Fusco?" the kid asked, a male voice, local accent.

Fusco nodded.

"ID?"

With a sigh he shifted onto one ass cheek and pulled out his badge. The kid handed over an envelope, waved, and roared off. Fusco looked down. It was, for some reason, Hackney Tower Hotel stationery. He didn't want to know.

Then he drove to Kips Bay, where the nation's largest DNA crime lab hummed away. The staff worked around the clock in a sterile facility, breathing purified air, processing the more than fourteen thousand pieces of evidence that would be handled that year. Fortunately for Fusco, one of those staff owed him a big favor. He'd gotten pulled over for DUI, not for the first time, and Fusco had made it disappear.

Now he laid the envelope on the desk. Dooley, the red-haired, red-eyed scientist, looked at it unhappily.

"There are hair samples in here," Fusco told him. "First run them against the victim on that open homicide, Ioana Petrescu. Try the sample marked *I* first."

"The floater?"

"Right. Then try the others against any other unidentified young females you've got, just in case."

"But this won't be admissible. It's not logged in properly, there's no chain of custody."

"I won't be submitting it. That's why I'm bringing it to you, privately. I'm just running down an anonymous tip. If it hits, we will follow it up. Whatever, that's not your problem."

Dooley sighed. "And when do you need this?"

"Now. Tonight." Dooley started squirming, but Fusco leaned into him, looked him in the eye. "Just get it done, Dooley, and then you can finish your shift and drive home safely, with a clear conscience. Right?"

Dooley nodded. He sighed as he pulled on gloves, the latex snapping, and turned over the envelope. "But this isn't even an evidence bag. Why's it in here?"

Fusco turned to leave. "You don't want to know."

Donna checked the hotel.

At the end of the day, she'd tried Daisy again, leaving a pissed-off message this time—she was gumming up the works and Donna's boss, and his boss, wanted this case wrapped up with a bow. But then felt bad—Daisy had been traumatized, after all, and maybe she was having some kind of PTSD breakdown. So she left another, compassionate message just before leaving to go home. Then it was homework and dollhouse and dinner with Larissa. Then bathtime and bedtime.

She was also deliberately not checking her phone because she was trying not to notice that Joe had not called—although of course she did not intend to answer if he did. Still she wanted him to try, at least, which she knew was, well, sick, yet appropriate in that it perfectly summed up her conflicted feelings. But of course it was early for Joe. He came late, like a thief in the night, or a stray cat meowing on the fire escape.

So it was after nine when she checked her phone, checked her work line, and finally decided she had to do something. Her first move was to call her mom, who agreed to come across the hall and watch *The Crown* at Donna's. Then she went to the hotel where they'd put Daisy and, showing her badge, got the manager to open the door to her room.

Her belongings, such as they were, were scattered around, her duffel bag was there, and there were towels and makeup out, suggesting, at least, that Daisy had not taken off for any reason. Nor were there any signs of struggle. That was the good news. On the other hand, the bed, made up hotel-tight, had clearly not been slept in. That was not so good.

⚬━✦━⚬

Daisy's darkness was total. It was the darkness of a bank vault, or of (she tried to keep herself from thinking, over and over) the grave. She was in concrete, not dirt, and she could breathe, thank God, but otherwise she was buried alive. Entombed. Already dead.

She knew, from the weak light that filtered in from shafts here and there, that a day had passed. A day without water or food. It was also very cold, and she felt herself slowly going numb, though she tried to keep her blood pumping by moving as much as she could, as much as the chains would allow. She'd given up yelling or scheming how to get out, and now she just focused on living, on staying alive and not thinking about dying, but even that was getting harder. Then in the darkness, she heard the rats come out. One nibbled her toe, just testing, a tickle really, and she freaked, kicking out and screaming, and they ran away chattering as her voice echoed down the tunnel. Then she heard them eating the other woman. And she started to cry.

49

Next morning, Jim Hackney checked the news.

Though *news* was a relative term, especially these days. He had already looked over the *Times* at breakfast—he had a print edition delivered—and he skimmed through his *Wall Street Journal* now as his assistant brought coffee, pausing only if he thought the article concerned his interests directly or if it detailed the triumph or downfall of someone he considered a peer, friend, or rival. Then, his obligations fulfilled, he checked the news that really mattered to him. First up was the *Real News* website. He grinned in anticipation: Would someone he knew or looked up to or down upon be exposed and humiliated, going bankrupt or getting divorced, or perhaps caught checking into rehab or sneaking out of a psych ward? Instead, he saw himself and his son.

> "Caught in the Wild Westlands: Dirty Developers Collude with Corrupt Councilwoman. Jim Hackney, would-be developer of the controversial Westlands project, along with his son, party boy and big-game hunter Jim Jr., have been caught red-handed conspiring with Councilwoman Amy Schlitz, as the treacherous trio discuss payoffs, fixed city council votes, and rigged contract bidding on the multi-billion-dollar deal . . ."

"What the goddamn fuck?" He clicked on the video and it began to play. It was indeed himself, Junior, and Amy Schlitz, in this very office the day before:

"But the council vote," Hackney saw himself saying on-screen, leaning forward just as he was now, elbows on the desk. *"That's a done deal?"*

"Bought and paid for, as you well know," the councilwoman was saying, sitting back in her white overcoat. *"The question is, do you have the funds on hand?"*

Panicked, he hit Mute, as if that would protect him. "Junior, quick! Come look at this . . ." His son came around to stand behind his chair. Flustered, he fumbled with the buttons, then got the video going again.

Now he was smoking a cigar on-screen, waving it as he spoke: *"Government bureaucracy is your department, you tell me. But paperwork aside, after the vote, the lease becomes official, and we make the payment. Then we can start awarding the contracts and taking in investment."*

"Oh my God," Junior said, leaning over his dad's shoulder as he watched himself chime in on-screen.

"There's no problem there," he was saying. *"Two hundred million from Russian banks, ready to flow."*

"And the first round of bids on excavation, hauling, concrete, steel, already set with our friends," Hackney added. *"Don't worry, Councilwoman, you're going to have a very well-feathered nest down there in the Caribbean."*

They both continued to mutter "Jesus" and "Christ" and "Oh my God" which were prayers, in a sense, as well as curses—as they read the comments, which were mounting rapidly and calling for them to be publicly hanged. They checked *Celebrity Report* and *TSI*. Both sites had it too. It was bad. Very, very bad.

"How did they get this? How?" Hackney demanded. He felt like he was on *The Twilight Zone*. "I mean, that is this office!"

"There must be a camera in here," Junior said, and then, as the idea dawned on him, "They could be taping this right now!"

At first both men began just wildly searching, which alarmed Juno, since Hackney, flailing about, almost dislodged the second backup camera on the shelf. But his son figured the angle, got a chair, and looked up in the corner by the ceiling. He found the camera and ripped it out. Juno got the second camera going. Jem meanwhile was exhausting herself, typing till her fingers ached, filling the comments section with: *They should be in jail! Crooks!*

Now seen in profile, both Hackneys were pacing, Senior puffing like a chimney, as they decided what to do.

"Listen, they haven't proven anything yet," Junior pointed out. "It's bad PR, but you know how long these investigations take. Let's just call the lawyers and sit tight. Say nothing. I doubt we even go to jail, and if we do, it will just be a little time in minimum security. We're white-collar, for crying out loud."

Hackney stared at him. "What the hell are you talking about? Are you too stupid to even understand what this means? Jail?" He snorted. "We'll be lucky to go to jail—at least it's safe. But not really. They can get us there, too. And by them I do not mean police."

"But that's not fair. It's not our fault. And we can spin it." Now Junior was the anxious one, pacing like a trapped animal, and his father was weirdly calm.

"These are gangsters. Killers. They don't care about fair or the color of our collars. They only have one way of spinning it."

"So what do we do, Dad?"

Hackney sat behind his desk. He glanced at the offending screen and turned it off. He looked at his son and shrugged. "We run."

In his basement, Juno sighed with relief. "That's it," he said, reaching for his phone. "That's a wrap."

Jem sat back, wriggling her cramped fingers. "Now what?" she asked. This was, she thought, the most exciting thing she'd ever done.

"Now we call Joe."

50

When the top bosses of the city's crime world began to gather in his basement, Juno thought to himself, *Thank God my mom's at work.* It was a busy day at the salon, he knew, and she would not be home till eight or nine, no doubt with some takeout in hand, some Jamaican jerk chicken or Dominican chicken and rice.

Even so, to avoid nosy neighbors, Gio had the line of Escalades, BMWs, Lexuses, and Mercedes pull up around the block in front of the DeVries place, which was behind Juno's. They were out of town. One at a time, Rebbe, Alonzo, Uncle Chen, Little Maria, and Jack Madigan each shuffled down the DeVries driveway, passing the old Caddy Mr. DeVries was always working on, cutting through the backyard with its birdbath and flower borders under burlap for winter, ducking through the shrubs where Cash was on hand to hold back the branches and direct them around Juno's mom's vegetable garden, to knock on the side door, where Juno waited to show them down to the basement. He and Jem had done their best to clean up, and Cash had helped them carry down extra chairs from the dining room.

"Careful, sir, that step's a little loose, sorry . . ." Juno said nervously as Rebbe edged down, regal in his black coat, high fur hat, and white beard, like a Satanic Santa. The hat hit the ceiling and wobbled. He muttered in Yiddish, catching it, and Uncle Chen steadied him, leaning in turn on Cash's shoulder. Chen wore a goose down coat, a wool hat, and gloves, but ordinary slacks and slip-on dress shoes.

Alonzo, dressed in a cashmere topcoat and scarf, put his hand out to help Little Maria, whose prosthetic was hidden by knee-high black boots, which did reveal sheer-stockinged legs under her long fur coat and matching hat. But she didn't need help. She had become so proficient on her shockproof limb that she came right down, limping only slightly.

It was short notice—word had gone out just a couple of hours before—but Gio assured them it was necessary. So they came. Still, it was a bit awkward. They greeted Gio and stood around. No one took off their coat. Alonzo, who knew Juno, greeted the young man warmly, but he had never been here. He looked around, removing his gloves, curiously noting both the high-tech equipment and the washer and dryer hidden behind a sheet. The last to enter were Joe and Yelena, she in a ski jacket now instead of the fur, Joe finally back in his own jeans and sweatshirt. Everyone looked over, acknowledging him expectantly, but he only nodded and stood against the wall.

"Welcome, everyone, it's an honor to have you," Juno nervously began, as if giving a speech at a wedding. "Please have a seat." He gestured to Rebbe and Uncle Chen, the seniors. "Mr. Um. Sir. Would you like to take the couch?"

"If I did, I'd have to take it home with me," Rebbe said. "Because I'd never get back out. I'll take a chair, thanks." He descended carefully onto one of the dining room chairs, and Uncle Chen took the one next to him.

"Mrs. Ms.?" Juno said to Little Maria, who ignored the hand he held out toward the couch and perched on his Aeron desk chair. He frowned but wisely said nothing. Gio, Alonzo, and Jack shared the couch. Cash tapped Jem on the shoulder and took her to sit quietly on the stairs, as if in the bleacher seats. Yelena perched on the arm of the couch.

"Would anyone like a drink?" Juno was asking. "We have orange soda, or pop. Grape Snapple. Or water. Or I can make coffee or tea."

At first they all shook their heads. Then Uncle Chen nodded. "I will take a Snapple." Juno rushed to get it.

Rebbe shrugged. "Orange soda."

"OK," Alonzo said. "Give me an orange, too."

The others stayed put as Juno handed out the drinks. Gio had a water already. He drank from it now, then he stood.

"Thanks everyone for coming so fast and so far. I know this is not our usual kind of hangout."

They chuckled.

"But to get all this technology set up and going someplace else would take too long, and you will see in a minute how important it is for our discussion. And how urgent." He nodded at Juno.

Now in the second-best chair, Juno rolled to the desk and politely inched the keyboard from in front of Maria. He tapped a few keys, and the live feed from Hackney's office came up.

"This is live," Juno said.

"That's Jim Hackney," Rebbe said.

"And his kid," Jack added.

"Correct," Juno said. "We have cameras and a mic in his office."

The two men were discussing flights, luggage, packing.

"So they are taking a trip," Maria said. "So what?"

"Juno, can you show us the screen?" Gio asked.

"Yes sir." He brought up the live mirror of Hackney's computer. "This is his computer right now. As you see, they are booking flights to the Cayman Islands, where their offshore accounts are, then Maldives."

"Which has no extradition to the U.S.," Gio noted.

"It also has nice beaches. And it is damn cold here. What is all this?" Maria said.

"Juno, the bank . . ." Gio prodded.

"Right . . ." He tapped madly. His throat was dry, but he didn't dare pause, and anyway, Uncle Chen had his last Snapple. He coughed.

"About one hour ago, Hackney and his son accessed the ten million dollars that was in the Hackney Realty Development Corporation account, ready to be paid out to the city as rent on the Westlands property, and transferred it to their offshore Caymans account." He brought up the account and logged in with the passwords he had obtained from Hackney earlier.

Now Maria was concerned. "*Hijo de la gran puta*," she muttered. "That is our money."

"Exactly," Gio said. "That is the ten million we staked Hackney for the Westlands project."

"Are we sure about this?" Alonzo asked. "Dead sure? I shook the man's hand, and honestly I don't think he has the balls to fuck all of us."

Uncle Chen spoke calmly. "I have a friend at the bank. Let me see." He drew a cell from his pocket and made a call, speaking Mandarin. The others watched Hackney and his son on the screen, shredding papers.

"That's never a good sign." Rebbe sighed.

Chen hung up. "It's true," he said. "The money is gone."

Now Yelena spoke: "Not gone. Just hiding."

Everyone looked at her.

"Joe suspected this might happen, so he had Juno take some precautions." She patted the young man on the shoulder. "Maybe you can explain it better. But keep it simple," she whispered.

"Yes, ma'am. When I hacked into Hackney's computer, Joe had me find all his banking info, including the records of transfers to the offshore account. He deletes that stuff, but I could still dig it out by—" Yelena prodded him, and he cleared his throat. "Right. Never mind. Anyway, we created a dummy version of the Caymans bank website and reprogrammed his browser to reroute traffic—"

Yelena interrupted. "He tried to steal your money. But when he thought he was transferring it to his Caymans account, it really went into another account. Our account."

This got a warm response. Uncle Chen patted Juno on the back and Maria gave him a kiss on the cheek.

"But why? That's the question," Jack said, sitting forward, peering at the screen. "He stood to make so much more by working with us. Ten million was barely lunch money on this job."

"That was my fault," Joe said from his spot at the back. Heads turned.

"How?" Maria asked. "Why?"

"We hired you to catch a killer," Alonzo said, "not scare off the golden goose."

Gio stood. "We brought Joe in to track someone down. That's where the trail led. Think about it. Rebbe? Uncle Chen? Alonzo? How do you all know him? As a customer in your brothels."

"A big customer," Chen said, shaking his head in dismay. "He spends a lot of money in my places. For a long time."

"That's right," Joe said, stepping into the center of the room. "He spent big money at all your places, hired all the top girls, and then one by one, they disappeared. Ioana, the girl they pulled out of the river? I found a witness who put her with Hackney just before she died."

At this Jem stiffened, like a cat, ears and back prickling, but Joe's eyes never looked her way.

"Then I found a pattern. All your missing girls, they took cars to Hackney Tower Hotel the night they went missing. I think he reached out to them behind your backs, lured them into moonlighting with lucrative offers, and made secret dates at a suite he kept in the hotel. No one else had access to it or knew about it, and he could use his private elevator to bring them in and out."

"So he is the *mamaguevo* killing our girls?" Maria asked. "I never like that pig. I thought he was just *aqueroso*, you know, talking shit. But this . . ." She shuddered and crossed herself.

"That's still not proof, Joey," Rebbe said.

"It's all circumstantial," Alonzo said. "We all know enough law to know that."

Now Gio pulled a printed sheet from his pocket. "Here's the proof." While he passed it around, Juno brought the photos Yelena had taken up on the screen.

Yelena spoke. "There's a safe in Hackney's secret suite. Me and Joe broke into it and found these gold lockets with hair and the missing girls' initials. We took samples."

"And I had my cop run the tests," Gio said. "That hair matches the DNA from Ioana."

Now there was silence, as the paper found its way back to Gio. For a moment, no one spoke or moved. Then, with a long sigh, Rebbe stood.

"Gio," he said, and kissed his cheek. "Give my love to the family." Then he clasped Joe's hand in both of his. "And, Joey, it's always a pleasure. But I'm late for my pinochle game." He turned to Chen. "Coming?"

With a nod, Uncle Chen, too, rose, as Cash hurried to open the door. The others quickly followed. In a minute, only Gio, Joe, Yelena, and Juno remained, with Jem still watching from the shadows.

Joe unstrapped the Patek Philippe watch and handed it to Gio, who slid it into his pocket. Gio leaned over to Juno. "Nice work."

"Thank you, sir," Juno said, eyeing the hand on his shoulder.

"Now make damned sure you delete all that shit we saw."

"Yes sir."

He squeezed the shoulder. "And whatever the fuck else you did that we didn't see."

Juno's eyes went to Joe, who smiled slyly and gave a little shrug.

"Yes sir," Juno repeated.

"You're a good kid," Gio said, and with a nod to the others, he left.

Jem didn't know what she had expected after Gio left, but the sudden change in demeanor, the calm but very focused, businesslike feeling in the air, made her stay still and quiet. The look on Joe's face was one she had never seen before. He didn't look angry or mean or anything, but all the warmth and good humor were gone. He looked cold. Cash appeared on the stairs.

"Car's ready, Joe."

Joe nodded. "Good." He turned to Juno. "Call Liam and tell him it's time to fold it up. And tell Josh I'm on the way." He asked Yelena, "You got that stuff for me?"

She told him, "In the car," and then turned to Jem, acknowledging her for the first time. "You have the keys?"

"Yes."

"Good. I will see you later."

Then she and Joe followed Cash rapidly up the steps. The door closed behind them.

Jem exhaled. "Gosh," she said.

"Yeah," Juno agreed. "*Gosh* is the word."

"What just happened, exactly? I mean, who were those people?"

Juno shifted, juggling his thoughts. "They're kind of like the board of directors, I guess."

Jem frowned. "Directors of what?"

"Well, you know, the Justice League or SHIELD, right? It's kind of like that except, you know, real." He shrugged. "And illegal."

"I don't know," Jem said. "Those old guys. And that lady with one foot. They don't look much like superheroes."

Juno sighed, weighing her words. "I guess that's relative."

"Relative to what?" she asked.

"The villain."

She squeezed his hand sympathetically, and he squeezed back. Then he got to work, typing rapidly, erasing forever much of the work they had just spent hours creating. Jem thought to herself, this had not been a corporate meeting, or a scene from the comics; it had been a trial. Those gathered in this basement had been the jury and the judges. A sentence had now been passed. And the executioner unleashed.

51

I n the car, on the way back into the city, Joe pulled a dark blue work-
man's coverall on over his clothes and added a matching visored cap
and tool bag, transforming himself into a standard-issue repairman,
another effective urban camouflage. He put in his earpiece and slid his
copy of *Ulysses*, which lay on the seat, into his tool bag. He wouldn't
see this car or his other luggage again.

Cash drove into the parking structure and Joe slipped out, proceeding
to the service elevator while Cash parked and opened the door for Yelena.
They took the guest elevator back up to the suite, where they immediately
joined Liam in packing and cleaning; soon every trace of their presence
would be gone. The luggage would be driven out in the Rolls by Cash,
while Yelena and Liam, now dressed in ordinary street clothes, would
leave separately to avoid notice. If their arrival had been a giant splash
designed to draw attention, their exit would barely cause a ripple.

Josh meanwhile was in security, watching the monitors and whispering to Joe over his earpiece when he could.

"Any location on the target?" Joe asked as he rode the elevator up.

"Juno says he and his son are still in their office, but the limo's on
standby, so they should be up soon. Remember Mama, though."

"How could I forget?" Joe said. "Remind Juno to kill that camera
as soon as they leave."

A moment later his elevator reached the top. "I'm on their floor," he
said, holding the Door Close button. Josh turned off the hall camera,
though he could see that the private elevator was rising.

"You're clear but hurry. They're on the way up."

"Roger that," Joe said, and opened the elevator. He hurried to the stairwell and shut the door behind him. Then he climbed the stairs quickly and let himself onto the roof. It was a winter sunset, gorgeous, cold, and quick, the sky bleeding out orange and red while darkness closed in fast. The wind up here was terrific. Joe held his hat.

"I'm outside," Joe told Josh.

"Right," Josh coached him. "Target's bedroom is the northwest corner. Terrace on your left."

Joe ran, keeping low enough to be hidden by the wall along the edge of the roof, then peeked over at the terrace. It was sectioned off from the rest of the penthouse's outdoor space, a private area with planters, a few evergreen shrubs toughing it out along with wooden benches and cast-iron chairs. Joe slipped on gloves, then, from the tool bag, he got out a length of nylon rope with snap hooks at both ends. He attached one end to a chimney pipe by looping it around the pipe and clamping it to itself. He dropped the other end over the edge and went down, landing softly on the tiles, then draped the end of the rope over the frame of the sliding glass door to hide it. Inside, Hackney's bedroom was dark and quiet.

"Hurry up, Joe," Josh said. "They're getting off the elevator."

"Right," Joe said, removing a jimmy from his bag. He slid the narrow strip of metal along the groove where the doors joined and forced the lock up, then drew it open, entered, and pulled it back shut. In the dim light he could make out a sumptuously male bedroom in a vaguely Edwardian style—huge bed with wooden headboard, polished, chunky wood bureaus and night tables, shaded lamps, and thick carpets.

"They're home," Josh said. "Just went in."

Joe opened the closet and stepped in. He closed the door, leaving just a thin crack to peek through. Then he reached into the bag and removed the long Ka-Bar knife.

"I'm in, too," he said. "And you're out."

"Right." Josh signed off with Joe, then walked into the main security office.

"Where's Riley?" he asked the guy on duty.

The guy shrugged, face in his phone. "He said he's at Westlands tonight."

"OK. Well, I'm going on break," Josh said.

The guy shrugged again without looking up. Josh took the stairs up from the basement and exited via the staff door. As he walked downtown, he unclipped his ID and tore it to bits, which he tossed in a garbage can. He had just resigned.

Like many cheats, Jim Hackney was a natural optimist. No matter what, he always believed, against all odds, that he was somehow going to pull it off, that he was going to win. And like most compulsive liars, he lied so consistently and earnestly that he began to believe his own bullshit. In fact, the lies he told others were nothing compared to the lies he told himself, to the point where he not only felt confident that he would win, he knew that he already had. In his mind, the long trail of bankruptcies, closures, and lawsuits were transformed into triumphs: after all, here he was, still standing, in his golden penthouse, on top of a tower with his name on it.

Hackney wanted a shower before he started packing. His private bathroom had a fantastic shower, the kind that was a glass box separate from the tub, with a built-in bench, that transformed into a little steam room. Who knew what the bathroom in his next place would be like? His plan was to get a house on the beach, maybe even look into beachfront properties for development. He and Junior would go first, then send for Anne. He wished he could send for Olga, too, or convince her to leave with him. But that would have to remain a fantasy, at least for now. Survival came first. His and his family's.

He shut his bedroom door behind him, padded across the thick carpet that contained his family crest—not just printed but really woven in—and undressed, tossing his suit and shirt onto the bed. Then, still in his white briefs and black socks, he went into the bathroom to turn the water on, get it nice and steamy. As he came back out, some worker in a repairman's coverall and hat was locking the bedroom door. Maybe he was here to fix something.

"Hey, get the hell out of here, I'm busy," he began, but then recognized the face. "What is this, some kind of goddamn joke?" Then he saw the knife.

"Look," he said, raising his hands. "The money I owe you. I'll pay, all right? Just let me call Junior. He'll bring the cash right up."

But Joe said nothing, just closed in.

"Is it the girl? Olga? I don't know what she told you, but she was the one who came on to me, all right? It's true. I swear. Women just come after me all the time." He backed away. "OK, I admit I wanted her, but nothing happened. She's all yours, I promise . . ."

Hackney turned, thinking he'd flee to the bathroom and lock the door, but Joe quickly looped an arm around his neck from behind, catching him in the crook of his elbow while kicking his leg out from under him, and Hackney was on his back, flailing like an upside-down turtle. Joe pinned him with a knee and his left hand, planted on his chest, while the right hand brought up the knife.

That was when the FBI showed up.

52

Donna was looking for Daisy. After the visit to the hotel, she got worried. She called Andy, who made the reasonable suggestion that Daisy went out to celebrate or even meet someone and convinced her to go home and wait till the morning. In the morning, she tried Daisy's phone again and checked with the hotel desk—nothing. Then, at work, she had her morning meeting, and afterward she followed her boss, Tom, back into his office.

"I understand your concern," he said, after she told him. "It's your first time leading a team like this. You feel responsible. That's good. That's commendable. But the operation is over, and she is not an FBI agent. If she wants to ditch out, she can. Who knows what her deal is? Maybe she has connections you don't know about. Family in the city. A boyfriend."

"She said she had nobody. Why would she lie?"

"Gee, I wonder . . ."

Donna nodded. "If they're illegal."

"Bingo," Tom said. "Or engaged in illegal activities."

"That's possible," Donna admitted, biting her lip.

"You think?" He shrugged. "I'm just being honest here. CIs are like feral cats. You can't control them. Chances are she'll come crawling back, sooner or later. But sometimes they just revert." He sat in his chair. "That's your lesson for today. Leadership 101."

And that was how they left it. Donna got busy with other things and was distracted until hotel housekeeping called late in the day. Daisy had still not returned. Despite what Tom had said, that just didn't seem right. Not to even want to change or get clean clothes? Not to fetch her already humble belongings?

"What are you afraid of?" Andy asked. "The case is over, the bad guys are locked up."

"I'm not sure. Maybe she had some kind of breakdown. Maybe she's in a hospital or passed out somewhere. It happens."

So Andy checked the hospitals while Donna called Fusco, asked him to put the word out to patrols. There was nothing. And it was already getting dark outside—or would be, if she had had a window in her office—when Andy had the genius idea.

"The tracker."

"Sorry?" Donna asked, putting down the phone. "Track her? I'm trying, if you haven't noticed."

"No," Andy said, sitting on the edge of her desk. "The tracking device. The chip. I mean, it's been deactivated, but if she's MIA then she never turned it in, right? Maybe we can turn it back on, get a reading on her location now."

"Brilliant," she said, standing up and kissing him on the cheek. "Why didn't I think of that?"

He grinned. "Because that's what you have me for."

Elated, they went to the tech guy, Mario, who was in his dungeon, a basement room even deeper and darker than hers, and got him to reboot the tracking program and search for her GPS. But there was no signal.

"What does that mean? I thought you could turn it on remotely."

Mario sighed. He liked Donna, but it was always frustrating to explain things to nontech folks who assumed what he did was magic.

"I mean, I can't just tap a key right now and like turn on your blender at home, can I?"

"I don't have a blender."

"My point is it was programmed to send out a signal every ten minutes until the battery died, even in off mode. But until it transmits its location to the GPS, I can't exactly map it."

"What, in your opinion, could have happened?" Andy asked soothingly. "Hypothetically."

"Well, let's see. The battery should still be good, but it might have gotten damaged. Stepped on. She could be out in the woods somewhere or someplace without a signal. Or she could just be in a basement like this," he said, waving a hand at his surroundings. "Minus the kick-ass Wi-Fi. Or just driving through a tunnel."

Donna nodded. "Mario, let me ask you this. And sorry if it's a dumb question. But can you tell me where she was the last time that you got a reading?"

He laughed. "Of course. That's easy." He tapped some keys and zoomed in on a map, then cross-checked the address. "She was in the Hackney Tower Hotel the night before last till midnight. I can even tell you what room number."

Twenty minutes later, citing exigent circumstances, they were at the hotel, with a team, demanding the key card to Suite 3003. There was nothing there. It was a very nice suite, with a swell view, but it had been cleaned and there was not a trace of Daisy, nor the slightest suggestion of anything suspicious. Still, she had been here. Why?

"Who rented this suite the night before last?" Donna asked the very nervous assistant manager, who looked at the FBI agents surrounding him as if certain they would take him down in a hail of gunfire any second.

"No one, ma'am," he blurted. "I mean, Agent."

"It was empty?"

"I don't know. The hotel keeps it for private use or to offer to special guests. I really don't know anything about it." He looked on the verge of panic as he watched Andy go through the couch cushions. "I swear."

"So who does know?"

"Well, the owners, ma'am. Mr. Hackney and his son, I guess."

"And where are they right now?" Donna asked him.

"And how do they unlock this safe?" Andy added, holding the painting in his hands.

At this point, the assistant manager wanted to call the manager, but Hackney had just fired him, so finally he took them up to the penthouse, his fear of being shot or arrested now morphing into the much more realistic fear of being fired himself. He knocked. No answer.

"Open it," Donna told him.

The assistant manager took a deep breath and used his master card key to swipe in. The agents surged past him into the apartment, calling out, "FBI!"

53

When Joe heard the voices calling out "FBI," the point of the knife was right over Hackney's throat. In that split second, he had to make a choice. With a sigh, he withdrew the blade, and jumped up onto his feet, and while Hackney stared in fascination, he backed away, grabbing his tool bag, slid the glass door open, and slipped out onto the terrace. He shut the door behind him, put up the knife, shouldered the bag, and clutched the dangling rope, grateful for his gloves as he climbed back up onto the roof, yanking the rope up behind him just as he heard the yelling Feds bust into Hackney's room. He unhooked the rope from the pipe, then sprinted to the door and clambered downstairs to the penthouse floor, where he carefully eased the door back to peek into the hall.

Guys in FBI windbreakers stood around, talking on walkies, hands on their holstered guns. The private elevator opened and some uniformed cops got off. Joe considered just strolling out, hoping to pass as a repairman, but he had to assume Hackney had given them a description. He considered walking all the way downstairs, but he knew that the exits would be crawling with law, and quite possibly the elevators and stairways, too. And he knew there was no point in contacting any of his team, who were all away clean. He was on his own.

"In here! Help!"

Hackney was still on his back when Donna kicked his bedroom door in. Hearing the cries for help, and finding the door locked, she had drawn her weapon and busted in, only to find the hotel's owner in his undies, writhing on his carpet in the center of what looked like a crest. Steam billowed from the bathroom where the shower was going full blast.

"FBI," she yelled. "What's going on here?"

"Thank God you're here," he said. "He just tried to kill me."

"Who did, sir?" Donna asked, checking the closet as another agent came in behind her, gun drawn.

"He went out on the terrace."

"Check the bathroom," she told the agent while she moved to the glass doors, staying close to the wall. She slid it open fast and ducked out. Cold wind howled around her head. That was it.

"Terrace is clear," she called as she went back in.

"Clear," the agent in the bathroom called. He shut off the shower.

"Sir," she told Hackney, who was still lying on the floor, though more relaxed. "We are here seeking information regarding the whereabouts of Daisy Gonzalez."

"Who?" Hackney asked now, starting to look more confused and less terrified as the agent helped him up. "Is she part of this?"

"Part of what?" Donna asked, holstering her weapon.

"The plot to kill me. Look, I need protection, all right?" Hackney said. "I'm sorry I tried to run, but when the news broke, I knew they'd come after me. I just never guessed it would be them. Or maybe it was about the poker money. Or Mistress Olga."

"What news, sir? Who's trying to kill you?"

"Who do you think? The Mafia," he yelled, then frowned. "And some of my hotel guests."

When they entered the penthouse and Donna broke left, leading a couple of agents toward the cries for help, Andy went right, leading the group who cleared the rest of the place. There was a lot to cover, so it took a few minutes for him to find his way to what looked to him like a royal bedchamber, maybe from medieval Rome, considering all the religious art, the crosses and candles. Most immediately disturbing, though, was a toppled electric wheelchair. Where was its owner? He heard a toilet flush in the bathroom.

"Hello? Anyone here? FBI coming in," he called as he crossed the room, weapon out. He banged on the door. "Open up. FBI!"

"Don't come in," a woman's voice shouted. "I'm . . . I'm using the toilet." It flushed again.

"Ma'am, you need to open up," he yelled.

"No!" she cried, flushing yet again, as he kicked in the door. An older white lady was standing over the toilet, fully dressed.

"Step back, please," he said, and looked in. It appeared to be clogged with gold necklaces. "What is your name, ma'am? And what is going on here?"

She raised her head high and sniffed. "My name is Anne Hackney. This is my private residence. And that jewelry belongs to me. If I want to flush my own property down my own private toilet, that is my prerogative."

When she saw Andy snapping on a latex glove and, with a sigh, leaning in to check the contents of the toilet, she yelled, "No," and tried to grab his arm, then suddenly turned and fled, running across the room.

"Stop her," Andy called.

Another agent, just coming in, caught her at the door. She fought wildly, and he had to toss her on the bed, where she took a pretty high bounce. By then Andy was coming out with a dripping fistful of small gold locks on golden chains.

"Mrs. Hackney," he asked, concerned about another victim. "Whose wheelchair is that?"

"It's mine," she said, sitting up, smoothing her hair, and trying to resume a pose of dignity.

"OK," Andy said, letting that one go for now. "And do you have any knowledge of the whereabouts of Daisy Gonzalez?"

"Is she the room service waitress?"

"No, ma'am."

Mrs. Hackney shrugged. "Then no, I don't. Unless she is one of my husband's whores. Then I might have killed her."

<hr />

Yelena was on her way downtown in a taxi when Hackney texted.

> *Dear Mistress,*
>> *My plans have changed, and I have to leave town.*
>> *But I'd give anything to see you once more. Please, I beg you, meet me on my boat. It's moored at the Westlands dock. I will offer the tribute I promised.*
>> *Your grateful servant*
>> *Jim*

She was now in street clothes, black jeans and a sweater under her ski jacket and wool cap, with one small pack containing items she was planning to safely dispose of, including the burner cell Hackney had just contacted. She sighed. Despite the boredom and the craving for action that had made her eager to join in this caper, she now felt ready to go home, to her own quiet and private space, her bath and bed. She knew of course that Jem was still there, and Midnight, so there was that to be resolved. Permanent arrangements weren't her style. There was also her job, with its host of day-to-day responsibilities that had gone untended: money uncollected, petty disputes unresolved. And that was fine. She'd had her fling, and now it was time to get back to her real life.

But not if it meant letting that poisonous insect crawl away. A monster who preyed on vulnerable women. If somehow he had slipped by Joe, then fine, her blade would fit in his heart just as well. Luckily she had that, too, in her bag. She tapped the Plexiglas.

"Driver," she called. "Turn around."

Then she texted Joe to let him know what was happening.

54

Joe did not get the text. He was busy. Back on the roof, he jogged to the edges and looked over. Police cars had now parked in front of the grand entrance, closing off the street, and cops stood on the steps and in front of the black granite planters that loomed over the sidewalk. They were stationed by the staff and garage entrances, too. No way he was walking out. But he couldn't stay here, either. For one thing, it was too cold.

He climbed over some planters to the private roof deck, where the personal elevator would arrive and park in a freestanding structure that housed the shaft. He pulled over a chair and climbed on top of it. He got a hand drill from the tool bag and pulled the screws that held the service panel in place, then removed them from their holes with numb fingers. The latex gloves guarded against fingerprints, not frostbite. Tears filled his eyes as the wind whipped his face. Finally he slid the panel aside and exposed the shaft.

The private elevator was far below. The shaft opened beneath him like a well. Directly under him was the pulley system, its cables dangling into the dark depths, where they connected to the car. On this end, the cables joined the counterweight, which sat parked in its hoistway. These slabs of metal were designed to equal the weight of the car plus half of its total capacity. As the elevator itself moved up and down, the counterweight rose and fell, decreasing the amount of energy needed, just as lifting someone on a seesaw is easier than lifting them with your arms. With the elevator at or near the bottom, the counterweight was right below Joe.

Very carefully, he climbed onto the structure that held the pulley gears and then stood on top of the weights, his back an inch from the wall of the hoistway. He looped the rope around his waist and then around the metal pole on which the weights slid before hooking the two ends together. Then he held on and waited. A few minutes passed, till he heard a humming sound and the cables pulled taut. A metallic groan echoed up as the elevator began to move, and suddenly, smoothly, Joe was sinking, riding the counterweight down the shaft as the elevator car rose.

He tried to remain steady, feet planted on the weight and rope brushing lightly on the pole that it ran on, for balance only. He tried not to think about the speed and height, any more than you did riding inside the car, standing still and staring straight ahead. Then, as the car sped up toward him, he held his breath and tried to freeze completely. Like a train in a tunnel, the car rushed past him, flying up just inches from his face, while he slid down, the wall just inches from his back. Then the car was above him, soaring up into the building while the cables before him slackened, and he sank, his stomach dropping, as they plunged into the shaft. Below him, the bottom rose, the vanishing point flying toward him, the pit where the shaft ended and four giant springs stood, ready to cushion the car. And then, miraculously, the weight shifted, and he came to a gentle stop, right below the basement.

He unhooked the rope, winding it over one shoulder, and jumped down from the weight to the bottom of the shaft. He took just a second to breathe and get his bearings. His legs felt rubbery, like he was getting off a boat or a nauseating carnival ride. But that was all. He knew that what went up must come down, and if the car descended this far it would crush him. Grabbing a screwdriver from his tool bag and holding it in his teeth, he clutched the arm that drew the door open and shut from inside and pulled himself up, balancing his toes on the lip of the door opening and grasping the edge of the doorframe like a rock climber. Behind him, the cables tightened as the elevator moved and the counterweight rose. The elevator was descending. Trying to ignore the ominous hum, he took the screwdriver and worked it under the arm, moving around until he found the mechanism that triggered the door, beneath the hole where a fireman or repairman's key would be inserted from the other side. The mechanism engaged and the door opened. Joe swung himself in, grabbing the door as it slid by to keep from falling back in. Two maids, passing on their way to punch in, looked at him with vague curiosity, just another maintenance worker doing something mildly unusual. The door shut.

Catching his breath, Joe wanted to lie down on the floor with his eyes closed for a while, but he just nodded and smiled at the two women and walked by as they nodded back. He found his way to the male employees' locker room and loitered about, sitting on a bench tying and untying his shoes, until he saw a young guy come in wearing a valet jacket and hang it on a hook before going to wash up. Joe grabbed it, buttoned up the jacket, and stuffed his cap in the tool bag.

The garage was full of cops, and the exit was sealed tight. But the cops were just standing around watching, while the actual valets, temporarily off duty, hung around talking or watching the cops. No one took any notice of Joe. He sauntered over to the valet's booth and ducked in, scanning the board full of keys. He grabbed the ones with the Ducati emblem.

He strolled to where the bike was parked and strapped the tool bag down. Then, using the key to release the brake, he walked the bike back toward the valet drop-off area, in front of the elevators. The cops were holding people back, surrounding the private elevator, whose signal light indicated it was coming down.

"Back it up, back it up," the cops called, as a black windowless FBI van pulled in.

"Move that bike back," a cop told Joe, who nodded obediently and rolled the bike to a discreet spot behind a garbage can, just to the side of the private elevator. He unsnapped the helmet from the seat and slipped it on. The doors slid open and Joe saw Donna go by, in a huddle of suits and FBI jackets, with Jim Hackney in the center. He stood stock still and silent, but some part of him reached out as her eyes scanned the garage professionally, mechanically, her gaze flashing over his helmet-masked face, which merely reflected her own warped image. The group boarded the van. And as the cops closed in around them, providing cover, Joe rolled his bike behind their backs, pushing it on board the private elevator and letting the doors close. He pressed the button for the lobby, and the elevator started to rise.

He came out fast. In the elevator, he ditched the valet jacket, then climbed on the bike, and while keeping the brake depressed, he revved the throttle till it was growling and threatening to roar. The doors opened, and he released the brake, zooming forward into the lobby. At first no one even noticed as all attention was on the phalanx of police vehicles blocking the front of the hotel. Then, as Joe rode by, heads turned, and eyes popped open wide. He swerved around a luggage cart, tore across the carpet, skirted a shocked woman who stopped, petrified, right in his path and closed her eyes, and skidded over the polished entrance floor, before speeding past a doorman holding a door for a bellman wheeling luggage. It all took about four seconds.

It took about half a second for the first cop to spot him when he came out the door. He was stationed, along with a loose row of other police, along the steps leading down to the sidewalk, about eight feet below. The rest of the front was comprised of black granite benches spaced along the frontage, dense planters full of evergreen shrubs, and a wheelchair-accessible ramp that would have been perfect for Joe if it hadn't been completely sealed by two cops standing side by side. The sidewalk was cleared, and cop cars were parked at the curb, lights flashing. Mostly they were just loitering, though, as Hackney was removed through the garage, and the FBI led the search inside for Hackney's supposed assailant.

"Hey!" the cop yelled. As Joe let out the throttle, propelling the bike forward, the cop, wide and low in his winter padding, seemed to try to both block Joe and avoid him at once, swaying side to side, arms out, like a hula dancer. Several other cops turned and quickly closed off the stairs, forming a defensive line. Joe ignored them completely, like a quarterback suddenly deciding to run instead of pass, and drove straight into the shrubs, throttle open, engine now roaring loud enough to make an impression even on Broadway. Head down, he plowed through the greenery, branches scratching his helmet and the bike's finish, and came shooting out the other side. Yanking the handlebars up, he came off the outside edge of the granite wall like a rocket, soared over the cops like a warning shot fired over their heads, and landed with a thump on the roof of a cop car. He skidded right off onto the street, wobbling and dragging his legs but quickly gaining traction and momentum. Before anyone quite knew what to do, he had crossed Broadway, in a chorus of horns, and come up on the opposite sidewalk, heading west.

Several cops tried to pursue on foot, a couple even drawing guns, pointlessly, as Joe swerved through fearful pedestrians and past parked cars, and vanished down the block. Others jumped into their cars and began trying to pull out, executing awkward three-point turns while jockeying for position among one another. Finally, a ranking officer, screaming and blowing his whistle, managed to get them to take turns while others held back the traffic, and a row of squad cars squealed off after Joe.

55

Yelena arrived at the Westlands gate.

The guard saw her coming and banged on the door of the little heated hut. The chain-link fencing ran down the block, and behind that lay a dark mass through which, here and there, one glimpsed the river beyond. Streetlights dotted the sidewalk, and smaller lamps lit a path behind the gate. The wind was very cold. Another guy came out. His name tag read *Riley / Supervisor.*

"Can I help you?" he asked.

She stepped into his puddle of light. In the cab, she had removed the knife from her bag and slid it under her sleeve. The handle was nestled in the hand she held at her thigh.

"I'm here to see Mr. Hackney," she told him, and he nodded. His underling unlocked the gate.

"He's on the boat, miss. Just follow the path down to the river."

She nodded and began to walk the curving path, the remnants of a crumbling asphalt road. It was hemmed in on both sides by overgrowth, partly lit with standing lamps, though many were broken or knocked over or obscured by dangling branches. As she walked, she could make out concrete ruins, weather-stained, half-sunken blocks and broken pillars with rebar sticking out, rusty girders and toppled heaps of rubble that reminded her more than anything of certain godawful parts of Russia she hoped never to see again.

Then she found the river. The path ended at the water's edge, where it joined a wide expanse of broken concrete, cracked with weeds and glittering with decades of smashed glass. A massive pier stretched out into the river. Set on giant pylons, the whole structure, once a warehouse or loading site of some kind, now listed like a sinking ship, a carcass of bent metal, broken windows, and rotting wood. Another pier was gone completely. All that remained were the stumps of wooden supports, now broken rows of rotten teeth emerging from the river like the jaw of an immense, prehistoric beast too sick and lazy to rise. On each stump sat a white seagull curled up against the chill, plump drops of white against the black.

There was the boat. It looked to her to be about twenty meters long. She didn't know much about boats. This one looked rich, but it was still a fishing boat, not a pleasure craft. It had an open back deck, with the controls in a sheltered front cabin and more room below. She peered onto the deck, confused by the heap of what at first looked like trash. Then in the moonlight, she saw. They were bones, human bones, with a skull resting on top. She heard a footstep behind her, and as she turned, a flashlight hit her eyes.

"You . . ." she said, confused. Her hand came up, ready to throw the knife, but she was blinded, and her blade arced into the river. And by then he had fired the dart gun in his other hand, and the tranquilizer was in her chest.

⚬⚬

Jim Hackney's interrogation did not go as Donna expected. For one thing, he seemed genuinely clueless, until he was finally shown a surveillance photo of Daisy leaving the brothel.

"Oh, her . . ." he said, at last, even grinning lasciviously for a second before reality hit. "Jesus, Sandra was a cop? I mean, agent or whatever?"

"She was an informer. Thanks to her, we busted that whole prostitution ring, including the human trafficking pipeline that smuggled the women into the country."

"Jesus," he said again. "*Trafficking* makes it sound so bad. I thought of it as harmless fun, you know, like gambling."

"Gambling is illegal, too," Donna pointed out, but Hackney interrupted her.

"Wait. I didn't even screw her! So you can't frame me for that. Did she say I did? I demand a test."

"She's missing, sir. And her last known location was your suite."

"I swear I never saw her there. I don't understand. And what does this have to do with the guy who tried to kill me? That's what I want to talk about. There's a contract out on me. I'm the victim. If you're charging me with something, then call my lawyer."

She took a breath. "And why exactly do you think this contract is out on you?"

He laughed. "Don't you read the news?"

"I read the *Times* and the *Daily News* today," she said. "You weren't in either."

"OK, not that news . . . yet. But check out *Real News*. It's a website. Or *Celebrity Report*."

So she googled those sites. One featured a model getting divorced from a soccer player. Another featured a rapper getting married to a heavily tattooed celebrity chef. She showed him the screen. "Either of these guys look like you?" she asked.

"What the hell?" he asked. "Check on my laptop. It was there!"

So they pulled his machine from its evidence bag and he entered the password for her. She looked. Same thing.

"I don't understand. I must be dreaming," he muttered.

"What is it you thought they said?" Donna asked.

"What?"

"What was the scandal that you thought these gangsters were trying to kill you over?"

Hackney stared at her blankly. "What?"

"Sir, you heard the question."

"Nothing. I mean, it was just a mix-up. Let's just forget the whole thing."

This turn of events was made even more confusing when Donna's intercom buzzed. She ducked into the hall, where an agent informed her that a man answering the description of Hackney's assassin had actually been spotted. He'd fled the building on a motorcycle and NYPD units were in pursuit. She went back into the room, where Hackney was squirming anxiously.

"So let's review," she said, taking her seat. "You're now saying that no one tried to kill you? You made it all up?"

"Right. I must have dreamed it. I'm sorry. Can I go now?"

<hr />

"When did you regain the ability to walk?"

Andy was with Anne Hackney in her room. He was not yet sure if there was any reason to arrest her. She'd confessed to a murder, but whose? She was back in her wheelchair now, if only because it was where she was still most at home.

"Last year, at a clinic in Switzerland. It was a miracle." She smiled. "Do you believe in God, Agent Newton?"

"Sometimes."

"I prayed for years. And tried every treatment. To be honest, I'd long given up. The stay in Gstaad was really just a way to get away from my husband for a while, but there was a new treatment and it worked. My prayer was answered. But then I realized the only reason my husband stayed with me was guilt. I knew if that burden was lifted, that chain broken, he would replace me in a second with one of his whores. So I said nothing. At first I was very weak, anyway. I stayed at the clinic for three months. Then I kept up my exercises when I was alone, which was all the time. We are only together for dinner. And my son comes every night to pray with me." She grabbed Andy's hand. "Agent, I'm worried about my boy. Will you pray with me now?"

⚬══⚬

When Joe escaped from the hotel he rode west, deliberately going the wrong way down a one-way street so that the cops couldn't follow, though a couple tried, boxing themselves in and bringing traffic to a standstill. He swam against the flow on the avenue, swerving around the oncoming cars and trucks, slaloming through honks and curses, sliding between an SUV and a parked van, swerving right to avoid an opening car door, and almost getting plowed under by a bus. He slipped through a narrow space, shearing the side mirror off a parked car, and swung onto the sidewalk when a looming truck, honking madly, threatened to flatten him. He took the corner, scattering pedestrians, and rejoined traffic heading uptown.

By then a cruiser had spotted him and hit its siren. Another cop car fell in behind it. Joe looked back to see it gaining and popped the bike into high gear. He flew forward with scary power, streaking through red lights until, facing increased traffic near Lincoln Center, he cut left, crossed the sidewalk island, and humped the bike up the steps to the wide plaza of the Lincoln Center for the Performing Arts. The cops pulled up and jumped from their cars, yakking into radios and trying to pursue on foot. Joe scattered tourists like pigeons, chasing them from where they posed by the fountain. He frightened a well-dressed crowd outside the opera and sped into the Damrosch Park area, which was darker and less populated, with just a few smokers or romantic couples willing to brave the cold.

He began looking for a place to hide. Free of pursuers for the moment, he pulled in behind some garbage cans and stopped. He could see police now, lights turning, as they began to close off the area. The smart thing now was to ditch the bike, lose the helmet and outer gear, and try to blend in with the crowd, drift into one of the buildings to wait it out in a warm bar or café. He removed the helmet and checked his pockets, and that was when he saw the text from Yelena on his phone. He tried to call, but it went straight to voice mail.

"God damn it," he muttered, and put back on the helmet. Keeping the throttle low and his head down, he pointed the bike toward the river.

"Are you ordering me to release him?" Donna was in her office, talking on the phone to Tom, her increasingly impatient boss. "I mean, he's clearly lying."

"About what?"

"Everything! I can charge him with lying to a federal officer."

"Small potatoes, isn't it? After all this? It might help if he was lying about an actual crime under our jurisdiction. Has there been one? He admits to being at the brothel."

Donna remained silent. It was true that Daisy's last known location was his suite, but there was no evidence yet that she was a victim of anything or had gone there under duress. All the other suspicious factors—the scandalous news stories and secret videos, all topped with an assassination attempt—only existed in Hackney's garbled narrative. Which he had now retracted. Still, her gut and her common sense agreed that unless he was completely stupid or insane—correction, *even* if he was stupid or insane—there was something else going on here. And, a little voice kept reminding her, it just might have something to do with Joe. God damn him.

"Are you there, Agent Zamora?" Tom said, which is what he called her when he was angry, like a dad using your full name.

"Yes, sir," she said. "And no, sir, as of this moment we have no knowledge of any new federal crime."

"Then for fuck's sake let him go, quickly, before someone finds one and I'm up all night, again," he barked, and hung up the phone.

"Fuck!" she yelled, slamming her receiver down. And then, "What?" picking it back up again and dialing an extension as she saw Mario standing timidly in her door.

"Um . . ." he began, clearly afraid, but she held up a finger as her call was picked up.

"It's me," she said into the phone. "Let him go. Yes, that's what I said. Fuck it." And then, slamming the receiver again and sitting back heavily in her chair, she repeated, more resigned now than angry, "Sorry, Mario, what is it?"

"Um . . ." he faltered. He found Donna a bit frightening, in an extremely impressive way, even at the best of times, but now he was worried about triggering another outburst. "I don't mean to bother you. It's probably not important anymore. But."

"Please, it's been a very long day after a long night and an endless week. Can you just?"

"Right. Sorry. It's just that tracker? The one you had me, um, tracking? Well, I kind of forgot about it because of this other rush job that came in for Agent Fontenelli working on that car theft thing?"

"Yes?" she said, edge rising in her voice.

"Even though I was busy, the system still automatically sent a ping out every fifteen minutes, and fifteen minutes ago it got an answer."

"Wait. Daisy's tracker answered? What does that mean exactly?"

"I don't know but it turned back on."

"And you have a location?"

He nodded. "Uh-huh."

"Show me. Now."

She hurried him back to his burrow and had him map it. Sure enough, the chip at least was alive and well, apparently, right on the river, maybe even in it. The closest address was an abandoned dockside, now a part of the Westlands Development site, controlled by none other than the Hackney Realty Development Corporation.

"Thank you! Thank you!" she shouted, and hugged him, running out before he could even blush. "Send any updates to my phone." She stopped by her desk to grab her bag, retrieved her weapon, and rushed up to the motor pool to get a car. She'd call for backup on the way. For now, she got behind the wheel and drove, fast, toward the river.

56

Joe cranked it. As he sped toward the exit of Damrosch Park, he knew the cops would see him, so his only hope was to punch through the perimeter and break for cover. Cover, in this case, was the Amsterdam housing projects, right across the street but a world away, like a parallel dimension separated by one avenue of traffic from the lights and glitz of Lincoln Center. Comprising thirteen buildings on nine acres, with more than one thousand apartments plus playgrounds, a clinic, a nursery, and a community center, it was a good place to get lost. And though, compared to some projects, crime was low due to the proximity to Lincoln Center and intense gentrification of the neighborhood, it was still the projects, home to crews selling weed or hustling stolen goods or just hanging out getting high and drinking, host to the occasional playground shooting, and generally not a spot where the citizens are going to run up and tell the cops which way the guy on the yellow-and-orange motorcycle went.

And so, like a rabbit going to ground, Joe was at full speed when he shot out of the park's exit, across the sidewalk, and onto Amsterdam Avenue, blasting past a cop car's headlights and headlong into traffic, which frantically honked and swerved. He veered uptown, with the flow, for half a block, merged left, and then banged over the curb, smiling as he passed the sign that read *Welcome to Amsterdam Houses*.

He began to weave among the paths, drawing the notice of residents who yelled as he passed, some demanding he slow down, some urging him on. The cops followed.

"Holy shit, look at him go!" an old man warming himself with brandy called out to his cronies as Joe snaked around some benches and rushed into a playground, a cop car screaming behind him. A bunch of teens were smoking weed by the concrete chess tables and Joe made right for them.

"He's coming this way!" they shouted, scattering. Holding the handlebars steady, and holding his breath, he shot through the narrow gap between two tables. The cop car braked but banged into one, crumpling its front end. "Go, motherfucker, go!" a teenager yelled while his friends laughed at the cops struggling with their airbags. "Damn cops broke our table!"

Then, as more cops entered the projects, a chorus of "Five-Oh" went up, and the dealers scattered, running into the buildings or ditching their stashes and looking innocent, all of which confused the cops. Some, like easily distracted hunting dogs, immediately chased the dealers down instead, while others stopped and demanded to know where the guy on the motorcycle went. They met a wall of silence. The locals had no idea who Joe was, but they figured if he had a reason to run from the police, that was his business, and they had learned to mind their own.

Frustrated, the cops began searching systematically, as Joe slowed his pace, nosing his way around the dark paths and landscaped shrubs while folks watched from their windows. The beams of high-powered searchlights crossed his path, and the glow of cop flashers splashed the buildings. A little girl with braids watching from a window waved in warning, and he turned down a maintenance alley, cutting his engine as a car rolled by. When it passed he crept out, waving thanks. Then a teenage boy on a kid's scooter pulled up, wearing a Knicks beanie and a down parka trimmed with fake fur.

"Yo," he asked, voice low. "Why you running?"

"'Cause they're chasing," Joe told him.

The kid nodded. "Fair enough. Can you pay?"

Joe nodded.

"Cool. Follow me," he said, and kicked off, darting along on his scooter. Joe followed. The kid rode to the edge of a building, then down a ramp to a basement door. He used a fob to open it, and interior light shined out like a beacon in the darkness.

"In here, man," he said, and Joe rolled the bike past him, cutting the engine. He shut the door.

"Thanks," Joe said, taking off his helmet.

"That's some nice riding, bro. That bike is fucking dope."

"Yeah, but a little hard to blend into the scenery," Joe said. "I should have painted it."

"No way, bro, the color is smoking. What's that, German?"

"Italian. Ducati."

He shook his head in admiration. "Someday I'mma get me one of them." Then he shrugged amiably at his kick scooter, which seemed more like something his kid brother would ride. "So check it, I can hide you in the boiler room, for say fifty? Hang out an hour or two till they give up. For twenty more I can get you some weed and beer to pass the time."

Joe smiled. "You know, I think I have a better idea."

<hr/>

Five minutes later, Joe emerged from the projects on the west side. Instead of his coveralls and helmet, he now wore a goose down coat and wool Knicks cap. And instead of a Ducati motorcycle he now wheeled a cheap scooter, his tool bag over his shoulder.

"Hey you, where you going?" The cops were blocking the way onto West End Avenue, right by the Western Beef supermarket. The one who talked was pretty beefy himself, a big white guy with a red nose in the cold. His partner, an equally large black guy, pointed a flashlight in Joe's face.

Joe shrugged, blinking in the light. "Going to get me a beer and some chips. That all right, chief?"

"What's in the tool bag?" Officer Beef asked, while his partner helpfully shined the light on Joe's tool bag.

"Tools," Joe explained.

Officer Beef waved him over. "Let's have a look."

Joe had expected this. As a top-notch professional criminal, he had a healthy respect for his counterparts, top-notch professional law enforcement. In a sense, he depended on them: if there were no smart cops around, crime would be so easy there would be no need for his services. But, just as most criminals are foolish and get themselves caught for that reason, so there are some dim cops out there, especially those stuck hunting motorcycles through the projects in the freezing cold. And this cop was doing just as Joe expected: randomly rousting the first guy he saw and bullying him a little on the vague chance he'd stumble across Al Capone. Joe lifted his tool bag onto the hood of the cop car and opened it up. Officer Beef poked around in it.

"What kind of work you do?" he asked, as a keen investigator.

"Handyman," Joe said. And the cop nodded wisely, looking over the rope, tape, screwdriver, wire cutters, and so forth. Meanwhile Cop Two patted him down.

"Arms up," he said, and frisked him. "OK," he said finally, "you can go."

Joe nodded and rode off, steering the scooter across West End. On the whole, it had gone pretty well. He was particularly glad that, as he approached the street, he had ditched his combat knife in a trash can.

57

Yelena woke up in shadows. The first thing she was conscious of was cold and damp and hardness. Then, coming fully awake, she leapt forward and was pulled rudely back. Her right hand was chained to a long pipe. She was on the concrete floor of a basement or bunker or tunnel. It was lit, with accidental artistry, by a couple of battery-powered camping lamps that revealed the weather-stained and graffiti-covered walls and dripping, rusted-out pipes. Chained up next to her, against the wall, was a young woman, dark-haired, stripped to her undergarments. Around her neck was another small gold lock.

At first Yelena thought she was dead, but on closer inspection there was shallow breathing, and when she stretched herself to the limit of her chain, a weak, fluttery pulse in the wrist. Then, in the gloom beyond, she realized there was another chained body, this one a rotted corpse, so decomposed that only the hair and some bits of flesh suggested it had once been female. Beyond that were skeletons, their wrists, like branches, still hooked to the pipe. The end of the pipe had broken, crumbled by rust, and been reattached with a clamp and fresh bolts. No doubt that was how Ioana had escaped. For all the good it did her.

Then Yelena heard steps and saw movement, a looming shadow, and she looked up. It was Junior, pushing an empty wheelbarrow.

"I'm disposing of the dead ones first," he said, huffing a bit as he entered. "But don't worry. I will get to you shortly."

"You killed all these women?" Yelena asked as he knelt and unhooked a skeleton, then loaded it into the barrow.

"All but one," he said. "The first one. She was my mother's. But she had every right. She was a whore, a vile bitch who tried to use her sex to enslave my father. He would have succumbed—he's very weak despite all his bullying. Or because of it. He would have left her, left us, for her, but like all strong women, like all true mothers, she protected the family. She found her in the suite where he takes them. And she stabbed her. She needed my help, though, to remove the body. I took it out in a suit bag, on a luggage trolley, in the private elevator. And stashed it here. And then, I assured her, she didn't have to worry. I would be her protector. Like any good son."

He looked up from his work. "I realize you're different, of course. You and your friends set us up, you conned us. But that still makes you a loose end. The last of my father's women. And now, thanks to you, we need to leave the country. And that means this place will be found, so I have to clean up before I go. So you see, it's really your own fault that you're here. You should have minded your own business."

Yelena looked at the row of victims, one still clinging on. "They were people. Like you. Just because they are poor. Or illegal here. Or you don't like how they choose to have sex."

"Not how. Who. They wanted to use their sex to steal my father. To replace my mother and then, with their foul little babies, replace me."

Yelena laughed bitterly.

"You think that's funny?"

"Very," she said. "It seems I know your father better than you do."

"What do you mean?"

"He was impotent. It was all for show, or ego. Or his own twisted sense of shame. Anyway, he did not have sex with them. He told me. So you see, all this was for nothing. There would be no babies. You killed these poor women for nothing."

Junior dropped the barrow and stormed over. "You're lying! You're trying to confuse me, succubus! Just like my mother said." He shook with rage, fists clenched, then slumped, shaking his head. "It doesn't matter now. Anyway, nobody missed these useless sluts. They're trash. All I did was dispose of them properly. And now, all their bones and clothes and crap, it all goes into the river. And you, too, right after this one."

He began to move toward the unconscious girl. "You know," Yelena called, raising her voice, "my mother was a whore. In Russia. My father was a trick, some man I never met, maybe a married asshole like your dad. So you see it's very fitting. The child of a whore has destroyed your whole empire. Now you're running like a nobody. And your daddy is already dead. My friend has cut him open like the pig he is."

"You're lying!" He swung toward her, hands out. "You are the whore of Babylon, the demon sent to confuse me."

Yelena prepared herself. If he came close enough, tried to strangle her, then she thought maybe she could kill him, or at least die trying. But his phone beeped. He snatched it up.

"Yes? What now?" he barked into it, still the executive being disturbed by an underling. Then he grinned. "Thank you. And, Riley . . . turn out all the lights." He turned back to Yelena. "Well, it looks like your friend is here after all. The last loose end. Maybe we can ask him before he dies."

Joe ditched the scooter by the fence.

He'd saved some time by hitching a ride on a bus, grabbing the rear fender and trying not to inhale too much exhaust while it towed him along. But now he approached the Westlands on foot. About a hundred yards from the entrance, he used his wire cutters to cut a hole in the fencing. Then he rolled under and was in.

He clicked on his flashlight, holding his fingers over the front to narrow the beam, and made his way through the overgrowth, trying not to trip over roots or scratch himself too badly. After a few minutes, he reached a path, lit haphazardly by lamps that dotted the way to the river. He was about halfway down when all the lamps went dark.

Instantly, he dropped to the ground. It was remotely possible that there had been a sudden power outage, that a fuse box had blown, but another explanation seemed more likely. Someone knew he was here. He guessed there were motion detectors or cameras. He crawled rapidly off the path into the woods and then jumped up and ran, zigzagging both to avoid the trees that seemed to leap out at him in the dark and to make a poor target, looping south before turning back to the river. He had just stopped for a second to catch his breath when a bullet from nowhere took off his Knicks hat, which he had, mercifully, pushed back from his sweaty forehead. A second shot tore through the tool bag. He dove into the dirt and rolled away, scrambling in the trash and broken glass, then crawling on hands and knees until he found a large heap of debris—vine-covered shards of broken concrete studded with rebar, the back seat of an old car, a charred picnic table—and crept into its shadows. He had come here on a search-and-rescue mission, hunting his target—but that, he realized, had changed. Someone was hunting him.

⚬━✦━⚬

When he got the word that Joe was in the Westlands, Junior was actually quite pleased. Since the moment his father had decided to flee the country, he'd been anxious to get here and cover his own tracks. He had also used his ploy one last time: he'd texted this Olga, as he had his father's other women, pretending to be him. He completed his mission, avenging his mother and protecting his own birthright, while also eliminating one of the only people who might connect himself or his father to a crime. Joe, of course, was another. Now he got the chance to snip that loose end. And he got to kill the man he blamed for much of his trouble.

He also got to pursue his own greatest passion. He had, out of necessity, indulged and shared his father's obsessions for gambling, whoring, and making money, but his own pleasures lay elsewhere: in fighting—martial arts, particularly—and in hunting big game. Now he had both. The Westlands were like his own private hunting preserve, one he knew intimately, and through it he would track a prize trophy, a man he'd wanted to kill from the moment they met. His father was the sexual predator, not him. In the end, he'd rather hunt Joe.

Junior hurried to his duffel bag and drew out his hunting rifle, then put extra ammo in his pocket and checked to be sure his sidearm, a Glock 9, was loaded. Then he pulled out his night goggles. He checked to be sure that bitch Olga's cuffs were secure. He didn't need another one going loose. She would keep, for now.

"Be right back," he told her, as he headed up to the ground.

Joe couldn't be sure who was after him, but he knew they had the advantage. He was unarmed, in the dark and cold, and on unfamiliar terrain. He also had to suspect the shooter had a night scope or night-vision goggles. And was an excellent shot. A former sniper himself, he had to admire the skill. He did not like his chances if he ran. He also knew he was doomed if he stood still. He had to do something.

He took off his jacket. Then, straining to see in the dark, he opened his tool bag and pulled out what he guessed were the most useful items—the rope, which he pulled over his left shoulder and under his right arm, like a bandolier; the duct tape, which he slid over a wrist; and the flashlight and screwdriver, which he tucked into back pockets. He abandoned the canvas bag as too cumbersome and too nice a target.

He felt a pang of regret abandoning the book, until he realized the bullet had drilled a hole through its heart. So much for *Ulysses*. He tossed it with the rest.

Then he felt around on the ground and found a fallen stick. He unwound some tape and secured the stick to the inside of the coat, poking it up into the hood like a puppet. Moving very slowly, he lifted the stick above him and hung the coat by its hood from a low branch. Then he picked up a couple of rocks and began, very slowly, to creep away.

In this dense foliage, the shooter would still want to get fairly close for a clear shot, so Joe tried to position himself as the third point in a triangle between the rifle and his coat, which was now silhouetted in the moonlight and rippling in the wind. It was black, but the snaps and zippers glittered slightly, and the logo caught the moonlight. He threw a rock so that it landed, with a clatter, back where he'd been hiding beneath the coat. Then he held still, listening and staring into the darkness.

In a few seconds there was a report. A shot cracked out and a hole tore through the coat. It was impossible to judge distance accurately, but a muzzle flashed in the woods ahead of him and slightly to the left. He began to run toward it, tossing another rock, hard, toward the coat. The muzzle flashed twice more, and two more holes appeared through the coat, which was blown from its perch and dropped out of sight. The first flash gave Joe a location, and by the second flash he had seen his man, down on one knee, braced against a tree trunk. Joe froze again, now just a few yards away. The figure hesitated. Then very slowly and carefully, he stood, slid his night-vision goggles into place, and began to move toward the fallen coat. Joe drew the flashlight and took the last couple steps.

"Hey," he whispered.

The guy jumped, spinning around, just as Joe flicked on the flashlight and hit him full force in the face. When the goggled eyes faced him, like a B-movie frogman, Joe realized it was Junior. Junior fired, but his shot went wide: the goggles had bloomed out in the powerful light, showing a totally greenish white or black view. That was when Joe jumped him, knocking him over and sending the rifle flying off into the woods.

Together, they fell to the ground. Joe got in some good shots—short, quick blows to the kidneys—but his opponent was well padded and in excellent shape. Trying to get an arm around his throat was impossible through his winter coat, and the goggles kept Joe from gouging an eye. Meanwhile, Junior, after being caught off guard, was now working his arms and legs into place, searching for leverage to flip himself onto Joe. They rolled, pummeling each other with fists and leaving welts on jaws, backs, stomachs. They clawed and kicked. Joe got a leg free and drove it between Junior's thighs. Junior gasped and pulled back, freeing Joe to try getting up. But Junior recovered instantly, rolling back onto his shoulders and kicking up, catching Joe on the jaw before he could get to his feet. Joe flew back, landing painfully on the rocks. He tasted blood. He reached for the screwdriver, planning to shove it into the soft part of the throat, but as he sprang forward Junior's own hand came up, holding a pistol. Joe dove to the side as Junior fired. The bullet tore through Joe's clothes and grazed his hip, cutting through the flesh like a hot knife through butter.

He rolled and scrambled, ducking behind some trees while two more shots rang out and whistled into the darkness above him. He tore his way downhill, heading for the river and the concrete structures whose outlines he could make out through the trees, where he hoped to find shelter and a better position from which to make a stand. Then, as he ran on in the dark, the ground disappeared beneath him. His foot plunged into space and he stumbled, tumbling into a hole hidden in the undergrowth and crashing down. His fall was broken, sort of, by a heap of twigs, leaves, dirt, and other debris that had fallen in before him, accumulating over the years.

He lay still, catching his breath, listening for Junior, and trying to feel out his new surroundings. He could feel the blood spreading on his side, the only warm spot on his body. Then, as a vague mental map came into place, he began to understand where he was. Concrete walls and floors. Broken glass and the sound of water dripping from afar. He was in the tunnels.

58

Donna pulled up to the Westlands entrance.

She had driven with one eye on her phone, which lay on the seat beside her. The map locating Daisy's tracker was showing a tiny green dot, blinking on and off, as if between hope and dread. Now she pulled right onto the sidewalk, headlight beams on the locked gate and the little guard shack behind it, leaning on the horn until two men emerged. She got out, tucking her phone in her pocket and pulling out her ID.

"What?" the larger one called out. "This is private property," he added, which was not exactly true.

"FBI," she yelled, showing her badge. "Open up."

But before she could say any more, the bigger guard turned to run, while the smaller looked on in alarm. She drew her weapon.

"Hold it!" she yelled, and fired a warning shot. The runner stopped, his back turned, still leaning forward as if waiting for the signal to resume running. "Next one to move gets a bullet in the ass," she added. "Now raise your hands. High."

They did. She called to the sprinter, "Turn around and get on your knees. Slow."

He did, grunting a little as he lowered himself.

"Now you," she told the one who hadn't moved. "Unlock the gate. Carefully."

He did. Donna tried asking them where Daisy was or what they had seen but they were totally unresponsive, so she cuffed them, putting one bracelet on Tweedle Dum and passing it through the fence before clapping the other on Tweedle Dee. Then she got a flashlight and, following her tracker, began to make her way into the Westlands.

⊙━┿━◦

Yelena grabbed the lock.

Reaching as far as she could, she managed to grasp the unconscious woman by the wrist and pull her closer, dragging her a few inches on the concrete and flopping her in her direction. The woman mumbled and groaned, eyes shut, like a troubled sleeper. Next, Yelena was able, at the extreme limit of her reach, to curl a finger around the chain that hung from the girl's neck and yank it hard. It snapped, but the lock fell to the ground, eliciting a bitter Russian curse. Now Yelena had to contort herself, curling onto her side with her chained hand jutting above her, and drag the little gold lock closer, inch by inch, first with a toe, and then a finger, and finally closing it in her fist.

Eagerly, she began to press the little lock against the concrete wall, gripping the case and bending all her strength against the shackle, which was slender but remained stubbornly locked in place. More curses. Searching the ground with hands and eyes, she found a loose chunk of concrete and dug it up, breaking a couple of her fancy, expensive nails. They had just been for show anyway, part of her costume—as a burglar she was in the habit of keeping them short. She placed the little lock on the edge of the shallow hole she'd made in the floor and began to hammer it with the broken concrete piece, striking her own fingers several times before she got a good blow in and the little shackle, a fine curve of slender gold, snapped. Now she had something to work with. Peering closely in the dim light, she began to hammer it out carefully, getting it somewhat straight but leaving a slight curve at the end, following the original shape. A lockpick made out of a lock.

Now came the easy part. It took her barely a minute to trigger the mechanism in the cuff that held her wrist to the pipe. Then she went to work on the girl's.

Joe was in an art gallery.

As he walked, his steps echoing, his eyes slowly adapting to the murk, he began to make out faint bits of light leaking through places where the roof had collapsed or where moonlight filtered in, bouncing off pipes and gleaming in dirty puddles. As Frank had described, the walls were covered in graffiti, much of it spectacularly colorful, even Day-Glo here and there, though it was also grimy, faded, and stained with weather and time. In letters taller than him, names from decades ago still called out, dancing across the walls in a riot of typography, sharp as razors or soft as clouds. Cartoon characters and elegantly shaded designs bloomed alongside curses and crudely sketched genitalia.

Around one corner, he entered a huge space, like a warehouse. Its high windows, way above Joe's head, were now all shattered, so that like a broken cathedral it displayed the heavens, while another galaxy of broken glass glittered on the floor. These walls were painted with faces and bodies, realistically if expressionistically rendered, some ten feet high. Another narrow hall was striped like a funhouse. The next chamber, a basement with heavy concrete columns, was full of sculptures of a sort: mannequins were posed, painted, their body parts recombined. There was furniture stacked and arranged, a pyramid of TVs with images from old magazines glued to the screens, a baby carriage full of doll heads. Above the door, it said, in ornate lettering: *Welcome to the Wild West Lands.*

He turned a corner, or would have, except the ceiling had collapsed, so he merely circled a freestanding wall. On the other side was an enormous nude woman, lying on her side, her abundant curves blown up as if she were a balloon intended for the parade. Something about the splashy strokes and bold colors stopped him. There, in the corner, it still read: *F. Jones.*

"Impressive, isn't it?" Junior's voice rang out. Joe hid behind the wall. Junior was just entering the large outer chamber. "Too bad it will all vanish soon in the name of progress."

Joe scurried like a rat along the edge of the room and darted into another tunnel, headed down, to a deeper level. He made a couple of blind turns and then stopped. In a pool of light he could see the steady drip of blood running down his ankle and over his boot, creating a trail that Junior, with his goggles, could easily follow. Joe grabbed the tape and, biting down hard, wrapped it around his hips like a belt, binding his wound. Then he ran into the darkest tunnel he could find. The walls narrowed, scraping his shoulders, and suddenly he stepped into water, or sewage; the floor had dipped and was flooded. He waded in, splashing along up to his knees. The stench was nauseating, and he could hear rats paddling around him. Worse, he could hear Junior, armed and sighted, stomping along somewhere above him, his voice echoing through the tunnels.

"Fi, fie, fo, fum, I smell the blood of a stupid schmuck!"

Then Joe hit a dead end. The walls and ceiling, which had been steadily shrinking, came to an end, and he walked right into a wall. He felt to the sides and above. He was blocked in, perhaps by a collapse. But he couldn't go back. Breathing slow to hold off panic, he felt around in the blackness, checking everywhere with his fingertips, up and down the walls from floor to ceiling. There, under the surface of the sludge, he felt an open space. The collapse left a passage, which had flooded. Taking a deep breath and trying not to think about it, he ducked under the filthy liquid and half crawled, half swam through, emerging into a slightly wider passage on the other side, then crept out of the foul muck onto higher ground. For once he was glad he couldn't see.

A few minutes later he saw the lights.

Yelena popped the cuffs open. The girl was free, her wrists raw from where she'd been bound, and she was alive, breathing shallowly and with a weak pulse, but she was like a dead weight.

"Can you hear me?" Yelena whispered into her ear, urgently. "Wake up, please." She shook her and rubbed her hands. She even slapped her, cruel as that seemed. No use. She tried lifting her and could just about manage it, using a fireman's hold, but she wouldn't get far, especially if she had to be quick. Then she thought of the wheelbarrow. Setting the girl back down—she whimpered, a heartrending but hopeful sign of life—she ran to fetch the wheelbarrow, then lifted the girl into it, settling her as gently as she could.

Then she heard a sound. A footstep, she was sure, coming from one of the tunnels that fed into this chamber. She turned, fists clenched, ready to fight.

59

"Hello Joe," Yelena said, smiling.

Joe didn't look good. He was covered in some kind of muck that she could smell from here, and he was trailing blood, but he smiled back.

"What a coincidence," he said, then saw that there was a body in the barrow. "Is she alive?"

"Just barely," Yelena said, brushing the girl's hair back. She nodded at the remains along the wall. "We are too late for them."

That's when Joe noticed the bodies, chained in a row, in various states of decomposition. He felt a surge of mingled horror and grief and fought it back. No time for that now. He had to attend to the living. The dead would wait. He grabbed one of the lanterns and hung it on the handle of the barrow. "You take her out." He pointed toward the end of the chamber. "I think if you keep heading downhill you should come out by the river."

"What about Junior? He's armed."

"Don't worry," Joe said. "I'll think of something."

She frowned at him. "That's what we will put on your tombstone."

Joe laughed. Then he heard steps coming, and faint singing. "Go," he whispered, and she went. Joe looked around, trying to come up with something.

Donna saw the boat.

She spotted it when the path she was on reached the waterfront. Weapon drawn, she ran over and checked it from the dockside first, then jumped down to search the cabin quickly using her phone's flashlight. No one was there. But when she climbed back out, she noticed a heap of what looked like trash on the deck. She trained the beam on it and gasped. There were bones with scraps of tissue on them, a human skull patched with hair, part of a rib cage. Also, a heap of clothing, a purse, a glove. And in the pile, partially covered, was a red dress that she recognized as the last thing Daisy had been wearing. She felt the seams of the dress, and there it was, tucked into the lining of the bust, the little silver button, the tracker.

She's dead, Donna thought with sudden certainty. *I knew it.* Till now she had foolishly pretended that as long as the tracker was alive, beeping like a little heart, then Daisy was, too. But she was buried here, somewhere, and this chip, with its long-life battery, had simply come back online when her killer dug up the evidence for disposal.

That was when she looked over and saw, coming as if from an open tomb, a haggard but determined blond woman pushing something heavy in a wheelbarrow.

"Hold it right there," she yelled, pointing the gun and the light, but the woman didn't stop, she pushed onward, revealing the shape in the wheelbarrow. Arms. A bent leg. A head.

"Hurry, she needs help," the woman called, in some kind of accent. Donna thought she looked familiar and was just remembering where she'd seen her before when she also realized that the woman in the wheelbarrow was Daisy. Back from the dead.

Joe was out of time.

"Heigh ho, heigh ho, it's off to work we go," Junior's voice came booming down the tunnel, his heels echoing.

Joe tried frantically to think. He was in a long, narrow chamber, with pipes running along the walls and ceiling, lit by one remaining lamp, and with a row of skeletons chained to the wall. One set of cuffs—which once held Yelena, no doubt—hung loose, one end open, the other still shackled to the pipe. He could flee, keep limping down the tunnel toward the open dockside, but then what? He was getting weaker, and his armed opponent could see and smell him, here or in the open, where he'd make an easy target and lead him right to Yelena. He had at his disposal only a rope, a little bit more tape, and one lamp, none of which really counted for much against a gun. And gathering at his feet, like a metaphor for his waning life-span, was a puddle of blood. The same blood that trailed across the floor and that Junior no doubt was following here right now. Then he got an idea.

First he got the rope off and clamped the hook on one end to the rope itself, making a loose loop, like a lasso. He tossed it over the pipe directly above his head. Then, balancing on one foot, he slid off his boot and dumped out the blood that had gathered inside, adding to the puddle at his feet, before slipping it back on. Next, he grabbed the tape and pulled off what was left, tossing the cardboard roll into the shadows. He patched his wound, tight as he could, to stanch the blood flow. Then, taking the other end of the rope in hand, he carefully walked back to the wall and hooked that end to the pipe, before hiding out of sight in the nearest tunnel. Then he held still and waited as the footsteps came near.

"Idiot," Junior called, as he entered the chamber, removing his goggles. "You really are clueless, aren't you? I mean, you're clever enough, when it comes to cheating at cards. But you're just an urban creature. Weak and hopeless in the wild. Talk about survival of the fittest. Don't you realize that with these goggles I just followed your blood trail here, easy as breadcrumbs? Man is the most dangerous game? What a joke. I've hunted rabbits smarter than you. What the fuck?" He stopped suddenly.

Joe peered from the shadows. Junior was standing where Yelena and the other woman had been chained.

"Shit. Well, she can't have gone far. This whole game preserve is mine. At least for one more night." Then he looked down, tracking the drips of Joe's blood as they crossed the space. He cocked his gun and crept forward, the hunter closing in on his kill. He reached the large blood puddle where Joe had stood thinking, a bootprint outlined in its border. And around it, nothing. The trail seemed to just end, as if Joe had reached this spot and then vanished or flown away. Junior stared at it thoughtfully. He looked all around. He bent way over and closely examined it.

That was when Joe moved. He crept up behind Junior, fast and quiet as he could, and slid the loose loop of rope over his head. Junior reacted, his gun hand rising, but Joe jumped him, grabbed on tight, and bore down with all his weight. The rope pulled tight, choking Junior off like a noose, with both their bodies hanging from it. Junior struggled mightily, and he was strong, but Joe hung on. Junior's own mass worked against him, the rope cinching tighter the harder he fought. He pulled the trigger, desperately, but the bullets rang out against the concrete floor and walls. Finally, his air cut off, he began to slump, and Joe felt him go limp. The gun clattered. Joe felt for Junior's pulse. He was unconscious.

Exhausted, and bleeding through the tape again, Joe quickly moved to where the rope was hooked to the pipe and detached it, yanking back on the rope with all his strength, drawing it back over the ceiling pipe and slowly hoisting Junior. He came to, recovering consciousness as he realized what was happening. Or perhaps it was nerves and instinct, the body reacting, as Joe lifted him a foot off the ground, hanging by his neck from the noose. He kicked, but that only made it worse, working the rope in tighter as Joe pulled, hand over hand, raising him higher. Junior's hands clawed at his throat, while Joe backed away, moving alongside the skeletons cuffed to the pipe. He slid the hook over the open bracelet from Yelena's cuff and snapped it shut. Then he let go. Junior bucked wildly, but that was just reflex, and after a few more grunts and gasps, he stopped, while Joe kicked an old crate under the dangling feet. His body hung still, one more corpse in this death chamber. He was done.

Donna called for EMTs, giving her location, warning that an ambulance probably couldn't get down the path. They'd have to bring the stretcher on foot. Meanwhile, the woman, the blond, turned to go back into the tunnel.

"Hey, where are you going? Wait here for help."

"I can't. He needs help now."

"Who does?" she asked, then suddenly knew: "Joe?"

The woman nodded and turned to go. Donna cocked her gun and started to follow. Then Joe came staggering out, holding his side. He was covered in what looked like shit, and blood oozed from between his fingers.

By now sirens could be heard on the street above and red lights bounced through the trees. Donna ran to Joe, forgetting everything in the moment, and touched his wound.

"You're hurt," she told him. "Don't worry. Help is coming."

He smiled. "Thanks, but I'm kind of in a hurry." He nodded toward Daisy. "Help her. She needs you."

"Don't you?" she asked. "Need me?"

"Always," he said, and squeezed her hand. Then an engine started. Yelena was on the boat, firing up the motor.

"Joe!" she yelled.

"I've got to go," he told Donna, letting go of her hand. "There are more bodies back in there. Victims. And a suspect."

"Dead?" Donna asked.

Joe nodded. "He hung himself. Remorse."

Then he limped to the boat and climbed on. They cast off, steering into the dark current, and were swallowed up by the fog. Donna looked down at her fingers. They were covered in blood.

60

Anne Hackney was taken into custody. However, her lawyers withdrew her spontaneous confession and argued vociferously that her mental state made her not responsible for her statement or, indeed, her actions. Nor was there any direct evidence connecting her to any deaths, aside from the gold locks. Her sudden confession and attempt to destroy evidence were, they insisted, both incompetent attempts to protect her son, Jim Junior. She was therefore transferred to a mental health facility on the Long Island Sound, where she remains.

Eventually, the official FBI and NYPD investigations concluded that Jim Hackney Jr. was a serial killer, responsible for at least eight deaths, including those of Ioana Petrescu, Maxine Waters, Jeri Calvert, and Mingmei Chong, though the true number may never be known. He was in the act of disposing of evidence when the arrival of law enforcement inspired him to take his own life rather than face justice.

Jim Hackney Sr. was released from custody. There was no evidence implicating him in the murders directly, nor did any of his wilder allegations pan out. Upon his release he immediately checked his Caymans account and found it empty. With his Westlands project in shambles and no money to repay his partners, he got on a plane to Moscow, where he still had some strong relationships with bankers he hoped might help him restart his career. Unfortunately for him, his Russian associates had another acquaintance in common—Yelena. Hackney was met at the airport by a limo and never seen or heard from again.

The bounty was paid. On a cold day, in an empty storage space deep in a Mini-King warehouse, Joe met with the bosses. Despite harboring certain suspicions about his investigative techniques, they asked no questions and expressed their satisfaction with the results. Their people and their fortunes were safe.

Later, the crew met at Club Rendezvous and the cash was split eight ways: Joe, Yelena, Liam, Josh, Cash, Juno, Jem, and Gladys. Afterward, they headed off to celebrate, each in their own way. Liam and Josh had booked a table for a romantic dinner at a new French place in Tribeca. Juno, Cash, and Jem went to an arcade. Gladys had her standing mahjongg game at a neighbor's. Yelena went home alone. She considered calling her lover, but decided she was going to take a long bath and enjoy the silence first. Joe caught a ride into the city with Gio.

For the first part of the ride, they were silent. The radio was playing a rock block of Pink Floyd, and neither of them had heard these songs in years, so they turned it up. Then a commercial came on, and Gio lowered the volume. Silence returned.

"How's the healing coming?" Gio asked finally.

"OK. Just some stitches. But it seems to ache more than other times. Must be the cold."

Gio grinned. "Did you say 'must be you're old'?"

Joe laughed. "Yeah, that too."

"Speaking of which, you sure you don't want me to swing by your place? That's a lot of money you got there. You might get jumped."

Joe laughed. "Thanks, but I need it."

"Buying something?"

"Yeah, a book." He glanced at Gio. "What about you? Business in town?"

"Yeah, I got a meeting after I drop you."

There was another moment of silence. The radio, lowered now, played the Stones softly, but Gio didn't turn it up. "Listen," he said. "I know we said it officially back there, but I wanted to thank you personally for handling this. I consider it a favor."

"No need. It was the right thing to do."

"Yeah. It was. Even if it caused a bit more collateral damage than some of our friends would have liked."

Joe nodded slowly. "Everyone thinks they want justice, but once you start down that path, no one can say where it will end. I'm not sure anyone can ever really be satisfied."

Gio laughed. "Almost makes you feel sorry for the real cops."

"Almost."

Gio dropped Joe at the impossible intersection of West Eleventh and West Fourth Streets. As usual, there were a few deeply confused tourists standing and contemplating the street signs. Perhaps they would wander down the block and into the bookshop for directions and end up buying something, but not yet. Alexis was in there, smoking, and the only customer was the cat, spread out on the desk getting her belly rubbed.

"Hey, it's the last real reader," he said as Joe came down the aisle. "Take a seat. I hope you came to spend big."

Joe sat, careful of the tightness by his stitches. "Actually, I did," he said, and tossed a fat envelope on the desk. "What will that buy me?"

Alexis opened it, whistled, did a rough count, and then closed it again. He sat back, ashing his smoke. "It would buy my virtue if I had any left. What about a first edition of *Tropic of Cancer* and the cat?"

"My grandmother wouldn't approve of either of them. How about a stake in the store?"

Alexis stubbed out his butt. "What kind of stake?"

"A minority share. You're behind on your mortgage. This would catch you up, right?"

Alexis nodded. "And then some." He leaned back, crossing his legs, and thoughtfully drew a fresh cigarette from his case. He tapped it on the lid. "Now, I want to put this carefully. I gather you have certain connections, which are none of my business. But this isn't some kind of clever scheme to take this place over and use it as a cover for something? Not that I'm judgmental, God knows. I'm just too old to go to prison and really enjoy it properly."

Joe laughed. "Nothing like that. Just a cover for when I want to sit around and look at old books. And maybe something to do when I'm too old for my other activities. Here's what I propose. You make me a junior partner, with an option to buy the business and the building, when and if you decide to give it up. Meanwhile, you run it as always, but I'm free to come by anytime, read anything, and play with the cat."

Alexis lit his smoke. "I can't speak for the cat, she makes her own decisions," he said, blowing out a plume. "But I think I like your terms—better than the bank's anyway."

"One more thing."

"There always is."

"I need a new copy of *Ulysses*."

Cookie poured them both a Scotch. They were back in her private salon, with a fire going and the lamps low. The thick velvet curtains were drawn, and the tapestries and fabrics cushioned the walls. The hustle of the city was muted and felt far away. So did the hustle going on just beyond her walls, as her employees and her clients traded pain and pleasure, feeding off one another's secrets and desires, hopes and dreams.

"Anyway," Gio was saying, "I wanted to come by and let you know personally. The man who killed Ioana won't ever hurt anyone again."

"Thank you, Gio. I just hope that helps her rest in peace." She held her glass up. "To Ioana." They toasted and drank.

"That reminds me," Gio said. "I pulled some strings about getting her remains released, since she doesn't have any next of kin here. Her friend Jem is going to have her cremated and then organize some kind of memorial. If you want to come, or maybe kick in."

"I'd like that very much."

"And Jem also asked me to tell you that she won't be coming back to work here. She was nervous about quitting, you know, without giving proper notice."

Cookie leaned back, shaking her head, and shook a thick, jeweled finger. "No one gets pressured to do anything they don't want to here, Gio. You know that. It's not necessary, for one thing. I got more volunteers than I can handle as it is." She shrugged and poured more Scotch. "Besides, you're the boss." She took a sip, licking her lips. "Speaking of which, I put Brendan on hold. In case you wanted to see him."

Gio hesitated, looking at his watch. His wife was making eggplant parm, a family favorite. Still, he could call and say something came up. An emergency. "No," he said, "that's OK. I've got a long drive home." He stood and kissed her cheek. "I'll be back, though."

She kissed him back on both cheeks. "Of course, *cher*. Cookie knows you will. Everyone comes back sooner or later."

⚬━✦━⚬

Joe met Frank and Kiran for dinner. It was a feast at a Bengali restaurant, to celebrate the defeat of the Westlands project. Kiran insisted that it was her treat.

"Why? I had nothing to do with it," Joe asked.

"I understand," she said, smiling big, huddled with Frank across from Joe in the booth as dishes began to fill the table. "Frank made that very clear. You had nothing at all to do with it."

"And it's only a temporary reprieve," Frank pointed out. "Somebody else will come along. They're already talking about new plans. There's just too much money."

"Yes, thank you, Mr. Glass Half Empty," she said. "But for tonight, I still want to celebrate that something good happened in this cold, dark world." She raised her beer. "And I still want to say thank you, Joe, on behalf of the community."

Frank, too, raised his beer. "And on behalf of all the rats and cats and pigeons and crackheads and hookers and cruisers and weirdo artists and all the other wildlife you spared."

Joe smiled and lifted his can of Coke. He wished now that he had taken a picture of Frank's painting or could even remember where it was. "To the wild life," he said.

When Joe tapped on her window, Donna was both startled and relieved. She had never returned his messages, though she was glad to get the last one, since she knew that meant he was OK. She had been worried about him terribly, but she was also afraid to begin a conversation without knowing where it would end. But she missed him. So much so that she'd been tempted to confide in her friends and mother, especially when they started noticing that her happy glow and good cheer were now gone. But of course she did not.

"Hey," she said, softly, raising the window and helping him in. "It's the mystery man."

"Hey, it's the most special of agents." He stepped down carefully, making sure not to wince, but she saw how he held his hand over his side.

"How's the carcass?" she asked, shutting the window.

He shrugged. "One more scar for the collection."

"Luckily some women find that sexy."

"Anyone I know?" he asked.

She shrugged. "We'll see." They sat side by side on her bed but didn't touch.

"Also," he said, "in the eligible bachelor category, I found a job."

"Seriously?"

"Yup. As of a few hours ago, I am now junior part owner of a failing used bookshop in the West Village."

"You've gone from best-read strip-club bouncer to most dangerous bookshop nerd," she said. "I guess that's movement of some kind. Congrats."

"Thanks," Joe said. Then, after a beat, he asked, "How is your CI?"

Now she sighed. "She's alive." Daisy had been treated for hypothermia and severe dehydration but was otherwise unharmed, physically. Mentally and emotionally, it was not so clear. "I pushed her into it, you know? Because of my ambitions. I put her in harm's way."

"Think of all the women you saved. Now and in the future."

"And the ones we couldn't save?"

"You got them justice."

"Right. Justice. Justice is blind on the statue, because she's supposedly fair and impartial. But she's still a fucking bitch, isn't she? There's always a price."

Joe smiled. "Or maybe it's just because she is swinging that sword around with a blindfold on."

Donna chuckled.

"It's nice to hear you laugh again," Joe said. "Even if just a little."

"Well, your joke wasn't that funny," she said, then adjusted her position so that she was facing him. "Look. I want to get this out in the open. I saw you, that night, with Hackney, coming out of the brothel."

"Oh," Joe said, then, "For what it's worth, nothing happened. With me, I mean, and those women. And not with . . . my Russian friend, either, since us. Not with anyone else. I know you probably don't believe me."

"Actually, I do," Donna said. "That's what's weird. I think you're an honest man, in your own completely illegal, amoral, and antisocial way. And I know you caught a killer when no one else was going to, especially not us. And I realize now it was insane of me to suggest you stop, that you get a regular job, because you're not a regular guy, and you're doing what you're meant to do."

She sighed deeply. "But that's the problem. Because I was jealous and upset. Possessive, I guess, like a real girlfriend. And I was terrified when I thought you were in danger. My whole instinct was to run in there and help you, fuck everything else. Just like I would if, God forbid, it was my daughter or my mom or anybody else that"—she hesitated—"that I loved." Now she looked into his eyes. "You see, that's the problem. If this goes on. If we go on. I'm going to fall in love. And I can't be in love with you."

Joe stared back at her. "I can't be in love with you, either," he said. "But I am."

Now they both fell silent, eye to eye, their mouths just inches apart, as if on the precipice of a leap that both were afraid to take but that neither could back away from. One gesture, one word, one kiss could change everything. Joe was afraid to move.

ACKNOWLEDGEMENTS

I would like to thank my editor, Otto Penzler, who has been my collaborator and accomplice throughout this series, for his taste, his wisdom, and his faith. I would also like to thank everyone at Mysterious Press and Mysterious Bookshop, particularly Charles Perry and Tom Wickersham. As always, I am immensely grateful to my agent, Doug Stewart, for his patience, guidance, and loyalty, as well as everyone at Sterling Lord Literistic, especially the intrepid Maria Bell, the essential Danielle Bukowski, and the amazing Szilvia Molnar. Thanks to Nivia Hernandez for help with languages and to Matilde Huseby and William Fitch for being my first readers. I would like to express my gratitude for the help and support of all my friends and most of all to my family for their patience, their kindness, and their love.